# Charmed

## A Death Escorts Novel

By Cambria Hebert

Other books by Cambria Hebert

Heven and Hell Series

*Before*

*Masquerade*

*Between*

*Charade*

*Bewitched*

*Tirade*

*Beneath*

*Renegade*

*Heven & Hell Anthology*

Death Escorts

*Recalled*

# Dedication

To anyone who's ever been charmed.

# Charmed

*'I'm selfish, impatient, and a little insecure. I make mistakes,*

*I am out of control, and at times hard to handle,*

*but if you can't handle me at my worst,*

*then you sure as hell don't deserve me at my best.''*

—Marilyn Monroe

# Prologue

*"Boxing - the act, activity, or sport of fighting with the fists, especially according to rules requiring the use of boxing gloves and limiting legal blows to those striking above the waist and on the front or sides of the opponent."*

## Charming
*1920 New York*

The moment when the course of your life will be defined forever.

I was in that moment.

The pungent odor of sweat and adrenaline permeated the air around me. The crowd, sizeable and energized, bellowed. It was an all-encompassing sound, the many individual voices creating a singular roar that echoed through the warehouse we occupied.

In just a few moments, my life was going to change forever. And damn, it was going to be sweet. Everyone here was going to know my name. After tonight they would say it with reverence, with awe. I would go down in the history books as the unknown scrapper who literally fought his way to the top and beat out the reigning champion.

The managers I couldn't get, the representatives who looked at me and sneered, were going to eat every last *you'll never make it* they ever said. I felt a few gazes from across the room and I glanced their way. They were from the reigning champ's camp. They looked at me with a mix of surprise and disbelief—like they still couldn't figure out how I made it this far without anyone to help me.

The answer was simple.

Determination.

I jerked my chin in acknowledgement of their stare, and their looks changed.

To arrogance, to pity.

I rolled my head on my shoulders, enjoying the sound of the cracks and pops in my muscles. The arrogance, that was to be expected, but the pity… that was something else entirely. It was fuel. Fuel to my fire, fuel to succeed. They thought I was going to get my ass beat in front of a sold-out crowd, in front of anyone who mattered in the boxing world.

They were wrong.

The announcer stepped into the ring, ducking between the ropes and straightening to his full height—which was still a full head shorter than me—and began to introduce the reigning king of boxing and then me, the unexpected, no name challenger.

I didn't bother to listen. Instead, I made sure the laces on my gloves were tight. I concentrated on the familiar rush of power into my limbs and I called up an image in my head, the reason I did any of this at all.

The crowd roared as the champ took his place in the ring. As I walked to my place, I picked out a few voices in the onslaught of noise. They were betting against me. Wagering I wouldn't make it past round one. Without thinking, I stopped my steady progress to the ring, halted where I stood and then pivoted back around. A hush fell over the crowd; they waited to see what I would do… if I was going to chicken out and leave without trying.

I walked to where the men were betting against me. They looked up, one of them visibly swallowing.

"Add me to that roster," I told the man with the paper and pencil.

"Excuse me?" he said.

"I want to place a bet." I said it extra slow like he was stupid.

His face flushed red. "I… boxers don't usually bet."

"My money isn't good enough?" I lifted a single brow.

"Of course," he said, recovering. "What's the bet?"

"I'll win in the third round. A complete knockout."

There were gasps all around me.

"Are you sure you want to do that, kid?" the man with the pencil asked.

I grinned. "Twenty dollars."

His eyes bulged. "That's a lot of money…"

"I'm a sure thing," I replied and turned around to walk away.

Someone behind me laughed. "That kid has balls."

The murmurs of "what's his name again?" did not escape my ears.

I climbed in the ring, my eyes going directly to my opponent's corner. He sat there with his team around him and a white towel draped over his shoulder. I made it a point to meet his eyes. I did it every fight. I wanted whoever I fought that night to know that I wasn't intimidated by their backers, their titles, and their name.

I was here to take it all away.

The clamor of a bell signaled the start of the match. We came out of our corners, circling each other a few times, sizing each other up, looking for weaknesses, for patterns, for anything that might give us the edge.

He threw the first punch. I dodged it; spinning away and then coming right back. He threw another and I blocked it, hitting away his glove like it was a gnat and I was annoyed.

The more blows I blocked, the more flustered he became. Halfway through the first round and I hadn't even taken a shot. I hadn't been hit either.

He drew back to attempt another shot when I struck out, the uppercut snapping his head on his shoulders. The crowd went nuts as he stumbled back.

His eyes locked on mine and like a freight train he came at me, knocking into me, back against the ropes, and I used their momentum to push him backward and hit him again.

After that, the fight got real. Fast.

I took several slams that made my vision go blurry, but I stayed on my feet and delivered a few vision robbers of my own. By the end of the second round, we were both breathing heavy, pouring sweat, and bleeding. I fumbled around with the water in my corner, trying to get it in my mouth. It was hard with gloves on and no one to help me.

Someone appeared next to me, standing outside the ring. He grabbed the water and squirted it in my face. I opened my mouth automatically to get some of the cool liquid.

"That's some good fighting, kid," the man said. "You just might win."

I glanced at my helper, not really seeing him because everything was blurry. All I knew was that he wasn't that big and he had dark hair. "Thanks," I said, opening my mouth for more water.

"The other side looks pissed. Word is they got a lot riding on this fight. They thought it was going to be cake. You're making it harder."

I grunted. "I'm going to win."

"My money's on you."

The announcer called out and I turned back.

"Keep an eye out, kid," the man behind me whispered. "Some people like to win dirty."

I didn't really hear his words because the bell rang and we moved out of our corners. My eyes went to my opponent's. There was a glint in them that hadn't been there before. A sort of clarity that could only come from confidence.

I shot my fist out to wipe the look off his face. He dodged me.

We locked arms, our upper bodies colliding as we tried to muscle the other toward the ground. "Give it up, kid," the guy whispered. "I'm not giving up this title."

I shoved my fist into his ribs and the crowd roared.

He collapsed a little farther against me, my body taking on more of his weight. "Give up now, or else."

I wanted to laugh, would have if I wasn't busy punching him again.

This time he fell over onto the floor. I bounced from foot to foot, waiting for him to pick himself up.

He lifted onto his hands and knees, his back heaving with heavy breaths.

Everything seemed to slow down then—like in a car accident when you know you're about to die and every last second is painfully drawn out so you know exactly what is about to happen.

My opponent glanced to his corner. His handler nodded once and then slid his cold eyes to me. The boxer got up and turned, looking at me with a hard expression. I saw his glove coming, but I didn't move fast enough. It hit me square in the face and I fell back, down onto my butt.

The guy was on me then, straddling my waist and hammering his glove into my face. My vision went dark. I'd taken thousands of hits like that before and not one of them ever took away my vision.

His glove. It was weighted.

He hit me again and warmth rushed from my nose. He must have put on a new glove, one with brass sewn inside. He was dirty.

I tried to get up, to hit him again.

"I told you I wasn't going to lose," the man rasped.

I heard the ref calling out for him to get off me, that he was supposed to back off. I heard the hush that fell over the crowd.

I looked up at him. He saw it in my eyes.

I wasn't giving up. This title, the money that came with it, was mine.

He reared back one last time, the ref screaming for him to stop.

He drove his glove into my face, up under my nose, driving the bones straight into my brain.

I collapsed beneath him.

As life faded from my limbs, a single flicker of emotion was felt.

For her. She needed me and I failed. What would happen to her now?

Death swallowed me then, taking what was left of my thoughts, my life. Turns out the moment in which my life was defined forever was not what I expected.

In fact, it seemed that my life was now defined by death.

* * *

*Red.* It's all I could see. It was all around me, everywhere. At this rate I wouldn't have one drop of blood left in my body. How long did it take someone to bleed out? How long until their organs, their heart had nothing left to fuel them? A minute? Five?

What I couldn't understand is why I wasn't in pain. Surely with this much blood pouring out of my skin I would feel some kind of raw pain. But there was nothing.

Nothing but red.

Why was it suddenly so quiet? I could hear nothing—not even the sound of my own breathing. Then I realized. The hush in the air was because everyone was watching me die. They were likely wondering the same thing I had been moments before: *How long?* I needed to get up, to prove to them that I wasn't going down like this. I wasn't going to die in a fight I should have won—a fight that was rightfully mine.

I stopped thinking completely when I practically flew up off the ground. An overwhelming dizziness overcame me, so disorienting and unsettling that my insides buzzed with discomfort.

I was upright, my body springing up so fast that I hadn't even consciously tried to move it. Still, all I saw was red. How could someone bleed so much and move so fast?

I looked down at myself, taking stock, mentally preparing for the sight of my blood-drenched body...

Only I wasn't bleeding.

And my body... it wasn't there.

In the place of skin and bone was nothing but a fine red mist—a red cloud that was shaped like a man—*like me.*

Tentatively, I reached out my arm (was it really still my arm?) and watched the red mist dissipate like smoke from a cigar.

I must already be dead.

This cloud—this red—was all that was left of me, left of my life?

I looked up, beyond myself, and saw that I wasn't in the ring anymore. I was in a room. An office. It was large, uncluttered and had a huge row of floor-to-ceiling closets lining the wall behind a massive desk.

It was clear this wasn't heaven. But it didn't seem like hell either.

I watched as the large leather chair behind the desk began to swivel around, slowly turning, and if I had a throat I would have swallowed thickly.

There was something ominous about the way that chair turned, something final. I knew it down to my core.

A boney man with a wide forehead and shrewd eyes appeared, steepling his fingers beneath his chin and regarding me in a way that did nothing to soothe my confusion.

"You're dead," the man said simply. "But you don't have to be for very long."

"I don't?" I replied, surprised when my voice echoed through the room. How does one speak without a mouth?

He smiled. It was the kind of smile that I'd seen before. The kind the boxer gave me right before he killed me in that dirty fight.

"I have a proposition for you," he began, pulling his hands down from under his chin and pushing out of the chair. "One that you won't be able to refuse."

And so just minutes after I lived the moment that defined my life forever... I also lived the moment that would forever define my death.

# Chapter One

*"Death Escort - an assassin employed by the Grim Reaper. Will kill a target by any means necessary. Including charm."*

## Charming
*Present day*

You would think being a Death Escort—a killer by trade—would make a man above getting a lecture from his boss. Apparently when you work for the Grim Reaper, the ultimate death dealer, it doesn't matter who you are, how many times you've killed, or how ruthless you might be because he is better.

After over ninety years of working for him, it's still annoying as hell.

And so are his lectures.

The fact is it gets old working for someone who is the be-all, end-all in life and death. So when I saw the chance to allow someone to get the best of him, I took it. I mean, it isn't every day when someone manages to get around the iron-clad rules of the Grim Reaper himself.

So yeah, I talked and wasted time. I "forgot" to mention that one of his new Escorts had figured out a way to break the call of death that was placed on a Target. Turns out in the eyes of the Reaper (who strangely looked a lot like Mr. Burns from that cartoon *The Simpsons*), that made me an accessory.

And now, after weeks of delaying the inevitable, I was getting my punishment.

Goody gumdrops.

Instead of listening to what a disappointment I was, how he should just Recall me right now and let me twist away in an eternity far worse than hell, blah, blah, blah, I turned my attention instead toward the floor-to-ceiling row of closets that lined the wall behind his massive desk.

The closets where he kept his bodies.

Some people collect coins, artifacts, or tools. G.R. collects bodies.

The doors were open, making me think he was displaying his collection to me for a certain reason. Shock value maybe? Though he must know that seeing a bunch of bodies wasn't something that would shock me. These bodies were all groomed and hanging in perfect rows. I was used to seeing bodies in… less than perfect condition.

Maybe it was to make me think that the very body I inhabited at this moment might end up back with the others and I would be nothing but the red mist that makes up my soul.

I scanned the bodies, my eyes looking for one that probably should have been familiar, but after so many years I wondered if it would be. I had done this occasionally through the years, but just like today, I didn't see it. I wondered what had become of my original body, the one I was born in. The one I died in. I couldn't imagine G.R. got rid of it; I mean, he was practically a body hoarder, yet in all my years of working as an escort, of rotating bodies, I hadn't seen it.

And I wasn't about to ask. Because asking would let him know I wondered; it would give him even more power over me… something he didn't need more of.

"I have a new Target for you," G.R. announced, effectively ending my thinking.

"A Target?" I asked, surprised, wondering if I somehow missed the punishment I was supposed to get.

"That is your job, is it not?" he mused, staring at me through narrowed eyes. His cheekbones jutted out and his wide forehead was further widened by the way he combed his dark hair back and away from his face. He wasn't a big man, but I guess when the merest touch could kill, muscles didn't really matter.

"I thought we were here to discuss the status of my job," I replied, looking right at him. I was careful to keep my posture bordering on lazy to give off the impression I could care less about whatever he dished out.

"Active," he said, irritation flashing through his eyes. "That's the status of your job. Like it or not, you're one of the best escorts I have."

I flashed a smile. I wasn't *one* of the best. I was *the* best. We both knew it. I guess that was the reason my punishment was lacking.

"Here," he said, holding out a file. I got up and took the folder, opening it up and staring down at the picture clipped to the front of the page. It was a young woman, in her twenties—long dark hair, brown eyes, and full lips. She was gorgeous, which could be considered a bonus. She had the bone structure of fine breeding and about four names, which spoke of old money.

She'd be dead by the end of the week.

I scanned the information, looking for her address, looking for the place I'd be flying off to next. Hopefully it was somewhere warm, with miles of beaches. Or perhaps the dessert where it seemed the sun always shined. I didn't really care as long as it wasn't here. Alaska sucked. I hoped I never came here again.

My eyes found the zip code and I stiffened. "Is this right?" I asked, turning to look at G.R.

"Have I ever given you faulty information?"

Here. The woman was here, in this godforsaken, cold, and dark town.

Something niggled at the back of my brain. I looked at her name again. *Rosalyn Elizabeth Kennedy Sinclair.* Her last name… I'd heard it before. I glanced down at the short paragraph on known information about the Target.

*Daughter of Senator Jack Sinclair.*

The file slapped my thigh when I jerked and spun around to look at G.R. "You've got to be kidding."

"I don't joke about business."

"She's the daughter of Jack Sinclair, the *Alaskan* senator. He's practically a celebrity around here," I said, thinking of all the times I watched the news or some show on TV. The press here loved him. They practically camped out on his lawn, just hoping for a glimpse of him.

"Yes. He is. His daughter is worth thirty million dollars."

"Money. So this Target is all about money," I said. I don't know why this irritated me, but it did. It certainly wasn't the first time I'd killed for money. It wouldn't be the last. In fact, I killed for money more than I killed for abilities because finding people with some sort of ability wasn't as easy as finding one with money.

"You have something against money, Charming?"

"No. But you have to know this girl has got to have security practically feeding her breakfast. Not to mention she probably has fifteen financial advisors and lawyers that will make actually getting to her money impossible."

"So are you saying you can't do this job? That you refuse?"

Ahhhh. And here it was.

Understanding dawned like the sun of a new day.

He was dolling out my punishment in the form of a job. He assigned me a Target that would practically guarantee failure. Failure would get me Recalled, would get my soul pulled out of my body and sent into an empty vast space of nothingness for all eternity. A place where I could hear the tortured wails of those lost around me, a place where I could think but feel nothing but pain, and a place where I would know no peace *ever*.

And if I refused this job?

Same thing. So here was an interesting dilemma. I could refuse and get Recalled. I could fail and get Recalled. Or I could pull off the most impossible kill in the history of escorting and I could make Mr. Death himself finally realize who he was attempting to mess with.

Really, there was no dilemma at all.

"You know this job is going to take longer. To infiltrate the camp of this woman, of this family… it isn't something I can do overnight."

G.R.'s eyes gleamed. "Yes, I'm aware. I'll give you six months."

I kept my face smooth, my posture relaxed as his timeline sucker punched me in the gut. *Six months?* That was insane. A job of this magnitude would take a year. I underestimated just how angry I had made him.

My eyes slid to the bowl of light-colored stones that sat on the corner of his desk. The stones that he always left in exchange for a life that he took. Once a stone was placed, the death—the end of a life—was sealed. There was no getting out of it.

Except for once.

Turns out if you can manage to break the stone, then you break the claim of the Grim Reaper. One of the new Escorts figured it out. It got him Recalled. It got me into this predicament.

"I want more than my usual cut," I said. Punishment or not, if I pulled this off I wanted what I earned. "Ten million."

"That's a lot of money," G.R. replied, leaning back in his chair as he appraised me. "You're in no position to be making demands."

I shrugged. "You're convinced I'll fail anyway. Who cares how much I ask for?"

Again, he rested chin atop his fingers. "Fine. Ten million."

I resisted the urge to smile.

"You get six months. Get into her life. Get into her bank accounts. Make sure when she is dead, it's all yours. And if you succeed…" He paused and looked at me. "Then I'll overlook your betrayal."

My betrayal? He acted like I was the one who broke his claim, who bested him. All I did was keep my mouth shut. If I had known I was going to be punished like this, then I would've made it worth it.

"Fine. I'll take the job." Like I really had a choice.

G.R. clapped his hands like a kid on Christmas morning. "Wonderful."

Yeah, great. Not only was I given the most impossible Target ever, but I was also being sentenced to this icy, dark prison that was Alaska.

I gripped the file and headed for the door. I was ready to go.

"Oh, Charming," G.R. called behind me.

I turned.

"You remember the rules. You fail, you get Recalled. You get caught or put in jail, I won't come get you. I'll let you rot in a cell until your body dies or you get out, and then I'll come get you… to Recall you. Basically, if you do anything but complete the job, life as you know it is over."

I left the room, closing the massive double wooden doors behind me. I took a moment to lean against them, sagging under the weight of this new assignment. I allowed myself maybe thirty seconds of wallowing before pushing away from the door and straightening.

He thought he had me. He thought he had a way—a reason—to finally get the best of me.

He was wrong.

Game on.

# Chapter Two

*"Hate - to feel hostility or animosity toward."*

## *Frankie*

Sugar. I needed more of it if I was going to make it through this day. The chocolate croissant and caramel latte I had this morning wasn't near enough to combat the massive lines, the noise, and disgruntled people that filled the DMV. Whatever in hell made me think that working at the Department of Motor Vehicles, here in Alaska, was a good idea?

Maybe it was the good pay. Maybe it was because I got weekends off.

Or maybe it was because I had a moment of temporary insanity that unfortunately coincided with me saying, "I accept," when I got offered this job.

Besides the fact that the lines were permanently out the door, the computer systems were temperamental at best, and my boss was a complete broom rider, my stash of chocolate and Sour Patch Kids was empty.

That meant someone was going to die today.

I glanced back up at the ninety-year-old woman whose head barely cleared the insanely high counters we stood behind and tried to hold on to my patience. "Mrs. Eldridge," I said extremely loudly. "Like I told you last week, you have to go and get new glasses before I can renew your driver's license."

"I have new glasses," she insisted.

Lord, save me now.

"You got those ten years ago. You need some from this year." *Or decade* I finished silently.

She shuffled out of the line like a turtle and I took her slowness as a chance to really search beneath my station and chair for a long-lost piece of sugar. Anything. Even a stray jellybean would likely find its way into my blood stream at this point. Of course there was nothing. I briefly considered hiding beneath my desk until five o'clock. *My car.* I had an emergency stash in my car. I glanced at my watch. I had another hour until I was able to take a fifteen-minute break.

A pair of black pumps appeared before me and I inwardly groaned. Just what I needed—a run-in with the witch. But instead of being greeted by her condescending, screechy tone, an icy-cold red can appeared before me.

Hallelujah, praise the Lord, it was caffeine *and* sugar!

I snatched the Coke out of her hand and popped the top, taking a large, satisfying chug. The bubbles crowded down my throat, slightly burning, and I took another swallow.

"I love you," I murmured to Lela, the girl who worked right beside me.

She laughed. "I know that look when I see it." Then she straightened and whispered. "Witch alert."

I shot up, my head bumping into the counter on the way. I wanted to shout out in pain, but I clamped my mouth shut, not wanting to draw the attention of my boss, Satan's assistant.

I turned back to my line, my eyes colliding with a broad chest. I looked up, and the can slid out of my hand, hitting the floor with a thud while fizzy liquid poured over my favorite boots.

I didn't even notice.

"What the hell are you doing here?" I growled as I looked around for something sharp I could stab him with.

A thick brow arched. "So is this where you spend your days? As if the DMV isn't a horrible enough place to visit without the poor people of Alaska having to tolerate you."

There wasn't enough sugar on this planet that would save him. I reached out and picked up the black phone. If I couldn't bludgeon him to death here at my place of employment, then I could at least call the cops. I began dialing, but he reached over and cut the connection.

I slammed the phone down on his hand, which was still pressed on the hang-up button. Breath hissed between his teeth and his green eyes shot to mine. "Careful, George, you're pissing off the wrong man."

"My name isn't George."

He shrugged, pulling his hand away from the phone. "When you have a man's name, does it really matter?"

Forget the police; I was going to kill him. "I do *not*—" I began, but then I stopped. I didn't have to explain my name to him.

He seemed to take my silence as some sort of victory and smirked.

I rolled my eyes. "Please, like you're one to talk about names. *Charming,*" I spat. "You have got to be the least charming person I've ever had the displeasure of meeting."

Of course Hagatha the Great chose that exact minute to walk up behind me. "Frankie, did I just hear you disrespect one of the citizens in this building?"

I held back my wince. Charming snickered. *I will not lose it. I will not lose it. I need my job,* I told myself as I slowly pivoted around to face my boss from hell.

"Ms. Toth," I began, trying to think up some excuse for why I was treating this douche like, well, a douche.

To my surprise he cleared his throat and spoke. "That scarf is beautiful. It brings out the blue of your eyes," he said, his voice smooth as butter. "You must have exquisite taste to be able to pair it with that blouse."

Ms. Toth completely forgot I was standing there and her body practically slid into a puddle as she leaned forward closer to him. Then she giggled.

I tried not to gag.

I turned around and saw Charming leaning across the counter, his right elbow planted wide, causing his black leather jacket to fall open to reveal a cerulean dress shirt stretched across his chest. He flashed his perfectly straight, perfectly white teeth at her, and I swear I heard her stutter.

"You'll have to forgive me," he said. "I was giving your employee a hard time. I guess I was feeling a little temperamental for being in such a long line."

"Oh, well." Her hand fluttered to her neck. "The lines are very long today. End of the month and all," she explained. He flashed his teeth again and she stopped talking to stare.

Very artfully, he pushed off the counter and ran his very long fingers through his cleverly messy hair, and I swear it made it look even more perfect. If I didn't know what a complete and utter loser he was, I might fall prey to his… well…. his *charm*. Damn it.

"I promise to behave," he said solemnly, pulling a paper from the inside of his jacket.

She was still staring, completely dumbstruck. Thankfully, Lela called out her name for assistance with her computer and Ms. Toth managed to tear her eyes away from the oversized Ken doll and walk away.

His eyes, full of smugness, found mine. "What was it you were saying again? That I wasn't deserving of my name?"

"What the hell are you doing here?" I hissed.

He stretched the paper on the counter before me. "I need to get the registration for my car renewed."

I smiled sweetly. "I'm so sorry, sir. I'm afraid you've been standing in the wrong line. Registration renewals are in that line over there," I pointed to the longest line in the building and I felt myself grin with evil glee. Who needed a sugar rush when you could torture the people you hated?

"You're lying," he growled.

"Nope." I waved a couple fingers in his direction. "Buh-bye now,"

He leaned over the counter once more, all trace of his fake charm gone. "I know you can do whatever needs done on that ancient-ass computer in front of you."

I gasped prudently. "Sir, I take offense to your tone. I can assure you that if I could help you with what you need I would." I batted my eyes at him.

His perfect teeth formed a grimace and he was about to say something very un-charming, I was sure, when an older man with a cane stepped up behind him. "You heard the lady," he said, "Now quit holding up the line."

Before he could shove away, he leaned closer, his eyes narrowing. Gone was the charming air he used on my boss. Replacing it was something cold and calculating, more in line with the man I remembered who came into my best friend's apartment not too long ago with a gun and kidnapped her. I reached for the phone again, fully intending to call the police and turn in his ass.

"I wouldn't do that if I were you," he said low. "You know exactly what I'm capable of."

Unease slithered down my spine. I tossed the blond curls away from my face and held his stare. "But you have no idea what *I* am capable of. Get the hell outta my line."

I watched him go to the other line and insert himself at the end. My heart was beating so fast that I had to gasp for breath. I wanted to demand an early break, to leave this room, which now felt contaminated by his very presence.

I didn't do any of those things. I picked up my half-empty Coke, took a swig, and called for the next person in line. I worked on autopilot all the while keeping an eye on him as he moved up the line. I should have just bypassed the system and did what he needed. Then he would've been gone. And I wouldn't be stuck in this room, which now felt entirely too small, with a Death Escort.

When he finally made it through and got his stupid little sticker for his license plate, he walked toward the exit, and I swear every single female in the place turned and watched him go. If they only knew what I did—that he was an assassin for the most deadly person on the planet.

Before disappearing into the cold Alaskan spring, he stopped and turned, his eyes spearing mine, and then he smiled, a cocky, arrogant grin. Fury spiked through my limbs, making me shake. I hated guys like him. Guys that thought nothing could touch them. Guys that thought they were God's gift to the world.

He was right about one thing, though. I couldn't call the police. Turning him in would only backfire on me and further hurt Piper, who lost too much at the hands of Charming and his boss. But there were other ways to pay someone back for the wrongs they committed.

I felt a smile tug my lips.

Payback was a bitch.

# Chapter Three

*"Steam shower - a type of bathing where a humidifying steam generator produces water vapor that is dispersed around a person's body."*

## Charming

Rosalyn Elizabeth Kennedy Sinclair wasn't a woman I could just "bump" into at the local grocery store in town. She wasn't the kind of girl that went to the same coffee place every morning for some frou-frou no calorie coffee drink, either. She had people that got that for her. She wasn't insecure, unpopular, or isolated—all the things that would make her an easy Target. In fact, she was overly popular, beautiful, and had probably been trained since birth to be cautious of people that weren't in her immediate circle of friends.

For a regular con man, stalker, or assassin, she was practically untouchable.

I wasn't a regular kind of guy. I was an Escort.

Still, setting up the perfect way to "meet" someone like her took some creative thinking. I needed an in that wouldn't raise suspicion or look even slightly contrived.

I clicked through another link on the computer and then sat back, rubbing my eye with the palm of my hand. This was the part of the job I hated. Research, learning… work. Rarely did I have to actually try hard on a job. Usually my charm, looks, and money got me to the finish line. Usually I could skate on what I saw and could figure out the rest. It was rare I had to do this amount of research on someone whose days were numbered. It really never made sense. Why bother learning the favorite color, food, and movie of someone I would never really know anyway? It was all about time management. It seemed like a more effective use of my time was to charm my way in and finish the job.

*Maybe that's why the last couple jobs weren't complete successes,* an annoying voice in the back of my mind whispered.

"I got the job done," I muttered, arguing with my inner conscience.

I was still here, after all. And it was abundantly clear that if I'd actually failed a job, I would have been Recalled on the spot. Yes, all the Targets I've ever been assigned (I lost count over fifty years ago) were dead. Their souls were gone (I had yet to figure out what exactly G.R. did with them), and most of the bodies had become a collector's item for Mr. Death himself. But… I hated when there was a but. As of late, a few of the jobs… I wasn't able to collect the money. Paperwork fell through, was lost, or loopholes were found.

*Maybe you're getting sloppy,* the voice taunted. *Maybe you're losing your charm.*

My growl cut through the silence of the kitchen, a firm denial and warning for that voice to shut the hell up. Something on the screen caught my eye and I leaned forward, scanning the information provided, taking in the list of attendees and the guest speaker. I grinned and slapped my hand down on the file and scattered papers across the tabletop.

Bingo.

Research might suck, but it usually paid off. I clicked through a few more links and then picked up my iPhone and made a call.

He answered on the third ring.

"Make sure my background is in place. Make sure it's good. You know who we're dealing with."

"I've done my part. When you fail, the only person you will have to blame is yourself," G.R. said, his voice calm in my ear.

The fact he was underestimating me made me very, very angry. "You remember that when you're cutting me a check for ten million dollars."

He chuckled. "Yes, well, all your documents and IDs will be there in the morning."

I didn't bother to point out that it took him three days to deliver the documents I usually got mere hours after every assignment. I knew it was on purpose, and so, I purposely acted like I had all the time in the world.

I pulled the phone away from my ear to end the call and the echo of his smug laughter when he spoke again. Even though his words were muffled, I heard them clear as a bell.

"Overconfidence isn't always a good thing. Even if you have the skills for a job—for a *fight*—it doesn't mean you're going to win." His words touched a part of me that I hadn't felt in so long I was mildly surprised it was still there. "I would think that you of all people would know this."

"Was that a reference to my past?" I asked, amusement clear in my tone. "Only people scared of their present drudge up the past." I lowered my voice, pulling the phone close to my mouth. "Tell me, G.R., are you scared I'll prove you wrong?"

"Death is scared of nothing," he intoned and hung up the phone. The cut connection rang with finality.

I stared at the computer screen for long minutes before a slow smile curved my lips. I pushed away from the table and headed for the stairs.

Death might not be scared of anything, but perhaps this time he should be.

*   *   *

Searing, thick steam rolled through the air, creating a cloudlike effect around me. The humid heat that it carried wrapped around my limbs and turned my tense muscles languid. All the extra energy coiled within me, waiting to be expended, evaporated, leaving me with a feeling that was quite close to relaxed.

This is exactly why I had a steam shower installed in this house. If I had to spend time in this godforsaken place, then I was going to make myself very comfortable. I knew the next six months of my life were going to be as close to hell as I ever wanted to be, so if there was a chance for me to steal any kind of peace—if even only during my shower—then I was going to take it.

I leaned back against the stone tiles and closed my eyes, taking in a deep breath of the fog-like vapor. Research? Check. A plan for a first meeting? Check. Background story, IDs, a home, car, and bank accounts all in my name? Check, check, and check. All I had to do now was go buy a brand new tux (if I could even find one in this town) and the biggest kill I've ever attempted would begin.

Energy slammed into me hard and fast, causing my eyes to snap open and my body to shove away from the tiles. I swatted at the steam like I could push it away, and when it didn't obey, I hit a few buttons on the control panel on the side of the wall.

Someone was in this house.

Not only were they not invited, but they'd also just cut short the only enjoyable thing about my day.

I might not be allowed to kill someone other than a Target, but I could damn sure make them regret they chose this house to creep into.

I opened the glass door to the stall and stepped out, reaching for a towel and slinging it around my hips as I went. I crept, not making a sound, light on my feet from years of practice. I inhaled, taking in the chaotic energy that buzzed through the house. It was a woman, had to be. A man's energy was more stable, less all over the place. But a woman… a woman's energy was exactly like the gender it inhabited: irrational and all over the place.

And this lady in particular must be crazy because her energy was practically shoving into me. I'd only felt this kind of forceful, *bossy* kind of vibe a couple times before.

*Shit.*

It better not be who I thought it was.

A sadistic smile curved my lips and I crept to the top of the stairs where I paused to listen to the sounds of papers being rustled, heavy breathing, and the erratic pounding of a heart.

Pulling another deep breath of her energy, I let it expand within me and then I took off, moving at the speed of light—so fast no one would hear or see me until I wanted them to.

I rushed toward the table where a figure dressed completely in black from head to toe was standing, peering at the screen of my laptop. On my way past, I snapped the lid closed and the force of my speed blew several papers up and away, sending them fluttering to the floor.

The woman gasped—turning around, her back going up against the edge of the table. Her eyes searched the room for me, but I wasn't done bouncing around. I went from one end of the room to the other, flipping on and off the lamps, turning on the flat screen hanging above the fireplace, and then hitting a button causing the logs in the hearth to burst into flames.

The woman pushed away from the table, rushing toward the set of French doors that led outside, but I caught her around the waist before she took three steps and yanked her back so she was firmly against me, pinned between my arms.

She didn't miss a beat and stomped down on my bare foot with her stiletto heal, causing me to howl in pain and release her. She ran forward as I recovered, reaching out and grabbing at her, only coming away with the black knit cap she'd stuffed over her head.

A flash of blond filled my vision before I caught her arm and yanked her back against me once more. Her chest was heaving and her nails dug into my arms, but I ignored it all.

"Who are you and what the hell are you doing in my house?" I growled into her ear.

"How did you move that fast?" She gasped.

Her voice. I knew that voice. It grated on my nerves like nails on a chalkboard. So much for it not being the infuriating girl with a man's name.

"You better have a damn good explanation for why I found you in my house, going through my things, George."

She stiffened and I felt her retort rise up inside her.

"Ah—ah—ah," I sang in her ear. "Now is not the time to piss me off any more than you already have," I warned.

Wisely, her mouth snapped shut as I spun her around to face me.

# Chapter Four

*"Cat suit - a close-fitting one-piece garment that covers the torso and the legs and frequently the arms."*

## Frankie

Once my shift from hell at work was over I drove straight to the closest gas station and filled my arms with enough sugary goodness to get me through the next week, or maybe just tonight, and dumped it all on the counter in front of the cashier who took in my haul with his usual disdain. I ignored him and went to grab some Dr. Pepper, Cherry Coke, and Yoo-hoo and added that to my pile.

At the last minute, I added a pack of pink bubblegum and winked when I got a glare in return.

Once inside my Jeep Wrangler, I cranked up the heat and tore into a bag of Sour Patch Kids, popping about five into my mouth at once. I enjoyed the way the sour coating on the outside burned my tongue. I backed out of the lot and drove the short drive to my apartment, with the radio too loud and too much candy in my mouth.

I let myself into my apartment, flipping on the light as I shut the door, and then leaned back against the painted-wood finish and sighed. Peace at last. I wasn't a loner, I wasn't a quiet person who enjoyed staying in rather than going out, but after the day I had… it was nice to be alone.

I took in the Tiffany-blue walls (hey, every girl need's a little Tiffany's in her life, even if it is only paint), the cream-colored sofa, mirrored coffee table, and the scattered magazines around the room. It wasn't much, but it was all mine. I dropped my bag of goodies on the floor beside the couch and shrugged out of my coat as I walked to the wall of posters all hung in vintage frames.

All the posters were of the same person. The woman I respected, was intrigued by, and yeah, maybe slightly obsessed with: Marilyn Monroe. She died before I was born, but even still her class, beauty, and the way she took life by the horns was still quite evident.

"Marilyn," I said to her, "what would you do if there was someone hanging around—someone that you just knew was up to no good?"

I smiled. She hadn't answered (if she had, I would probably check myself into a mental ward), but I found my answer anyway.

"This calls for a good old-fashioned cat burglary." I spun away from the pictures, grabbed a Dr. Pepper and the rest of my Sour Patch Kids, and went into my bedroom.

I opened up the closet doors to my very packed, too-small closet and several articles of clothing fell out and buried my feet. I ignored them and started pulling out all the black items I could find.

A knock on my front door echoed into my room and I began pawing my way out of the closet, tripping on a few items and spilling some of the soda over onto my hand. Now that was just a waste of perfectly good sugar.

"Come in!" I yelled, giving up trying to break free of the clothes.

A few seconds later Piper, my best friend, appeared in the doorway. "What the heck are you doing?"

"Inventory," I said, sipping the soda and scrutinizing her appearance. She looked tired, but that wasn't anything new. Going to school, working, and volunteering at a health clinic would do that to anyone. I looked past her lack of energy for something more, for the grief that she seemed to wear like a second skin. It was there, but it wasn't any worse than before—if anything, it seemed just a little lighter. "What are you doing?"

She held up a sack. "I brought Chinese."

"Well, why didn't you say so?" I said, holding out my can so she could take it. "Here, take this. I'm about to go ninja style on all these clothes holding me hostage."

Then I winced at my word choice. *Good one, Frankie, remind her all about the time she was kidnapped at gunpoint and thrown in a trunk and held hostage by a killer.* A killer who walked into the DMV today like he wasn't a criminal.

I snuck a peak at her to see if what I said caused some horrible flashback, but she was grinning, no doubt wondering how I was going to escape my closet.

I began kicking at the shirts and pants, but all that did was wind them further around my feet. I took a step forward and toppled over, right into the giant pile of black that I'd made. I squealed, landing face first, and pushed myself up onto hands and knees and proceeded to crawl out of the mess. On my way, I found the knit black cap I'd been searching for.

"Score!" I exclaimed and paused to pull it over my head.

"What's with all the black?" Piper asked as we left the mess behind and went into my galley-style kitchen.

"Guess I'm feeling moody," I said non-committedly. I still wasn't sure what I should tell her about today.

"What happened in here?!" Piper exclaimed, staring at the explosion that was my counters. Bowls, spatulas, and several appliances with awry cords cluttered the countertop. Cupcake liners were scattered about and there were multicolored sprinkles making a rainbow in the sink.

"I did some baking last night," I said. "I was hoping the maid would come by today while I was at work. Good help is so hard to find these days." I sighed.

"You don't have a maid, Frankie."

"Shh! Don't ruin my fantasy."

"Well, where are the cupcakes?" Piper asked, snooping through the cupboards.

"I threw them away."

"That's a crime against sugar!" she said and then gasped.

I laughed. "Actually, the crime was the way they tasted."

"Everything you make tastes great. You're just too hard on yourself."

"Yeah, well, when there's a place like the Iced Princess to compare yourself to, standards are high."

Piper made a tsking sound as she pulled out the Chinese from her bag. I grabbed some plates and we loaded up on noodles, veggies, and chicken. We ate in silence at the tiny table on the far end of the kitchen for a few minutes before I brought up the hard stuff.

"So how ya doing?" I asked.

She knew it wasn't a general question. She set down her fork and looked at me. "Better, I think. I still miss him. It helps, you know, knowing that he's not somewhere suffering."

I nodded. Piper fell in love with a Death Escort, a guy who worked for the Grim Reaper, and was assigned the job of killing her. But in the end he couldn't kill her, and it cost him his life. He somehow got a message to her that he wasn't suffering in death, but he was still dead. And she was alive, but left to deal with everything that happened alone.

I wasn't sure if I should tell her who I saw today or not. I thought she had a right to know that Charming was here, but I also didn't want to disrupt any kind of healing she was doing.

"Out with it," Piper said, cutting into my mental ping-pong.

"With what?" I asked, batting my eyes at her.

"Uh-uh." She shook her head. "That won't work on me. I know you are far from innocent."

I pushed away from the table and went to the living room to grab my bag of stash, stopping at the fridge to put away the Yoo-hoo and Cherry Coke. Then I grabbed a pack of Junior Mints from the back and carried them back to the table.

This conversation required chocolate.

"I saw Charming today." I didn't bother beating around the bush. It wouldn't make the news any less hard.

Her fork clattered against her plate and her skin paled a little. "Where?"

"He came into the DMV. He was registering his car in this state."

"He's staying here?" she whispered.

"I don't really know. Seems that way."

She nodded. "Thanks for telling me."

My eyes about fell out of my head. "That's it? That's all you're going to say about the guy who stuffed you in a trunk and tried to kill you?"

"What else am I gonna say, Frank?" She pushed away from the table and stood. "That I hate him? That I blame him for Dex's death? That we should call the cops and have him arrested?" She sank back down in the chair and looked at me. "What's the point? We can't fight him. We can't fight the Grim Reaper. I'm tired. I just want to move on."

I pushed the Junior Mints toward her. "Have some candy."

She snorted. But she picked up the box and dug out a piece. "You got his address, didn't you?" she asked me quietly.

I helped myself to a piece of minty goodness. "Yep."

She moved fast, faster than I expected, her hand shooting out to grab my wrist, and she pinned me with serious brown eyes. "Stay away from him, Frankie. Promise me."

How did a girl get around making promises she had no intention of keeping?

I used my free hand to shove a couple more candies in my mouth. "It's not polite to speak with a full mouth," I mumbled.

"I'm serious. These people… they live by their own rules. I almost died. Dex did die. Going around them, it's like lighting a match in a room full of gasoline. Stay away from them before you become death's next Target."

"Piper," I protested, but she shook her head vehemently and squeezed my wrist.

"Promise me, Frankie. I don't know what I would do if I lost you too."

She looked down at where she held me and let go like I burned her skin.

"What did you see?" I asked, watching her face. Piper had this ability to see visions of the future. All she had to do was touch someone.

"Nothing," she said. "I'd like to keep it that way." She cleared her throat. "I've had enough visions to last me a lifetime."

"Come on," I said, abandoning my plate and grabbing up the box of candy. "Let's go watch something completely trashy on TV. I'm sure there's some reality show on that will make us feel better about ourselves."

She laughed but pinned me with a serious gaze. "Promise me, Frankie."

"I promise," I agreed.

That seemed to make her feel better, her steps lighter as we walked toward the TV. I wondered what she would say if she knew the promise I made wasn't the one she'd exactly asked for.

I had no intention of staying away from Charming. I fully intended to find out what the hell he was up to. I just promised not to die while doing it.

*　*　*

It was after ten by the time Piper left for her apartment. She stayed later than she usually did, and I wasn't sure if it was because she needed the company or if she was afraid that the minute she left I'd be up to no good.

She was right, of course.

The minute she left, I ran into my bedroom and ransacked the pile of black clothing lying on the floor. I pulled out a pair of black leggings and a long-sleeved black T-shirt and quickly pulled them on. The clothes felt like a second skin against me. I checked myself out in the floor-to-ceiling mirror, leaning against my bedroom wall, and smiled with satisfaction.

I wasn't a girl that suffered from low self-esteem.

I liked the way I looked and I worked hard to maintain the curves that shaped my body. I wasn't fat, though by today's standards (which basically said you should look like a stick with a head), some people probably thought I was, but I didn't really care what those people thought. In my opinion, a woman should have a shape; she should be a body of swells and valleys. She should have something for a man to grab on to in bed—a solid form to hold on to in the night—not some twig that he couldn't even find between the sheets.

I stood at average height, 5'5", and had a classic hourglass shape (just like Marilyn Monroe) with full hips that gave way to a waist that dipped in on each side and rose up to meet an ample chest and a strong set of shoulders. My thighs rubbed together when I walked and someone once compared my booty to an onion (he said it made a brother want to cry).

I wore my golden-blond hair short (just past my chin), and I liked to style it in messy curls or waves that framed blue eyes and a creamy complexion.

To finish off the body-hugging outfit, I pulled on a pair of high-heeled black boots and the black cap I'd found earlier. Cat Woman could eat her heart out. On my way out the door, I grabbed a black coat and my bag that contained the address I got illegally out of the DMV computer system. What? What's the point in working at a job you hate if you can't benefit from it sometimes?

It took about forty-five minutes to get to his house. Of course he lived in some ritzy part of town. What was surprising and to my advantage was that his house sat apart from everyone else's. I guess I shouldn't be surprised that he would value privacy—I mean, he *was* a killer.

The house was dark and instead of parking close to the yard, I turned around and went back the way I came, parking near a cluster of houses just down the road. Making sure there wasn't anyone else lurking around (besides me), I walked the rest of the way to his property.

I wasn't about to knock on the door so I went around the side of the house, peaking into darkened windows and snooping through the bushes. The house was large, made of some kind of stone, and had a lot of wide windows. When I came around to the back, I noticed there was a light on in what appeared to be a family room with an adjoining kitchen.

I tiptoed up onto the back deck, creeping closer to a nearby window. I pressed myself up against the side of the house and then stealthily peaked around and into the house. There was a really tall dining table with four leather chairs sitting in the center, acting as a divider between the spaces. On it was an open laptop and papers scattered all around.

There was no one there. I heard no sounds, even after I stood there for a good ten minutes. No other lights went on or off. The back of the yard remained dark; not even a neighbor's dog barked.

Maybe he wasn't home.

I wanted to know what was written on all those papers.

I pushed off the stone and stepped up to the French doors, pulling out a credit card from my coat pocket. Before I attempted to jimmy open the door with my plastic, I had a twinge of doubt… This guy was a Death Escort—an assassin. His house was probably wired to the max with some high-tech security to keep out the crazies.

Then again… wasn't he one of the crazies?

Besides, Charming practically had a God complex. He probably hadn't bothered with an alarm because he thought he was invincible.

I snorted in amusement but then froze, afraid someone heard me.

Seconds ticked by and no one yelled, "Hey, you!" or "Freeze!" so I figured I was good to go. I had the door open in seconds, grinning to myself about my expert use of a credit card as I slid it back into my pocket.

The door closed soundlessly and I crept over to the table, my heart pounding so hard that I actually looked over my shoulder, thinking someone else was there.

I was still alone.

I reached out and touched one of the keys on the computer and it sprang to life out of slumber. It was some sort of confirmation for something purchased. A ticket of some kind. I hit back a couple times and was redirected to a website advertising some sort of charity ball.

Interesting.

Charming didn't really seem like the charitable type.

Next I looked through the papers that were scattered out of a vanilla-colored folder. It was all facts and information about a woman… I came across her photo and recognized her immediately. It was the senator's daughter.

What was he up to?

I looked back at the screen and I was hit in the face with a gust of wind. The laptop's lid slammed closed and the papers blew, some of them falling onto the floor.

Startled, I gasped, drawing back away from the table and spinning around to run for the door. But the weird just kept on coming.

The lights flickered off and on, the TV roared to life, and flames exploded out of the fireplace.

I almost peed my pants.

Was this place haunted? Is that why he didn't have a security system? It would be just like him to buy some creepy place filled with ghosts—ghosts of people he probably killed—and use it to scare the crap out of anyone who stopped by.

The door was just steps away, the darkness like a beacon. It promised concealment if I could just get there… Someone or something grabbed me from behind, locking their arms around me like a set of vices.

A scream caught in my throat and I swallowed it. I wasn't going down like this. I stomped down, using the heel on my booth as a weapon. When the man howled in pain, I took off again. He grabbed at me and the cap on my head was ripped away, but I kept going. I could buy a new hat… but the rest of me…

Piper's words echoed through my head. *I don't know what I would do if I lost you too.* And I bit back a cry. *I'm so sorry, Piper,* I thought.

He caught me again, this time around the waist, and hauled me backward up against his chest, which was solid and much wider than me. *I will not scream, I will not scream,* I ordered myself.

"Who are you and what the hell are you doing in my house?" he growled into my ear.

Are you freaking kidding me? That was *him*? Forget peeing my pants. I was going to give him a black eye for scaring me like that! "How did you move that fast?" I demanded.

I caught his heavy sigh once he heard my voice. I hope I was irritating the hell out of him right now. "You better have a damn good explanation for why I found you in my house, going through my things, George."

*George!* He called me that just to drive me insane. Clearly, I hadn't done enough damage the first time I stomped on his foot, so I prepared to do it again.

"Ah—ah—ah," he warned. "Now is not the time to piss me off any more than you already have."

Before I could do anything, he spun me around, his fingers digging into my arms, but I barely noticed the pain. I barely thought about the way he'd scared me—the way he moved so fast.

He wasn't wearing any clothes.

His skin was bare and carried the sheen of being slightly damp. His muscles… *Dear Lord…* He was wearing a towel. A towel that was dipping dangerously low on his narrow hips…

*Why!* someone inside me demanded. *Why is it fair for someone so damn deadly to look so damn good?*

The thought shook me and I squeezed my eyes shut. Man candy or not, this guy was not made of sugar.

So I kept my eyes closed and began to scream.

# Chapter Five

*"Infuriating - to make furious; enrage."*

## Charming

"I'm blind!" she screeched. "My eyes!" She began to struggle against my hold and I gladly let her go, giving her a little shove away from me.

"I think I'm scarred for life now!" she said, bringing her hands up to cover her eyes. "Get some clothes!"

"You break into my house and then demand I get dressed?" I growled.

"I see now why you don't have an alarm. You just walk around half naked. That's enough to keep anyone out." She lowered her hands but kept her eyes trained on the floor.

"I was taking a shower," I ground out, so annoyed that I explained myself without even thinking about it. Then I stopped. I didn't have to explain myself to anyone.

I took a step toward her, watching as she took a step back. I did it again, angling myself away from the door so she would have to do the same.

I kept prowling closer, reducing the space between us, and she kept scrambling backward trying to gain it back.

And then she came up against the back of the couch.

I saw her swallow thickly, her gaze traveling up my body, past my shoulders, until her eyes collided with mine. "You don't have the look of a woman scarred for life. If anything, you look like a woman who likes what she sees."

She snorted and opened her mouth for another of her sarcastic comebacks, but whatever she was about to say died on her lips when I took one last step forward, closing the little space left between us.

I reached out, resting my hands on both sides of the back of the couch, caging her between my arms. She made a sound and brought her hands up to push me back but then dropped them before actually touching me. "What's a matter, love?" I whispered. "Are you afraid if you touch me you won't be able to stop?"

"Oh my God!" she burst out, ducking beneath my arm and trying to get away. "You are so gross."

I caught her arm and yanked her around. "How did you find me? What the hell are you doing here?"

She pulled herself free and glared at me. "How did you move so fast before?"

"Answering a question with a question. I'm not the one who owes any answers." I crossed my arms over my chest. "You broke into my house."

She rolled her eyes dramatically. "Please, your back door opened with a credit card. With locks like that you were practically asking for it."

"I don't need locks. I'm an Escort."

She snorted. It was a habit I found very unbecoming. "I knew you'd say that," she muttered to herself. "Arrogant, pigheaded…"

"Excuse me?" I lifted a brow.

"What's up with all those papers?" she asked, hitching a chin toward where they had fallen to the floor. "Why are you so interested in the senator's daughter?"

"I suddenly don't care why you're here or what you want. It's time for you to go. Don't even think about coming back here again," I threatened, shoving her toward the French doors.

"Or what?" she taunted. "You'll kill me?"

I didn't have time to reply because she gasped and stopped in her tracks. I had to move fast to avoid bumping into her. She spun around and pinned me with a hard blue stare.

"You're going to kill her, aren't you?"

I just stared at her.

"I knew you were up to something!" she burst out. "Is she your Target? Or is she just for fun?"

"I do not kill for fun," I said mildly.

"Well, you must not hate doing it because you do it all the time."

Her words struck something inside me that I hadn't felt in a long time, and I pushed it back, I didn't think about those kinds of things anymore. I didn't *feel*.

"What I do is none of your business."

"It is when you burst into my friend's house and pull out a gun, then kidnap her."

I sighed. She was exhausting. "So we're back to that, are we? Your friend is still alive. I am no threat to her anymore," I said and then pinned her with a stare. "Which is more than I can say about you."

"Go ahead and try," she shot out, leaning toward me and narrowing her eyes.

"So you aren't afraid of me at all?" I asked slyly. I reached out and brushed a wild lock of blond hair from her cheek and then slowly let my fingertips travel down her face, making a path all the way down her neck. I felt her heartbeat speed up and I smiled. I shifted, angling my body toward hers and leaning down so that my lips were near her ear.

"You're not afraid to be alone with a man without a conscience? With someone who kills for money and power? Who possesses more strength in one hand than you have in your entire body?" As I spoke I splayed my fingers out along her neck.

Her breath hitched and I moved fast, slamming her body up against the door, wrapping my hand around her throat and applying just enough pressure to make her eyes widen in surprise.

"There is nothing stopping me from killing you right here, right now," I growled.

Her hands came up to grab at where I squeezed her neck. "Please, don't." she said. It was a soft plea that I might not have heard if I hadn't been so close.

I pushed away from her, putting several feet between us. I heard her gasp from behind and imagined her sinking back against the door and bringing her hands up to her tight throat.

But that isn't what she was doing.

She shoved me hard from behind, sending me forward, tripping a little, and then she shoved me again. "You jerk!" she spat as I caught myself on the edge of the kitchen island and spun around.

I couldn't help it. I laughed.

"I'm not going to let you kill her!"

That wiped the smile off my face. "Don't get in my way."

She smiled a flat, unfriendly smile. "Oh, I'm already there."

*　*　*

I don't know how long we stood there glaring at each other across the room, but when the start of some bad infomercial came on the TV, it snapped me out of it and I flew across the room at her. It made me extremely satisfied when she flinched like she was afraid.

As much as I wanted to ring her neck, I wanted her gone more. She was officially the most infuriating person I'd ever met. I tossed her off the deck and into the dark yard and then stalked back into the house and slammed the door, locking the lock she made fun of.

Then I snatched up the remote on the coffee table and hit a button, lowering all the blinds on the windows. I ran upstairs and threw on a pair of jeans and then stood in the darkened window that faced the street and watched as she made her way down the road toward a red Jeep Wrangler.

I stood there long after she was out of sight, watching to be sure she didn't come back.

Tonight was a first for me.

The first time anyone ever dared to break into my house. The first time anyone ever snooped in my business. The first time the sight of my naked chest didn't turn a woman into a puddle at my feet.

But most of all…

The first time I ever *felt* anything other than death in a very, very long time.

# Chapter Six

*"Vending machine - a coin-operated machine that dispenses merchandise."*

## *Frankie*

Okay, so maybe breaking into his house wasn't the smartest thing I've ever done. But I did accomplish something. Besides getting scared to death, annoyed, and slightly turned on (just because he's good-looking doesn't mean I have to turn into some obsessive groupie)…

I learned what he was up to.

I should have known it wasn't going to be something as simple as wanting to set up a legitimate residence.

He had a new Target.

A high-profile one.

My hands curled around the steering wheel and squeezed until my joints ached. What was it with this guy? How could he be so casual about killing—about robbing someone of their life?

I should have listened to Piper. I should have stayed away from him.

But I didn't.

Now I knew.

I couldn't just let him kill her.

The Jeep slowed as I pulled into the parking lot of a place I didn't even realize I was driving to. It was one of my most favorite places ever. The Iced Princess. The Iced Princess was this completely posh, over-the-top bakery. They were famous here in Alaska for their cupcakes and all pink decor. Everything inside was pink—pink rugs, pink couches, and pink chairs sitting at pink tables.

They had a bakery counter that would make anyone drool. The cupcakes were piled high with homemade icing and usually with some sort of edible decoration. Not every cupcake was pink, but they did always have their signature treat: Princess for a Day. It was a white cupcake in a hot-pink wrapper, piped high with pastel-pink icing and an edible sugar tiara balanced on top.

They also had a coffee bar where even the paper cups were pink. The coffee was so good that not even the most macho of men cared to be seen with a pink cup.

Charming probably wouldn't be caught dead drinking from a pink cup.

I pushed him out of my mind. I was taking a brain break from the killer.

My sugar stores were running low and I needed an emergency pick-me-up. The Iced Princess was closed—they didn't open until six a.m. for the coffee crowd, but I didn't have to resort to breaking and entering again that night just to get what I wanted.

I left the Jeep running and went toward the giant pink machine topped with a glittery tiara sitting by the front entrance. I checked out the electronic menu for my choices and couldn't decide. I swiped my card and hit a button. Seconds later, I lifted the door on the front and withdrew a pink box. Inside was a chocolate cupcake. Then I repeated the process twice more and collected another two cupcakes. This time selecting the classic Princess for a Day and a Rock Me Raspberry flavors.

I mean seriously.

A vending machine filled with the best cupcakes on the planet? If I could figure out a way to tow this thing home, I would so do it.

I stacked the boxes and climbed back into the Jeep, not bothering to wait until I got home. I needed sugar now. I opened up the Choc-o-holic cupcake and dug in.

It was filled with fudge sauce.

I groaned with joy. "Thank you, Jesus," I prayed.

After licking all the chocolate off my fingers, I backed out of the lot and drove home, eyeing the other two boxes the entire way. If that place was closer to my apartment, my fine balance between curvy and fat might be in danger.

My brain break lasted until I arrived in the safety of my home, where I ate another cupcake. But it couldn't last forever. I had a decision to make.

I could forget I ever saw Charming today, forget I knew what he was planning.

Or…

I could make it my life's mission to stop him.

Who was I kidding? There was no choice here. I wasn't about the let him charm someone to death.

It was about time his charm ran out.

# Chapter Seven

*"Charity ball - an event where the practice of benevolent giving
is carried out."*

## Charming

I might consider Alaska a boring place, a forgotten and cold bare landscape where nothing interesting resided. But the upper class, the high-society of the state, seemed to know how to party.

The charity ball that was being held for land conservation and historic preservation drew quite the crowd of upper-crust socialites. It was being held in one of said socialite's homes—practically a mansion—that sat away from everything else on the edge of a wide piece of land. We were in what only could be described as a ballroom, with gleaming marble floors, soaring ceilings, and what appeared to be hand-painted murals on the walls. On the end of the room was a wall of windows and in the center were wide glass doors that led out onto a stone balcony with a rounded edge and stone railings. Beyond the balcony was a view that could draw the eye for hours and still leave more to see. It wasn't of a cityscape or a body of water. It was endless land covered in trees and foliage. In the distance were mountains that seemed to rise up into the dark sky and were capped with white— snow that probably never melted.

Even though it was spring, there was still some snow on the ground. I was beginning to wonder if the snow down here ever melted. I mean, what was the point of having a huge balcony if one could never open the doors, let in the night air, and enjoy the view?

I turned away from the sight; it was making me want to go home.

*Six months*, I reminded myself. *Do this job and then you can get the hell out of here.*

A waiter in a perfectly tailored suit walked by and I snagged a flute of champagne from his golden tray and took a long drink. What I wouldn't give to just drain the glass and then another. But I had to restrain myself. Appearances were everything. And while it might not seem that anyone was paying any attention to me, they could be.

An Escort could never afford to forget his place. His job.

A job was why I was here.

I looked around the room—servers with trays, a man at a piano playing some boring ballad, and people dressed in gowns and tuxedos. The women dripped in jewels and perfume, laughing their fake laughs and sipping champagne without a care in the world. Security was placed discreetly at all the exits, the windows, and near the staircase at the far end of the room.

I knew the senator must be here already and it wasn't hard to spot him in the crowd. People surrounded him, laughing and talking. I gazed through his friends, his followers, and the wannabe's looking for Rosalyn, his daughter. I didn't see her and I figured perhaps she wasn't here yet, waiting for a time to walk in and be fashionably late to draw the stares of everyone already in the room.

I suppressed a sigh at the thought. Dealing with a diva was never fun.

I set down my empty glass and snagged another from a passing tray and then worked the room, introducing myself and pretending to be interested in the charity.

As far as events went this one was pretty good. Over my many years of being an Escort, I had grown accustomed to nice things. I liked money. I liked being in places where everyone around me had money too.

Across the room there were a few paintings on display, and I went and stood in front of one and stared at it. It was a decent piece, especially considering the art scene here must be dismal.

Someone came up beside me, stopping to stare at the same painting. I turned my head just a fraction to see who it was.

It was her. Rosalyn.

I turned back to the painting, pretending to study it some more while sipping the champagne. I could feel her eyes on me, but I still didn't acknowledge her.

"It's a beautiful painting," she said finally.

I glanced at her. She was wearing a black gown, the fabric close to her tall, willowy frame. Her dark hair was pulled up away from her face and she wore a necklace that probably cost three million dollars. Vaguely, my mind started running scenarios of how I could snatch it without being caught. If sold on the right market, I could make quite a little profit on a piece like that.

I met her eyes—they were brown—and saw she was waiting for my reply. She expected me to say something vague and non-committal about the art. She thought I was just another one of these rich airheads here tonight to throw around my excessive money.

I looked back at the painting, taking another slow sip of my drink. "I think it's very sorrowful," I said. "The lines seem heavy. The shadows there"—I pointed—"behind the man seem to come forward as if to consume him, surround him." Then I looked back at her. She was watching me with interest and I held back my smile. *Gotcha.* "But you're right; it is a beautiful piece of art. Sometimes there is beauty in sorrow."

And then I walked away.

I didn't look back.

I didn't pause.

I stopped beside the piano and dropped a twenty into the glass fishbowl sitting on the top and asked him to play something a little less monotonous.

I felt her eyes follow me as I moved around the room. She watched me with interest. I was the man who gave her an unexpected answer. The man who didn't seem to care or even know who she was. And then I just walked away without so much as a backward glance.

I knew her type.

I was driving her crazy.

Good. Let her think it was her idea to come to me. Let her think she was the cat who got the mouse.

When really… it was exactly what I wanted.

* * *

I was speaking with the mayor when she approached. I saw her out of the corner of my eye. The mayor, of course, stopped talking the minute she arrived and he turned to her and smiled. "Rosalyn, you look beautiful tonight."

"Thank you, Mayor Hayes," she said, her eyes sliding to me.

"Rosalyn, this is…" He began to introduce me only to realize he never bothered to learn my name.

I smiled. "I could bore you with all four of my stodgy names or you could just call me what my friends do."

"And what is that?" she asked.

"If you'll excuse me a moment," the mayor said, already pulling away.

"Of course," Rosalyn said and I shook his hand before he walked off to no doubt try to secure another sizeable donation.

"You were saying?" Rosalyn asked when he was gone.

"Charming. Everyone calls me Charming."

She lifted a delicately shaped brow.

I grinned my best devilish grin. "I left my white horse with the valet."

She laughed. "That's probably for the best. Whatever would they say if you brought a horse into the ballroom?"

"Want to find out?" I grinned again.

"Funny and art savvy," she mused. "I haven't seen you at any of these functions before."

"I just arrived in town not too long ago. I'm in real estate. Thought I would come and see if there were any opportunities to grow my business here in Fairbanks."

"And what do you think of Fairbanks so far?"

"It's very cold."

She laughed again. I noticed she hadn't sipped her drink once since arriving at my side. I caught the eye of a nearby waiter and he came over, clearing his throat. I gently took her half-empty glass from her fingers and then slid a fresh one in place.

"How did you know I wanted a new one?" she asked.

"You just seemed like the kind of woman who enjoyed her champagne chilled."

She smiled and took a sip, stepping just a fraction closer to me than before.

*Got her.*

Maybe getting this job done in six months wouldn't be so hard after all.

I smiled down at the Target when a flash of red caught my eye. I looked up and saw a woman in a red silk dress enter the room.

Red was my color.

It was powerful, unforgettable… and it stood out in this room among the people who were all dressed in black.

The woman wearing it didn't look like anyone else here. She filled that dress out in a way that made every man in the room turn to look. The dress was low-cut and instead of just showing off her skin, she wore a very long strand of pearls that looped around her throat and then draped all the way to her navel.

Her throat…

There was something familiar about it.

I tore my eyes away from the gown and looked up. Blond hair. Curls. Blue eyes.

What the hell was she doing here?

Just as I was about to turn away, she caught my eye and I swear a sadistic smile curved her lips. Her steps picked up and before I knew it she was at my side, slipping her hand around my elbow and inserting herself into my job.

"There you are," she said like she'd been searching the entire room for me. "I swear the ladies room must be half a mile away." She batted her eyes at me and I thought about dumping my drink down her chest.

"Is this your girlfriend?" the Target asked, a closed look coming over her face.

*No, no, no.* I didn't have time for this!

I opened my mouth to vehemently deny that accusation, but she beat me to it.

"His girlfriend?!" she asked, horrified. "Good Lord, no."

Rosalyn smiled and I breathed a sigh of relief.

But George wasn't done talking. "I'm his sister."

I choked on my champagne.

George started pounding on my back, like that would somehow help. "Go easy on the booze there, brother."

Then she looked at Rosalyn and whispered conspiratorially. "This one likes the bottle."

She. Was. Dead.

"Does he now?" Rosalyn said, glancing at me with a smile.

"Ignore her. She doesn't get out much," I replied.

"It's true," George sighed. "It's why I tag along with Charming here"—she hitched her thumb at me—"to all his events." She released me and turned to Rosalyn. "He told you we call him Charming, right?"

She nodded and smiled. "Yes, and I can certainly see why."

*Ha! Take that!* I thought smugly.

"When I saw him talking to you, I said to myself, Frankie get yourself over there and save that poor girl."

"So your name is Frankie?" Rosalyn asked.

"Francesca," she said and held out her hand.

*Francesca.* She would take a name like that and butcher it all to hell.

"What a beautiful name."

"Thank you. Rosalyn is beautiful as well," Frankie said and I took a long drink of champagne, wishing it were scotch. Neat.

When I got *Francesca* alone, I was going to ring her neck for real this time.

The two women stood there and ran their mouths about everything they could think of. It was annoying as hell and my patience was wearing very thin. I excused myself, ignoring the glint in Frankie's eye, and went off in search of that scotch.

There was a bar near the front entrance and I got in the back of the line behind a bunch of men who were also no doubt looking for something that would help them put up with the women in the room.

After I collected my scotch in a crystal decanter, I moved off to the side and took a swallow. I was still feeling murderous so I figured I needed a few more minutes to chill.

I lifted the liquid to my lips again and through the clear glass someone caught my eye. I swallowed so quickly that the alcohol felt like a hard knot going down my throat. It was painful, but I didn't notice.

I blinked, staring at the woman who practically glided by just feet away.

It couldn't be.

I blinked and looked again. She was wearing a golden dress that caught the light when she walked. It was the kind of dress that women wore… a long time ago. *Back then.* The kind that hugged a woman's chest but then flared out into a full skirt that went all the way to the floor. She was tall and thin, the natural kind of thin that no amount of eating would add any weight to her frame. Pale-blond hair fell perfectly straight over her shoulders and down her back.

My throat went dry. My vision seemed to blur.

It wasn't her. I knew it wasn't.

But, my God, she was so familiar.

The woman turned to go up the stairs, pausing as if she sensed my stare. She looked over her shoulder. Her green eyes met mine.

The glass in my hand slid to the floor and shattered on impact.

# Chapter Eight

*"Ghost - the soul or spirit of a deceased person or animal that can appear, in visible form or other manifestation, to the living."*

## Frankie

Priceless. The look on Charming's face when he saw me in that ballroom was priceless. It took everything I had inside me not to laugh out loud at the horror on his face when I declared I was his sister.

Of course, horror wasn't all I saw…

When he first looked up, when he saw me in this sinful red dress, he liked it. I could tell the way his eyes roamed over the silk, the way he took in every curve. It gave me a funny feeling in my stomach… one I couldn't really describe. It wasn't the first time; it was just the first time I actually acknowledged it was he that made me feel that way.

But then he looked at my face.

And that's when the fun began.

I knew when he excused himself from our conversation that he was angry. A little warning bell went off in my head, telling me maybe I was pushing him too far. But it was too late to turn back. I was in this.

Rosalyn was actually a pretty down-to-earth girl for being a senator's daughter. I actually liked talking to her. I saw the way she watched him as he walked away, her eyes following him until he was out of sight. He probably had, what, fifteen minutes tops with her? How in the hell did he manage to wrap her around his finger that fast?

Something had to be done about that.

Of course there were other people there vying for her attention. When her father called her name, she looked at me apologetically and I smiled. "Duty calls."

She sighed. "I suppose so. I enjoyed talking with you tonight. I thought this event would be like every other one I get dragged to." She stuck out her tongue. "But this one turned out to be pretty entertaining."

I smiled again and turned to go when she caught my hand and pressed a business card into it. "Maybe we can have lunch soon?"

I guess I looked surprised because she made a face and said, "Most people I spend time with are, like, over fifty."

I laughed. "I'm sorry. Sure, lunch would be fun."

"Bring your brother, too."

Oh, yay. She wanted me to bring Charming.

"Are you sure about that?" I asked, wondering if what I told her had fallen on deaf ears.

"A girl can never have too many friends," Rosalyn replied. "Especially young ones."

I gave her a wave and went off to see who Charming was torturing with his presence now. I rounded the corner in time to see him standing off by himself with this weird look on his face. Almost as if he'd seen a ghost.

And then the glass he held fell from his hand and shattered everywhere, causing everyone near him to flinch at the sound.

Waiters rushed to clean up the mess and Charming just stood there pale and staring at the staircase, unmoving.

I walked up to him and grabbed his arm. "What's the matter with you?" I demanded. "Did you need some extra attention?"

He blinked and looked at me, his expression clearing a bit. "Did you see her?" he asked.

"Who?"

"The blonde in the gold dress…" He glanced at the stairs again. Without another word he took off, rushing up the stairs and out of sight.

A woman dressed in a black beaded lace gown came rushing over. "All guests are to remain downstairs," she said, then looked down at the half-cleaned-up mess. "What happened?"

I don't know why I tried to smooth things over. I wasn't here to help him. But the words just came out anyway. "I'm sorry. I startled him and he dropped the glass." One of the waiters looked up at me sharply. He knew I was lying. I gave him the evil eye and turned back to the woman who was likely hosting the party.

"I think he was embarrassed and just wanted a moment alone to compose himself."

As if on cue, Charming descended the stairs, looking unruffled and polished as ever.

"I didn't mean to cause a commotion," I said, drawing away her stare. "This is a lovely event, one of the best I've ever attended. And your gown is just stunning. I bet that beading was all hand sewn."

She straightened under the compliments and was about to reply when Charming arrived at my side. "Madam," he said ultra smoothly. "Please allow me to pay for the broken glass."

"That isn't necessary. Accidents happen."

He grinned, showing off his perfect white teeth. "Well, then allow me to make a second donation this evening. Would you care to lead the way?"

He held out his arm and she all but tripped, wrapping her wrist and arm around him. They began to walk away toward the donation table when he glanced over his shoulder. "Sister, dear," he said, his voice sickeningly sweet. "Don't go anywhere just yet."

And that was my cue to leave.

I dug my coat check ticket out of my clutch and turned it in, wondering after several minutes if the guy decided to go to the store and buy me a new one because it took so long for him to bring it back. When he did arrive, I snatched it out of his hand and didn't bother to put it on but went out the great double doors and onto the porch (if you could even call it that. It was bigger than my entire apartment).

On my way to the stairs, I wondered how long the valet would take to find my Jeep.

Charming appeared out of nowhere, taking me by the elbow and pulling me around. "Where do you think you're going?" he growled.

"Away from you."

Someone passed by and glanced at us. Charming dropped my arm and smiled. "You shouldn't be out here without your coat. You'll catch a cold." He took my coat and held it out like any gentleman would.

The passerby smiled and moved out of earshot.

"Wouldn't want you to *die*," Charming intoned when I slipped my arms into the sleeves.

"Gee, how thoughtful of you to be concerned," I said dryly.

"What the hell are you doing here?" he said low.

"I'm here for charity," I said innocently.

"What's the cause and how much did you donate?" he asked, rocking back on his heels and slipping his hands into his slacks.

Even when he was acting like a pompous ass, he looked like a perfect Ken doll. Idiot.

"It's called the save-an-innocent-woman fund. And thankfully, screwing up your plans didn't cost me a thing."

"You can show up here tonight, try and make me look like an idiot, ruin my chance of getting to know the Target—"

"Her name is Rosalyn," I interjected.

He talked right over me.

"But there is always tomorrow. And the next day. I'm not going to give up."

"I told her you were gay."

That got his attention.

He stood there for long moments, his perfect jaw practically unhinged from his face. "You did *what?*" he finally asked, shocked.

"I admit, you're good. You managed to impress her already. I had to do something to lessen the blow of that charm that seems to work on everyone *but* me."

The look—the anger—that crossed his face made me take a step back. Again, I wondered if I was acting like a fool by baiting the wrong man.

I certainly didn't stand around and wait to see what he would do. I rushed down the stairs and gave my ticket to the valet and prayed he would hurry the hell up and that my Jeep wasn't parked in the nosebleed section of this property.

The valet went off in search of my car and then I was alone. Outside. In the dark.

"She couldn't possibly have believed you," he said from behind. His voice was low and calm. Something about that made that feeling in my stomach start up all over again. Full force.

I looked over my shoulder, tossing my curls, and I moved my head. I might feel jumbled up on the inside, but damned if I would show it. "Why is that? All I am is a very concerned sister about her extremely charming brother who just doesn't understand the effect he has on the opposite sex." I put my hand on my hip. "Why wouldn't she believe me?"

His chin dropped down and he pinned me with an aggressive green gaze. The muscles in the side of his jaw worked and I glanced around for the valet. He was nowhere in sight.

Charming's perfectly polished black dress shoes made a hollow sound when he stepped forward. I turned fully around to face him, standing my ground.

I pretended not to notice the way my knees began to shake as he prowled toward me.

"The valet is going to be right back." I reminded him we weren't alone.

He said nothing, just took another step closer, his eyes not once leaving my face.

"Someone could come out here at any moment."

He stopped in front of me, so close I could feel the body heat he emanated, and his shoulders were wide enough that I could see nothing but him.

He reached out, his hand delving inside my open coat and sliding over my hip, his fingers digging in just slightly. "I like that dress," he growled. "Red is my color."

"Is it?" I lifted a brow and ignored the heat searing my body. "I hadn't realized you'd staked your claim over a color."

He took another step forward and I had no choice but to step back. He was like a solid wall that bulldozed me wherever he wanted.

"From now on," he said low, "you aren't allowed to wear this color." As he spoke, his other hand also found its way beneath my coat and curved around the other side of my hip.

"I don't take orders from you." Damn my breathless voice!

"No?" he asked, amused, the corner of his lips tilting slightly. "What *will* you take from me?"

My back hit the nearby brick retaining wall. And I was completely surrounded. One of his hands crawled around to the small of my back and grabbed a handful of the red silk.

I didn't have time to say anything. To declare I couldn't even stand his presence. I wouldn't have been able to form a sentence anyway because he yanked me forward and his mouth covered mine.

Aggressive. That's how he kissed. Like he was staking a claim, not only on my lips, but my entire body.

I couldn't think.

I couldn't breathe.

I didn't care.

I only wanted his lips to never leave mine.

He kissed continuously, endlessly. His lips moved over mine over and over again with the perfect amount of demand. And his hands... Oh mother, his hands.

They had minds of their own. They started out at my hips and around my waist, but they didn't stay there long.

They smoothed out the silk he'd bunched at my back and then cupped my body, sliding up my sides and around until my breasts were filling his very large, very warm hands. He squeezed—not enough so it would cause me pain, but enough that my body arched forward begging for more.

And boy did he give it. His mouth pulled away from mine and my head fell back, my hair sticking to the rough brick wall as he dropped kisses down the hollow of my neck, sucking and licking until I thought I would melt into a puddle right there on the street. His hands fell lower so he could draw lazy circles over my belly, the repeated movement almost making me mad as his lips dropped even lower into the exposed cleavage on my chest.

My hands found his hair and pushed in, ruffling the perfect style and tangling at the base of his head.

I might have moaned.

It was all a blur.

My body was on overdrive and he was the one in control.

And then his hands cupped my face, anchoring it, holding it hostage as his lips ravaged mine some more. I met him kiss for kiss, and when his tongue tangled with mine, every muscle inside my body went lax.

Finally, he ripped his mouth free of mine.

His chest heaved, and with every deep draw of breath he took, he brushed against my chest, which felt swollen and sensitive. I bit my lip to keep from making a sound.

He gazed down at me, and even in the darkness I saw the intensity in those very green eyes. He looked completely and utterly satisfied with himself.

He reached out and ran his thumb along the bottom of my lower lip. The lip I knew without a doubt was swollen and pink.

"Tell me," he murmured, caressing the fragile flesh of my mouth one last time. "If I kiss her like that, will she still believe you?"

His words penetrated the cloud around my head, the heavy fuzz of being extremely, thoroughly kissed.

*It was all to prove a point.*

He did this to me, revved my engine, made a complete and utter fool of me to prove a point.

And what was worse?

It worked.

I kicked him in the shin.

He groaned and bent forward.

"How freaking dare you!" I hissed. "Don't you ever…" I paused to suck in a much-needed gulp of air. "*Ever* come near me with that lizard-like tongue of yours, ever again."

He laughed.

He actually started laughing.

I kicked him again.

He groaned but then lunged at me, grabbing my arm and yanking me up against his chest.

My freaking body was a traitor and it shifted toward him. He chuckled knowingly.

I was about to scream bloody murder and create the scene to end all scenes when the valet cleared his throat behind us.

Charming stiffened and released me, spinning around so fast that I wobbled on my feet.

"Your car, ma'am," he said.

I stepped around Charming, avoiding any and all contact with him. Touching him again was the *last* thing I wanted. I stopped in front of the valet with my chin held high. "Thank you," I said and jerked my head in Charming's direction. "The gentleman there has your tip."

Charming made a sound and I smiled at the young valet. "He's loaded. Don't take less than a twenty."

Then I walked, very steadily I might add, over to my Jeep, climbed in, and slammed the door. I didn't look back as I drove away.

I didn't need to.

I knew exactly what I was leaving behind.

And I was very afraid that this time I was in way over my head.

# Chapter Nine

*"Pizza - an oven-baked, flat, disc-shaped bread typically topped with a tomato sauce, cheese (usually mozzarella), and various toppings, depending on the culture."*

## Charming

I handed the valet a twenty as the taillights of her Jeep disappeared around the corner. She was a piece of work. Showing up here tonight, hell-bent on screwing up my plans, telling everyone she was my sister.

I made a sound of disgust in the back of my throat as I headed up the stairs, back into the ball, where hopefully I could reverse whatever damage she had done.

Gay. She freaking told my Target I was gay.

I should have strangled her for that.

But I had my revenge. I got her curvy, sassy body all turned on. It must suck to be so turned on by someone you hate.

There was some movement off to my right, over in the darkened part of the huge stone patio that wrapped itself around the entire front of the home. It was a shadow within a shadow.

A low curse fell off my lips. As if this night hadn't been screwed up enough.

Making sure that no one outside paid me any attention, I made my way over into the darkness, away from prying eyes. I leaned up against the side of the house and looked around for more movement. He was there to my left, trying, I would guess, not to be seen.

"I thought Ghost Escorts were supposed to be invisible," I said flat. Ghost Escorts were another version of a Death Escort. Except they didn't kill. Their job was to stay in their "ghost" form—meaning G.R. wouldn't let them have a body—and they used their "ghost" status to follow Targets around and watch them. They also watched the Death Escorts and reported everything they saw back to G.R.

A very colorful twist on a curse word came out of the dark, and I was impressed. But I didn't show it. He was following me. If I wasn't already on G.R.'s shit list, I would have killed him right then, but killing another Escort is definitely against company policy.

"Why are you following me?"

"Shit, man. You saw me?"

"I think that much is obvious."

"Not again," he muttered and I glanced in his direction.

"You mean this isn't the first time you got caught spying on someone?"

"For the record, it isn't spying when you're being paid to do it. It's surveillance. And yeah… I got caught before. On my last job."

"Which one are you?" It annoyed me that all the Ghost Escorts were black. I knew being so dark was what made them blend so well into the shadows, but it also made it very hard to tell them apart.

"Storm."

"You were the Ghost assigned to Dex," I said, my interest perking a bit.

"Yeah. He was cool. We were gonna chill on a beach once his job was done. But then you screwed it all up for him and he got Recalled."

"*I* screwed it all up for him?"

"Maybe if you hadn't been so hardcore after his Target, he wouldn't have felt the need to protect her instead of kill her."

"I wouldn't have been so hardcore if he'd just done his damn job." I growled.

"Guess it doesn't really matter now."

"Why are you following me?"

"Man, I don't know what the hell you did, but G.R. is hating on you hard right now. So hard I didn't even get a vacation between jobs. He wants you watched twenty-four-seven."

First he gives me a lecture, assigns me an impossible Target, stations me in this godforsaken iceberg, and now he's having me followed? I was really beginning to hate that guy.

"Yeah, well, I don't want or need a babysitter. So you can just go on and spy on someone else."

"I don't take orders from you," Storm said, his voice going cold.

"You'll be taking something if I see you creeping around me again." To prove my point, I shot my hand out toward the darkness where I could see just enough of where he was.

When my hand didn't go through him, but rather connected, we both froze.

"What the hell?" I muttered. I hadn't expected that at all. All I was trying to do was scatter around some of the mist that made up his form. It would only annoy him, but it was the only thing that you could really do to a guy with no body. But that was exactly my point. He didn't have a body…

So how did I just touch him?

"Care to explain how a guy with no body is partially solid?" I asked dryly.

"Nope."

"Really. I wonder what G.R. would say if he knew he was employing a Ghost Escort who is lacking the actual ghost qualities."

Another one of those colorful words slipped out and I grinned. This guy was pretty entertaining. "Where'd you learn to cuss like that?"

"I grew up in Brooklyn."

"I'm from New York, too," I said, thinking that things from my past just kept coming up tonight.

"Yeah? Well, then you must be good people."

I was about to make a sarcastic remark, but he started telling me things I wanted to know so I bit back my comments.

"At first, not having a body wasn't too bad. I mean, without a body, I never really got hungry. I never had to take a bathroom break or worry about taking a shower. I liked watching people when they didn't know they were being watched—I actually still like that part. You learn a lot about the human population by what they do when no one's looking."

He paused and I could feel his gaze, so I nodded. "Go on."

"But the thing about being a ghost is that no one ever sees you. It's like you don't even exist. All my thoughts, my feelings, my opinions… they're all unheard. Without the mundane things like showering, sleeping, and eating, every day just stretches out before you like a one long endless event. And man, sometimes a dude just wants to eat a slice of pizza."

"Hear that," I said, and without thinking I held up my fist for a fist bump. When I realized what I'd done, I went to lower it, but he stopped me by saying, "Wait."

So I stopped and held my fist in the air.

I watched as a dark shadow, a black shape in the form of a fist came forward and bumped mine. The force of the impact caused some of his form to slip and spread out like smoke, but some of his shape held and I felt the impact.

"Sitting around and watching people all day gets kind of boring. So I started experimenting, seeing if I could figure out a way to make myself solid. It started working. Now when I try, I can hold a cell phone, make a call. Or sometimes if I'm really bored, I can manage to play a game on it for a while. It just started out as something I wanted to see if I could do. I was kind of shocked when it worked… Then it became an obsession. Only, now…" His voice trailed away.

"Now, what?"

"Only now my body doesn't seem to ever go all the way back to being a ghost. It makes it harder to do my job. Dex saw me. You saw me… If I keep getting caught, word is gonna get back to G.R., and if that happens…"

"You'll get Recalled."

"Being a ghost might not be ideal, but it's better than that."

"Maybe we can turn this less into a 'you spy on me' job and more into a partnership," I suggested.

"What do you mean?"

"Meaning, I won't tell G.R. about your, uh, problem and instead of watching me all the time, you can watch the Target and tell me what she says about me when I'm not around. It will give me an edge if I know what she's thinking, if I know what angle to play."

"I can get on board that train," Storm said thoughtfully.

I didn't point out I wasn't giving him a choice. "Just don't get caught. The last thing I need is another person hanging around and messing up my job."

He snorted. "That blonde is a piece of work, isn't she?"

Something short of irritation flashed through me. "You've been watching Frankie?"

"She's kind of hard to miss."

"She's not part of the job."

"Seems to me she made herself part of it when she announced to your Target that she was your sister." He was silent a moment, then laughed. "She told her you're gay."

Maybe this "partnership" wasn't such a good idea. I felt like I was surrounded by idiots.

"I'm not gay," I growled.

"Hey, dude, it's cool."

"Forget it," I said and turned to walk away. The last thing I needed right now was to be seen having an argument with myself in a darkened corner of the terrace.

"If it makes you feel any better, I'm not sure your Target believed her."

I swung back around. "Why do you say that?"

"Because right before the blonde came to find you, the Target asked her to have lunch. Then she mentioned she should bring you along."

Frankie, the little brat, didn't mention that to me. "Interesting," I said, feeling suddenly better about tonight. Maybe all the progress I made with the Target hadn't been lost after all.

"Thanks for the info," I told Storm.

"Does that mean you won't say anything to G.R.?"

"No, I won't. He's been nothing but a colossal pain in my ass since Dex got around his claim on Piper, so not telling him something he might be interested in is the least I can do to pay him back."

"Thanks," Storm said, relieved.

"Don't thank me just yet. Don't forget the deal. You keep an eye on my Target."

"Will do."

I started to walk away, but then I realized he probably knew something else I needed. "Before I go, I'm gonna need to get an address."

And just like that, I got what I wanted.

# Chapter Ten

*"Breakfast - The English word derives from the concept
that sleep prevents eating, thus an involuntary fast occurs during sleep;
this fast is broken by the first meal."*

## *Frankie*

The incessant knocking on my door far too early the
next morning dragged me out of the steamy bathroom and
through my chilled apartment. I hated the morning. I hated
getting out of bed at some ungodly hour when humans were
meant to be sleeping. But noooo, I had to drag my still half-
asleep butt into the DMV where the lines never went away
and my boss was likely in her office sticking needles in her
voodoo dolls that looked exactly like all of us poor
unfortunate employees.

And oh happy day, it was also Monday.

The knocking just wouldn't stop, and it was beginning to
give me a headache, so I rushed a little faster toward the
door, tripping over the striped rug and almost doing a face
plant into the sofa.

"Hold your freakin' horses, Piper!" I yelled. "Gheesh. I
know I didn't call you back last night—" My words died off
midsentence when I flung open the door and saw it was not
my best friend trying to give me hell for a missed phone call.

It was Charming.

I slammed the door in his face and headed back to my
bathroom where likely all the nice warm steam from my
shower had now evaporated and I would have to finish
getting ready in a cold room. Perhaps I would ask my boss if
she had any extra dolls so I could pretend one was him and
stab it repeatedly with a needle.

The door opened and closed behind me and I stopped, pivoted around, and stared at the man who just let himself into my apartment. Damn, I should have thrown the lock. It was just too early to think of such details.

"I'm sorry, but did you not understand the way I slammed the door in your face?" I said coldly. "It means I don't want you here."

"Charming place you have here," he said, ignoring me completely and walking around my house, looking at all of my things.

"Get out," I said, flat.

He stopped in front of my wall of Marilyn Monroe and stood looking up at her for long moments. "She was even prettier in person," he said, still staring at one of the posters.

"You met Marilyn Monroe?" I asked, partially in awe.

He shrugged. "We used to run in the same circles."

I snorted. "I highly doubt she would go anywhere near you."

He turned and looked at me. "She liked men. Charming ones at that."

"You *are not* charming."

"Your idol thought so."

The headache that had been forming since the pounding on my door started erupted full force. "It's far too early to deal with you." I went to the door, opened it, and then stared at him pointedly.

"Have breakfast with me."

I looked at him like he had fifteen heads and not one of those fifteen had a brain. "Are you on drugs?"

His white teeth flashed when he smiled. "Get your coat."

I looked at myself. "I'm still wearing my pajamas."

He looked at my sleep pants and T-shirt pointedly. "Oh, is that what those are? I can't tell the difference between your day clothes and these. Both are equally ridiculous."

My mouth fell open. Then snapped shut. Then fell open again. "What did you just say to me?" I growled.

"Time's a wasting. Wouldn't want you to be late for work," he said, pointing at the insanely expensive watch on his wrist.

Of course even at six a.m. he looked completely put together wearing dark trousers, black shoes, and a navy-colored crewneck sweater (probably cashmere) with a white T-shirt beneath it, and topping it all off was a black wool coat. Even his hair was perfectly styled to look effortlessly messy.

"You're completely insane if you think I'm going anywhere with you," I said, still holding the door.

He came over, and just when I thought he'd finally gotten the hint and was taking his sorry butt out the door, he stopped, grabbed the door from my grasp, and slammed it closed.

"We can do this the easy way or we can do it the hard way," he said softly. There was a dangerous note to his voice. "You can come willingly or I can drag you out of this apartment by that blond hair of yours."

"You wouldn't dare." I seethed.

"Try me." He glared back.

We stood there glaring daggers at one another until I sighed. "Fine. But you're buying me a coffee with caramel. And whipped cream."

He smiled; it wasn't a pleasant sight.

"Ugh! Put those white teeth away. It's too early for me to have to see that."

I swore I heard him laughing when I walked away. I didn't bother to look back on my way to my closet, but I did yell over my shoulder, "Oh, and I'm going to need a donut! A big one."

* * *

He took me to the Dunkin Donuts not far from the DMV. He wouldn't let me drive, saying he knew the minute I got into my Jeep I would speed off into the morning and he didn't feel like having to hunt me down.

Of course I was angry and hurled insults at him the entire time he was shoving me into his car. But once he shut the door behind me and I sank back against the buttery soft leather of the seat, I decided that maybe riding with him wouldn't be *that* bad.

He was driving a Porsche Cayenne, a crossover SUV that I knew probably set him back at least one hundred and fifty thousand dollars. It was white with a butter-colored leather interior and boasted upgrades such as heated seats (in the front and the back), navigation, surround sound, satellite radio, interior ambient light (which was actually rather soothing to my headache), and a freaking heated windshield. I didn't even know you could heat a windshield.

I stopped checking out everything the minute he opened his door and slid in. The last thing I wanted him to see was that I actually liked his car. Then he might start thinking I liked him. Which was never gonna happen.

"Do me a favor and say nothing," I said as he turned the car on and the seat warmer began to spread heat throughout my back. I wanted to sigh in pleasure.

Don't get me wrong, I loved my Jeep and it was great in the snow, but it wasn't luxurious at all. I mean my windows *zipped* open and closed. This car was just pure luxury.

To my surprise he actually did as requested. The ride to the Dunkin Donuts was just too short. I actually found myself wishing it were further away so I could sit here longer, in the heat and leather with the soft hum of classical music playing in the background. Even after he parked and climbed out, I sat there, not ready to deal with whatever reason he dragged me out to breakfast.

In truth, I was exhausted. I didn't get to bed until late because I'd been at that stupid charity ball and it took me an hour to get home. Then I tossed and turned half the night. I kept dreaming he was putting his hands all over me, and his lips… His lips were in places I actually never wanted them to be. So I would wake up frustrated and annoyed only to fall back asleep and have it happen all over again.

I was still committed to ruining his plans and hopefully run him out of Alaska to never be seen again, but I was also hoping for a little space, a little time to get over my embarrassment over how my body responded to him last night.

He opened the car door and leaned in, his face just inches from mine. "Did you plan on getting out?"

"Ugh!" I said, pushing his face away with my hand. "I was trying to avoid you for as long as humanly possible."

I followed him inside where amazingly the line wasn't that long. I usually avoided coming inside on the way to work (I opted for the drive-thru) because it was usually insanely busy. I went ahead of him in the line and ordered the biggest caramel coffee they had and one of the giant coffee rolls that looked fresh out of the oven. I didn't bother to stand with him while he ordered but left him to pay and wandered down the line where an incredibly fast barista handed me my coffee. "Bless you," I told her.

I took my coffee and went to sit by the window, hoping I could people watch instead of listen to whatever it is he dragged me here for. A few minutes later he came over and dropped a paper sack in front of me, along with several napkins. He sat down and popped the lid off his black coffee (gross) and then unwrapped a sandwich that appeared to be made on wheat toast and consisted of egg whites and ham.

"Are you one of those freaks that counts every calorie they put in their mouth?" I asked as I dug out the giant coffee roll and took a huge bite.

"Clearly, you are not."

"My breakfast tastes better than yours," I sang and took another bite.

"Food is fuel. Not… enjoyment."

I ignored him and savored my sugar.

"When were you going to tell me we were invited to lunch?" he said after a few minutes.

I choked on my coffee. "How did you know about that?"

He gave me one of those looks that would cause lesser, healthy-eating girls, to run away screaming. I just sat there and waited for him to get to the point.

"Call her. Make the date for this week sometime," he demanded.

"If you think I'm going to help you—" I began, sitting up a little straighter.

"I wouldn't need your help if you hadn't involved yourself in my business, befriended my Target, and told her I was gay!" he growled over the rim of his coffee.

"You know what they say," I told him. "When the going gets tough, the tough get going. Maybe you should take that as your cue and leave."

"What part of this is my job do you not understand?" he ground out. "Do you think I want to be here in this reject of a place? Do you think I want to be sitting here with you? I don't have a choice. I do this job or…" His words fell away and I leaned forward.

"Or what?"

"Are you finished?" he asked, looking around at a few of the other tables. Apparently we were drawing an audience.

"Yeah," I said, dropping my half-eaten donut in the sack and rolling down the top. I stood up and grabbed my coffee and the bag while he threw everything away except for his coffee, which now had its lid.

I followed him out of the shop and sank back into the leather of his Porsche. The seats were still warm.

He turned on the engine but didn't put the care into drive. He just sat there staring out over the dashboard. "Make the date or I'll kill you."

"You will not." I rolled my eyes.

He turned hard, cold green eyes on me and stared me down. I stared back, refusing to buckle under the pressure of his threat.

"All it would take," he said softly, "is one little call to the Grim Reaper himself. All I would have to do is tell him that you were getting in my way and I wouldn't have to kill you. I think you know once the Reaper makes a claim, there's no going back."

I thought about Piper. I thought about the price she would pay if he actually made good on his threat and sent the Reaper after me.

"I can't do it until Saturday. I only get an hour for lunch during the week."

"Good. Make it a weekday. Then you won't have to stay the entire time."

"Fine. Now take me to work. I can't stand to be in your presence any longer." I felt defeated, in over my head, and it was barely eight a.m. I didn't even feel like hurling insults at him anymore; it was all just too much for the moment.

He didn't say anything the rest of the drive and when he pulled up to my building, I climbed out of the car, not even caring I was early (usually, I liked to be there right at eight so I didn't have to spend any extra time here).

He grabbed my arm, stopping me from getting out completely. "Make the call today, Frankie. I'll be checking in to see that you did."

I jerked my arm free and got out of the car, slamming the door behind me. I didn't look back but went straight inside and to my spot behind the counters. It was only then I realized I left my coffee and the rest of my breakfast in his car.

I sighed.

Headache + Charming - Sugar = one very bad day.

# Chapter Eleven

*"Haunted - to come to the mind of continually; obsess."*

## Charming

I dreamt about her last night. I heard her voice calling my name. I heard her laughter and then I heard her cry. I pushed the covers off before daybreak and the air was still frigid due to lack of the sun. I went to make coffee, thinking the brew would help chase away my thoughts (and yeah, maybe the brandy I was going to pour in), but I found myself staring at the coffee maker and wondering what she would have thought about all these modern day appliances.

I couldn't stay here. I couldn't be alone. The minute I left Storm last night and climbed into my Porsche, I'd thought of little else other than her. I needed a distraction. A face to look at other than the one that haunted me.

I pulled up the address on my phone, got dressed, and drove to her apartment. I knew she would be pissed; I was actually looking forward to her hideous attitude and screechy voice. Anything to drown out my own memories.

Her apartment had been a little bit of a surprise. It wasn't gaudy and over the top like I thought it would be. It was almost classy. And the posters of Marilyn Monroe reminded me of old Hollywood. She, however, had been over the top.

She pushed me so far with her attitude that I threatened her with G.R.'s wrath. That was the first time I ever threatened to sic him on someone. Usually I fought my own fights. She just knew how to push all my buttons and piss me off like no one else could.

Still, the way she climbed out of my car, without looking back, leaving her precious sugar behind, had made me feel… bad.

I told myself it was because of who I thought I'd seen last night. The reason I was feeling things. The reason I was so on edge.

So now instead of being haunted by one woman, I was being haunted by two.

I wasn't good with idle time to fill. I was used to working… on pursuing a Target, a job, until it was complete. But this one was different. I couldn't pursue the senator's daughter like I would any other woman. I had to wait. I had to be patient. Building up trust wasn't something I could do overnight.

I went to a gym in the bad part of town. Pulled my Porsche into the alley next to the entrance. There was a bum sitting near the dumpster, reading a tattered paper. He eyed my car and my clothes when I got out.

I fished a couple twenties from my pocket and extended them to him. "Watch my car. Don't let anyone touch it. If you have problems, come get me. If it's still here and undamaged when I come out, I'll give you two hundred bucks."

He eyed the cash in my hand.

"This now. Two hundred after. Got me?"

He nodded and took the cash.

I went toward the back door.

"You know there are better gyms on the other side of town. Gyms for your kind of folk," he said.

"Yeah," I replied and went through the door.

There were better gyms. But he was wrong about my kind of folk. I might look the part of a high-society man. I might have the money and the connections. But deep down beneath it all… I was a fighter.

The gym was one large square and smelled like no one had cleaned it since it was built. I walked past the free weights, the heavy bags hanging from the ceiling, and the many jump ropes hanging on the wall and into the tiny locker room where I kept a locker. I undid the lock and pulled out my gym clothes, stripping away the high-society man and putting on the one I was born as. When my wifebeater, shorts, and shoes were on, I went out to the ring.

There was a guy there, a little bigger than me, and I made eye contact with him. We both laced up some gloves and got in the ring.

I didn't hold back. The mood I was in wouldn't have allowed me to anyway. Even after all these years, after all the bodies I'd been through, I still remembered how to box. There wasn't anything like it. Just two guys and their fists. Back in my days of boxing, I used to think that sheer will was what won fights. I still believed that. But I also learned that those who didn't have enough will to win cheated.

I took a glove to the eye, felt the skin around it split and the warm trickle of blood down my face. The cut stung instantly because my salty sweat mixed in with the blood. The guy that hit me backed off, figuring I would get out of the ring.

I wasn't getting out of the ring.

I sprang forward and delivered a series of rapid hits that had him shaking his head to clear his vision. I pounced again, dropping him to the mat but still punching, still delivering blows. It took two guys to pull me off. It wasn't until they literally tossed me out of the ring that I snapped back to reality. I stood up, wiping at the blood on my face and peering into the ring.

The guy was unconscious. He had a split lip and it looked like a broken nose. The way he lay so still, I wondered if he was dead. *Is that what I looked like the night I died? Was I that still and pale with blood on my face?*

I realized the room was entirely too quiet. I glanced around. People were staring. Everyone was staring. Except for the men who were bent over the man I pummeled.

I hadn't been trying to kill him. I was just trying to forget.

And then I realized if he were dead, I would have broken yet another one of G.R.'s rules: kill no one but a Target.

I'd gotten away with it once… many years ago. Something else I really didn't want to remember. Afterward I'd walked around in a state of panic thinking G.R. would find out and Recall me. But he never did.

I didn't think I would get that lucky twice.

The man in the ring moaned and relief poured through me. He wasn't dead. It wasn't really that I valued his life so much—I had no value for life at all.

I just didn't want to make this job any harder than it already was.

# Chapter Twelve

*"Bandage - a strip of material such as gauze used to protect, immobilize, compress, or support a wound or injured body part."*

## *Frankie*

The best part about today? It was almost over. The lines at the DMV today had been longer and more hellacious than usual. Or maybe my mood was just more hellacious that usual. Starting my day with a demanding, self-important moron banging on my door at the crack of dawn just set me off on the wrong path.

On my way out the door, I rummaged through my endless bag of things I might need but never actually used, searching for my keys. When I couldn't find them, a little tingle of panic shot through me, the kind of panic I always felt when I thought I lost something important.

Except I didn't lose my keys.

I didn't have them because I didn't drive to work today.

"Ugh!" I burst out, stomping my foot on the pavement, and turned to go back into the building. A flash of red caught my eye. I did a double take over my shoulder and sure enough, my Jeep was sitting in the parking lot.

I had no idea how it got there, but I wasn't about to complain. Now I didn't have to call a cab. I hurried over to the driver's side and opened the door; my keys were in the ignition.

Charming had to have done this. He's the only one that knew I hadn't driven to work. He's also the only idiot I knew that would park my Jeep in the parking lot and leave the keys in the ignition.

"Well, I guess that's better than him actually walking inside. Then I would've had to see him again," I said out loud, disgust lacing my tone.

"Are you referring to me?" someone said from the back seat.

"Agh!" I practically fell out of the Jeep as I was climbing in.

"What are you *doing*?" I demanded, swinging my purse behind me to whack him on the leg.

He dodged the blow and sat up. "Well, I'll tell you what I'm *not* doing and that's being comfortable. The back seat in this thing is worse than a Porta Potty on a hot day."

I snorted. "Like you ever use a Porta Potty."

"I brought your Jeep here because I knew you didn't have a way home. I was trying to be nice."

"Please. You aren't nice. What do you want?"

"Can we go now?" he asked, sitting up from his reclined position. "I left my car at your apartment."

I turned around to glare at him, but my glare fell away. "What happened to your face?"

"Nothing."

It wasn't nothing. He had an angry red gash on his eye that was starting to blacken. "You need to put some ice on that."

"I'll do that. Just as soon as I get out of this torture chamber."

I started up the Jeep and pulled out of the parking lot. "Let me guess, you treated someone else to your winning personality and they punched you in the face?"

He grunted but otherwise said nothing else.

At my apartment, I pulled up behind his Porsche and parked, moving the seat so he could climb out of the back. I started to walk away but then stopped. "Thanks for bringing my Jeep. The cabs around here take forever."

"Did you make that phone call yet?"

Ahh, and there it was. The real reason he brought my Jeep. It was just an excuse to check up on me.

I sighed. "No."

"I'm not leaving until you make the call."

"Fine. Come upstairs. I'll call her inside."

At my door, I used my keys to unlock it and let us in, pausing once the door was open. "You left the door unlocked this morning when we left."

"You locked it when you left, then?"

He nodded. "Leaving your doors unlocked isn't safe."

I almost made a quip about him not caring about whether or not I was safe, but I didn't bother. I was tired.

He sat down in the nearby club chair and dabbed at his eye.

I went in the kitchen and grabbed an icepack and towel. "Here," I said, jabbing it in front of his face. "That looks like it hurts."

"I've had worse."

I leaned in and looked at it. It was still oozing. "Did you even clean it?"

"I rinsed it out. You gonna make that call?" he asked, holding the ice up to his face. He didn't even wince when the pack made contact with his wound.

I grabbed up my phone and dialed Rosalyn's number. I was aware of Charming's brooding stare as the phone rang. Rosalyn answered on the third ring.

"Hello?" Her voice was a little questioning, probably because my number was new.

"Hi, Rosalyn. This is Frankie. We met the other night…"

"Oh, yes! How are you?"

"I'm great. How are you?"

"Nothing wrong that a greasy slice of pizza can't fix."

I laughed. "I don't think there is anything pizza can't fix."

"Hey, you wouldn't want to grab some in a bit would you?"

"Oh. Well…" Charming appeared next to me and nodded. "I'm just getting off work—" Before I could finish my sentence, he snatched the phone out of my hand.

"Rosalyn," he purred into the line. "This is Charming. We met the other night." He grinned at whatever she was saying. "Yes, I'm here with Frankie. She was having some car trouble so I picked her up from work."

I wondered if he would like a gash on his left eye to match the one on his right.

"Pizza?" he was saying. "Sure, we'd love to." His eyes slid to mine and he smirked. I walked into the kitchen and grabbed a soda out of the fridge and sat down at the table. This day just kept on getting better.

A few minutes later he pulled out a chair across from me and sat down. "Hope you like pizza, sister dear, because we have plans."

"Can't you just tell her I'm sick?"

He shook his head. "Nope."

"I don't want to go."

"Too bad. You're the one who told her we were related. Then you told her I was gay. You're going to come tonight and tell her I'm not. That you were just being an overprotective sister and didn't want your only brother to get hurt."

"And why would I do that?"

"Because once she knows I'm not gay, I can start dating her and then I won't have to use my 'sister' as an excuse to see her."

Well, at least then I wouldn't have to see him every five minutes. Maybe once he wasn't watching my every move, I could actually come up with a plan to get rid of him.

I got up and pulled out a small first-aid kit near the sink and returned to the table, pulling my chair directly in front of his. "At least let me clean up that eye. I don't want to have to look at it while I'm eating."

When he didn't protest or make some nasty comment, I tore open a small cleansing wipe and reached up to dab at the corner of his eye. I expected him to wince or suck in a breath, but he didn't do either. He just sat there staring at me without blinking as I worked.

"It really does look like someone punched you."

He grunted.

"Was that a yes?"

"It was a 'you should have seen the other guy.'"

I paused, wondering if he was being serious and deciding I really didn't want to know, then finished dabbing at the cut and dropped the wipe on the table. "So, the other night… when I was in your apartment—"

"You mean the night you broke into my house?" he interrupted.

"Yeah, that one." I said, opening up a butterfly bandage and reaching for the antibiotic cream. "You moved really fast. How'd you do that?"

I dabbed a little ointment around the edges of the cut. His shoulder's tightened, but he made no other acknowledgement about my movements.

"It's one of my abilities."

"Moving fast?"

"Sort of. It's called kinetic absorption. It's the ability to absorb energy from other people and things around me. My body then can use the extra power by converting it to extra strength, super speed, or even sometimes using it to create power blasts."

"Like from your hands?" I asked, forgetting I was cleaning his eye and just sitting there listening to him.

He nodded.

"Wow. I never heard of that before." It might even be unbelievable if I hadn't seen him do it. Or if I didn't know the Grim Reaper existed.

"So is that all you can do?"

"I have super hearing too."

"So that's how you knew I was in the house."

He shook his head. "The energy level in the house changed. You have lots of energy."

I glared at him. "You used my energy that night?"

He shrugged.

"But I didn't feel tired."

"It doesn't work that way. I take the *extra* energy; I don't suck all of yours away."

"Oh." I picked up the bandage.

"Actually, that ability pretty much is the only one I have beyond the hearing. But it allows me to do a lot. It pretty much turns me into a super-powered human."

"Human is debatable," I muttered.

His shoulders began to shake with his laugh.

"Hold still," I commanded and leaned closer to apply the bandage.

He smelled good. Like really expensive cologne. I knew it was expensive because all the cheap ones were overpowering; they smelled too strong. But this one wasn't like that. It was light and clean with just a hint of spice.

I cleared my throat and sat back. "It's actually not that bad. The cut, I mean. Those kinds of things always look worse than they are. The swelling will probably be gone in the morning."

I began gathering up the supplies and wrappers. When I turned from the trashcan, he was inches from me. I gasped. "Just because you can move that fast and apparently silently doesn't mean you should."

"Frankie," he said. He leaned down close, so close I could see the different shades of green that all worked together to create the vibrant shade that made up his eyes. I swallowed; my stupid heart began to race with his closeness.

"What?"

"Don't forget what you're supposed to do tonight. At dinner."

I made a sound of disgust and shoved him away. I swear he laughed beneath his breath. "Oh, I won't forget." I promised, leaving the room.

At this point I would tell her anything he wanted just so I could get a little space.

# *Chapter Thirteen*

*"Fiber - the parts of grains, fruits, and vegetables that contain cellulose and are not digested by the body. Fiber helps the intestines absorb water, which increases the bulk of the stool and causes it to move more quickly through the colon."*

## Charming

We met at a small local pizza place that specialized in wood-fired pizza. Frankie refused to ride with me and I wasn't going to argue. I had enough of her already to last me an entire lifetime.

I don't know what I'd been thinking telling her about my abilities. Talk about giving away the home court advantage. One minute she was putting that shit that burned like hell on my face and the next I was answering her questions without even thinking about it.

It had to be the head injury.

It was making me behave foolishly.

But after tonight I wouldn't have to see her as much. My *sister* could just be a topic of conversation between the Target and me while we were out on dates. I wasn't fool enough to think that the minute I announced I wasn't actually gay she would jump into my wholly available and waiting arms.

I had no doubt that her people would be running background check after background check on me. It didn't matter. They wouldn't find anything other than what I wanted them to see. To her I was just a businessman who worked in real estate and property development. I went to an Ivy League college and worked my way up to the self-made millionaire that I was today. I was divorced (because a guy like me would have to be damaged goods to never have been married before) and I had no kids.

In fact, on paper I looked like the perfect guy for a senator's daughter to date. I would even look good in the family photo.

It was going to be tricky to insert myself in her life so quickly, but I knew I could do it. The key was to move slowly at first, gain her trust, pass all the checks they wanted to do, and appear uninterested in the fact that she was a senator's daughter and worth a lot of money.

Acting uninterested in her money wouldn't be hard at all. They would never know it, but I had way more money that she would ever have.

I parked my car in a spot in the back of the lot beneath a streetlight and cut the engine. I sat there and watched as Frankie pulled in and parked that tin can of a Jeep on the other side of the lot. That thing was hideous. It had vinyl seats a basic interior.

I frowned.

It probably wasn't safe at all.

I shook off the stray thought (I wasn't hit that hard, but my brain sure was acting scrambled) and got back to business. The hardest thing about this job was going to be acting interested in the Target. She was attractive and I was sure she was well educated and all, but she wasn't my type. She was one of those girls that people built a glass house around because everyone thought she was important. She probably never had an ounce of fun because of the duties that had been bestowed upon her just because her father chose the career he did.

Maybe that was it. Maybe the key to getting to her heart fast wasn't romance. Maybe it was fun. Excitement. Maybe I should break down that glass house and show her what life on the outside was all about.

I sighed. I didn't really know what life was about either. All I did was plot and kill.

I watched Frankie walk across the parking lot. She was wearing a pair of loose-fitting black cotton pants and a pair of heels. The red pea coat she wore flared out around her waist and swung around as she stepped. She would know all about how to have fun. Like I told her before, she was brimming with energy.

But I wasn't going to involve her any more than necessary. Not like she would cooperate anyway. She was more stubborn than a mule's ass.

A black BMW pulled into the lot and parked in the row right in front of me. I caught a flash of long dark hair and knew it was the Target. Time to get to work.

I waited until she pushed open her door, and then got out of my car, pressing the lock button on my key fob. The SUV beeped and just like I hoped, she looked over her shoulder at me.

I smiled and held up my hand. "Fancy meeting you here."

"Charming, glad you could make it." Her eyes swept over me quickly and then settled on my face, or rather the injury that was unnoticeable.

"What on earth happened to you?" she asked just as I fell into step beside her.

"I was at the grocery store earlier and I saw this little old lady trying to reach onto the top shelf for the last box of cereal. I reached up to get it for her and would you believe she thought I was taking it for myself and she clobbered me."

She laughed. "Actually, I don't believe that."

I shook my head. "I had no idea how serious old people were about their fiber."

She laughed again as we approached the entrance. I stepped ahead to pull open the door and hold it for her. The scent of wood-fired pizza and bread wafted out onto the sidewalk.

"That smells so good," she said.

We stepped in and my eyes found Frankie immediately. She was sitting in a booth toward the back. She saw us and waved.

When we arrived at the table, the Target slid into the booth, opposite of Frankie, and I wasn't sure what she would think if I slid in next to her so I gave Frankie a light shove and sat down beside her.

"So that's your story, huh?" the Target asked, picking up her menu. "Black eye by old lady?"

Frankie gave me a look.

I smiled sheepishly at the Target. "Actually, no. I was at the gym earlier. I do some boxing and some guy got in a lucky shot."

"You box?" Frankie said, surprised.

"Been boxing since I was a kid. You know that," I told her. She was a lousy con.

"Right. Sorry. I didn't realize you still did it."

I nodded. "When work allows me to get away."

"Oh, I know how that is. I was in meetings all day."

"What do you do, Rosalyn?" Frankie asked.

"Mostly I just head up some of my father's foundations and causes. I wanted to go to law school, but my father needed me." She shrugged.

"Not me. I hated school. College sounded like torture. Of course, now I'm stuck in a job that's like torture so I guess I traded one for the other."

"There has to be something you want to do that wouldn't be torture. What is it?"

I knew I should interrupt their conversation, swing it in my favor, captivate the Target's attention, but I kind of wanted to hear the answer.

Frankie's cheeks turned pink. "I kind of like to bake."

I suppressed the urge to roll my eyes. I should have known it involved sugar.

"Yum, what's your favorite thing to make?"

"Cupcakes," she replied. "But it's just a hobby."

"Have you ever been to the Iced Princess?" Rosalyn asked.

Frankie's eyes lit up. "That is my favorite place ever."

"What's the Iced Princess?" I asked.

"This ultra-fabulous cupcakery about an hour or so away."

Frankie nodded. "There's nowhere else like it."

The two ladies launched into some discussion about cupcakes and pink and I totally tuned out. I was about to change the subject when someone walked in front of the window by our table.

All the air in my lungs seemed to disappear.

It was the same girl from the other night. From the charity ball.

Long blond hair, willowy figure. She was alone, her hands stuffed into a royal-blue coat. As I watched, she stopped walking, directly in front of our window and pulled a beeping phone out of her pocket. She glanced at the screen and smiled—*I knew that smile*—and glanced up.

Our eyes connected.

Hers were green.

My body jerked like it had been shocked and my mouth went bone dry.

The woman turned away and started walking again. I craned my neck to watch her until she disappeared from sight.

"Charming, are you okay?" Frankie was looking at me with a funny look on her face.

I cleared my throat, glancing at her hand, which was resting on my forearm. The Target was watching me as well. "I'm fine. I thought I recognized that woman, but then I realized I was wrong."

"Some people just have those faces," the Target was saying. "You know the kind that everyone thinks they know."

Frankie agreed with her and removed her hand from my arm. I kind of wished she'd left it there another moment. It made me feel grounded. *That looked just like her.*

It wasn't. And I wasn't going to do this. Not now. Not here. I finally had my chance to get in with the Target and I wasn't going to let anything blow it for me.

The waiter came around and took out orders and then came back with drinks all around. After that I tried to keep the conversation about the Target, figuring it wouldn't hurt to appear interested but also maybe learn something about her that could be useful.

Frankie kept butting her big mouth in to talk about shoes, celebrities, and TV shows.

"Speaking of clothes," Rosalyn said, turning away from me to look directly at Frankie. "I loved the gown you were wearing at the ball. Where did you get it?"

"Oh, there is this great little vintage shop downtown. Not many people know about it."

"We should go!" the Target exclaimed.

The two made plans to go shopping that weekend and I couldn't help but feel like Frankie was trying to move in on my Target.

When Rosalyn got up to use the ladies room, I leaned in close. "Quit being nice," I growled in her ear.

She made a face. "Not everyone has the disposition of a turd like you do."

"When she comes back to the table, we're going to tell her that I am not gay. You're going to play the worried sister."

"And if I don't?" she challenged.

"I'm going to show up at your apartment every day at six a.m. and pound on your door."

Her eyes narrowed.

Rosalyn slid back into the booth. "Hey, so what did I miss?"

We both looked up and smiled. "Actually, Frankie here had something she wanted to tell you."

The Target turned to Frankie.

Just then the waiter appeared with our pizzas. Talk about the worst timing ever. He handed out the food and then picked up a pitcher of water to refill our glasses.

As he reached for my glass, someone bumped him from behind and about half the pitcher went pouring into my lap.

I jerked up immediately, brushing the ice and water off my pants. But it didn't matter. They were soaked.

Frankie sat there and giggled while Rosalyn handed me her napkin, her lips twitching.

"Very funny," I said, trying to control my temper and not verbally assault the waiter who stood there staring at me open mouthed.

"Oh, dude, I am so sorry. I must have slipped," he said. Dude? What kind of talk was that for a waiter to use?

"Don't worry about it," I said, then excused myself and went to the men's room where I would, oh, I don't know, punch something.

As soon as I went into the bathroom, the door burst open behind me. I turned around to see the waiter drag the huge trashcan in front of the door.

What the hell?

"Ah, man you should have seen the look on your face!" he said.

"What?"

"Sorry about your pants," he said, looking down at the huge stain that made it look like I peed myself. A laugh slipped from between his lips. "Dex would have loved to see that."

*Dex?* How did he know about Dex?

"It's me, man. Storm."

*"Storm?"*

He nodded. "Yeah. I really needed to talk to you and I didn't know how else to get your attention in the middle of the restaurant."

"You have a body now?" I asked, trying to understand. "And why don't you have a black ring around yourself?"

"I don't have a body, so I borrowed this one."

"You *borrowed* a body?"

"Yeah. It's ah… something else I'm not supposed to be doing."

So he was able to get into other people's bodies and control them? That was really scary… but also really cool. "If you ever get in my body, I will kill you."

He snorted. "Being in your body would hurt too much anyway. I have a feeling you take up every last inch of real estate you got inside there."

"What?"

"It can get kind of crowded, you know? Two souls instead of one. The bigger the soul, the more painful it is."

"Does it hurt now?"

"Not much. This guy's not too bright."

"You are so going to owe me for keeping all this to myself."

"That's why I'm here," he explained. "I know you're getting ready to tell your Target you aren't gay. You shouldn't do that."

"What? Why?" Telling the Target I was gay was exactly what I needed to do.

"I've been watching her like you said. Turns out she just went through a bad breakup. I heard her telling her friend she didn't want to date anyone."

Great. Could this job get any worse?

"So if you stay gay, you won't be a threat, you know? She won't have to worry about you hitting on her all the time."

"We could be friends?" I said, trying to work it out in my mind. I was so used to dating the Targets I never really tried to be their friend.

"Exactly. Her very gay, nonthreatening, and unavailable friend."

It wasn't a bad idea. I was already unenthusiastic about trying to romance her anyway. At least this way I would only have to pretend to like her as a friend.

"Are you sure about this?" I asked.

He made a face like he was uncomfortable and shifted. "Yeah, I'm sure." He shifted again. "Oh, and I heard her making plans today for some fundraiser. The person who was helping her put it together bailed. You should offer to help."

I liked it. "Okay, I will. Thanks, man."

"Sure thing. Now I gotta get out of here, drop this body. He's starting to get annoyed."

"Where are you going to do that?" I asked, still amazed he could take over someone's body.

"Probably outside behind the building. If he doesn't come back to refill your water anytime soon, it's because he's still waking up."

"You mean that puts them to sleep?"

"Yeah, kind of. It wears off fast though."

I glanced toward the door. I needed to get back out there. "I'll talk to you later," I said as he pushed the trashcan away from the door.

We both exited the bathroom, him going in one direction and me in the other. I wasn't looking forward to sitting around with wet pants the rest of the night, but I couldn't leave. I had too much to accomplish. My plans had changed. I was no longer going to try and date the Target. Instead, I was going to be the fun, gay friend who offers to help organize fundraisers.

This might actually work out better than I originally hoped.

Frankie and Rosalyn were laughing when I rejoined them at the table. "Ladies, sorry about that."

"You look like you peed yourself," Frankie said.

"My sister, the joker," I said, trying to sound affectionate, and pulled on a strand of her hair. She looked at me like I lost my mind.

Maybe I had.

"So what did you want to tell me before?" the Target said.

For once I was thankful Frankie didn't do what I told her to do.

I put my hand under the table on her thigh and squeezed. "Actually, I should be the one to tell you. After all, I was the one embarrassed."

"Embarrassed about what?"

"My sister told me that she confided my secret to you."

"Your secret?" she asked. A second ticked by and realization dawned in her eyes. "So it's true. You're gay?"

I squeezed Frankie's thigh again just to be sure she got the message. I nodded. "Yes, it's true. I don't normally go around telling everyone, though. I know it can make some people uncomfortable."

"Oh." Understanding came into her eyes and she reached her hand across the table for the one that was lying next to my plate. "I assure you it doesn't make me uncomfortable in the least. And for anyone that it does… who needs them anyway?"

I smiled and released Frankie's thigh. I could feel her questioning gaze on my face, but I ignored her and focused on the Target. "I'm relieved to hear you say that. A guy can never have too many friends."

She smiled. "Absolutely."

Score.

After a few minutes of small talk, I mentioned I was looking for a few charities and fundraising organizations to get involved with to help me and my business get established in the community since I was fairly new in town.

What a surprise that the Target needed help with one she was planning.

Score again.

I was feeling quite pleased with myself when dinner came to an end. I was also feeling confident that this job might not be as hard as I originally thought.

On the way out of the restaurant, Frankie leaned in close and hissed, "What are you up to?"

I just smiled and continued on my merry way.

It was none of her damn business.

# Chapter Fourteen

*"Question — an expression of inquiry that invites or calls for a reply."*

## Frankie

I went shopping with Rosalyn. She called me about a week after our pizza dinner and asked me to take her to that vintage store I told her about. I almost said no, but I hadn't seen Charming either since that night; he was being quiet. Too quiet. I wanted to know what he was up to.

So I said yes and we went shopping. It was actually really fun. Until she started talking about Charming. Apparently, the reason he'd been leaving me alone was because he was devoting all his time to annoying her. Only she didn't think he was annoying. She liked him. At one point she actually sighed and wished he wasn't gay.

I actually threw up in my mouth when she said that.

But then she went on about how sweet and fun he was. About how he took her to the local ice arena to go ice-skating and then they went to a fondue restaurant for chocolate.

I had to act all happy and make noises about how fabulous my *brother* was. I could have spoken up and admitted to all my lies right then and made him look bad. But I would have made myself look bad too. I didn't want to look bad to her; I liked her.

Ahhh, the tangled web I weaved.

But the worst part? The fact that he ate sugar. That's right, he who said food was merely fuel. It made me so angry my stomach began to churn. But when I went into the fitting room and looked in the mirror, I saw it.

It was right there in my eyes.

I wasn't angry about the stupid chocolate.

I was jealous.

And now here I was two hours after our shopping trip and I was still driving around trying to figure out why I had that look in my eye. How could I possibly be jealous about Rosalyn spending time with someone who literally wanted to kill her?

My mind was swirling; it felt like I was on the Internet with about twenty different tabs open and running all at once. And about seventeen of those tabs all had something to do with a positively hideous man with really striking green eyes.

Why, oh why were all the best-looking guys the ones who were the worst kind of trouble?

*Frankie,* I told myself, *what you need to do is forget about him and go back to the original plan. Meet a doctor. A rich one who is average looking. Get married. Be spoiled.*

Yep, that was my plan. Had been my plan since before I graduated high school and decided I would rather eat glass than go to college. My parents didn't like that idea and I quickly became the world's worst daughter. So I moved across the state to put my plan into action. Funny, I hadn't thought about my plan much lately. And now that I was, those plans seemed… unappealing.

"Oh no," I scolded myself and turned the Jeep in the opposite direction from home. "Don't even go there." This kind of thoughts called for a special kind of sugar. And I needed it before my brain joined sides with my body. The next thing I knew, I would be giggling like a vapid airhead and hanging on Charming's every word.

Not. Going. To. Happen.

I turned the radio up too loud, hoping to drown out my thoughts, and drove to the Iced Princess. When I got there, the girl inside was just locking the doors and flipping over the closed sign. Figures I would be too late. At least I could still raid the vending machine.

I turned off the engine and sat there in the quiet, leaning my head back against the seat. I stared out through the windshield at the girl behind the counter. She was wiping everything down and taking all the days' leftover cupcakes out of the display case in the front. I could tell she had the music turned up by the way she moved to the beat.

She looked happy. Like she didn't have a care in the world and wasn't in a very big hurry to get home. By the time my shift was over at the DMV, I wanted to run screaming from the building every day. It must be nice to be able to do something you love every day.

I sighed and leaned down to pull my wallet out of my bag, getting ready to raid the cupcake machine. When I sat back up and turned toward the window, there was someone standing there, watching me.

I screamed and my wallet flew out of my hands and onto the floor by my feet.

"Geeze!" I cried, putting my hands to my racing heart. "You about scared me to death!"

He smirked.

I rolled my eyes and popped open the door, hitting him with it. "What are you even doing here?" I said, ignoring his grunt of pain. "Are you stalking me now?"

"I'm not a stalker."

"Right. Because that's so much more offensive than your actual line of work." I had to practically climb under my front seat to get my wallet. I swear it was trying to hide from him.

When I finally found it and pulled myself out, I nearly slammed into him. In my attempt not to touch him, I stumbled backward and he reached out and caught my arm, steadying me.

I glanced up, my eyes connecting with his. They were slightly heavy lidded. "Oh my gosh!" I said, pulling my arm free. "You were totally checking out my ass."

He smirked.

I suddenly felt like I was standing too close to a flame. Heat seared my skin. I made a rude noise and left him standing there while I headed across the parking lot toward the cupcake machine. Clearly my body was still malfunctioning where he was concerned. I would have thought the time I spent away from him would have helped. Judging from the way I felt right now, it hadn't helped at all.

Unfortunately, he followed.

"What is that thing?" he asked when I stuck my card in the slot and pushed a button.

"It has cupcakes inside."

"Why not just go into the bakery?"

"They're closed," I said. "I never make it here before they close," I muttered.

The next thing I knew he was knocking on the glass door and the girl inside pulled it open. "I'm sorry, we're already closed," she said.

He gave her that megawatt smiled of his and ran his hand through his hair. "Yeah, I see that. I know you're probably busy cleaning up, but do you think we could come in just for a few minutes? I'll pay double for whatever you have left over from the day and take it all off your hands."

"That's like fifty cupcakes," the girl said.

He smiled again. "My sister here"—he motioned to me and I wanted to smack him—"had a really rough day." He leaned in close to her and whispered, "Man troubles. I think fifty cupcakes should make her feel better."

The girl's eyes slid to me. "That's your sister?" Then she looked back at him, eyeing his designer coat and good looks all over again. "You're so sweet to do that for her." And then she was holding open the door and we were being invited inside.

Really.

He just charmed his way inside my favorite cupcake shop.

Of course I went inside. I was getting free cupcakes out of this.

Before I knew it, we were sitting at the table by the window with two coffees and a huge pink box filled with cupcakes in front of us.

"I hate you," I told him around a bite of a sinfully good chocolate cake. "But I love these."

He smiled. This smile wasn't the kind filled with ego. It was a nice smile.

"Aren't you going to eat one?" I asked him, setting it down and picking up my bright-pink cup filled with coffee. Somehow he managed to get his coffee in a plain white cup. I didn't even know they had those here.

He shook his head. "I'll leave the sugar consumption to you."

"You don't know what you're missing."

"Maybe not," he said, watching me. I swear his pupils dilated when I poked my tongue out to lick away some frosting from my lips.

I took another bite, purposely leaving frosting behind, and then used my tongue once again to get it.

His eyes narrowed. "Are you doing that on purpose?"

"What?" I asked innocently while inside I did a little happy dance. It thrilled me to no end to know he wasn't as unaffected by me as I previously thought. I felt less horrified by the way my body reacted to him.

"What kind of game are you trying to play, love?" he asked, leaning over the table and lowering his voice. Desire spiked within me.

I swallowed, knowing if I tried to make some smart reply, I would only end up babbling or making a fool out of myself. I looked at him, telling myself there was a lot more to him than a pair of green eyes and a sexy body.

It worked.

I sat back in my chair and set down the treat. "Can I ask you something?"

His eyes widened a little when he realized I wasn't going to be falling all over him like the girl behind the counter.

"What?" he asked warily.

"Is it hard?" I began. "You know… what you do?"

His face and eyes seemed to close up. That little peak of genuineness I saw in his smile earlier completely disappeared. "I've been doing my job for a very long time."

"How long?" I asked, remembering the time he said he knew Marilyn Monroe.

"Ninety or so years."

Surprise had me sitting up a little straighter. I hadn't really expected him to answer and I sure as sugar didn't expect that amount of time.

"Ninety years," I whispered to myself. Then I looked back up at him. "So, that body… your body… that's not yours?"

"It's mine, has been for a while. But it wasn't my first one."

Wow. I couldn't imagine what it would be like to wake up one day in a completely different body. Seems like it would be hard to know who you were.

I cleared my throat, wanting to get back to my original question. It was one of the thoughts that sent me here tonight, one of the thoughts that seemed to eat away at me.

"So is it?"

"Is it what?" he asked, picking up his coffee.

He knew what I was asking. Was he avoiding the question?

"Is it hard to kill people?" I lowered my voice, leaning in.

"No."

Just like that.

I didn't believe him. A man couldn't kill for over ninety years and it never bother him. That just wasn't natural… It wasn't human. "I don't believe you."

His eyes snapped to my face and he set his coffee between us on the table. "Believe it. Killing isn't as hard as you think. Most of the time it's over in seconds, before the person even knows what's happening. It's not something I drag out."

*It's not something I drag out.* His statement was more telling than he realized. It was like he was saying he did it quickly to get it over with because it was something he didn't enjoy.

"But what about the ones like Rosalyn?" I said, my stomach tightening at her name. "The ones you have to spend time with, the ones you get to know. Doesn't it bother you then? Don't you feel bad for all the things—all the life— you're robbing from them?"

"It's getting to you," he said softly.

"What?"

"You've gone out to lunch and off shopping. You've inserted yourself into her life. You've made her your friend. And now you feel guilty."

It didn't surprise me that he knew I spent a little time with her on my own. I shrugged and picked at the top of a cupcake. "Why don't you?"

He leaned forward even farther, a snarl curling his lips. "She isn't my friend. Yes, I smile and make jokes, I pretend to listen to the words that fall from her lips, but I'm not really hearing. She's not a person to me. She's a job. A means to an end. It's her or me."

"She's a person," I said, not knowing what to feel or think about his words.

He shook his head. "She's an assignment and if I don't finish my assignment then I'm the one who gets Recalled. Death isn't a place for a girl like you," he said, his words taking on an angry tone. "Death is cold. It's mean and it's unforgiving. It's every man for himself in my world and if I don't do the job, someone else will."

And that's when I realized.

He really meant it when he said it wasn't hard to kill. But the reason it wasn't hard wasn't because he'd done it so many times. It was because he wasn't completely human. Yes, I joked about it before, but I never really considered that it might be true. This was a man who should have been dead. This was a man who walked around in a body that really wasn't his. The reason he seemed so detached sometimes was because he was… Charming was completely detached from life, from living. All he knew was death.

I stood up from the table abruptly. My chair would have fallen back onto the floor, but I caught it, sliding it beneath the table and gripping the back with both my hands. I didn't know what to say to him. All sarcastic remarks had completely faded from my brain.

"I have to go," I said.

And then I rushed out into the night.

# Chapter Fifteen

*"Kiss - to engage in mutual touching or caressing with the lips."*

## Charming

I finally said something that got to her. Yeah, I said stuff constantly that drove her crazy or made her mad, but I don't think I ever said something that got this far under her skin so fast.

I watched her go, thinking I finally found the thing that would drive her away.

Maybe now I could finish this job without issue.

Funny, I thought I would be happier. I thought I'd feel lighter without having to worry about what she was up to that might ruin me.

I didn't feel lighter.

I didn't feel satisfied at all.

I dropped a five on the table, picked up the huge box, the coffee, and waved good-bye to the girl who let us in. She told me her name, but I wasn't listening. I pointed to my cup where she'd scrawled her phone number and I grinned, making her think I was eager to call her. I wasn't ever going to call her.

She blushed and disappeared into the back. I took the opportunity to increase my speed, stopping just behind Frankie who was fumbling to get inside her Jeep.

"You forgot your cupcakes," I said, shifting the load to one arm and reaching around her with the other to open her door.

She didn't turn around.

"Why are you here?" Her voice was slightly hoarse and my body tightened.

I set the box and coffee on the hood of her car, not bothering to say a word. I really didn't have an answer anyway.

When my hands cupped her shoulders, she flinched. I told myself it didn't bother me. That I knew she didn't like me. It didn't matter if she liked me or not. I was used to taking what I wanted.

I turned her around, my grip never leaving her shoulders, and pulled her closer so the space between us was maybe an inch at best. She looked up, her blue eyes confused and slightly hurt. My right hand found its way up to the back of her neck while the left tipped back her chin.

"Don't," she whispered.

I had to.

I lowered my lips to hers, wrapping my arm around her back and pulling her so close that there wasn't even room for air between us. She never appeared short, but when she was up against me like this, she felt it. My body had to hunch itself around her so I could taste her the way I really wanted to.

The last time I kissed her was to prove a point.

This time it was because I couldn't *not* kiss her.

There was no resistance where I expected. It was almost as if she hadn't just said, "don't," but instead murmured "please." Her mouth was soft and pliable, warm and adept. She kissed like she had nowhere else to be but right here in my arms. It made me hold her tighter. It made me groan in the back of my throat and when I did, her tongue delved inside my mouth like it was trying to capture that sound, capture it and swallow it away so she would be the only one to have heard it.

Adrenaline poured through my limbs and they began to shake, a fine tremor that I would have denied if she called me on it. But thankfully, she didn't. Because she was too busy kissing me back. I wanted to tear my mouth from hers, to kiss more than just one place on her body, but her lips were like a drug. A lethal drug that claimed me with a single dose.

I ran my hands down her sides and across her back, dipping lower so they cupped the roundness of her bottom. She made a sound, stretching up on tiptoes, wrapping her arms around my neck, trying to get closer. I kissed her harder, with more intent. My lips finally broke free of hers and blazed a path across her cheekbone toward her ear. Her chin tipped back, giving me greater access, and I sucked her earlobe into my mouth and kneaded it with my tongue. She made a sound that caused me to smile, and I pulled back to look down.

Her cheeks were flushed, her lips were swollen, and her eyes were unfocused like she had one too many drinks.

I kissed her again, a series of four short rapid kisses that blended into one.

This time when I pulled away, she sucked her bottom lip into her mouth and held it there. I told myself it was because she wanted every last taste of my kiss.

"Why did you do that?" she asked, her voice husky and low. "Why are you even here?"

"Do you need a reason for everything I do?" The truth was I didn't know why I was here. I was out driving and the next thing I knew I was here.

"I think I do."

I pulled the cupcakes and the coffee off her hood and held them out. When she took them, I lifted my cup off the top. "Because I wanted to."

"You wanted to kiss me?" she stuttered out.

I wanted to wipe that look off her face—the one of contempt and disdain. The way she looked at me before leaving the bakery… had been like I was a complete and utter stranger. I didn't want to be a stranger to her. I wanted to know I could make her feel something other than death.

By the look on her face, by the way her body hummed against mine, I would say I was successful. Which really wasn't a surprise.

What I hadn't expected was, for the first time in a very long time, I felt something other than death too.

# Chapter Sixteen

*"Human - subject to or indicative of the weaknesses, imperfections, and fragility associated with humans: a mistake that shows he's only human; human frailty."*

## *Frankie*

I baked about one hundred cupcakes. My little kitchen had never seen so much icing and batter. When the cupcakes were done, I started on cookies and then moved on to sticky buns with a vanilla glaze.

I called in sick to work. The thought of facing that depressing place was too much to bear. I couldn't be trapped like that. Not today. Not after.

When the phone rang, I ignored it. When Piper texted, I put my phone on silent. I didn't want to talk to anyone. I didn't want to think. I had flour in my hair, batter on my apron, and cinnamon under my nails.

But it didn't matter how filled up my kitchen got with desserts because my mind was still filled up with him.

Damn it.

How dare he kiss me like that? How dare he make me feel something for him other than hatred? His heart might beat like mine. His lungs might fill with air. He might walk and talk like everyone else out on the streets, but he was different. He wasn't really human.

He was a machine.

A robot.

A killer.

He looked me in the eye and told me it didn't bother him. He told me that he killed over and over again without regret.

But, really, I guess the problem wasn't him. The problem was me. Because even knowing all those things, even knowing that he would kill again, I still felt things for him. Things I didn't want to feel.

*Death isn't a place for a girl like you.*

His words haunted me. He was right. And so I was going to stay away from death—from him. I was going to bake until I ran out of flour and move on with my life. I never should have gotten involved with him; it was stupid to think I could stop him, that I could chase him out of town.

No more.

From here on out, Charming could be someone else's problem.

*But what about Rosalyn?* a voice inside me whispered. She deserved some kind of warning that Charming wasn't who she thought. She'd become my friend and I couldn't just let her walk right into her own death.

I was going to have to talk with her. But after that I couldn't be friends with her anymore. It was too complicated and it made me feel guilty. Every time I was around her I felt like a liar. I didn't like feeling that way.

I glanced at my phone, then away again. Not today. I couldn't deal with this—with her today. Maybe later this week I would feel less shaky and more like myself. Then I would call her.

Then I would somehow tell her the truth about Charming.

# Chapter Seventeen

*"Socialite - a person who is or seeks to be prominent in fashionable society."*

## *Charming*

I liked money. I liked cars and clothes. I liked having nice things and the ability to buy whatever I wanted. But sometimes the things I had to do to earn my money really sucked. And I didn't mean the killing. Killing didn't require much talking or much listening.

But spending time with a Target—specifically Rosalyn—required both.

I was starting to think that eventually going to hell wasn't my punishment for murder—it was spending time with her.

It was a Saturday, a day most socialites would be lounging in bed, playing golf, or sitting by a pool. Not Rosalyn. No, she would rather drag me all over Fairbanks to scout locations for the fundraiser that I offered to help her chair.

What surprised me was that there were so many viable locations for such an event. I didn't think this town consisted of much more than snow.

"Are you even listening to a word I'm saying?" she said, wrapping her hand around my elbow and looking up.

"I'm sorry, my brain's starting to shut down from lack of caffeine," I said and gave her my best smile.

"It has been a long morning. Let's get some lunch and caffeine," she said.

"Now you're talking."

"It will give us a chance to discuss all the venues and pick one."

Internally, I groaned.

Her phone rang inside the designer bag she wore over her shoulder and she pulled it out. "Oh, it's your sister!" she said, smiling.

My sister…

"Frankie, hi!" the Target said enthusiastically when she answered the phone.

Oh, yes. My *sister.*

I hadn't seen or heard from her in over a week. Since I kissed her. Ever since that night, I went out of my way to avoid her. As much as I hated to admit it to myself, that kiss had shaken me. It made me *feel* things I didn't want to feel.

After several days, I started to get the feeling I wasn't the only one avoiding someone. She never showed up when I had plans with the Target, she didn't show up to snoop around my house, and she never once tried to call.

Frankie was avoiding me too. Her avoidance irritated me for reasons I didn't understand. I should be happy she was finally backing off. It's what I wanted.

Even still, I had Storm check up on her. She could have been up to something that I needed to know about. He said she wasn't. He said the only place she ever went was work except for two trips to a soup kitchen in the bad part of town where she delivered boxes of cupcakes and cookies.

It didn't seem like her to give away all that sugar.

"It's been too long," the Target was saying into the phone. "You've been a stranger!"

I listened closely to hear what Frankie would say.

"I was hoping we could meet? I would really like to explain why I haven't called."

What exactly did Frankie plan on *explaining* to my Target? A feeling of alarm washed over me and I knew Frankie was going to somehow rat me out.

"I was just about to go have lunch with…" The Target looked up, about to tell *my sister* I was with her. I caught her eye and shook my head, placing a finger over my lips. "Umm, would you like to meet now?"

I nodded and she smiled.

Frankie suggested a nearby café and the Target agreed.

"What was that all about?" she said after she ended the call and was stuffing her phone back into her bag.

"I haven't seen her in a while either. I thought I would surprise her."

"You're sweet," she said, taking my arm again. "What's it like to have a sister?"

"It definitely keeps me on my toes," I replied, guiding her down the street toward the café. I couldn't help but wonder what Frankie would do when she walked in and saw me at the table.

I would know in seconds if she really were planning on somehow turning the Target against me. I didn't think she would go so far as telling her I was a Death Escort. I mean, that would only make her sound insane. But even just the slightest hint that I wasn't exactly who I said I was would make this Target suspicious.

It seemed that my very boring day with the socialite was about to become a lot more interesting.

# Chapter Eighteen

*"Stranger - one who is neither a friend nor an acquaintance."*

## *Frankie*

This was it. The moment I would warn Rosalyn about Charming. And then I could wash my hands completely of the both of them. It took me longer than I thought to make this call, but I did and that was all that mattered.

I lied and told Piper I was sick, that all I wanted to do was sleep after work. It wasn't really a lie. Physically, I was fine, but mentally… I still felt kind of sick.

But the past few days had been better. I finally stopped baking, I cleaned up my kitchen, and I was ready to get on with it. There was just one more thing I had to do.

I took a deep breath, reaching out for the door, and stepped into the café. It was pretty busy inside; almost all the tables were full of people. The servers were moving about the room, trying to keep up with their sections, and the hostess at the door smiled warmly at me.

"I'm meeting someone… Rosalyn," I said, knowing the hostess would know who Rosalyn was.

The hostess nodded and weaved her way toward the back of the room. I saw the discreet security guard sitting at the end of the bar, a water with lemon and a menu in front of him. I wondered if he really was going to eat or if he just wanted it to look like he was. What would his reaction be if he knew Rosalyn was spending time with a murderer right under his nose?

He caught me looking at him so I looked away, toward the table where the hostess was gesturing me. My feet stopped, almost as if I'd stepped in a giant puddle of glue and they were now permanently rooted to that spot.

He was here.

My eyes swept over his dark hair, green eyes, and perfect clothes. He looked exactly the same as he always did. How had he known? He couldn't possibly have figured out I was going to try to advise Rosalyn away from him.

The way his eyes narrowed on my face told me that he definitely suspected it.

I tore my eyes away from him and looked at Rosalyn, giving her a genuine smile. If he thought his presence could scare me away, then he was wrong.

I yanked my feet out of the glue and covered the remaining steps to the table, pulling out a chair across from him and Rosalyn.

"You didn't tell me you were with my brother," I said.

"He wanted to surprise you." She smiled. "Apparently, I'm not the only one who hasn't seen you lately."

"I admit, I've been very busy." Maybe I should kick him under the table.

"Well, now we can all catch up!" Rosalyn said, glancing at Charming. I wondered if she realized it was awkward he had yet to say a word.

"You look well, Frankie. I've been wondering what you've been up to." He said the words casually, but I caught their underlying meaning.

"You know me," I said. "Always planning something."

His eyes narrowed.

The waitress brought over waters for everyone and then took our order. I pointed to the first thing I saw on the menu. The last thing I wanted to think about was food. Maybe I should just pretend I had an emergency and leave. When the waitress walked off, I laid my cell on the table, hoping that any kind of text would come through and I could play it off and go.

Charming reached across the table and snatched it away, sticking it into his trouser pocket. "No phones today, sis. We want your complete attention."

That's it. When I left this café, I was finding his car and slashing his tires.

"Brothers can be so annoying," I said to Rosalyn and then rolled my eyes.

She laughed and her shoulders seemed to relax slightly. I really didn't want to make her uncomfortable with all the undercurrents between Charming and me. I decided I was just going to ignore him.

"So what have you two been up to this morning?"

"Scouting venues for the fundraiser that Charming is helping me with. I'm sure he told you."

"Actually, he didn't." Yes, I knew they were doing charity work together, but since then I tried to know as little as possible.

Rosalyn began explaining everything in great detail. I did my best to pretend I was interested and even asked a few questions here and there. But the truth was I could barely pay attention. I couldn't think about anything with him sitting right there staring at me.

The waitress brought our food, thankfully giving me a moment to compose myself. 'Course the minute she walked away, he had to open his mouth and speak.

"Are you on a diet?" he asked, looking at my salad.

"No. I like salad." Okay, I didn't really like salad.

"You look too thin."

I tried not to gape. "I do not!"

"You look tired too. You have bags under your eyes." He turned to Rosalyn. "Does she look tired to you?"

Rosalyn glanced at me. "I think you look beautiful but maybe a little tired." She shrugged her shoulders apologetically.

"I've been busy," I mumbled, then turned to Rosalyn. "Show me some of those places you were looking at." I pointed to a stack of papers near her elbow.

I listened politely while she rattled on while I tried not to look at Charming. I couldn't believe he would insult me like that. Okay, I could believe it, but it still made me mad.

A woman in a nearby booth laughed and Charming's fork clattered against his plate. He looked up, his cheeks losing some of their color, staring in the direction of the laugh. I snuck a glance over my shoulder to see a young woman, with pale-blond hair, standing up from her seat. She looked over at Charming, a flash of something I didn't understand in her eyes.

He made a sound, a faint one that no one else seemed to hear. But I heard. I watched as all the color left in his face completely drained away. His eyes never left the woman and as she began to walk away, he stood abruptly, knocking over his chair.

"Charming?" Rosalyn said, looking up from her papers.

"I think I see someone I know. I'll be right back." He didn't give her a chance to reply but followed the woman, bumping into servers and pushing his way through the crowd. When she turned the corner toward the ladies' room, he seemed desperate to catch up, desperate not to lose sight of her.

I saw his lips move, like he called out a name, but what he said I couldn't hear. But the look on his face… it did something to me.

"Would you excuse me?" I said to Rosalyn. "I need to use the ladies' room."

"Of course."

Charming was just outside the ladies' room, leaning against the wall with his head down, looking utterly defeated, when I saw him.

"Charming?"

His head snapped up and he grabbed my arm. "She went in there."

"Who? The girl with blond hair?"

He nodded. "Go in there and get her. Make her come out."

Okay, this was weird. Even for him. "You want me to go in there and yank some stranger out here?"

"She isn't a stranger," he ground out. *"Please."*

"Why didn't you just go in after her?" I highly doubted he had a problem with storming the ladies' bathroom.

He glanced back the way we came.

"Oh. Right. Wouldn't want the Target to think you're a weirdo."

"*Please*," he pleaded again.

There was something in his voice. Something that made me do what he asked. The inside of the bathroom wasn't very large. There were only four stalls and four sinks. The first two stalls were empty; the last one had a little girl in it who was singing "Twinkle, Twinkle Little Star" at the top of her lungs. The stall in the center had its door closed, but I walked over to it anyway, prepared for the "someone's in here!" so I could apologize and wait for her to come out.

But the stall was empty.

When my hand pushed on it, the door swung all the way open.

I glanced back at the only other stall with someone in it. Did that woman have a little girl with her that I hadn't seen? I washed my hands at the sink until the little girl finished her song and they came out to wash her hands. I smiled at the mother through the mirror.

She had dark hair.

The blonde wasn't in here.

Charming straightened away from the wall when I came out, his eyes searching all around me, hopeful for a glance at her face. When he realized I was alone, a flash of pain shot through his eyes, so real that I actually felt it.

"She wasn't in there," I said, my voice hushed.

The mother and daughter came out behind me and disappeared around the corner.

"You're lying." He snarled and pushed past me and rushed into the bathroom.

After several minutes, he still hadn't come out, so I went in quietly behind him.

He was standing in the center, staring at an open window on the far side of the room. He didn't say anything, not a word, when I stopped beside him.

There was something about his silence that was tangible. It wrapped around us both, pressing in until I couldn't be silent anymore.

"What's going on?"

"It's him," he said, almost like he was talking to himself. "He's messing with me."

Who was he talking about? The Grim Reaper?

"Charming, who was that?" I asked. I didn't actually think he would tell me.

He turned abruptly and stared down into my face. Stark. That's the only word that came to mind when I looked at him just then. There was no mask of perfection, no look of arrogance, no hint of a lie.

"My sister." It was a whisper, a barely there confession.

Shock rippled through me. Charming had a sister? A real one?

Before I could say or do anything, he left, making excuses to Rosalyn about something that just couldn't wait and promising to call her later.

After he had gone, I realized my opportunity to warn her away had presented itself. His odd behavior just now would help back up whatever I said.

I opened my mouth to tell her, to ruin everything for Charming.

Only the words that came out had nothing to do with Charming at all.

The more I talked, the more I realized I wasn't going to be confessing anything today.

I couldn't do it.

# Chapter Nineteen

*"Exhume - to revive or restore after neglect or a period of forgetting; bring to light."*

## Charming

I drove straight to his house. That bastard had gone too far this time. I knew he was doing this. He had to be. There was no other explanation.

He opened the front door before I even knocked. He was wearing a long, black trench coat and his hand was clutched around something I couldn't see.

I didn't care what it was anyway.

I wasn't leaving here until I got some answers.

"Charming. How nice of you to come unannounced, but I am on my way out." He flipped up the collar of his coat and I saw that his hand was full of stones.

"Your killing spree is going to wait. We need to talk."

"I suppose I have a few minutes." He dropped the stones back into the bowl sitting on the table near the door.

I had a notion to reach out and shove them all to the ground, just to see his face when I did.

"Come along, then," he called like I was some sort of dog.

In his office, he took a seat in the black chair he likely thought of as his throne and looked at me expectantly.

"Playing games with me isn't going to work," I said, not bothering to veil the anger in my tone.

"I'm afraid I don't know what you mean," he replied, but his eyes shined with glee.

I stepped forward and slammed both my palms onto the surface of his desk. The bowl of stones sitting nearby rattled. "Don't play stupid with me!" I yelled.

He looked at his disturbed stones and then back at me, anger igniting in his eyes. "I will do whatever I want. I can see that my games are doing exactly what they are meant to."

So he was admitting it.

I had known it was him. But knowing it didn't stop the lance of pain that whipped over me. I couldn't help but hope that maybe he wouldn't know what I was talking about. That maybe somehow… *no*. It wasn't possible without him.

"Where is she?" I demanded, pushing away from his desk to pace the room.

"Who?"

I snapped. I came here for answers and was met with this. With a roar, I lunged forward, sweeping my arm across his desk with only one thing in my aim.

The glass bowl of stones went flying into the air and dropping onto the floor like a lead weight. The bowl shattered into millions of tiny glass shards and the stones went everywhere.

G.R. jumped out of his chair with an enraged cry and rushed to the mess, staring down at it like his children had all been murdered. "How dare you!" he screamed.

"How dare you!" I shot back. "I want to know where she is. I want to know what you've been doing with her all this time!"

"I don't have to tell you a thing." He snarled, reaching down to pick up the stones. "You answer to me!"

I pounced on him, moving so fast it took him off guard. I wrapped my hand around his neck and lifted, holding him up so his feet dangled in the air. He eyes bulged in surprise. I don't think he was shocked I was able to lift him like this—he knew I had abilities. I think he was shocked that I would dare touch him this way.

"Where is my sister?" I roared.

His office door flung open and two men rushed in. They grabbed me from behind, hauling me backward, but not before I could toss the Reaper against the wall. I smiled at the sickening thud his body made when it hit.

His minions wrenched me back, shoving me up against the wall and pinning me there. They were stupid if they thought they could pin me down. Using my super strength once again, I brought my arms around with great force and smashed the two men together. They collapsed onto the floor at my feet.

The Reaper was standing amongst his scattered stones, watching me, when I stepped forward.

He began to laugh. A deep laugh that started in his belly and reverberated outward until his entire body was rolling with sick pleasure. "You're starting to crack," he goaded. "I barely had to do a thing. A few sightings, the exhuming of the past. Why, Charming, I never knew how easy it would be to take you down."

"Do I look down to you?" I growled.

"Perhaps not," he replied. "But soon. It's going to eat you alive, you know. The wondering. Where is she? How is she? Is she frightened? Does she need me? After all, that is why you took this job in the first place, isn't it? Because *she* needed you."

I ground my teeth together so hard that pain radiated up my behind my eyes. Damn him. How did he even know about her? I never talked about anything personal with him. Not once. Not ever.

He laughed again when I said nothing. Then to the guys who finally picked themselves up off the ground, he ordered, "Get him out of here."

One of them had the balls to grab my arm. I swung around and decked him, busting open his lip and knocking him to the floor. The other one made a move like he would charge me, and I used the energy welling up inside me and released it from my palm, hitting him in the center of his chest.

He flew back and hit the wall, sliding down until he was nothing but a ragdoll sprawled on the floor.

I turned back to G.R. "This isn't over."

"We'll see," was all he said.

Yes. Yes, we would.

# Chapter Twenty

*"Talk - to speak of or discuss (something)."*

## Frankie

It was late when I heard a single knock on my front door. Late as in the hours that I am no longer decent looking. I wasn't asleep. I stopped trying to even pretend I was going to about an hour before. I figured Piper was no longer was buying the "I'm sick" story and since my cell phone was still in Charming's pants, I was guessing I'd missed a couple more texts or calls.

I tossed the TV remote down on the coffee table and padded to the door, swinging it open wide, not caring if Piper saw me at my most unattractive.

Only it wasn't Piper.

"Charming." I practically gasped his name. It was almost as if I had thought of him so much since lunch that my subconscious somehow conjured him here on my doorstep.

I wanted to cross my arms over my threadbare oversized T-shirt, to cringe from his stare and get a comeback ready for whatever insult he was sure to throw my way about the state of my appearance. But he didn't say a word. In fact, he acted like he didn't even notice my old as the hills shirt and holey sweats.

He was leaning on the doorjamb, like he was so tired he couldn't hold all his weight. My mind automatically went to the possibility that he was somehow injured or hurt and I looked him over for some kind of confirmation. But he looked perfect as always. Except of course for his heavy posture and silent tongue.

"Can we talk?" he asked, quietly.

"Uh, yeah," I replied, stepping back from the door while resisting the urge to ask him if he was playing some kind of joke on me.

He came inside, shutting the door, and trailed behind me as I went over to the couch and settled into the corner, draping a blanket over myself and tucking it around my bare feet.

He surprised me some more by sinking down on the opposite end of the couch. "I've never really had anyone to talk to before," he said, not looking at me.

"Is this about what happened today at the café?"

He rubbed a hand down his face. "Seeing her got to me."

"I didn't know you had a sister."

"I don't. Not anymore."

I wasn't used to seeing him like this. Morose and quiet. "I don't really understand what you're saying." Just from how well this conversation was going, I would have known he never actually talked to someone about this before even if he hadn't told me.

"I had a sister a long time ago. Before I died. Before I became an Escort."

A million questions sprang into my head. A million things I would love to know. I never really thought about Charming's story, but of course he had one. And looking at him now, it seemed his story was the key to who he really was.

*You know all you need to know.* I reminded myself. *You're supposed to be washing your hands of him.*

"He wants me to fail. I didn't really realize how much."

This time I didn't say anything. I figured he was having enough trouble saying whatever it was he wanted to say without me interrupting and asking questions.

"He knew the one thing, the *one thing* that could throw me off. He found my weakness and he used it against me."

"Now you know how it feels," I said. The words were just a thought, something I hadn't meant to say out loud.

He glanced up, his green stare pinning me in place. "What did you say?"

I swallowed and shook my head.

"Say it again," he insisted.

"I said now you know what it feels like. For someone to use your weakness against you. For someone to basically be working against you." He just kept staring, almost as if he were looking right through me. "Whatever he did to you… it sounds a lot like what you do to other people."

"You're right," he said, realization dawning on his features. "I'm the Target this time."

"So, the Grim Reaper wants you dead?"

He stared off into space. "I'm already dead. He just wants to Recall me."

"Do you want a beer?"

The side of his mouth pulled up. "Yeah."

I took the blanket with me into the kitchen, tiptoeing across the cold linoleum, and took out two bottles from the fridge and popped the tops. I juggled them with the blanket back into the living room where Charming had propped up his feet on the coffee table and had taken control of the remote.

"You're watching an old movie?"

"I like old movies," I defended.

"Yeah, me too."

I tried not to gape at him. He actually said he liked something. It was a miracle. I handed him a beer and set the other one by his feet.

"Is that one for me too?"

"I didn't think one was going to cut it."

"You trying to get me drunk so you can take advantage of me?" he said, tilting the bottle to his lips and taking a long pull. His throat worked as he swallowed and I noticed he unbuttoned the top few buttons of his button-down.

"Two beers will get you drunk?" I scoffed. "Lightweight."

I sat back down on the couch, squishing myself into the corner. He seemed to be taking up a lot of space.

"Why did you let me in tonight?" His serious tone caught me off guard.

So did his question.

"You looked kind of lonely," I replied, my voice hushed.

He took another long pull of the beer and turned up the TV. We sat there watching while he finished off both beers. He didn't talk anymore and I didn't ask him if he wanted to. I figured that the very little he said was more than he'd ever told anyone.

That knowledge changed something for me. It made me less angry with him, less appalled. It was hard to tell yourself that you shouldn't care about someone when that someone desperately needed you to care.

At some point I dozed off. I don't know how long I slept, but when I awoke, it was to the sounds of an infomercial for some kind of booty shaking workout. Charming was still beside me. He'd fallen asleep too. His arms were crossed over his chest as it rose and fell with every breath he took. He looked more relaxed than I'd ever seen him. Funny, I never realized how "on" he always looked until I caught a glimpse of him "off."

I decided not to wake him. Instead, I turned off the TV and used the blanket in my lap to cover him. As the cover settled over him, he wiggled a little deeper into the cushions. I resisted the urge to stroke his cheek, settling instead for taking advantage of his slumber to stare at him.

"You know what I think?" I whispered, knowing he couldn't hear me. "You aren't dead. You just don't remember how to live."

I turned the lock on the front door as I went past and then climbed into bed. I fell asleep almost instantly and slept more soundly than I had in weeks. I woke to the sun streaming through my curtains, but I didn't think about the weather or how I could languish in bed because it was

Sunday. My first thought was of Charming. I wondered if he would still be here. Of what I would say to him if he was.

*One way to find out.*

In the living room, I noted the door was still locked. My stomach began to flutter around as I peeked over the back of the couch. I expected him to still be there.

He wasn't.

But my cell phone was sitting on the coffee table beside his empty bottles.

I glanced back at the door, which was definitely locked. How had he gotten out and locked the door behind him?

I sighed and went to make coffee. It was just one more thing I could add to the very long list of things about Charming I wanted to know.

# Chapter Twenty-One

*"Weakness - something of which one is excessively fond or desirous."*

## *Charming*

*You aren't dead. You just don't remember how to live.*

I pretended not to hear her words. But I did. I lay there long after she'd gone to bed, half awake and half asleep. I couldn't seem to pass the threshold of being truly unconscious so in my half in, half out state I thought about her words.

She was wrong.

I remembered what it was like to live. To feel. To worry.

Living was too hard. Death was easy by comparison. With death, the only considerations were the when and the how. In some ways what I did was doing people a favor. I was taking them out of a world that most likely was making them miserable and sending them off somewhere that had to be better than this.

I still wasn't sure what exactly possessed me to go over there last night. The confrontation with G.R. had left me rattled. Then I saw the text on her phone… The next thing I knew I was standing on her doorstep, hoping she would let me in.

Chewing off my own arm would have been easier than my attempt at talking. For some reason I thought I would be able to spill everything, to lay out everything that happened like it was no big deal. Because it wasn't a big deal. Only I couldn't. What I did manage to say probably made no sense to her at all. But that was good because I shouldn't have gone there. I wasn't the kind of guy who could "talk" anyway. I lived the last ninety or so years without anyone and I would live the next ninety or so the same way.

For some reason that thought made my shoulders sag with exhaustion.

Of course after seeing G.R. yesterday, maybe I wouldn't live another ninety years at all. Maybe these last few months were all I was going to get.

Ah, hell, maybe it was time anyway. It wasn't like I got into this for some long-lasting career. Shit, I had no clue what I was getting myself into. I had only done it— I cut the thought off. I wasn't going to think about that. Those thoughts were too close to life. Too close to feeling. Besides, it didn't matter why I got into this; it only mattered that I did.

And fuck my previous thoughts. I wasn't going to let G.R. tell me when my time as an Escort was over. He wasn't going to get the best of me.

I stared up at the ceiling from the center of my California king bed and remembered a few more of Frankie's words. *Whatever he did to you… it sounds a lot like what you do to other people.*

She was right. He was doing exactly what I did to other people. Using my weaknesses against me. So he figured out my *one* weakness. Now that I knew what he was doing, it took away his advantage. But what about me? What were my advantages?

If a guy like me had a weakness, then that meant anyone could have one. Including the Grim Reaper. Crap, he'd been alive so long his closet was probably full of skeletons.

The thought had me sitting up straight.

That was it. All I had to do was find G.R.'s weakness and use it against him. And where did an Escort start when he was looking for dirt on his boss? A small smile curved my lips.

Why, of course, in his closet.

* * *

"Nice place you got here," said a voice from behind.

I spun around, catching the plate in my hand just before it crashed onto the floor. Storm was there, filling up my house with his black cloudlike self. "Seriously, man, don't you knock?"

"You called. I came."

"I called you hours ago."

"Well, spying on the boss isn't something that can be done in five minutes."

"What did you find out?" I said as I finished putting away the last of my dinner dishes.

"I really thought you would have a maid."

"You of all people know that I can't have some bonbon eating, phone gossiping woman snooping through my house and my life at all hours of the day and night."

"I didn't really mean a live-in maid… although, if that's your type." The black shape that was Storm shrugged his shoulders.

"Maids are not my type," I ground out. What was with this conversation? We were supposed to be talking business.

"No. What's your type, then?"

*Frankie,* the voice in the back of my head whispered. I told it to shut up. "Whoever's my assigned Target."

"C'mon, you can't honestly expect me to believe a guy like you survives with no nookie."

"What the hell is nookie?"

"If I didn't know better I would have thought you lived in a cave. A celibate cave."

Okay, so nookie was what he called sex. With language like that, I was sure he never got any. "I have sex."

"With women other than Targets?"

"I'm not going to discuss my sex life with you," I said, pulling a bottle of water out of the stainless-steel fridge.

"That's code for yes." He sighed. "You're wasting that body."

I grinned. "I guess not having a body makes getting some pretty hard."

"Yeah, well, I make up for it when he lets me have a body for a while."

Speaking of G.R. "What did you find?"

"Nothing. It was business as usual at his place, Escorts coming and going, security guards patrolling. The most exciting part was when the chef cooked his steak wrong and he ordered pizza."

"How was that exciting?"

"I haven't had pizza in a while, either," he mumbled.

"Was he still home when you left?"

"Yeah, but he was getting ready to go out. He was going to some dinner with the rich people. I don't know how he manages to never accidentally touch someone."

"Maybe he doesn't," I replied.

"What do you mean?"

"I mean maybe if he does accidentally kill someone, he just covers it up. I mean, it's the perfect crime scene—if you could even call it that. The cops certainly wouldn't with no fingerprints, no blood, and no sign of a struggle. They would likely call it a heart attack and drag the poor dead sap off to the morgue."

"Yeah, well, I guess that wouldn't be too hard of a stretch considering I don't have a body and you kill people professionally."

"Touché."

"Anyway, he was going to be gone most of the night."

"Good, let's go."

"Go where?"

"To his house. I'm assuming you can get us in?" The way he just let himself in here minutes ago must mean he was good at picking locks. I was too, but I wasn't practically invisible.

"What the hell do you want to go to his house for?"

"To search it. You know a man like him has got to have some skeletons mixed in with all those bodies in his closet."

"Man, you don't really think that someone like the Reaper is just going to leave his business out for anyone to find, do you?"

"Nope, but I don't mind digging around until I find it." I pinned him with a hard stare. "And you're going to help me."

"What makes you so sure?"

"For starters, you don't want him to know about your little visibility problem." I reminded him. "But also because you need a body and he has a hoarding problem."

"Okay, I'll help. I don't have anything better to do anyway."

"Good. Let's go."

*   *   *

You would think the home of the Grim Reaper would be a dark and creepy place. That it would be shrouded in shadows with winding trees draping the property and ominous-sounding nightlife to warn you away if you dare get to close.

Nope.

The Grim Reaper I knew and hated had his house lit up like the fourth of July on a hot summer night. It's like he stuck lights in every possible crevice and corner of his home. You would think *he* was scared of the dark. Of course he wasn't because whatever else went bump in the night had never met a man that could kill with a single touch.

"There's more security here now than earlier. And what is up with all these lights? This ain't New York City," Storm said from beside me.

"It's because he's not home. He's expecting me to pull something after last night."

"What the hell happened last night?"

"We had a little confrontation."

"Geez, man, we need to go. You should have known better than to come here."

I stood against the side of a four-car garage on the neighbor's property across the street. This house wasn't filled with light so the yard was dark, creating a lot of concealment. "No, that's exactly the reason we should stay."

"What?"

"He knows I'm pissed and won't go down without a fight. He expects me to try and pull something. So I do it now, while he thinks everything is on lockdown and I can't get in. I won't get caught and he'll never know I was here. Hell, if I'm lucky, he won't even notice anything's missing until I'm long gone." I paused and then added. "Besides, it has to be tonight. He's sending me out of town tomorrow on another job."

"Damn, a double?" Storm said, I looked in the direction of his voice, but I couldn't make him out in the night. He completely blended in.

"Yeah, so let's do this."

"What exactly do you think you're going to find?" The skepticism in his voice made the challenge of what we were about to do even more appealing.

"A weakness," I murmured.

He made a non-committal sound.

"Here's how this is going to work. You're going to go first, unlock the front door from the inside. On your way through the foyer, flick the porch light off and count to three, then flick it back on. Then get to G.R.'s office. I'll meet you there."

"You think you're going to walk through the front door?" He scoffed. "And if you think three seconds of darkness out there will be enough, you're a few chips shy of a Pringle can."

"Just do it."

"Fine. But if you get caught, I'm not going to play Cinderella to your Prince Charming."

"What the hell does that mean?"

"I'm not really sure," he muttered.

"Can we just do this please?"

"Fine. Be ready."

He didn't say anything else and I didn't see him move. I didn't hear the rustle of grass or feel the ripple in the air from a body cutting through it.

"Storm?" I whispered, but he wasn't there.

When he was in complete ghost form, he was pretty good.

I pushed away from the side of the garage and watched the house, looking for signs of Storm, waiting to see if he would get caught. Even though the yard and house was bright, I didn't see him once.

I really hoped he didn't screw this up.

I took a deep breath.

The lights over the front door went out.

One. I took off running, zipping across the street way faster than any human could go.

Two. I took advantage of all the excess kinetic energy around the house, courtesy of the guards, and propelled myself even faster.

Three. I opened the front door just wide enough to get through and rushed inside. I heard the shouts from a guard at the corner of the house as the door closed soundlessly behind me.

The light outside came back on.

I pressed myself up against the back of the front door and zeroed in on the guards who had just managed to rush to the other side. If they opened it...

"What the hell was that?" one of them asked.

"Probably a short in the breaker. All these damn lights," the other muttered.

They both moved away from the door and I let out a breath, pushing away and moving down the hall just as quickly as I got into the house. As I reached for the office door, it opened soundlessly, and my heart skipped a beat as I waited for G.R. to appear.

But he didn't.

From inside, Storm said, "Hurry up!"

Letting out the breath, I went in, the door pushing shut behind me. This room wasn't lit up like the outside. The only lighting in here was from a small lamp on the desk across the room.

"How the hell did you get in here so fast?"

"Fast is a talent of mine. Kind of like becoming solid is yours."

"Well, let's see how fast you can find some dirt on the Reaper."

"Where are you?" I asked, searching all the corners of the room.

He moved so he was closer to the desk, so I could make out a shadow near the lamp.

"How did you manage to go ghost all the way? Where are the solid parts of you?"

"They're still there. I'm just using the non-solid parts to kind of cloak them."

"Right," I said, still not completely understanding, but realizing I probably never would unless I spent all my time without a body.

I didn't have time to think about it anyway. I had an office to search.

# Chapter Twenty-Two

*"Addict - to occupy (oneself) with or involve (oneself) in something habitually or compulsively."*

## *Frankie*

I had come to the conclusion that I was an addict. It didn't matter how many times I told myself to stop thinking about him, I couldn't. My emotions were wide open, ranging from flat-out wanting to kick him all the way to daydreaming about the way he kissed.

I went from scheming up ways to get out of the situation I found myself in, which was between him and Rosalyn, to lecturing myself about getting involved in the first place, and then it seemed I always circled back to the way it felt to be in his arms.

Up until last night, I was determined to stay away from him. I made up my mind. He was no good for me and he was driving me insane. But then he showed up on my doorstep, looking wounded. His pathetic attempt at talking was… well, it was pathetic.

Yet also endearing.

Endearing because he'd been genuinely shaken and that seemed to confuse him. It's like he had no idea what to do or where to go and somehow he ended up at my door. I could see him try—try to express what he was thinking, what was going on, but he couldn't.

Just like I couldn't come clean to Rosalyn at lunch.

It's like he and I were stuck on a carousel—destined to go round and round but never actually getting anywhere.

I could vow to myself that I wouldn't see him again, that I was just going to wash my hands of the situation. But I wasn't going to do that. Because I wasn't a liar and if I said that, I would be lying to myself.

I blew out a breath. I needed a break. A brain break. I needed to stop thinking and stop worrying. I needed my best friend.

I was likely in hot water with her too. Because like any good addict would tell you, addicts pushed away the people who cared about them. Addicts isolated themselves so they only had one thing in their life and that was whatever they were addicted to.

I needed a twelve-step program.

No. That was too much work.

I settled for Chinese food instead. There wasn't anything some good Chinese food couldn't fix.

I called and placed an order for too much, making sure I got plenty of the vegetable lo mein Piper liked so much. I knew she would be home. It was Sunday night and the diner she worked at closed early.

When I knocked on her door with food and movies in hand, I actually felt a little nervous. I wondered if she would be upset with me for the way I'd been acting. I wasn't being a very good friend. I practically fell off the face of the earth and ignored a lot of her texts and calls. When I did answer, the replies were short and not at all the way they used to be.

She seemed a little surprised when she opened the door, but she smiled. "I'm starving!" she said, eyeing the bag in my arms.

"I got your favorite," I sang, going inside.

"I'll get some plates!" She dashed into the kitchen and rattled around and returned in record time with everything we needed to stuff our faces.

"You must really be hungry."

"I really am," she said, reaching into the bag. "But I also want to hang with you. Long time no see."

"I know. I'm sorry. Work's been busy." It wasn't a lie. Work's always busy. It just wasn't the reason I hadn't been around.

"Oh? I thought maybe there was a new man in your life."

I choked on the soda she'd given me when she came out of the kitchen. "A man?" I croaked.

She nodded, dumping a pile of lo mein onto her plate. Then she reached into the bag and pulled out the crab rangoon and added a few of those onto her plate as well.

"Nope, no man in my life worth talking about." Again, that wasn't really a lie. Charming wasn't worth talking about. I was trying to have a break from thinking about him anyway.

"Are you sure?" Piper said, pinning me with a stare. "Is everything okay with you?"

"Yep. Everything's fine. I just figured we were overdue for some girl time."

She didn't really seem convinced, but she let it go.

"So I brought us a movie." I put down my plate and reached into my bag. "It's about zombies."

"*Warm Bodies*?"

I nodded. "Any movie that combines brain eating with romance is a must see."

She laughed. "That's gross."

"Don't take this the wrong way, Piper," I said seriously, "but if I was a zombie, I would totally eat your brains."

"Of course you would. My brains are delicious."

"So what do you think? Should we watch and see how a zombie falls in love?"

"Let's do it."

We popped in the movie and settled back to watch it, chowing down on our food. I felt a little guilty because I had ulterior motives for choosing this movie. I wasn't interested so much in how a zombie fell in love but rather how a girl could fall in love with a zombie. Zombies were killers.

Like Charming.

Except Charming didn't eat brains (thank God).

Charming told me he wasn't really living. Zombies were dead.

Maybe if I could somehow see how a girl could love a zombie, I would be able to figure out why I couldn't get Charming out of my mind. I could understand why I didn't run screaming in the other direction.

Because really, the only direction I seemed to be going was toward him.

# Chapter Twenty-Three

*"Booby trap - an explosive device designed to be triggered when an unsuspecting victim touches or disturbs a seemingly harmless object."*

## Charming

The tricky thing about searching someone's personal space was making it appear it hadn't been searched at all. Just the slightest disturbance of something that seemed like it would go unnoticed is the one thing that could cause everything to blow up in my face.

"Look over there," I said in hushed tones, pointing to the bookcases across the room from the desk.

We searched in silence, not wanting to alert any of the staff that might be in the house. It was amazing to me that the Grim Reaper was able to employ so many people and never get caught. If I were him, I would want all the privacy I could get. Hell, I wasn't him and I still wanted that.

I started with his desk. I looked through the neat stack of papers that lay in the center, but it was all just stupid paperwork. Utility bills, invitations to events, and some spreadsheets and invoices for the legitimate business that he owned, which was luxury car sales. He had dealerships in Anchorage, Los Angeles, and New York.

I restacked the papers and moved on, looking over the surface of the desk. There wasn't anything else to search. My eyes settled briefly on the bowl of stones that sat on the corner and then moved away. I wasn't going to touch those things. His stones were his calling card, the only thing he left in place of a life he took. My luck, I would pick up one and alarms everywhere would start wailing.

I went through the contents of his desk drawers, looked through his calendar, his pens, and the roster of names that I knew were Death Escorts. The business was growing. He had more Escorts than I realized. Maybe that was one of the reasons he thought I was expendable. He thought he could replace me. I smirked. I wasn't replaceable.

"There's nothing here," Storm complained about ten minutes into the search.

I glanced up. "Did you look in those books?"

"All one hundred of them?" He moaned. "Yeah. Nothing but a bunch of words."

"Keep looking."

"I'm telling you, you aren't going to find anything."

I reached under the desk and pressed a button. All the closet doors containing his collection of bodies opened soundlessly. They all hung there in perfect, neat rows. Not a hair was out of place on any of them.

G.R. was definitely a neat freak, which made searching a pain for many reasons. One, I had to be sure everything was back exactly the way I found it. And two, everything was so decluttered that I was starting to think Storm was right, that there wasn't anything to find.

"We're going to have to search his bedroom after this."

"You wanna do what?" Storm said, disbelief crowding his tone.

I began looking through the bodies, sliding them back and forth on the rods. "I'm not leaving here until I have something I can use against him."

Storm came over beside me, stopping and I would assume staring at me, but I ignored him. I got down and searched under the bodies' feet, looking for anything that might be of use. But all the bottoms of the closets were completely empty. There wasn't even a speck of dust.

I stood up and looked up, above the racks, thinking there might be shelves with boxes for storage. Nope. The only thing in these closets were bodies. Lots of them, all hanging single file.

"Which one of these is yours?" I asked Storm, looking through one of the bodies pant pockets.

Storm was quiet a moment, moving all the way down to the last closet on the wall, and hovered near the center. "This one."

I reached out, pulled the hanger off the rack, and held up the body. He looked to be in his early twenties. He had skin the color of coffee mixed with cream, a smooth complexion, and all its hair was buzzed off. Storm had been a fairly tall guy, probably reaching at least six feet because when I held the body up, his feet about reached mine.

"I don't understand why he dresses all the bodies like we're students at prep school. Does anyone even wear khakis anymore? Where the hell are the jeans?"

I grinned. "I guess death doesn't come with fashion sense."

"Which one's yours?" Storm asked.

"It's not here."

"Where is it?"

"I don't know. I haven't seen it since I died."

"You mean he's never let you use it?"

"I don't even think he has it." The only thing I could think of was that it was too damaged to save.

"That man has everyone's body. It isn't right that yours isn't here."

I shrugged, like it didn't bother me. It really never had before. But now… now I kind of wondered where it was. I kind of wondered what it would be like to see it again. Would it feel familiar to me? Would it feel like home?

I pushed away those thoughts. They were stupid. "Want to take yours for a spin?" I asked, holding his body out to him. Even to me it seemed weird that I was offering someone a chance to use their own body.

"Hell no. If he noticed that body missing, the first place he would look was for me."

"Well, then, take your pick," I said, hanging Storm's body back in the closet and making sure it was equally spaced between the others.

"You want me to take a body?"

"Why the hell not? He's got so many he won't even notice. I've been listening to you whine about wanting one since we met."

He was quiet a long time. I knew he was tempted. I know I would have been.

Finally, he said, "No, I'll just stick with borrowing."

"Why borrow someone else's body and deal with their spirit when you could have your own."

"Because if I took one of these bodies, I would barely get to use it. I would have a black cloud around me that would point to me like a beacon. If one Escort saw me, they would know I shouldn't have it."

"So tell them you're on vacation."

"It's too risky. A borrowed body covers up my spirit."

"How?"

"Best I can figure is that their spirit cancels mine out."

"How did you figure that out?"

"Like everything else. Practice."

"And you're the only Ghost Escort that can do that?"

"As far as I know."

I finished searching through the length of closets, patting down pockets and peering under feet, looking for anything I could use.

But I found absolutely nothing.

After rechecking that all the bodies were hung exactly as they had been, I pressed the button and closed the doors. I sat down in G.R.'s leather desk chair and let out a sigh.

"There's nothing here. Let's go to his room."

"You're crazy."

I wasn't crazy, but I was starting to feel a little desperate. Both my hands gripped the seat of the chair, my fingers curling underneath it and squeezing the leather. I was so sure that I would find something. So sure he would be hiding some sort of secret.

I went to push myself up, but when I dragged my hand along the bottom of the chair, I felt something. Some sort of small round knob on the bottom of the seat. I ran my finger over it several times. It felt like a button. I pressed it.

There was a soft sound across the room. Both Storm and I whipped around, thinking we were somehow caught. But we weren't. The sound came from a secret door. A secret sliding door in the bookcase. It opened, the doorway wide enough for a man to fit through.

Excitement pounded through me. *Got you,* I thought.

I glanced at Storm. "I thought you searched over there."

"Shit, you expected me to find some kind of secret door? It's probably a booby trap that's going to suck us into the depths of hell."

"I'll say hello to the devil for you," I said, returning G.R's chair to the exact place it had been in and going over to the entrance and peering inside.

"Well?" Storm asked from close behind.

"No trips to hell today. It's just more closets." Three doors all in a row.

"What could he possibly keep in there?"

I wasn't about to wait to find out. When I stepped into the narrow hallway, I half expected an alarm to go off, but nothing happened so I took another small step and then another.

My heart was pounding in my ears, drowning out the quiet and making me more nervous. I told myself to calm down, that it was stupid to get this nervous. I mean, I didn't even act like this when I killed people. Guess my body was more afraid of the Reaper than my brain realized.

But fear of the Reaper was why I had to keep going. Being scared of him was unacceptable. I stopped in front of the first door I came to, staring at its cherry finish.

I was surprised when I opened the door.

I don't know what I was expecting. Something sinister and twisted.

I was a little let down when all I saw was more bodies. "It's just bodies," I said, irritation lining my tone.

Storm finally got over his fear this was a portal to hell and came inside. "What's so special about these bodies?"

What, indeed?

I looked closer, having to squint a little because the lighting in here was so dim. My eyes first went to a contrast in the dark. A body with blond hair. Overly long, messy blond hair.

I grabbed the body, gripping its shoulder and yanking it out so I could see it.

Like a freight train, recognition slammed into me.

It was me.

Memories of looking in the mirror when I was alive crashed over me. Wave after wave of broken clips of memories… of me brushing my teeth, combing my hair, studying a black eye or a busted lip.

This was the body I was born in. The body that carried me through my life. The body that used to laugh and eat cookies. The body that used to hug… them.

"Uh, Charming?"

I shook myself but still kept hold of my body. Of my past. "It's me," I said, then cleared my throat. "This is my body."

He let out a low whistle. "Why's it in here?"

I shook my head and carefully put it back where it was. Then I looked at the one beside it. It was a man I'd never seen before. He had dark hair parted on the side and combed over. It was an old hairstyle from a very long time ago. There wasn't anything remarkable or special about him so I moved on to the next body.

It was a woman.

I reached out and pulled her out for Storm to see. "Check her out."

She was wearing a long gown made of rich woven fabric. I couldn't tell exactly, but her hair looked like it was a shade of red and it was done up in a style of many curls all piled on her head. She had pale skin and what appeared to be freckles splattered across her cheeks. She was pretty attractive, if you liked redheads.

"When's the last time you saw a girl in G.R.'s closet?" I asked Storm, not taking my eyes off her.

"Um, never?"

"Exactly. He doesn't use women as Escorts. He thinks they're too soft to kill."

"Well, he hasn't met my ex," Storm quipped.

It was something I didn't agree with the Reaper about, though I never said anything. Who he chose to make an Escort wasn't something I cared about. I wasn't going to make friends with them and I worked alone so it didn't matter in terms of my job either. But if you asked me, a woman had the potential to be the perfect Escort. Because of a woman's softness, their girly-like qualities, they were often underestimated. They were too often thought of as innocent. Many Targets wouldn't see their death coming until it was already delivered.

"What's in the next one?" Storm asked.

It took me a second to close the door of the closet I was standing in front of. It was surprisingly hard to shut away the body I'd just found.

But I did. Because I knew I wasn't going to leave it there.

I pulled open the next door.

There was a single body.

I sucked in a breath.

It was *her*. My sister.

Sadness overcame me. Sadness for her… about a life cut way too short. A life lost that was all my fault. And now there she was, hanging in a secret, dark closet like she was someone's shirt. Like she wasn't once brimming with life with her own set of dreams and wants. She had been a person… a beautiful and innocent person. And now she was here. Held hostage by a man who shouldn't even have her. I should have known she was here. I should have done something.

Her light hair was around her shoulders and she was dressed in the same clothes she was wearing the last time I saw her.

"Another woman?" Storm said. "She's hot."

I spun around and snarled. "Watch your mouth."

"Whoa. I didn't mean nothing." He backtracked. After a short pause, he said, "I take it you know this one too?"

"Yeah," I said, my voice hoarse. "Yeah, I do."

But really, there wasn't anything here to know. Yes, I recognized the body, but it was merely a shell of the person who lived inside. It was she who I missed. I didn't think she was here. I would have known. After all these years of working for the Reaper, of butting heads with him, there was no way he could have kept the fact that my sister was still alive a secret.

Besides. I knew she was dead.

I was the one who killed her.

"I don't mean to interrupt your… uh, reunion," Storm said over my shoulder. "But we need to hurry."

He was right.

There was still one more closet to look in. Gently, I closed the closet containing my sister and faced the final door.

"If there isn't something besides bodies in that one, I'm going to be very disappointed," Storm told me. "I mean, really, what kind of Grim Reaper doesn't have at least one sinister thing in his secret stash?"

I was ready to go. For some reason I felt like I'd been in a ten-round boxing match and my body took most the hits.

I opened the door.

There was no body hanging inside. It wasn't a closet.

It was a room.

"It's a secret lair," Storm whispered.

I rolled my eyes and walked forward into the room. It looked like a mini apartment. The room was a large rectangle and off to the right was a couch, two upholstered chairs, and a round coffee table. On the wall was the hugest flat-screen TV I'd ever seen.

Off to the left was a small kitchenette, but it looked like it was never used. Everything was brand new and looked untouched.

But it wasn't dusty.

If this was a place he never used, then it would be dusty; it would smell stale and vacant.

It didn't.

"Ugh, Charming, You might want to look at this."

There was a small door leading out of the space. Presumably to a bedroom. But I wasn't concerned with how the room was used or decorated, but rather what was coming out of it.

It was a soul.

It looked just like Storm. Except it was bright pink.

The soul stopped just inside the room—just hovering there like it was shocked to see us.

Hell, it couldn't have been as shocked as we were.

Now *this* was interesting. In all my years, this was the first time I ever saw a soul wandering around—besides a Ghost Escort.

"Is it a Ghost Escort?" I asked Storm.

"Couldn't be. All of us are black and that is clearly not black."

"You're just like me," the soul said, floating a little closer to Storm. It had the voice of a woman. She seemed surprised to see someone like her.

Clearly she could talk. I guess that wasn't a surprise, considering the rest of us could talk when we weren't inside a body.

"No body here either," Storm agreed.

"Are you here to bring me a body?"

I glanced at Storm. She was waiting for a body?

"Uh," I began, for once not being able to come up with a rapid reply.

"Not that it matters," she said. "I probably won't be able to get inside that one either."

This just kept getting better and better.

The Grim Reaper was harboring the soul of a woman who, of her own admission, couldn't manage to get into a body.

"You can't get into a body?" Storm said, intrigued. "That's like G.R.'s specialty. He can take souls in and out of bodies in his sleep."

"Who are you?" she asked, suddenly realizing maybe she should be suspicious.

"We work with G.R.," I told her. "Why are you in here? Who are you to him?"

"This room was secret. How did you find it?" As she spoke she went backward, moving away from us.

"G.R. told us about it," I said, taking a step closer.

"I don't believe you."

And then she started to scream.

"Shhh!" Storm and I both exclaimed, looking back the way we came. Her screams weren't that loud. I guess she couldn't project her sound, but I knew if she yelled long enough, someone would hear and then shit would hit the fan.

"Shut her up!" I growled at Storm while I ran into the kitchenette to see if there was anything I could use to make her be quiet. But there are no real weapons you can use against someone that doesn't have a body.

Except another soul.

Storm tackled her, the black cloud that made up his form wrapping around her pink form, and the two colors began mixing together. A burst of pink would explode from the center of the black and Storm would make a grunting sound, but then the black would cover up the pink once more and he would swirl around her like an angry thundercloud just waiting to unleash its wrath. Her screams turned to strangled sounds and then died off completely.

"A little help here," Storm called as he struggled.

"What do you want me to do?" I asked, wondering if he was somehow killing her.

"Find something to put her in!"

That I could do. I reached into the cabinet where I saw a jar earlier and grabbed it, rushing across the room while I unscrewed the lid and held it out. Storm started circling her, like a spinning cyclone. Round and round he went, whipping up the air around us and creating what could only be described as a tornado inside the tiny apartment.

"Hold it steady," he called, and then like a baseball bat, he smacked the pink soul into the jar.

I stood there stunned that he actually made the shot on the first try. Pink funneled out around the jar and floated around my hand. I waited for it all to gather in on itself and follow the rest of the soul into the jar, praying it hurried up before she came to and tried to get out.

She didn't. Whatever Storm did seemed to put her down for the count. When all the pink went inside the jar, I jammed the lid on and screwed it shut, tight.

"What the hell was that?" I asked Storm.

"Spending time with the other Ghost Escorts can get a little… irritating. Sometimes we wrestle."

*"That was wrestling?"*

"Soul style."

Soul-style wrestling? Okay, then.

"We gotta get out of here," I said, glancing through the door. We were lucky no one heard her and came running.

"I can't believe he has a soul," Storm said. "What's he going to do with it?"

"I don't know, but I know what I'm going to do with it."

"Tell me you aren't," Storm said, his voice flat.

"You don't actually think I would leave this here? A soul in a jar?"

He let out a few more of those really artful swear words.

"It won't be easy to get out of here," I said thoughtfully. "The bodies are going to be more of a challenge."

*"You're taking the bodies too?"*

"Why do you keep acting so surprised?" I asked, irritated. "This is what we came for."

He mumbled something I didn't hear.

"Are you in or are you out?" I said coldly. I didn't have time for his pansy-ass ways. I had bodies and a soul to steal.

"I'm in," he said, not even stopping to think about it. Good thing too because I was starting to think he was turning into a woman, what with all his questions, incessant chattering, and gasping about my nefarious plans. Geez, next time I went on a mission I would just hire Barbie. She'd be easier to work with.

"Good. Let's get to it," I said, stuffing the jar containing the soul inside my jacket. "We have some bodies to steal."

# Chapter Twenty-Four

*"Vacation - a period of time devoted to pleasure, rest, or relaxation,
especially one with pay granted to an employee."*

## *Frankie*

I was pretty sure Mondays were invented to remind the
poor schmucks who had to work for a living at jobs they
hated that the weekend had been nothing but a tease and now
they had five long days of torture to look forward to.

Although really, my weekend hadn't been all puppies and
rainbows anyway. Today the torture was just being moved to
another place: the DMV. Although at least here at work, I
could get a break from my personal life. I snorted inwardly.
The day I started looking at my job as a vacation from life, I
had a problem.

Between lunch with Rosalyn and Charming, him
showing up at my apartment wanting to talk and falling asleep
on the couch only to disappear the next morning, to being
interrogated by Piper on Sunday, I guess I could understand
why I wanted to escape.

It was just too bad my escape had to be screening old
people's eyes for driver's license renewal and listening to
Hagatha tell me I was the worst employee ever, but she
wasn't going to bother to fire me because that would mean
she would actually have to work and train someone new.

Ahhh, to be on a tropical beach somewhere.

I threw myself into my work all day and ignored my
thoughts and the scathing remarks from the witch. I even
stayed late to enter some data into the computer that one of
the other girls forgot to do. By the time I left, it was almost
six and everyone but me and my boss was gone. She was shut
into her office and I wasn't about to go pretend I liked her

and say good-bye. Who knows what I would catch her doing in there anyway. Likely sharpening her claws on a dagger.

I walked out to the parking lot, digging through my bag for my keys. I didn't notice a white Porsche was parked next to me until I was standing beside it. I was sandwiched between his car and my Jeep when the passenger window rolled down.

"You stayed late," he said, leaning over so he could look through the window.

"What can I say? I love my job."

He smirked. "You hate this place and you know it."

I gasped in mock disdain. "Is it that obvious?"

"I just read you well."

I snorted. "If you read me at all, you wouldn't come around me. Go away," I said and turned to let myself into my car.

"I am going away."

My head snapped up and I turned around. "You're leaving town?"

He nodded. "On my way to the airport."

I was finally getting my wish. He was leaving. I would never have to look at his face again. Why did I not feel happy about this? "Well, I'd say I was sorry to see you go…" I shrugged, leaving the rest of my sentence dangling in the air.

He ignored my sarcasm. "Go home. Pack a bag."

"What?"

"You're coming with me."

I laughed. "I'm not going anywhere with you."

"It's not a request." His eyes narrowed.

"I don't take kindly to orders."

He opened his door and got out, coming around the back of his SUV. "I knew you were going to be difficult. That's why I took the liberty of packing a bag for you." He reached inside the back and pulled out a purple duffle bag. *My* purple duffle bag.

My mouth fell open. "You went to my house. You went through my things?"

"You need to clean out your closet."

"How the hell do you get in and out of my apartment?"

He smirked. "I have friends."

"*You* have friends? How much do you have to pay them to keep them around?"

"Very funny," he replied. "I don't have time to argue with you. I'll follow you home. Park your Jeep. Then we're going to the airport."

The depth of his idiocy was incredible. "I'm. Not. Going."

His green eyes flashed with impatience and he stalked toward me, burying both his hands into his jean pockets. He was wearing jeans. Not dress pants or trousers. Honest to God jeans. They were low slung, worn, and faded with a rip in one of the knees. I looked at his shirt. It was a plain, long-sleeved cotton tee with half the hem tucked into the front of said jeans.

Holy hell, could he wear a pair of jeans. If I looked like that in jeans, I would sleep in them. I certainly wouldn't wear dress pants.

He snapped his fingers in front of my face. "Earth to Frankie." When I looked at him, he continued. "I don't have time to argue with you. The plane is ready. I'm not leaving you here to wreak havoc on my life while I'm gone." He brought his jean-wearing self even closer, the toe of his Nike bumping into the toe of my heel. "Don't think I didn't know what you were up to at lunch the other day, what you were going to do."

I batted my eyes at him all innocent-like.

"Please," he muttered. "There isn't an innocent bone in your entire body."

I scowled. "You are so rude."

"If I was as rude as you think, I would have killed you for all the stuff you've pulled. Instead, I'm hauling you off on vacation and you're stupid enough to argue about it."

*Wait a minute. Vacation?*

A sly smile slipped over his features when he saw the interest in my eyes. Gah! I was so stupid. I should have acted like I was still annoyed.

"Have you ever been to California?" he asked, dangling a carrot in front of a very hungry rabbit (me). "The palm trees, the beaches…"

*Act like you don't care. Act like you don't care,* I repeated over and over in my head.

"Rodeo Drive…" he added.

A rabbit couldn't resist a carrot. How was I supposed to resist all that? "You're going to California?"

"No, we are."

"I can't go to California. I have to work. I have a life."

He rolled his eyes. "Please. You hate your life."

"I do not!" I burst out.

He raised an eyebrow and crossed his arms over that sexy body of his.

"Just my job and everything currently going on in my personal life… which is *all* your fault."

"Well then, take advantage of a free vacation to Los Angeles. I'll even give you my American Express card to go shopping."

I pursed my lips. "You really think I'm going to screw everything up, don't you?"

"Oh, I know you will, and I have enough to deal with already. Get in your car." He glanced at his watch. "We're already late."

"Oh, shucks. We'll miss the plane."

He grinned. "Private jets don't take off without their passengers, love."

I don't know if it was the "private jet" part or the "love" part that had me agreeing and climbing into my Jeep and driving home. But before I knew it, I was sitting in his Porsche heading toward the airport.

It was only then that I realized I hated flying. Planes made me extremely nervous. So obviously it hadn't been the "private jet" that got me here. It was the fact that the endearment "love" sometimes fell so naturally off his tongue.

Oh, and the way he looked in those jeans…

I never even stood a chance.

# Chapter Twenty-Five

*"Aviophobia - the fear of flying."*

## Charming

You could learn a lot from someone just by watching them. Really watching them. It was something I never realized when I was alive. If I had, I might not have died the way I did. Now, I had a lot of practice at watching people and I knew fear when I saw it.

I've witnessed a broad range of emotion from Frankie, but fear wasn't one of them. Unease? Yes. Nervousness? Yes. Flustered, annoyed, angry… Yes, yes, and yes. Desire? Desire was my favorite.

She was literally a kaleidoscope of feeling. You never knew which feelings of hers might blend together and what would happen when they did. I was shocked when she agreed to come with me so easily. I wondered if the dark circles beneath her eyes were part of the reason. That and the fact I hadn't seen her consume sugar at all the last few times I saw her. She was looking a little thin; I realized I liked her better filled out.

"Are you scared of flying?" I asked. Amusement sparked through me like a sparkler on the fourth of July as I watched her grip the armrests of her seat.

"No," she said harshly. Then she looked at the floor. "Maybe."

I grinned.

"Wipe that smile off your face before I do it for you," she growled.

"There's a stash of candy over there by the mini bar." I pointed to the other side of the plane where all the drinks were kept chilled.

The jet lurched forward as it began to taxi to the runway. Her skin turned green. I saw her swallow thickly.

I sighed. Watching her misery wasn't as entertaining as I thought it might be. I went to the mini bar and pulled out some clear rum and a can of sprite. I combined them both over ice in a crystal glass and took it over to her.

"Here, how about some sugar poured over liquor?"

"Thanks," she said, looking at the glass, but she made no move to loosen her death grip on the armrest so she could take it.

I sat down in the seat beside hers. "You ever been to L.A.?"

"No."

"Never? Wow. I think you'll like it. It's warm and sunny. The sun always shines. The people are tan and beautiful. The palm trees are taller than a lot of the buildings here and the beach—"

"I've never been to the beach." She interrupted.

That surprised me. "You've never seen the ocean?"

"Just on television."

"I think you're going to love it."

"How do you know?" she asked. I noticed her skin was now back to its original complexion. Her fingers seemed to be getting a little more circulation as well.

"Because," I said, leaning in closer to her, "it's a lot like you. Larger than life. It fills up the space in front of you as far as you can see. And it can be temperamental." I smiled when she made a face. "One minute it's crashing onto the sand with great ferocity, but the next moment the waves become gentle and it laps at your ankles like a soft caress."

She let go of the armrests completely and leaned a little closer. "Sounds like you're the one who really loves the ocean."

I stared at her for long minutes, her words not really penetrating my brain. All I could think about was how pretty she was sitting there with those loose blond curls framing her face and her nervous pink cheeks. But then the word love broke through the haze in my brain. I shook my head. "I don't love anything."

She sat back. I handed her the drink, which she took and downed about half in one great slurp. "We're in the air," she said.

"You didn't even notice we were taking off." I got up and moved across the plane to sit on a small couch over by a few small windows.

"It's those damn jeans," she murmured.

"What about my jeans?"

"Stupid superpower hearing," she muttered, taking another drink.

"You like my jeans, huh?" Smug satisfaction filled my chest.

"I'd like them better if you took them into another room and stayed there."

"You keep up that attitude, this is going to be a very long flight."

"How long is it anyway?"

"About nine hours."

She gaped at me. "Nine hours stuck on a plane with you?"

I grinned.

"What are we going to do for nine hours?"

"I can think of a few things." I wagged my eyebrows. "Want to see how my jeans look on the floor?"

She spit her drink halfway across the room and the back of her hand flew to her mouth. "Ew! You are so gross!"

I scowled. "That's not what you were saying the other night when I kissed you."

"Do not remind me."

"Why? Afraid you'll want to do it again?"

Her shoulders slumped a little and she swiveled her chair toward the window. "If I get fired for this little trip, you owe me a million dollars."

I would take her silence on the kissing subject as a yes. "A million dollars? I didn't realize DMV employees made so much money."

"They don't. Most of it would be for the mental abuse I'm suffering at your hands."

I laughed.

"I think a shopping spree on Rodeo drive will change your mind."

"I'm not going shopping on Rodeo drive."

"No?" I figured that was the first place she would go.

"No. I'm not spending your money."

"But you'll take a million?"

She looked around the back of her chair at me and rolled her eyes.

"So what's the first thing you're going to do?"

"Find the beach."

"We're staying on the beach. I have a house right on the sand."

Her chair spun back around to face me. "Are you serious?"

"Views from every room."

"How much money do you have?" she wondered.

More than she or I could ever spend. More money than some small countries. Killing paid well. Killing for over ninety years made a man very, very rich. I opened my mouth to answer and she held up her hand.

"Don't answer. It doesn't matter."

"No?"

"No."

"Why not?"

"Because of the way you earned it."

Irritation slammed through me. Figures she'd say that. "Money is just paper. It really doesn't have anything to do with the job."

"You do the job for the money," she spat.

"I do the job because I have to," I snapped, getting up and going to the bar. Shit, this was going to be a long plane ride. I should have just left her in Alaska and done damage control when I got home. It probably would have done me good to get away from her. She drove me mad. I poured half a glass of brandy and took a swallow.

"Because you'll get Recalled," she said softly.

"Yeah, and I'm in no hurry for that to happen."

"It's pretty terrible?" she asked.

"Don't worry about it, love," I said, wincing when the endearment slipped out. *Again.* I had no idea why I kept doing that. Calling people by anything other than their name was something I never did. "You won't feel a thing."

"But you will," she whispered. I figured I wasn't meant to hear that either so I didn't bother to reply. I wasn't naïve enough to think she actually cared.

"What's the purpose of this trip anyway? I thought you were all about your Target," she said with mock seriousness.

I didn't bother to sit back down, but paced the cabin instead. This jet was feeling smaller than usual.

"I am all about my Target. That's why you're here."

"Well, then?"

I took another drink of the alcohol and hoped it would numb my brain. She asked too many questions. "Work."

"Is Rosalyn traveling to L.A.?" she wondered out loud. Then she said, "Couldn't be, then you wouldn't have cared if I was there."

I stayed silent. I was tired of talking.

"If you're not going for Rosalyn, but it's still work…" She gasped. "You're going to kill someone. Aren't you?"

I closed my eyes. How did she make everything I did sound so awful? "It's really not any of your business."

"Are you kidding me?" she shouted. "You're making me an accessory to murder!"

"Keep your voice down," I said, glancing at the cockpit. "And you can't be an accessory to something you know nothing about."

She drained the rest of her drink, set the glass on a nearby table, and then spun her chair back toward the window. I guess that meant she was done bitching at me. Thank God.

We sat in silence for a long time. I finished my drink and had another, watched the sports highlights on the mini flat screen, and stared out the window into the dark. Flying didn't bother me—I did it all the time—but sitting here left me feeling restless. She still hadn't turned that chair around. She hadn't uttered a word.

It made me mad that I was sitting here even thinking about her pouting. I took my empty glass over to the bar and then grabbed her chair and turned it around. She was sitting with her knees pulled up and her chin resting on top. Her arms were wrapped around her legs and she tilted her head back and looked at me. "What?"

"Are you going move in the next eight hours?"

She sighed and unfolded herself from the chair. "Where's my bag?" she asked.

I motioned to the back of the cabin to the large closet where I put our bags. She pulled open the door and yanked out her bag so it was practically on top of her feet. Then she glanced at me and pointed to the garment bag hanging inside the closet. "Seriously? You put your clothes in a garment bag? How many pairs of trousers did you bring?"

I wondered what she would say if she knew there was a body in that bag and not my trousers. A body I stole from the Grim Reaper. And what the hell was wrong with trousers? They were classy. The way she said it, you would think I was running around in sweatpants. "If I had known you liked me in jeans so much, I would have brought more of those instead."

Her cheeks turned pink and she bent down to rummage through her bag. After a few minutes, she made a sound. "Didn't you bring me a sweatshirt?"

"We're going to California. It's hot there."

"But this plane is freezing."

"There's some blankets in the cabinet over here."

She abandoned the duffle and walked over to where I was pulling several blankets out of the cabinet. When she reached out for one, I noticed the goose bumps prickling her arms. I guess I should have packed her a sweater or something. Packing for a woman wasn't something I ever had to do. I snatched the blanket away and her eyes widened.

"Hey," she started, but she fell silent when I yanked the shirt I was wearing over my head. Then I swiftly pulled it down over her.

"You'll warm up faster this way," I said.

"I'm not going to freeze to death," she protested even as she pushed her arms through and fixed the hem. The white fabric fell mid-thigh. "How come men get all the good body heat?" she mumbled, reaching around me for the blanket and taking it over to her chair.

"What do you know about men and body heat?" I felt my eyes narrow as I watched her shapely behind move beneath my shirt.

"That they have more of it."

She yawned loudly and wrapped the blanket around herself.

"You might as well get some sleep. I have a feeling once you see the beach you won't want to go in the house."

"Good idea." She leaned her head back against the chair. If she slept like that she was going to get a neck cramp.

"Here, this would be more comfortable." I told her, grabbing a remote and pressing a button. The couch I sat on earlier slid out of the wall, widening so it was the size of a double bed.

She stared at me for a few minutes before getting up and going to the bed. I handed her a pillow. "Thank you."

"Don't thank me. I just didn't want to hear you whine about your neck from sleeping in a chair."

She made a rude noise and lay down, draping herself with the blanket and rolling away from me.

I hesitated a minute before dropping down so I crouched right beside her. "At first it was hard," I said softly. She would know I was talking about the killing.

She rolled over to look at me. The blanket was pulled up to her chin and her face was just inches from mine. "How come it stopped being hard?"

I glanced at her lips, distracted by their pink fullness. "Because I stopped living."

Her blue eyes stared at me as something danced between us. It was completely invisible to the eye, but it was impossible not to feel. I think the word for what I felt was chemistry. It was equal parts push and pull and it created a charge in the air surrounding us. I wanted to touch her. I wondered if she would pull away if I did.

Slowly, I reached out, and I watched her face as my hand drew closer. She stopped breathing for a moment. Everything about her paused, except for that unseen energy around her. That energy seemed to hum.

I skimmed the back of my knuckles down her cheek and then rolled my hand over and cupped her face with my palm. My thumb made lazy circles around the apple of her cheek.

Her eyes fluttered closed.

She drew in a deep breath.

Without opening her eyes, she replied, "Maybe it's time you started living again."

Her words caused something inside my chest to splinter apart. Kind of like a mini explosion that only I could feel. I crouched there beside her for a long time, my thumb still brushing over her skin. She fell asleep like that, her breathing turning even and deep.

Only after my legs and feet had gone numb from my awkward position did I get up to go sit down. All I could think about was what she said.

All I could think was that maybe she was right.

# Chapter Twenty-Six

*"Ocean - the entire body of salt water that covers more than seventy percent of the earth's surface."*

## Frankie

The sun was just lifting into the sky when Charming slid his cherry-red Audi R8 Spyder convertible through the security gates of what looked to be a super exclusive beach neighborhood. It was already so warm here that we were able to put the top down as soon as we left the airport. (Apparently, when you have your own plane, you get a mini hanger to put it in, and that's where his car was). We drove for about a mile when he slowed, turning into the driveway of a large modern house that was literally right on the beach.

I tried not to gape at the clean lines, large glass windows, and tropical landscaping. I admit it had always been my hope to snag a rich doctor and have a nice lifestyle, but not even I could fathom Charming's world. It was overfull with crazy expensive cars, private planes, houses on the beach… and that was just the stuff I knew about.

But he was alone. He didn't have anyone to enjoy it with. I don't think all the money in the world could make up for that.

He parked in the garage next to a fancy-looking motorcycle and climbed out. I yanked my bag from where I jammed it beneath my feet and slung it over my shoulder while he gathered his bags (I thought it was amusing that I was the girl, but he had more bags than me).

I knew the inside was going to be spectacular. But when we walked in, I barely saw any of the walls, the furnishings, or the type of countertops in the kitchen because my eyes went straight to the view.

The entire back of the house was glass. The bag thudded to my feet as the view sucked me closer, beckoning me like a fresh donut hot out of the fryer. It was the most breathtaking sight I'd ever seen. Nothing could compare to the way the ocean, an endless deep blue, stretched out for miles and miles. There were no trees, no buildings, nothing to block the sight.

I stopped just short of the thick window, resisting the urge to put my hand on the glass so as not to leave a print behind to get in the way of such perfection.

The waves never stopped, rising up and rolling in, crashing over one another and then hurrying up onto the shoreline, which was nothing but billions and billions of tiny grains of sand.

"It's a lot better than looking at snow, isn't it?"

I wanted to argue and tell him that Alaska, my home, was better, but that would be a lie. To me, this view was more beautiful than any view I'd seen in Alaska.

"I've never seen anything like it." I glanced at him. "Can I go outside?"

"You can do whatever you want here."

I stepped through the glass door and onto a wide deck that ran the entire length of the house. There was no overhang, no columns, nothing but a railing also made of glass. The wind immediately pulled at my hair, sending it this way and that way. The air smelled like the sea, salty and thick. There wasn't a single cloud in the perfectly blue sky.

I don't know how long I stood at the railing, just gazing out at it all, but eventually I pulled up one of the lounge chairs as close to the edge as I could get and sat down.

The sun was much higher in the sky and it was getting hot when a plate appeared under my nose. It was filled with scrambled eggs, bacon, and ruby-red strawberries.

"Please tell me you have a chef inside," I said, taking the plate and staring down at the food. If he told me he cooked, I might fling myself off the side of the balcony. Really. Being rich, good-looking, and sexy as hell wasn't enough for him?

"That's the thing about eating. It required learning how to cook."

I groaned and stuck a piece of bacon in my mouth. It was really good. I put my plans for taking a dive off the balcony on hold.

"I'm surprised you aren't already down there," he said, hitching his chin toward the beach.

"I can get down there from here?"

"Steps are over there." He pointed.

I started to get up, to abandon the food, but he reached out and pushed me back down. "Eat first. The water isn't going anywhere."

I felt like I was seven again and my mother told me I had to eat all my vegetables before I could go outside to play. I wanted to shove them all into my mouth and then rush out the door. I scowled at him.

"You slept the entire flight. When's the last time you ate?"

"Lunch. Yesterday."

He shook his head like my answer made him angry. I inhaled the food, which, dammit, was really good, and then picked up my plate to carry it in the house.

He'd already finished his plate as well, so I followed him inside where we abandoned the dishes in the sink. I looked for my bag, but I didn't see it anywhere.

"I put it upstairs in your room," he said, seeing me search. "First door on the right."

I wandered up the wide-open staircase, stumbling because I still couldn't tear my eyes away from the view, and then took the door he instructed.

Of course the room was gorgeous. It was all white—white walls, white bed, white canopy, white curtains billowing in the breeze because the sliding glass doors were open letting in the sound of the waves. The only color was from the dark hardwood floors and the view. I peaked briefly into the bathroom, which was all white marble and chrome fixtures. Not wanting to waste another minute, I dumped the contents of my bag onto the bed, scattering the clothes all around, and found a pair of loose white linen shorts and a fitted black T-shirt.

I changed quickly, only pausing for a second when I pulled off Charming's shirt to replace it with mine, and then I left the room barefoot, padding down the hall to another bedroom, the master, and pushed open the partially closed door.

The room was almost all white too, but his bed was much bigger and the trim on his bedding was black. I didn't bother to snoop around, I just tossed his shirt onto the bed and then hightailed it back downstairs so I could get outside.

Charming was standing by the back door, a new pair of jeans riding his hips and making his ass look like he should be an underwear model. Apparently it wasn't just one pair of jeans he looked good in, but all jeans.

He turned when I stopped behind him. He was wearing a Lucky Brand T-shirt the same vibrant green as his eyes. A pair of aviator sunglasses were pushed up on his head and he was rocking a five o'clock shadow.

His eyes started at my toes and raked up, lingering on my legs and then settling on my face. "Where are your sunglasses?"

"I guess my butler didn't grab them." I sighed. "Good help is so hard to find."

He rolled his eyes and pulled the aviators off his head and handed them over. "Here, you're going to go blind in that sun."

"What will you wear?"

"I have more than one pair of sunglasses."

Well, of course he did.

"Thank you," I said, taking the glasses. I barely knew how to act when he behaved so, so… *nice*. If I wasn't careful, I would fool myself into thinking he was someone other than exactly who he was.

"I have to go out. I have stuff to do," he said, watching me closely.

Well, there went my previous thoughts. "I have stuff to do" was code for "I'm going off to murder someone." I crossed my arms over my chest and glared at him.

"I don't know when I'll be back. Make yourself at home. I'll leave the keys to the convertible on the counter."

"You'd let me drive your car?"

"Why wouldn't I?"

I shrugged. He didn't really seem like the kind of guy who liked to share.

"If you wreck it, you owe me a million dollars," he said, winking.

I wasn't charmed. I wasn't.

"Don't turn into a lobster while I'm gone." He stepped away from the back door.

The reason he was leaving crashed over me all over again. Sharp pains cut through my middle. "As long as no one comes to murder me, I'll be just fine," I snapped coldly.

He stopped in his path but didn't turn around. I saw him flex his hands at his sides. "I wouldn't worry about that. All you'd have to do is open your mouth and anyone coming near you would run away as fast as they could."

He started walking again, but I didn't stand there to see if he looked back. I went out the back door, slamming it behind me. I wasn't going to think about him. I wasn't going to think about what he could be doing. I was going to take advantage of this beautiful place and not think at all. With any luck, the waves would carry away every single thought I had.

# Chapter Twenty-Seven

*"Kill - to deprive of life."*

## *Charming*

The Target was a man. I didn't get a huge folder of background information on him. Just his name, his whereabouts, and the fact that he was supposed to die. Frankly, I welcomed the fact that I didn't have to learn anything about him. It seemed like such a waste of time to get to know someone who was practically already dead.

I didn't even know why G.R. wanted him dead. It wasn't for money or the job wouldn't be an in-and-out type of thing. If he had an ability G.R. wanted for someone, he didn't say. All I was supposed to do was complete the job and then call him so he could come collect.

Although, I really wouldn't be surprised if this man had anything G.R. wanted. He was probably just some lame excuse to get me out of town and away from my real Target for a couple days.

I wasn't even sure what he did with the bodies, with the souls of the Targets. Once we called and he came, our part was through and we left. I never asked him and he never volunteered the information. I never really cared. Until now.

Robert "Bobby" Salzman worked in the entertainment industry. In Hollywood, that could mean anything from blockbuster movies to adult films. Whatever he did paid him pretty well, judging from the size of his house and cherry-red Dodge Viper sitting in the driveway.

But he should have spent his money on better security. I pulled the motorcycle I "borrowed" into his driveway, leaving my helmet on but flipping up the visor so it only looked like I was too lazy to pull it off and not like I was trying to hide. I kept the leather jacket and gloves on and then unstrapped the pizza that I picked up from the local pizza joint on the way and carried it toward the door.

To any wandering eye, it would appear I was just the pizza guy delivering lunch. I made it to the front door and rang the bell. From what I knew, he lived alone, but I wasn't sure if he was alone today, so ringing the bell would give me a chance to figure it out before I actually finished the job. It was never good when you realized there was a witness that you didn't know about. Then your single Target became two. Yes, the rules were you killed no one but the Target, but when the job was compromised, exceptions were made.

He answered the door. I checked a housekeeper off my list of potential witnesses. He was wearing a bathing suit and no shirt. He smelled like tanning lotion and his skin was slick with the stuff. "What?" he demanded.

"Pizza delivery," I said, holding up the pizza.

"I didn't order a pizza."

I read off the address—his address—on the order form attached to the pie.

"That's me, but I didn't order a pizza."

"Well, I'm already here and no more orders to fill. Here," I said, holding out the box, "on the house."

He grunted. "Yeah, okay. Thanks, kid."

I handed him the box and he went inside, shutting the door on my face. What? No tip? I stepped away from the door, but instead of getting on the bike, I zipped around the side of the house (super speed really comes in handy) and into the back yard. There were lots of foliage and tropical plants back here and the neighbor's house wasn't even visible, so it made the job even easier.

He was sitting in a patio chair with the open pizza box beside him. I stepped into his line of sight and he stiffened, standing up immediately. "What the hell are you doing, kid?"

He came over; his body language said he was ready for a fight. I kicked his legs out from under him and he fell back, hitting his head on the concrete. He lay there unmoving. I used my foot and pushed him into the pool.

If the body was found, it would appear that he slipped, hit his head, and fell into the pool and drowned.

When I was sure he was dead, I dialed G.R. "It's done," I said into the phone. Then I hung up.

He appeared two seconds later, stepping through the door/portal he created, and looked at the body floating in the pool.

"Job complete."

I started to walk away, but then I stopped. I had to ask. Even if he didn't answer. "Why this one?"

"That Viper in his driveway came from my lot. He hasn't paid his lease in six months."

Revenge, then. I nodded and walked away. I ignored the sick feeling in my stomach. When I stepped around the house and into the foliage, I heard the water in the pool ripple. Curious, I turned around, keeping myself concealed behind a large palm. I watched as the Reaper waded through the shallow end toward the body. He didn't touch him but hovered his palm over the man's back.

I watched, waiting to see what would happen. Just a few seconds ticked by and then the man's spirit began to rise up out of his body. It was green. I thought G.R. was going to talk to him—maybe recruit another Escort.

He wasn't looking for another Escort.

When the green spirit hovered over the Reaper's head, he raised up his arms, looked up toward the sky, and then he proceeded to eat the spirit.

He literally opened his mouth as wide as it would go and began to suck the spirit into his mouth. But the spirit didn't just go into his mouth; it seeped into his ears and up his nose. The spirit didn't struggle; it didn't try to get away. I wasn't even sure if it knew what was going on.

*I* wasn't sure if I knew what was going on.

Was this what he did to all the people he killed—that the Escorts killed?

This was some disturbing shit.

When he was done chowing down on spirit, he waded out of the pool, leaving the body right where it floated. Then with a single wave of his hand, the portal opened and he stepped through, leaving the scene of the crime—of his meal—behind.

I didn't loiter on the property. I zipped around the house and forced myself to jog to my bike like a guy who just delivered a pizza and who didn't witness the Grim Reaper eating the green spirit of a man he'd just killed.

I put the bike back in the parking garage where I found it (but kept the helmet—since my hair and therefore DNA was now in it) and climbed on the closest bus. I rode that and got off after three stops. I got on another bus, rode that for two stops. Then I got off and walked three blocks, passing a city garbage truck on the sidewalk. I tossed the helmet into the back and it was immediately crushed into the already huge pile of trash. Another block passed and I ducked into a parking garage. I went up three flights of stairs and climbed onto another motorcycle—this one mine. It was completely different than the one I borrowed earlier. This one was a bike built for speed—something flashy that rich people drove. If you wanted to blend in around Beverly Hills, then you drove something expensive.

I pointed the bike toward my beach house. Toward Frankie. I pictured her sitting on the beach, her toes buried in the sand. I wondered if she would talk to me when I got home. I probably didn't deserve it. I still hoped she would. Right then, I would have loved to hear her yell at me, to see her roll her eyes. Hell, I would've even listened to her insult me.

Anything to drown out my own thoughts.

Because right now I was thinking I didn't like myself.

Right now I was feeling guilty. Guilty about what I just did. And I was also feeling slightly freaked out that I kind of fed my boss.

Why would he eat a spirit? There was perfectly good pizza right there if he was hungry.

Something told me pizza wouldn't have conquered his kind of hunger.

It didn't matter anyway. This whole thing started out as being about getting the best of him and doing the job. And now… now I wasn't sure what anything was about.

The only thing I really knew for sure was that I wanted to see Frankie.

# Chapter Twenty-Eight

*"Sand - small, loose grains of worn or disintegrated rock."*

## Frankie

I came to the conclusion that I would never get tired of staring at the ocean. It didn't matter how long I sat here or how long I stared because the sights were forever changing. There was always a new wave to look at, a boat, a bird, or a person.

The ocean had a way of making a person feel small, but not in a bad way. In a way that made you feel like you were part of something bigger. It was humbling, but it was also inspiring.

Even though Charming left me here while he was off committing a crime, I couldn't feel sorry about experiencing this. I still felt thankful that I hadn't gone another day without seeing something outside the walls of Alaska.

The sun was beginning to sink behind the water when I felt his presence behind me. I didn't have to look to know it was him. My body had a way of knowing when he was near. He approached slowly and I stiffened. He didn't tell me where he was going today or what he was doing, but I knew.

I hated it.

"There enough sand here for the both of us?" he asked, standing just slightly behind me.

The insecurity in his voice had me patting the empty space beside me.

"You've been down here all day, haven't you?"

I glanced over. He was still wearing those jeans, but that was all. No shirt and no shoes. He stretched his legs out in front of him and propped himself up with the heel of each hand just slightly behind his back. I wondered if he was doing it on purpose, displaying his perfectly cut abs just to throw me off. It didn't matter because it wasn't going to work.

"I sat on the deck for a while," I answered. "But yeah, mostly I was down here all day."

"I knew you'd like it."

"I do."

We watched the sun slip lower and lower until it completely disappeared behind the endless sea. The breeze off the ocean turned cooler and the shoreline grew quiet except for the crashing of the waves against the sand.

"Rough day?" I asked him.

"I've had better."

I could have made a biting remark about why his day had been so shitty. Several scathing comments rose up in my mind, but even just thinking them made me tired. And there was something about him tonight, something about the air that surrounded him, that told me it didn't matter how many mean things I said because he was already saying worse things to himself. Part of me was glad. Part of me thought he deserved all those mean things and more. But there was this other part of me that felt sorry for him. In the end, it was the softer side of me that won out.

"Well, the sun will be up tomorrow and with it comes a new day. A fresh one."

"What if the day that comes before the fresh one is so full of clouds and they cast shadows that follow you all the way into the new day?"

"Usually even on the cloudiest day, the sun will find a way to peek through at least once."

His hand wrapped around mine. His fingers found their way in between mine and curled closed, pressing his palm against mine. My heart began to beat a little harder; nerves began to tingle throughout my body.

"I know I'll never be able to make up for the things I've done," he said. I had to lean a little closer so I would catch his words before the wind carried them away. "And I doubt I ever try. Feeling better isn't really something I deserve, and it seems that living with those things is part of the punishment."

I wondered if he realized he said the word living. Up until this point, he'd been adamant about the fact that he was dead.

"But when I'm around you, I feel like there might be some hope."

My heart lodged itself in my throat. I could barely swallow past it. "Hope for what?" I asked, my voice almost drowned out by the sound of the waves.

His fingers tightened around mine. "For a little more sunshine instead of just clouds."

Oh my God, what he did to me. I felt like a dishrag that had been used to mop up far too many spills and then rung out again and again. I felt twisted and damp, like I wasn't as clean as I was in the beginning.

He was right. There was no excuse for his actions. There was no excuse for him. But I still wanted to sit here with him. I still wanted to feel his hand hold mine. Nothing about Charming would ever be simple. And it also became quite clear that nothing was going to change the way I felt about him.

I guess the real question I had to ask myself was if I was going to feel all these things beside him or if I was going to feel them at home, alone. Because even if I walked away from him right now and didn't see him again for a year or ten, I would still get the lightheaded, slightly shaky, fluttery feeling that washed over me when he walked into a room.

It was a choice that wouldn't come easy. When you were so drawn to someone the way I was drawn to him, it was almost impossible to think about walking away. But that didn't mean I wouldn't do it because if he wasn't good for me, then I couldn't stay.

"What are you thinking about?" he asked.

"You."

He pushed me down in the sand, his body coming over mine and blocking out the stars that glistened like jewels in the night sky above us. "I'm going to kiss you now," he murmured, already brushing his lips across mine. "Don't bother to try to fight it. It's a fight you won't win."

"What if I want to lose?"

He groaned and crushed his mouth over mine. His lips were hot against my wind-chilled skin. My body began to shake all over, and I reached up, curving my hand around his waist and pulling him down so our bodies were tangled together. His skin tasted salty like the ocean air and his toes were chilly as they ran up my calf. He moved his body against mine, the roughness of his jeans brushing against the bare skin on my legs. Without thought, I opened my legs for him, so he could settle even closer. The moment he did, pressure began to build in my center and he kissed me more fiercely than before.

I was going to burn up, burn up from the inside out. Every time he touched me, ran his hand up my inner thigh, or teased the skin on my stomach, it was like he lit yet another match and added it to the fire.

He murmured my name against my lips and I ran my hand along the rough stubble lining his jaw. If we didn't slow down, he was going to take me right here.

Sleeping with him would only make things harder.

But it was hard to listen to your head when your body wanted something so badly that it shut off all thought.

He pulled away abruptly, coming up onto his knees and staring down at me lying in the sand. Grabbing a fistful of my shirt, he pulled me up and ripped the cotton fabric up over my head and threw it onto the sand. The sand was cool and rough against my back, but I barely noticed because my eyes couldn't get enough of his chiseled body leaning closer.

I was wearing a bra, but it must have been in his way because he yanked the cups down so they were bunched beneath my breasts and pushing upward so the sensitive and aching flesh was closer to his hands.

But he didn't touch them.

He latched onto them with his mouth. His lips were warm and moist as they trailed across each peak. My fingernails found his biceps and dug in as little shivers raced up and down my spine. When his tongue flicked over a very erect nipple, I arched up off the sand toward him and cried out. He looked up at me and smiled, then repeated the movement again.

My hands moved to his head and kneaded his scalp, silently begging for more. The wind off the waves carried away his throaty chuckle as his mouth covered my nipple completely, sucking it fully into his mouth.

Moisture pooled between my legs and I titled my hips closer to him, closer to the hardness pressing against the front of his jeans.

His mouth left my breast as he trailed kisses down my stomach, toward the top of my shorts. My hands fell on either side of me and pushed down into the sand as I stretched myself like a cat, trying to become longer so there was more of me for his lips to touch.

Just as he slipped several fingers beneath my waistband, a swell of water rushed up around us, making me squeal. Charming came back over me, laughing, and buried his face in my neck as the water began to recede. "Hold on," he said, kissing me below my ear and pinning me a little closer to the beach.

As the water receded, it pulled at us, making me dizzier than I already was. Before the wave could completely pull away, another one surrounded us and I squealed again. The water was cold without the sun to warm it, and I snuggled in a little closer to his heat. Once again, the water pulled away, going back into the sea where it belonged, and once again, it pulled at us, trying to claim us for its own.

But I was already taken.

By the man anchoring me to the sand.

Even if I forever remained single, my heart would never be free.

Once the water was gone, he pressed his forehead against mine and stared down into my eyes for a few silent moments before sighing and pulling away. Part of me was sorely disappointed. My body still tingled for his touch as he adjusted my bra and stood. Then he reached for me and my forgotten shirt and wrapped his arm around my shoulder. My body fit perfectly into his side and we walked together up to his half-glass beach house where he rinsed off my feet with the hose before pulling me close and kissing me senseless once more. Just when I was sure we would end up tangled in bed, he growled and pulled away, tucking his hands into the pockets of his jeans.

His whispered goodnight was lifted away by the wind as he disappeared into the house.

# Chapter Twenty-Nine

*"Text - to communicate by text message."*

## Charming

I woke as the sun was rising, lying there in my king-sized bed, watching the sky turn a peachy-pink as day broke over the water. I bought this house for the view, for the location. I didn't really expect to like it here as much as I did, but the house was comfortable and there was something calming and steady about the ocean.

Out of all my houses throughout the world, this one probably felt most like home, aside from the first one I ever purchased. That home was the biggest, the most private, and was the only place I've ever been where I could fully be myself. It's where the old me and the current me could blend together to create a total person. When I went there, I didn't have to be all about the job. I didn't have to think about the way I looked, the way I acted, or the impression I was giving someone else. I hadn't been there in a long time and thinking about it now made me realize how much I missed it.

I made a sound and rolled away from the view. Missing a place was stupid. I didn't have time to miss anything because I had a job to do and thanks to G.R., I was losing a couple days because I was here and not there.

It didn't matter though. We could leave tonight and I would be back to work tomorrow. It was time I stepped it up a bit. The Target was familiar with me now; she seemed to feel safe in my presence and no longer suspicious. It was time to come up with a plan to get to her money. When a Target was a lonely person, when they didn't have a large family or a network of people around them, it usually wasn't very hard, but this time was different.

I needed an angle. Maybe I could somehow get into her bank account through the fundraiser I was supposed to be helping her with. A dull ache began behind my eyes and I knew it was going to be a long day.

I would rather eat a bucket of nails and wash them down with a glass of bleach than go back to Alaska tomorrow and spend time with the Target.

Flinging the down-filled covers off me, I got out of bed and snatched my cell off the nightstand. I should send her a text, something just to keep myself in her thoughts, to endear her to me a little more. Maybe a picture of the empty morning beach.

Everything in my body rebelled at the idea of sharing any part of this place with her. If I could smack some sense into myself I probably would have because my body and my mind needed to get with the program. I'd never had a problem faking my feelings for any Target before. Hell, this Target should be even easier because I didn't have to pretend to have romantic feelings for her because she thought I was gay.

Maybe the pressure G.R. was putting on was getting to me. The impossible assignment, the extra job, my sister...

I was starting to crack under the pressure. I mean, I was *feeling* things for the love of God.

I walked to the wall of windows to snap the picture. Like it or not, I was going to do this job. When this was done and the Reaper understood that I wasn't someone he could yank around, then I would go home, take a break, and get back to normal.

Before I could lift the phone, something caught my eye. A person walking at the edge of the water. It was Frankie. She was already down there, slowly walking along the shore as the waves rushed in soaking her feet.

The ocean wind was pulling at the hem of the cotton dress she wore, pulling it back and molding the fabric to the curves of her body. A body that my hands had been all over last night.

My muscles tightened at the memory of how she felt beneath me. Sinful. It was the only word that could capture how it felt to have her in my arms. That woman was a ball of passion, a pot of bubbling water about to boil over. Her kind of passion wasn't something a person found every day.

I knew she felt something for me. I saw it in her eyes. I felt it crackle between us. But I also saw her disgust for me, the hatred of who I was and what I did. As I watched her bend down to pick up a few seashells in the sand, I wondered which side was bigger, the hate or the desire.

A text came through my phone and it beeped in my hand. Irritation cracked through me at the disruption. It was the irritation that gave me clarity. All these feelings I'd been having, the lack of interest in my job... *the guilt*. I wasn't cracking under the pressure from G.R.

It was her.

She was the reason I was changing. She was the reason I was losing focus on my goals.

Feeling disgusted with myself, I looked down at the text.

***Don't think he's noticed yet. Everything go as planned?***

It was from Storm. He was keeping an eye on G.R. so we would know when he noticed his secret collection was gone. It hadn't been easy getting those bodies and the soul out of there the other night, but we did it. Instead of keeping everything together in one place, we split up the bodies, Storm hiding two of them and me taking the girl and the jar with the soul in it.

I glanced inside my closet, making sure she was still there, and then looked under the bathroom sink at the jar.

***All went as planned. Will be home tomorrow,*** I typed back.

***Target is getting on a plane,*** he replied.

***When?***

***First thing in the morning.*** It wasn't morning yet in Alaska.

***Thanks for the heads up.***

Ugh. Where was she going? How long was she going to be gone? I didn't remember her mentioning a trip to me, yet I hadn't really talked to her since that day in the café when I rushed out of there. Ever since then I'd been too busy trying to find something to use against G.R. *And too busy thinking about Frankie,* the voice in my head whispered.

Damn. I was getting sloppy. Exactly what G.R. wanted. Shit, I wouldn't be surprised if he knew she was going out of town and he sent me here just so I would miss that much more time with her.

With a growl, I punched a button on my phone and dialed her. She answered on the first ring.

"Charming, this is a surprise," she said. Her voice was friendly yet slightly reserved. My weird behavior at lunch the other day clearly left an impression on her. And now here I was calling her at a very late hour (for her).

"Rosalyn," I began, interjecting warmth that I wasn't feeling into my tone. "It has been a few days, sorry about that. I had an unexpected business meeting and had to fly to Los Angeles."

"You don't have to explain, Charming," she replied. "It isn't as if your every move is my business."

I shut my eyes in frustration. See, this was the bad part about being "gay" because if we had some sort of romantic connection, she would feel entitled to knowing every move I made and I could likely romance her into forgiving the way I acted.

Still, the way I was feeling lately being her friend was hard enough, let alone trying to act like her boyfriend. My eyes strayed down onto the beach to look for Frankie. She was still picking up shells, using her dress as a bucket to hold them.

I laughed. "Well, of course not. But I figured since we were friends and also working on the fundraiser together, I should keep you informed."

"About the fundraiser," she began, and a ball of ice formed in my gut. If she told me she didn't need my help anymore I was going to freaking kill her just to be done with her and forget about the damn money. "We will have to postpone our planning for a few days. I'm actually at the airport now. I must go out of town."

The air in my lungs expelled. "That's no problem at all," I replied. "I can work on a few things on my end and then when you get back we can regroup."

I wanted to ask her where she was going. I wanted to ask her why, but I wasn't about to. Appearing too interested right now could be the nail in my coffin. She was already sounding a little distant and cool, and giving her any other reason to doubt my motives for hanging around her would be stupid on my part.

"Well, yes, that would be great," she replied, her tone losing some of its coolness.

"Just let me know when you arrive back in Alaska and have a safe flight."

"Thank you," she said. I thought she would hang up then and after a second I pulled the phone away from my ear, but when she began to speak again, I yanked it back up.

"Charming, is there another reason you called so early?"

"Not at all. I was just sitting here watching the sun rise and I realized the last time I saw you was kind of rushed. I figured I would take a chance and see if you were still up."

"Oh. Well, I'm sure the view there is much nicer than the one here."

"I don't want to make you jealous," I teased.

She laughed. "Yes, I would think so. Okay, well, as long as everything is okay with you…" Her words died off.

"Absolutely. The other day I'd gotten up to go talk with a business acquaintance and then I received a call that there was a fire at one of the properties I own. Naturally, I rushed over, but it wasn't nearly as bad as the man on the phone made it seem."

After that, I was glad most of her reserve had melted away and I hoped I managed to stay in her good graces.

When we finally hung up the phone, the ache in my head had turned into a pounding.

Looks like the job was delayed for… well, for I didn't know how long. I was going to have to have Storm find out where she was going and when she was returning.

I glanced at the clock. Not even eight a.m. and I was exhausted.

Frankie appeared on the deck below, dumping a huge pile of shells onto the floor by her feet. Sand scattered everywhere. Then she picked up the hose and started spraying them off creating puddles and globs of wet sand. I shook my head. This place had never seen such a mess. Not only was there sand and shells everywhere, but her towels were draped over the chairs, and her flip-flops lay forgotten near the stairs.

It looked like a home.

Like a place where people could be happy.

I thought again about the place I was missing earlier.

Without a second thought, I tore downstairs and out onto the deck, startling Frankie, who was still using the hose. She jumped, spun around, bringing the hose with her, and splattered me right across the chest.

I flinched and growled her name.

She burst out laughing. "That's what you get for scaring me."

I snatched her towel off the chair and began drying myself. "I came down here to tell you to pack up."

"You want to leave?" I didn't miss the disappointment clouding her tone.

"Yes, but we aren't going back to Alaska just yet."

"Where are we going?" she said, instantly suspicious. "Do you have another job?"

"No." The relief in my voice made me want to mentally kick myself. "I want to go home."

"I thought this was your house?"

"I have a lot of *houses*," I answered, hoping she would get
my meaning. I didn't want to explain the way I was feeling
right then. It was bad enough I was feeling it.
She nodded. "Where is home?"
"Scotland."

# Chapter Thirty

*"Majestic - having or displaying majesty or great dignity; grand; lofty."*

## *Frankie*

I was so getting fired. There was no way the dragon lady was going to let me call off sick the rest of the week from work without demanding pictures of me at the hospital, unconscious and with an IV sticking out of my arm.

But I got the impression Charming wasn't ready to go back to Alaska yet, and to be honest, neither was I. This was my chance to see places I'd never seen before, to be spontaneous and do something exciting. If I got fired from the job I hated, then I guess I would get another one. I mean there had to be tons of crappy jobs just waiting to suck away my soul when I got back.

And then there was Charming.

He was as bossy and demanding as ever, hogging the remote on the plane, slinging insults about everything I did, and generally annoying the crap out of me, but even still, there was something different about him.

I couldn't quite put my finger on what I was sensing other than… something about him was changing.

His insults weren't quite as nasty, he handed me a blanket on the plane before I even asked for it, and on the way to the airport he stopped and bought a box of donuts and ordered me a coffee loaded with sugar. And he hadn't once put on a pair of trousers.

It seemed that our time on the beach had created some kind of tumultuous truce between us. It was kind of nice.

Of course, Charming had yet another crazy expensive car waiting at the hangar when we touched down at the airport.

This time it was a black Ferrari. But not even a car as nice as a Ferrari could steal my attention from the sights of Scotland.

It was majestic.

No other word could even come close to the rolling hills that seemed to be carpeted in a grass so thick and green it almost looked made up. I really only thought that places like this existed in books. But here I was breathing in the incredibly fresh air and looking out over miles of green.

After we left the airport, Charming drove to this tiny market where he picked up a few essentials for the fridge, explaining it was easier to get those things here than where we were going. Not too much later, he was pulling the Ferrari onto a ferry of all things and we were setting out across the sea toward the Shetland Islands. I didn't know Scotland consisted of islands. I thought it was just a big lump of land like every other country, but oh my, was it so much more. The Shetland Islands were comprised of many islands, the largest one simply called Mainland. Charming explained that this was where his home was.

Once we were able to disembark the ferry, we drove in silence (I had my face plastered to the window) down a two-lane winding road. We passed sheep farms, more endless rolling hills, and sea views that were incredible. The farms all had stone cottages plopped down in the center, with grass all around. It was the most peaceful place I'd ever been.

And I wasn't the only one affected by this place.

If I had thought Charming was changing before, I knew it now. It was almost like night and day. I kept sneaking glances at him out of the corner of my eye as he drove, wondering what side of him I would see next.

"Aren't the sights to your liking?" he said, glancing at me, then looking back to the curving road.

"Are you kidding? This place is amazing. I won't even make you pay me a million dollars when I get fired. This place is worth it."

He flashed his teeth. "Then why do you keep looking over here?"

I paused. I thought about making a smart-ass crack. I decided I would try being real. "Because of the way you look here."

"And how do I look?"

"Like you're finally somewhere you can breathe."

He didn't say anything for a long time, and then all he said was, "We're almost there."

Not too much longer, he pulled down a long and private road that took us around a wide curve. When the Ferrari made it around the bend, a house came into view. It wasn't what I was expecting after seeing the modern glass place on the beach.

But it was so much better.

It looked like an old giant farmhouse that was built nestled into the side of one of those sweeping hills and hadn't been touched since. It was all white brick, painted and worn. The windows were small, but there were many and they lined the house in rows, each with its own pair of painted black shutters. Those were pealing and chipped as well. The roof was a traditional roof with black shingles (those actually looked fairly new) and it was in the traditional shape (kind of like a big triangle perched on top of many boxes). The grass around the building itself was trimmed, but everything else around the property was long and shaggy; the tall green blades swayed back and forth with a gentle breeze.

As we drove along the narrow road toward the house, I looked over toward Charming, but my eyes didn't see him. They went directly to the sweeping view of the sea that sat miles away, facing the house. Calm, dark-blue water met a rugged and rocky coastline, and I instantly wished I had a pair of boots to go exploring on the stones.

"How long have you owned this place?" I asked, my voice an awed whisper.

"Longer than you've been alive."

That was… wow. I didn't know whether to be amazed or creeped out.

The driveway wasn't paved and I was partially shocked when he drove the Ferrari right across the dirt road and pushed a button, lifting a black barn-style door. Clearly, he had modernized the house in some ways.

"I had the interior of the place gutted. It's completely new inside. When I bought the house, it wasn't livable."

"By whose standards?" I scoffed.

"Well, not even the wayward sheep who had found their way inside appreciated the leaky roof." When he looked at me, his eyes twinkled and I realized the green in his irises matched the green that surrounded us here.

I smiled. "Well, give me the grand tour," I exclaimed and scrambled out of the car to meet him eagerly at the door.

I could tell he was excited to show me his home, the only place he truly loved to be. I think it was his excitement that made me so excited because I knew this place had to be special if it elicited this kind of reaction from someone like him.

The home was… It was everything anyone could ever want but never dream up. Exposed beams, floors made of old barn wood, and accent walls of the same white brick as the outside filled this house. Hand-braided rugs, richly upholstered furniture, and rooms without the boundaries of walls made it feel like more than a refurbished building, more like a place that someone loved. Of course, mixed in with all the old elements were all the new ones—a huge stone fireplace, a huge open kitchen with granite surfaces and stainless-steel appliances, and the amenities of remodeled bathrooms and a home theater. The house was so large that he didn't even show me the entire place.

The last stop on his tour was my room, which had a view of the sea. It was a large room with a queen-sized bed, luxurious bedding, and an adjoining bath that was made up of natural stone and contemporary fixtures.

"Well, what do you think?" he said, watching me gaze around the room.

"It's the most beautiful place I'll ever see."

He grinned. "How do you know?"

"I know."

"It took me years to get this place like this."

"Most people wouldn't have had the time and the money," I said, running my hand over the ultra-soft and thick comforter.

"I guess being a Death Escort has some advantages."

The coldness in his tone had me looking up. He thought I was insulting him. In truth, I'd been thinking out loud.

"I wasn't trying to insult you."

"What, then? Were you trying to remind me what you think about my money and how I earned it?"

"No." I defended. "I—" I stopped trying to explain myself and sighed. "It was just a comment, a slip of the tongue. I don't have to remind you what you do. You remind yourself enough on your own."

His eyes narrowed.

"The truth is you're a Death Escort. You kill people. Repeatedly. I'm just trying to figure out if that's something I can live with."

"Something you can live with?" he repeated. "Are you saying you thought of me and you… together?"

"I—well—" Words failed me. I felt like a complete idiot. Maybe I was suffering from a major case of jetlag. I have no idea what would possess me to say that stuff out loud.

Well, no. I did know what it was. It was the pull, the attraction that was always there between us. It was the swirl of energy that seemed to only encompass him and me when we were in the same room. It was the beat of butterfly wings inside my stomach and the way my skin vibrated beneath his touch. Hadn't he felt those things too?

The way he kissed me, the way his fingers reached for mine… the way he sometimes whispered the truths that lay deep inside him. I wasn't making those things up. The electricity between us was so thick I could almost scoop it out of the air. Why would he pretend it wasn't there?

"So is it?" he said. His tone sounded weird and it broke through my inner monologue of panic. "Is what I do something you could live with?"

I wanted to say yes. I wanted to know without a doubt that I could look him in the eyes every day when he came home and not wonder about who he killed that day, who he plotted against. I wish I wouldn't have to think about the person he was taking away from loved ones, tearing an entire family apart with a senseless death.

I looked up. "I don't know," I whispered.

"Don't look so upset," he replied, his voice even. "It isn't like we have a future together anyway. There is no happily ever after for someone like me. There is only death."

He turned and left the room then, exiting so quietly and quickly that it was almost like he'd never been there at all.

But even if my eyes and ears were fooled by his departure, the rest of me wasn't. My heart would bear the marks from those words, the echo of finality in them, forever.

# Chapter Thirty-One

*"Storm - an atmospheric disturbance manifested in strong winds accompanied by rain, snow, or other precipitation and often by thunder and lightning."*

## Charming

The minute we drove onto the Mainland, here on the Shetland Islands, I felt like a weight the size of a walrus was lifted off my chest. I wasn't sure how long it was since I visited here last—a year, maybe two? But even after all that time, it still felt like home to me. It felt that way from the very first time I came here on some job for G.R. to escort a Target. After the job was done, I stayed on and bought a house, a house that took me years and years to remodel. It was probably the only thing I've done in the past ninety years that gave me any pleasure.

The pull to come here had been stronger than ever before. I wanted to feel linked to something, something other than the job—something other than death. Something that was mine and no one else's. That was why I should have stayed away. It was an assault to my already confused senses. My only excuse was that being around Frankie was seriously messing with my head.

And with my heart.

I reached up and rubbed the spot in the center of my chest where the organ that pumped blood throughout my body lay just below my ribs. It felt weird. Almost like it hurt.

I dropped my hand and rummaged around through the kitchen cabinets, looking for the antacid tablets. It was probably just heartburn.

Crunching on the chalky tablets, I glanced at the clock. It was afternoon, still too early for dinner, which was a good thing because I wasn't hungry and I didn't feel like cooking. Frankie was still out of sight, likely off snooping through the house. I hadn't seen her since she told me she thought about us beyond a temporary annoying relationship.

The words caught me off guard. I knew she was attracted to me; her body responded every time I touched her and the pounding of her heart did not fall on deaf ears. Still, hearing she even considered anything more was just unsettling.

She wasn't the first girl to ever have feelings for me or imagine a future together. It happened all the time, because I wanted it to. Making a woman fall in love with me or so close to it was my job. It's what I did. Hell, a couple times I'd gone so far as to propose marriage. But those times were different. This was different.

I never tried to make Frankie feel anything other than hate for me.

But she did. She admitted as much.

I was just too charming for my own good.

I moved away from the kitchen and into the great room, where I knelt in front of the stone fireplace and lit the kindling already laid out in the hearth. It wasn't cold here, but it was chilly, and after coming from L.A. the extra warmth was needed.

I didn't want feelings between Frankie and me. I didn't want anything from her other than for her to stay out of my business.

*That's not true*, something inside me whispered.

I rubbed at my chest again. Those damn pills weren't helping.

I accepted my solitary existence. It suited me. Trying for anything more would just end badly.

I heard her soft footfalls coming toward me and the muscles in my body tightened, getting ready to face her anger.

"Is there a path or road that will lead down toward the coast?"

She was asking me about a walking path? She didn't want to yell at me? I stood away from the fire and looked at her. She wasn't scowling. She didn't look like she was going to throw something at my head. She was calm.

Well, this was different.

"Yeah, it might be a bit overgrown. It's a couple miles, though, to get down by the water."

"That's okay. I feel like walking."

"I should probably go with you. The ground is a bit uneven and if the path is overgrown, you might get lost."

She looked slightly alarmed at the mention of me tagging along, but she covered up the look very quickly. "I'm sure I'll be fine."

"I don't want to have to come looking for you when you get lost," I growled, irritation running rampant through my veins. Was I that easy to get over, then? Did my rebuff not affect her at all?

"I won't get lost with this giant house to use as my reference."

"Fine. Go." Time away from her would likely do me some good anyway. "The path starts behind the house."

She nodded and left without another word.

I picked up a book written by Mark Twain and sat down, determined not to think about her anymore.

An hour later, a heavy rainstorm seemed to appear out of nowhere. The blue in the sky was taken over by angry dark clouds and swirling winds.

I smirked at the idea of her getting rained on even as my ears listened for her retreat back into the house.

Not too much later, thunder rolled overhead and the rain began to fall in a downpour. She still wasn't back. Worry crept into me, and I put the book down and looked out the window, overlooking the direction the path would have taken her.

Through the heavy rain, I saw her, a moving spot maybe half a mile from the house. She was moving quickly, trying to get out of the storm.

And then she fell, her body disappearing completely from sight.

A low swear tripped out of my mouth and before I knew it, I was grabbing a slicker off the hook by the door and racing out into the storm. As I went, lightning lit up the sky, creating an angry electric streak that bolted toward the ground. The crack of thunder that followed left a hollow ringing in my ears.

I picked up my pace, worrying she was hurt and lying there out in the open, vulnerable to the elements.

"Frankie!" I yelled, my voice cutting through the gusting wind. My shirt and jeans were soaked in minutes, my shoes were saturated, and I felt like I was walking in a puddle. Wet grass slapped against my legs and water dripped into my eyes.

I heard her call my name, the wind carrying the sound over to my ears. I ran faster, tapping into the reserve of energy my body always had, zipping over the wet grass across the slopping ground.

I stopped when I saw her. She was trudging up one of the slight hills, mud and rain soaking her hair and body. She looked like a drowned cat.

She was a few yards away when she saw me, her feet quickening their pace, but in her haste she slipped again.

She flung out her arms, trying to steady herself, to catch some balance and not fall, but there was no use. The ground was too slick and the mud too slippery.

I caught her around the waist just before she landed in a heap.

"I told you not to come out here alone," I snapped, pulling her back onto her feet.

"I thought you said you weren't going to come after me!"

"Shut up!" I yelled, yanking the slicker down over her head and putting up the hood. My heart was still beating too fast from watching her fall before.

"I'm already soaked," she yelled over another rumble of thunder.

I didn't bother to reply. I knew she was soaked—we both were—but I felt like I had to do something. I tugged her hand to pull her along behind me, and she made a soft whimper in the back of her throat.

I spun around, my eyes sweeping over her. "Are you hurt?"

"I'm fine," she lied. Her lips were turning an ugly shade of blue.

"Don't lie to me!" I yelled, grabbing her by the shoulders. Rain was pelting us from every angle and it felt like a million tiny needles against my skin.

"I twisted my ankle." Her shoulders sagged, like admitting she was hurt was somehow giving in and letting me win.

Which it was. She should have listened to me in the first place.

I turned around and crouched down, giving her my back. "Let's go," I called out.

She hesitated only a moment before climbing onto my back and wrapping her arms and legs around me. "Hold on!"

Even though I kind of liked having her wrapped around me, I moved quickly, trying to get us away from a storm that was far too violent.

I let us into the mudroom, setting her on a wooden bench by the door and pushing the wet hair off my forehead.

"Going off alone like that was stupid!" I burst out, anger ripping through me. Now that we were out of the rain and she was safe, I was going to let her have it.

"I didn't know it was going to downpour!" she yelled back.

"You should have been more careful!"

"Why are you yelling at me?" she shouted, yanking off the slicker and throwing it on the floor. She was streaked with mud and dirt and her teeth were beginning to chatter.

My anger drained away like water in a sink. I knelt down and unlaced her ruined sneakers. "It's hard not to yell at you," I said gently.

She snorted but then made a sound when I slipped her shoe away from the ankle that she twisted. It was red and slightly puffy, but it didn't look too bad. I used a nearby towel to gingerly pat the water and mud off the sore part. "It doesn't look that bad. Should be fine by morning. We'll get some ice on it."

She didn't say anything and when I looked up, I caught her staring at me, watching me with this strained look on her face.

"Are you hurt somewhere else? Did you hit your head?" I reached up and fingered her scalp, searching for cuts.

"I'm fine." She caught my wrists and pulled them away from her head. "Why is it whenever I try to get away from you, I end up in your arms instead?"

"Because you're clumsy and pigheaded?" I offered.

She rolled her eyes.

"You went out there to get away from me?" I asked seriously. Something in my stomach churned and that feeling in my chest was back.

She pushed at her wet hair. "It's easier that way, you know?" she said quietly. "Like you said, there is no future for us."

That's why she went outside. Why she didn't want me to go with her. I hurt her. Telling her that I didn't want her actually hurt her feelings.

Having power over another person's emotions was always something I reveled in. But not now. Not this. It seemed like an awful lot to bear… I didn't want the responsibility of knowing I could hurt her. Hell, I just ran out into a raging, angry storm after her to keep her from getting hurt. Now she tells me she was out there in the first place because of me.

I dealt with her feelings the best way I knew how. Not at all.

"Are you hungry?" I asked.

If the change in topic surprised her, she didn't show it. "Yeah."

"Let's get changed and I'll make some spaghetti and you can ice that ankle." I helped her up the stairs and into her room where she assured me she could manage, and so I left her, going to change into a dry pair of jeans and shirt.

The fire was almost out so I added some more wood to it and then went to boil the water for the noodles. Frankie appeared when I was pulling a jar of sauce out of the cupboard. She grabbed some ice out of the freezer and hobbled over to the table and sat down, propping up her foot.

"I don't think it's that bad. Barely hurts anymore."

I made a sound and added the noodles to the boiling water.

We made small talk. Mostly she asked me about Scotland and I answered. The conversation stayed the same while we ate and the storm still raged outside. Underneath the light conversation, a tension was building. I didn't know if she felt it too or if it was purely my own frustrations starting to come to a head, but it made me feel restless and moody.

There was so much between us that wasn't said, and the hurt I was responsible for would flash in her eyes every so often, there only long enough for me to recognize it before it was gone again. It was a relief when she went to bed, saying the events of the day had made her tired.

I thought once she was gone and I was alone, the tension coiled inside me would lessen, that it would go away. It didn't. It got worse. It was like being away from her made my body want to search for her.

Maybe I should just admit it.

I wanted her.

I had feelings for her.

Frankie made me *feel*.

I growled in frustration. But even still, what I said earlier held true. There was no future for us; there couldn't be.

The next thing I knew I was standing in her doorway, peering into her dark room at the bed, wondering if she was asleep yet. She wasn't in the bed. She was standing at the window, looking out at the moon. She was wearing a pair of boxer shorts and a tank top, an outfit that left little to the imagination.

Lust slammed into me so quickly that I almost stumbled. The need to touch her, to claim her, almost had me across the room and pushing her onto the bed.

But I held back, needing to tell her.

"I've thought about it too."

She jumped, my voice startling her, and she turned, glancing at me over her shoulder through the dark.

"Since the other night on the beach, I've thought of little else." The more I did this talking thing, the easier it became. And when she looked at me like that, with her blue eyes wide like I was doing something extraordinary by just telling her what I was thinking, it made me want to make things up to say just so she would keep on looking at me.

"Charming, I—"

I held up my hand and she stopped. "I just wanted you to know that. I didn't want you to think that I hadn't thought of you at all. Because I have. You make me… *feel.* I thought I had bypassed that a long time ago. And that's why we—why *I* can't be with you. I can't even think about being with you. Because it's selfish. Because if I let you close to me, I would do what I do best. I would kill you."

"Charming, you would never kill me."

"Yes, I would. Just not the kind of killing I usually do. This kind would be slow. It would start with you pretending you were okay with who I am. I would take away pieces of you one by one until you were just like me: dead."

"Charming," she whispered, taking a step toward me.

"For the first time since becoming an Escort, I care if someone lives or dies," I whispered. "I won't kill you. I won't take the only life I value on this earth away."

"If you had wanted to push me away, you should have told me I was fat, thrown me out of the house, or left me out there today in that storm. But what you just said… those words… all they did was pull me closer to you."

See, this is what happens when a guy tries to talk.

It backfires.

"I should have known you were crazy enough to twist what I said into something romantic."

"Ahh, now you try the insults," she said, a smile creeping into her voice.

"If I was insulting you, you would feel insulted," I muttered.

"Hmmm," she said, taking a step toward me.

"I'm not trying to pull you closer."

She took another step and another. "What if I want to be closer?"

"Didn't you hear anything I just said?"

"I heard." She stopped directly in front of me, tipped her chin back, and looked up. "So you do this noble thing, you stay away from me, and you 'save my life' by not being with me."

She hooked her fingers in the belt loops on the front of my jeans and tugged, bringing me that much closer. "But what about you?"

"Me?" How was I supposed to think with her hands in such close proximity to the fly of my jeans?

She made a sound of agreement and released my belt loops, but instead of pulling back, she ran her hands along my sides and across my lower back.

It was the first time she ever touched me… well, touched me first. Usually she didn't touch me until my lips were devouring hers. Most of the blood flow left my brain and all rushed downward… into my jeans. I knew once the brain downstairs took over, I wouldn't be leaving this room. It took everything in me to reach around and pull her hands away, to gently return them to her sides.

I didn't look back as I left the room because if I had, I wouldn't have left it at all.

It occurred me then the reason I spent so much time doing the wrong thing was because doing the right thing was too damn hard.

# Chapter Thirty-Two

*"Butterfly - any of various insects of the order Lepidoptera, characteristically having slender bodies, knobbed antennae, and four broad, usually colorful wings."*

## Frankie

I couldn't sleep. I felt restless and hot, like someone left the oven door open in the house on a hot day. I gave up on the bed and left my room, wandering down the hall and stopping at Charming's door. It was open and a small lamp beside the bed showed me he wasn't in bed either.

The past two days had been like a rollercoaster ride. And the things he said, the words he whispered… it was official. He was it for me. That was the only thing I knew for sure right now. Well, that and I wanted him. Badly.

I wandered through the house, not finding him in the places I thought he would be. So I went down the stairs toward a part of the house I hadn't seen yet. As soon as my feet hit the floor, I knew he was down there. The sound of his heavy breathing and swift movements beckoned me onward until I was standing in the open door of the most impressive home gym I'd ever seen.

It was huge. But it would have to be because sitting in the center of the all-white room was a full-sized boxing ring.

Charming was in the center of the ring, going through movements that up until now I had only watched on TV.

I stood in the doorway a long time. Watching him move was mesmerizing. His body was so fluid, so strong. It's like he was exactly sure about every punch and jab he made. His skin glistened with the sheen of sweat and his usually perfect hair was ruffled and damp around his ears and forehead. The gloves on his hands were big. They looked heavy, but somehow strapped onto the ends of his arms, they seemed small.

He was in his element; that much was clear. The breath that whooshed and wheezed out of him as he practically danced around the ring created an odd sort of cadence that was like music as I stared.

I felt like a voyeur, like someone seeing something they weren't meant to see… Yet the idea of turning away, of leaving him to his privacy, was more than I could bear.

I needed to see him like this. I wanted to.

The changes in him, the changes that started in L.A. and followed us here… I finally knew what exactly I was feeling. He was becoming human. Where he once seemed cold and shutdown, he now looked more alive than half the people I knew.

*Butterflies with razorblade wings.*

That's how he made me feel. It was the feeling that plagued me since we had met, the feeling that took me so long to acknowledge and even longer to identify. It's exactly what he did to me.

Because the way I felt about him…

It hurt, but like a butterfly, it was beautiful. He made me feel like I was walking on the edge of a cliff. Like at any moment the bottom could fall out of my stomach. At any moment, the cliff's edge could tumble away and I would be left falling… plunging toward the unknown.

The fluttering in my belly was never gentle. It was as if a million wings were in there beating, making me breathless, but then the wings would come into contact with me and slice me open. Being with him hurt. Being without him… I wasn't sure, but I thought it might be worse.

I noticed he was no longer moving. He was standing in the center of the ring, watching me.

I pushed out of the doorframe, the heavy door swinging shut behind me and banging with an ominous finality.

When I got closer, he grabbed the ropes around the ring and created an opening, holding them while I ducked inside, straightening to face him.

"I couldn't sleep," I said, staring at his chest, following a rivulet of sweat that made a path all the way down his six-pack and disappeared beneath the thick waistband of the silver gym shorts hanging low on his hips.

"Me either."

It wasn't lost on me that the only thing separating me from him was the very flimsy fabric that made up those shorts.

"I didn't know you had a boxing ring," I said, my voice going hoarse.

"There's a lot of things you don't know about me."

I was beginning to understand that. There were so many layers to him. I was beginning to wonder if I would ever uncover them all.

One of those butterfly wings nipped at my belly, causing a stinging sensation inside me.

I wanted to uncover every single part of him.

My eyes locked on his. Without looking away, I grabbed his arm, pulling the glove up between us. My fingers tugged on the string that kept the laces tight. It unraveled, loosening the hold the glove had on his hand. I brought my other hand up and gently, slowly yanked the glove off and dropped it onto the mat.

He watched me, his eyes heavy, as a thick cloud of desire grew between us.

I repeated the same process with his other hand until both of his hands were free. He reached for me, but I shook my head and laced my fingers through his. We stood there for a long time, hands clasped, staring at each other without saying a single word.

Maybe I was waiting for my conscience. Maybe I was waiting for him to turn me away. Maybe I was drawing out the anticipation until everything inside me was pulled so taut that I was sure I would snap apart.

None of that mattered anymore. All that mattered was the here, the now.

I released his hands and reached out, laying my palm against his stomach. His muscles rippled beneath my touch and my skin instantly became slick with his perspiration.

I stepped forward, done with waiting, and slid both my hands into the waistband of his shorts.

"Frankie," he rasped, his voice stilling my movements.

Another one of those razorblades nicked me. If he turned me away right now, I would likely bleed to death. I raised my eyes, waiting for his decision.

"My name…" he began. "My real name is Oliver."

Everything beneath my skin vibrated. I felt like I couldn't stand still a second longer because all of the energy—all the emotion that was building inside me—was dying for release.

"Olly," I said, trying the name out on my tongue. I liked it.

He must have liked it too because he made a sound in the back of his throat and nodded.

The damn broke. Whatever thin barrier had lain between us until this point was now completely broken. I pulled my hands up and leapt at him, jumping up and wrapping my legs around his waist.

He caught me, stumbled back a bit, but the ropes were there to steady us as our lips finally met.

I'd been kissed by many men in my life before I met him, but I couldn't recall one of them now. It was like he was my first, my only.

"Say it again," he said as he trailed kisses down my neck.

"Olly," I purred and he sank to his knees.

He pulled back, robbing me of his lips, robbing me of the sensation of them upon me. His green eyes were practically electrified; they were so intense.

"Don't ever stop calling me that. No one has called me that—" His words dropped away and he shook his head. "It doesn't matter. Just don't stop."

I don't know why, but tears filled my eyes. I whispered his name again and he lowered me backward so I was sprawled out in the ring and he was on his knees between my thighs, staring down at me with lust in his eyes.

He reached out, grasping the hem of my boxers, and yanked them down. I lifted my foot as he slid them off one leg and then I kicked them away, over beside his discarded gloves. I was still wearing a pair of white lace panties and a white tank top, but by the look on his face you would think I was completely exposed.

"I don't think I've ever seen anyone as perfect as you."

I sat up, my face directly in line with his hard abs, and I hooked my hands into his waistband and pulled.

He wasn't wearing any boxers.

All the breath whooshed from my body and I was left with a dull buzzing sound in my head. He wanted me; that much was *very* clear.

I looked up, expecting to see the Charming I always saw, the Charming with the arrogant grin, the gleam in his eye… but that man was gone.

In his place was someone who was vulnerable, whose feelings were laid bare in his eyes and looked like he'd been alone far, far too long.

No, I wasn't seeing Charming. I was seeing the real man beneath the carefully built exterior. I was seeing Olly.

"I want you," I told him, reaching out my hand and grabbing the evidence of his want, wrapping my hand around it.

He closed his eyes and swallowed.

I leaned forward and placed my tongue at the base of his erection, licking upward like he was a giant lollipop that I couldn't get enough of. He jerked and all his muscles went tense as I wrapped my lips around him, taking every ounce of him inside me that I could. His fingers dug into my shoulder and I smiled as I pulled back, using my teeth to gently rake upward, across the sensitive skin, before pulling away and looking up.

He groaned my name and pushed me back, coming over me, fitting his body along mine. I wiggled, trying to get him even closer. He chuckled in my ear and pressed a kiss on the side of my neck.

"Patience, love," he murmured as his hand found the hem of my tank and traveled upward to cup the very sensitive flesh of my breast.

I groaned and leaned up to kiss his shoulder.

The next thing I knew, my tank was gone and the only thing between us was the lace panties I was starting to hate.

His mouth made me forget, though, and his tongue was like a magician who did things to my skin that I didn't know were possible. It danced across my cheekbone, trailed down my arm, and then he picked up my hand, bringing it to his lips where he pressed single kisses to each one of my fingers.

When he was done with my hand, he placed it on my knee, lowering his lips to that sensitive skin just behind, and then nibbled all the way down. "Do you always wear panties that look like this?" he asked, glancing up from the inside of my thigh.

I nodded. It was all I could manage.

"Sexy," he said and then licked right up my center, my swollen, damp flesh being teased by the snippets of his tongue that I felt through the lace.

My back arched up off the floor and I groaned. I wasn't sure how much more of his sweet torture I could take. He did it again, his fingertips playing with the edges of my panties, slipping just inside and then pulling back out and trailing down my thigh.

 Every part of my body began to tremble until I couldn't even hold myself still. I lay there under his gaze, beneath his feather-light teasing touch, and did nothing but shake and thrust myself closer to him.

He pulled up, placing an open palm on each knee, and spread my legs as wide as they would go, holding them there before lowering himself between me, pressing his very hard erection right at my core.

I couldn't take it anymore. I needed him.

"Olly," I said, knowing it was exactly the right word to say to get what I wanted.

He didn't even pause to remove the lace. Instead, he pushed it aside and entered me.

My mouth opened, but no sound came out. I'm pretty sure everything inside me splintered apart and then found its way back together again. All I could do was hold on. I wrapped my hands around his biceps and let sensation after sensation take me for a ride.

The contrast of the lace against the smoothness of his flesh was almost my undoing. But what truly pushed me over the edge was when he stopped. He pulled back slightly and looked down. Dark hair fell into his eyes and his arms trembled slightly.

I thought he might say something, but no words left his lips and then suddenly he pushed forward, filling me so deep that my eyes fluttered closed. He lowered himself so every inch of our bodies was in contact and he brought his lips to my ear.

It was then he whispered.

"I've been dead for so long that I forgot what it was like to live. I forgot what it was like to feel. Even still, I'm pretty sure nothing I had experienced was ever like this. You brought me back to life, Frankie. You make me want to live."

I whispered his name again, gripped his butt, and pulled him closer, pushing him as far inside me as he could possibly go. And then I ground myself down on him, grinding so deep that not even air could come between us. A low groan ripped from his throat as he hunched down over me, his body going stiff and convulsing over mine. All at once I felt like a firecracker went off inside me. Bright white pleasure burst in my center and spread out until my limbs were completely boneless and I collapsed against the floor, unable to move. I felt the beads of sweat slipping over my skin and I heard the rasping breaths he sucked in as he leveraged himself over me on shaking limbs, but beyond that I was completely senseless.

I knew being with him would be incredible. My body never reacted to anyone like this ever before. But damn, I hadn't known. I hadn't known it was possible to get so completely lost in another person. For a moment there I wouldn't have been able to tell where I ended and he began. It was amazing. And terrifying. Like it or not, Olly was now completely and utterly inside my heart.

# Chapter Thirty-Three

*"Truth - a statement proven to be or accepted as true."*

## Charming

My skin was tingling. My lungs expanded with air. I could feel the erratic beating of my heart against my ribs. I was lying on my back, collapsed on the mat, feeling things I hadn't felt in so long, things I thought for sure I would never feel again.

I turned my head to the side, looking at the person who started it all. Looking at the girl who practically dared me to live. Her blond hair was wild, her skin flushed, and every inch of her dangerously soft curves was exposed.

Something inside me yawned.

Something stretched and moved…

I was waking up.

Over ninety years of being dead—of being consumed by death… I was waking up.

Nothing had done it before. Not money, not power, not killing or having no consequences for anything I did or took. Up until now, I was asleep; I was completely dead.

But then Frankie came along. This woman who never shut up, annoyed the hell out of me, and ate way too much candy.

I loved her.

I loved her completely.

And it was because of her I wanted more. I was tired of death. I wanted to live.

"You told me your name," she said from beside me, her voice slipping into my thoughts and wrapping around my mind.

I'm not quite sure what possessed me to tell her the one thing I guarded so close. I had many names over the years, more than I could count, more than I cared to remember. But only one had meant anything. The one I was born with. The one that my mother gave me, the one that someone truly wanted me to have. My name was the only connection I had left of my past, of my life. It was the only part of me that I thought I had left.

I turned my head, looking over at her once more. She was watching me tentatively, almost warily… like she wasn't sure what to expect. She probably wondered if I'd even told her the truth and now that we'd slept together, if I was going to morph back into the man I'd always been with her.

I walked my fingers between the space between us, and her laugh was throaty as my fingers neared hers. Instead of linking them together, I wrapped my hand around her wrist and tugged, pulling her closer.

She came willingly, fitting herself against my side and resting her cheek on my shoulder. The toes on her right foot found their way between my calves and I smiled up at the ceiling.

"You're the first person I've ever told my real name since I've been dead."

"How did you die?" she asked quietly.

This was something I'd never told anyone either.

"I was a boxer. I died in a dirty fight."

"Did it hurt?" she asked, sorrow lacing her voice.

"I don't really remember," I lied, but I was tired of lying so I told her the truth. "Yeah, for a moment, but it didn't hurt very long."

"And then what happened? *He* came for you?"

*He* being the Grim Reaper.

I nodded. The movement of my head caused a couple strands of her blond hair to stick in my stubble and tickle my chin. I reached up to untangle the silky strands and smooth my palm over them. "Next thing I knew I was in his office.

Nothing but a cloud of red—basically just a soul—and he was offering me a job as an Escort."

"Did you know what an Escort was when you took the job?"

I knew eventually she would ask me this. It was a natural question—*did you know you were going to be a killer? Did you actually choose it?*

"Yes," I answered. "He told me what I would be doing."

We both lay there for long moments, quiet. I wasn't sure what she was thinking, if the realization—the knowledge that I actually chose this life—would be something she could ever accept.

*And if she didn't?* my brain asked me.

But I think the real question was *What if she did?*

Because if she didn't, I would understand. I could go on exactly as I had been before. Okay, not exactly as before because this had changed me—*she* had changed me. But I would go on, and I would continue to do exactly what I'd been doing for over ninety years.

But if she did… if she somehow found a way to accept me, I knew things—*life*—as it was now would have to change. Irrevocably and forever.

She lifted her head off my shoulder and propped her arm and chin on top my chest. Her blue eyes studied me and her wild hair was tangled around her chin. "So how come you agreed? Why do any of you agree?"

"I can't say for sure about the others, but I do know that when you've just suffered some kind of violent or sudden death, you're in shock. You find yourself basically a cloud of color standing in a room with a man and his closets full of bodies." At this she lifted both her eyebrows and stared at me in disbelief, but she said nothing else as I continued.

"It isn't really much of a choice. You can stay dead and be tossed into some kind of void that is a fate worse than hell for all of eternity, or you can take his offer, get a new body, a new life, and a shit-ton of money. Considering most people are still shocked that they're actually dead, choosing to live isn't that hard."

"But it's not living," she said softly.

"No. It's not." I took a minute to brush some of the wayward hair out her face. "But usually by the time you realize that, it's much too late. Once you make the deal, once you take on the title of Death Escort, there is no getting out."

"Like Dex," she whispered.

"Yeah, like Dex. You do the job or get Recalled, sent off to a place worse than hell."

"When did you realize you weren't really living?"

I brushed my thumb along the bare skin of her collarbone, back and forth, back and forth. Goosebumps broke out along her skin and I smiled. "Today."

I caught the skepticism in her eyes. "Don't try that charm on me," she warned.

"Are you saying you're immune to my charm?" I lifted a single brow.

"Oh yes," she said, her lips curving secretly. "It's your other, shall I say, gifts that I'm partial too." As she spoke her finger trailed across my chest and down my stomach.

I laughed. But then I sobered up. I wanted her to know this stuff. "For several months now I've been feeling restless. I always completed the jobs I was assigned, but sometimes things fell through the cracks."

"Money, you mean," she replied.

"Mostly," I rasped and rubbed a hand over my face. "It gets old… working for a man who can be as ruthless and cunning as he wants. He can play with your life, make threats, and withhold things that are rightfully yours." I paused and glanced at her. She nodded and so I went on. "And then Dex came along… He figured out a way to get around G.R.'s game. I did nothing to stop him."

"You *helped* Dex?" she said, her eyes going wide and her shoulders straightening.

"I didn't save your friend." I could see in her eyes that she was trying to make me into the hero. I wasn't a hero. I never would be. I was the bad guy. The killer. "All I did was look the other way and maybe keep G.R. busy while Dex did his thing."

She shivered.

"Are you cold?"

"A little."

"Come on," I said, starting to rise, but she made a sound deep in her throat.

"In a minute." She pushed me back down and pressed herself closer against me. "There's something else I want to know."

"Hmmm?" I asked, paying more attention to the way her body felt against mine than what she was saying.

"Did you take the job because you were angry you died?"

"You ask the hard questions," I murmured.

"Because those are the ones that tell me the most."

"Does it really matter?" I asked then. "The reason I became what I am? The reason I became a killer? Because it won't change the fact that I've killed over and over again for over ninety years."

"It matters to me."

I hesitated again. Was I really ready after all these years to tell my story to someone?

"Olly," she whispered.

I wasn't sure that I would ever get used to hearing her call me that. It brought a rush of emotion every single time she said it. "My sister used to call me that."

"Tell me about her."

I nodded. "Her name was Sarah." It was another name, another emotion… another blast from the past.

And then it was like I couldn't hold it in anymore. The words, the past came tumbling out of me.

"I died in nineteen twenty. The world was different back then. It wasn't as free—as liberal as it is now. Women's rights were on their way, but even still, women weren't regarded the way they are now. They still needed the protection of a man, the income of a man. They were vulnerable, easily exploited and taken advantage of."

I was aware of Frankie's fingers moving lightly over my chest, giving me courage to talk.

"My father wasn't much of a man. He left us when I was ten years old. Sarah was only five. A baby. My mother did what she could for us. She worked herself until she had circles beneath her eyes and holes in the bottom of her shoes. Still, she always smiled at us, always told us how much we meant to her. It would have been easy, I think, to blame us, to be angry and make us the target for that anger. But she never once let us see her cry. I heard her sometimes, at night, when I was supposed to be in bed."

Instead of saying she was sorry for what obviously had been something hard, she still said nothing. Instead, she kissed me just beneath my jaw and then pressed her face in the crook of my neck.

"I got my first job when I was twelve. I was bigger than most boys that age, so I lied and took on as many jobs as I could. It helped some and gave my mother more time with Sarah. When I was fifteen, I quit school to work fulltime. I brought home enough for us to live, but I wanted more for them. Mother was always there for us, and Sarah… Sarah was…" I swallowed past the lump that had formed in my throat. Thinking about my sister was something I tried to never do.

"She was important, huh?" Frankie said, sensing the emotion that welled up inside me.

"Yeah, she was," I replied. My sister meant everything to me. "So I started boxing. I got beat up a lot the first couple years. It seemed I always had some sort of injury—a black eye, a busted rib. But I didn't give up. I kept fighting. I liked it. I think I got all the anger my mother never seemed to carry. After a couple years, I started winning. You got a lot more money for winning than you did for losing. The night I died, I was fighting for the championship title. A title that could have made me over ten thousand dollars. I was naive to think someone wouldn't kill to keep their title."

"You took the job, you became an Escort for your family, didn't you?"

"Without me, without my income, they would have ended up in poverty or my mother would have married herself off to someone that didn't deserve her. So, yeah, I took the job. I killed and I sent almost all the money I made to my mother and my sister anonymously."

"Thank you for telling me. I probably would have done the exact same thing in your shoes."

She thought that was all there was to my story. That the killing machine I was today was solely based on the fact my family needed to survive. It definitely was what made me an Escort… but the emotionless killer… that took something else entirely to create.

"Is your sister a Death Escort too?"

"*No,*" I denied. The thought of my sister, of someone so pure as her doing what I do made me sick.

"Well, that day at the café when you said you saw her… wouldn't she be…?" Her words trailed away.

"Dead. Sarah is dead."

"But you said you saw her…"

"The Reaper has her body. I have no idea how he got it or why, but he does and he was using it to throw me off, to mess with my head."

"You said before he doesn't want you to complete this job."

"He wants me gone. For good. If I don't do this job, he's going to use it as an excuse to Recall me."

Her arms tightened around me, and her face buried against my neck. "I've been trying to mess it up for you too."

"You didn't know any better," I soothed, rubbing my hand over her back.

"I don't want you to get Recalled."

"That's not going to happen. I have a plan."

"What kind of plan?"

I shook my head. "The less you know the better. I don't want you involved in this."

"Charming?"

"Hmmm?"

"If your sister's body looks as young as it does, then…"

I swallowed against the memory of that day. Of the day I killed my sister. "She died a couple years after I became an Escort. She was barely eighteen."

I felt the breath she sucked in, but I was so lost in the memory of that day that I didn't hear if she said anything.

"After I died, the boys started coming around. And I say boys because none of the guys that showed interest in my sister were man enough to have her. It drove me crazy, seeing her with guys that didn't deserve her, that couldn't give her the life I wanted her to have. But once I was gone…"

"She was trying to find someone to fill the hole you left behind."

Yeah. Maybe. "She and my mother cried for weeks after I died," I recalled softly.

"We don't have to talk about this if it's too hard."

"No. I want you to know." I blew out a breath and finished the story. "Sarah got serious with this guy. When he wasn't around her, he gambled, he drank… he cheated. I couldn't just knock on the front door and warn her away. I mean, she didn't even know me. One night he showed up at the house after he'd been at the bar. Sarah told him she didn't like his drinking. He hit her."

I clenched my fist at the memory. I could still hear the slap against her skin. I could hear her cry.

"I killed him."

"You were protecting your sister."

"Yes, I was. But killing him is no different from killing anyone else. Except he wasn't a Target. One of the Reaper's rules is to never kill anyone but a Target. I walked around for days, terrified he would find out, that he would Recall me. But he never did. He never said a word. And so I went on killing and sending the money to my family."

"And then Sarah died."

"She didn't just die. She killed herself."

Frankie sucked in a breath. "But why?"

"Because I killed her boyfriend. I heard my mother talking to one of her friend's right after the funeral. Seems that losing me and then losing the only other man she ever loved sent her over the edge." Why she loved that jerk was beyond me. I thought she had better taste than that. Maybe I didn't know her as well as I thought. I was silent for a few minutes. "Because of me, my sister killed herself."

Frankie pushed up against my chest to stare down into my eyes. "You are not responsible for what your sister did."

There was no point in arguing what I knew to be true. "After that, I stopped caring. I figured out a way to shut down my feelings and just focus on my job. On death."

"What about your mother?"

"I sent money every week right up until the day she died at age eighty-five."

"I'm sorry," she whispered, stroking my cheek. I liked when she touched me.

"Don't be sorry. Everyone dies sooner or later. My mother lived longer than most." I wasn't about to let this conversation turn to pity. I wanted Frankie to know my story, but I didn't want her to pity me for it. I realized my life hadn't been easy, but it certainly could be worse.

"Come on, love," I said, reaching down and patting the side of her ass. "We're naked and you're cold. Why don't we take this conversation to the kitchen where the coffee is?"

She made no attempt to get up.

"Frankie?"

"I'm afraid the minute we step out of this ring that Olly is going to disappear. That Charming is going to come back."

Her words caused something inside me to tighten. "A part of me is always going to be Charming. I've spent more time as him than I ever spent as Olly."

"I know," she said softly, "and I'm sure you're going to drive me insane." She flashed her teeth at me. "Just promise me you won't let Olly run away from Charming."

I laughed and got to my feet, pulling her up alongside me.

"I'll make you a deal. You walk around naked all the time, and I'll forget Charming ever existed."

"Spoken like a true man," she said with a sigh. "I need coffee. With sugar."

I jumped out of the ring first, landing like a cat, and held open the ropes for her to step through, and then I lifted her off the platform, letting her body slide down mine. Just before her feet hit the ground, I caught her and captured her lips with mine.

She had full lips and she kissed like she did everything else, with passion and attitude.

It turned me on.

Her laugh caused me to break away and look down.

"You keep kissing me like that and we're never gonna leave this room."

I growled and bit her bottom lip. She returned the bite with one of her own.

I sat her down and grabbed her hand. "C'mon." I held the door open and she went ahead of me into the hall. Before stepping through, I looked back.

Our clothing and my gloves still lay scattered in the ring.

I lost my life in a ring a lot like that one.

It somehow seemed appropriate that was where I got it back.

# Chapter Thirty-Four

*"Gone - being away from a place; absent or having departed."*

## Frankie

My legs were still trembling and every other part of me
tingled with pleasure. The butterflies in my belly were still
fluttering wildly, but now their wings no longer felt sharp. I
knew sex with him would be amazing. My body practically
screamed out for him whenever he was near, but I had no
idea it would be like *that*. If I never had sex with Olly again, I
would spend my entire life trying to find someone who would
make me feel the way he did.

And I would fail.

There was no one else on this earth like him (which
probably was a good thing).

I groaned and stuck my head under the insanely large
waterfall showerhead that was raining water from the ceiling.
I was in so much trouble.

He was completely maddening. He was selfish, spoiled,
looked like a Ken doll, didn't like sugar, and constantly had to
have his way. Not to mention he worked for the Grim
Reaper, killed for a living, and kidnapped my best friend at
gunpoint. He was practically the poster guy for guys a girl
shouldn't bring home to Mom.

I grabbed the shampoo (which smelled insanely good
and probably cost a hundred dollars a bottle) and started
washing my hair.

He was all of those bad things and more. But there were
other parts too.

Parts that he hid from most of the world because they
made him vulnerable. Parts of him that if he allowed out
would slowly kill him. I had a feeling that when Olly hurt, he

didn't just hurt. He bled. If he allowed himself to feel everything that everyone else felt, his entire world would come crashing down. A Death Escort couldn't afford to feel—to *live*.

He made my heart race. He made me feel challenged, like every day wouldn't just be the same as the last. And he confided in me.

He told me things about his life, his family, that he hadn't told anyone. I realized that he could be lying, but I didn't think he was. It would have been easier to make up something simple or to say nothing at all. I couldn't imagine what it must have been like to die and then trap himself into a job that would never end to be able to take care of the women he left behind. And his sister… God, he'd walked around for years and years thinking she died because of something he did. And if that wasn't enough, the Reaper was using her against him, bringing it all back up, taunting him.

Not to mention he was completely loaded and kissed me like there was no tomorrow. I guess when you see death constantly, you learn to realize maybe there won't be a tomorrow.

Hell.

I didn't hate him.

I didn't just kind of like him.

I freaking loved him.

Like, no holds barred, give up donuts forever kind of love.

I hurried to finish my shower, partially bummed that he hadn't come to join me, and shut off the water. I wanted to see him. I wanted to know if he would look any different to me now that I admitted to myself how in love with him I really was. Mostly I wanted to assure myself that he was still Olly, still the same guy I left in the kitchen making coffee.

Once dried, I quickly blow-dried my hair, leaving it straight because he didn't pack my curling iron (he probably didn't even know what that was). When it was straight like this, it was longer than it usually appeared and it hung past my chin, falling into a messy bob. When I left the bathroom and entered my room, I smiled because there was a pile of clean clothes lying across my bed. They were Olly's. They were more casual than the other things I'd seen him wear—a pair of dark-gray Nike gym shorts and a white T-shirt with the Nike logo across the front. I picked up the shirt because it appeared well worn. It smelled like him. Like the expensive designer cologne he always wore.

I pulled on my bra, a tank top, another pair of lace panties and then stole his tee, sweeping it over my head. I wasn't a small girl, but his shirt was still big. I didn't bother with a pair of shorts and went off in search of Olly.

I looked in his room, his adjoining bathroom, and his office at the end of the hall. On the way downstairs, I looked in the family room, the library, and then finally wandered into the kitchen. The rich smell of coffee had me groaning.

"Want me to make some eggs?" I asked, expecting to see him at the table.

He wasn't there.

"Olly?" I turned, looking toward the fridge and then wandered into the giant pantry.

He wasn't anywhere.

I went the last place I thought he would be… downstairs in the ring. I smiled thinking of a repeat of this morning.

He wasn't there either, but our clothes still were.

A feeling of dread enveloped me as I made my way back to the kitchen to pour a cup of coffee. I staved it off as best as I could, but every second, every minute that passed without him bounding into the room to annoy me made the facts harder to ignore.

By the time my second cup of coffee was drained, the razorblades were back in my belly. He wasn't here. He left. He literally made it impossible not to love him and then he did the one thing he said he wasn't going to do: he let Olly run away.

Where he went I didn't know.

All I knew was that he was gone.

# Chapter Thirty-Five

*"Taunt - to reproach in a mocking, insulting, or contemptuous manner."*

## Charming

I got all of an entire hour of living before I was reminded that I wasn't allowed to live. That my life was over and technically it belonged to someone else.

Someone who just happened to be Death.

But I was done taking orders from him.

As soon as the coffee began brewing, I took the stairs two at a time, thinking I would slip into the shower with Frankie and have a little fun…

But I never made it that far.

I got close. Close enough that I was able to toss some clothes onto her bed.

But then I was yanked right out of my body. It dropped onto the thick carpeting like a stone and I was left—nothing but a red cloud—hovering above it.

"The state of your undress and the fact there is a woman in the shower makes me think you have other priorities besides your job," said an all too familiar voice from behind.

How in the hell did he find this place? The one place I thought I was actually free of him.

I turned. "I don't really think you care about me completing this job."

"You don't think I care about thirty million dollars?"

"I think you knew from the very beginning… The only reason you chose the *senator's daughter* as a Target was because the only thing you cared about was seeing me fail."

He smiled. "That's right. I knew you would fail. Just like I knew you were here. Did you think I didn't know about this house? Where you spend your time off? You should know by now that I know everything."

"You don't know where your secret bodies are."

That wiped every ounce of smugness right off his boney old face. I resisted the urge to look toward the bathroom, not wanting to show that I was worried for Frankie. If she came out here…

*No.* I wasn't going to let her get caught up in this. It was the reason I brought her here in the first place. Yes, I wanted to keep an eye on her, but not for the reasons she thought. I wanted to make sure she was safe from him.

"And what bodies would that be?" he asked like he was bored, but I saw the flicker in his eye… the fear.

"The ones you keep hidden. The ones you didn't want anyone to know about," I said casually.

"What do you know about those?" he demanded, his eyes narrowing into barely there slits.

"I know where they are. But otherwise, not as much as I want to. Unfortunately, the soul you have wandering around your house wouldn't tell me a thing."

"You little—" He snarled, lunging at me, but his hands went right through, making the red puff out around him.

"Bodily harm requires a body," I taunted.

And just like that I was back in my body and being dragged up from the floor. "You better hope those bodies are where they're supposed to be," he said, jutting his face up close to mine.

The water to the shower shut off.

"Better go see," I said, injecting a dare behind my words. There was a huge chunk of ice in my gut. *Get him the hell out of here!* the voice inside me was screaming. I looked at the bathroom door. *Stay in there.*

With a wave of his hand, a doorway appeared right beside the bed. The Reaper started forward, grabbing me and pulling me along with him. I didn't put up a fight. I wanted him out of here and as far away from Frankie as he could be.

And it seemed the fastest way for that to happen was for me to go with him.

And so I went, the door he created snapping shut behind us like it hadn't been there at all.

# Chapter Thirty-Six

*"Therapy - the treatment of physical, mental, or social disorders or disease."*

## *Frankie*

I drove his Ferrari to the airport and left it in the long-term parking lot. If it got stolen or damaged, it was his fault for being a wimp and disappearing on me like that.

I mean, really. Did he not know me well enough by now to know I wouldn't have dissolved in a puddle of simpering tears if he told me he only said those things because he was high on sex? Or maybe he was just trying to keep his precious face intact because he *did* know me and he knew I would have rearranged it.

At the ticket counter, I maxed out my credit card buying a flight back to Alaska and sat there at the gate, praying I wouldn't get sandwiched between someone who liked to talk and someone that smelled like bacon and sweat. Never mind that my eyes kept straying to the crowd and I hoped to see him pushing through, trying to stop me from leaving.

This wasn't some movie like *Pretty Woman* where the rich guy comes riding up in his limo with roses and begs the girl to take him back after he acted like an idiot.

After all, Charming hadn't *acted* like an idiot. He *was* an idiot.

And I certainly wasn't going to forgive him.

The flight was endless and far less comfortable than the private jet we took to get to Scotland. I kept praying that I wouldn't have a panic attack from all the turbulence I felt sitting on the very last seat on the plane. I knew if I started barfing I wouldn't stop and it would all likely be blood because those razorblade wings were back and they were making mincemeat out of my belly.

When we finally landed, I pulled my cell phone out of my purse and powered it on. I wasn't looking to see if he called. I knew he hadn't. It didn't stop my heart from plummeting when the only missed calls were from Piper.

Piper. That was a whole other huge mistake. I had four missed calls and four texts from her. We'd barely talked in weeks. I was not only stupid for giving away my heart to the wrong man, but I also ruined a friendship while doing it.

I sent her a quick text: **_Just getting back into town. We'll talk soon_**. And then I threw my phone back into the bottom of my bag.

I took a cab home, spending the last of my cash, and trudged up to my apartment. I dumped my bag on the floor and fell face first into the couch.

That's when I started crying.

Whoever said "big girls don't cry" never got their heart broken. It hurt. A lot. I wished I could just eat a box on donuts, go shopping and watch a bunch of movies where guys got the shaft and get over him, but I couldn't do that. I was too busy wondering where he was. If he was okay and if he knew I left.

I turned my head and caught a familiar scent that made me ache all over again. I looked down. I was still wearing his T-shirt. I forgot to take it off.

I should've taken it off and lit it on fire. I should've run into the kitchen and stick it in the garbage disposal.

I pulled it closer around me.

I was pathetic.

I looked at the posters of Marilyn. She understood heartbreak. She knew how shitty men were.

There was a knock at my door.

"Go away!" I groaned.

The knocking grew louder.

"I said go away!" I yelled.

"I will not go away!" Piper yelled through the wood. "I'm not leaving until you open this door!"

I dragged my pathetic self off the couch and opened the door, then went back to the sofa and did another faceplant. I heard the door shut, but I didn't bother to see if she took one look at me and hightailed it to safety.

"What happened to you?" she said, coming to stand beside the sofa.

I pushed myself up and swiped the hair out of my face to look at her. Her eyes widened when she looked at me. "Have you been crying?"

I sniffled.

She sighed. "You didn't stay away from him, did you?"

I shook my head.

She sighed again.

"You fell in love with him."

I groaned and fell sideways. "I'm so stupid!"

She sat down on the edge, where I wasn't completely taking up all the space, and patted my back. "Not stupid. I know how easy it is to fall in love with someone like him."

I blinked back the tears in my eyes. "I didn't know Dex, but I do know that he wasn't like Olly."

"Who?"

"Charming," I corrected and ignored her look of curiosity.

"It doesn't matter."

"Of course it does."

"I thought you would hate me. I was so scared to tell you about him."

"I could never hate you. But you shouldn't have been scared to tell me. I thought we were best friends. Friends tell each other stuff. Even the hard stuff."

"Yeah, I know," I said, my voice hoarse. I wanted to cry all over again. "But you told me to stay away from him. I promised."

She half-smiled. "That was selfish of me to make you promise. I knew by the look in your eye that day it was too late."

"What?" I said, incredulous. "I hated him back then. I never hated someone so much."

"There's a thin line between love and hate, Frank."

She was right. Aside from the fact he was completely horrible, I think part of me knew he had the capability of hurting me this way. That he *would* hurt me this way. I hated him for that too.

"He tried to kill you. How could I fall for someone like that?"

"Dex tried to kill me more than once. I loved him anyway. I still love him."

"We need therapy," I said.

She laughed. "Yeah, we really do."

"Maybe we should start a support group for women who love killers. Just think of all the women who love inmates across America…"

We both laughed.

"I'm really sorry," I confessed after our laughter died away.

"Aww, Frank, it's okay. I understand. But don't ever cut me off like that again. We're family. Even if I think you're being an idiot, I'll still love you."

"So you do think I'm an idiot," I said, trying not to get all emotional over her understanding.

"What happened?" she asked.

I got up and scooted over, making more room for her on the couch. Then I pulled the Tiffany-blue throw off the back and wrapped it around my shoulders. I didn't know where to start. I didn't know how much to say… Piper was my best friend, my family, but some of the things I shared with Charming had felt so private… so *mine* that I didn't really want to share them.

She must have sensed my hesitation because she got up and went into the kitchen, and I heard her opening and shutting cabinets and filling the kettle with water. A few minutes later she came back with two mugs of steaming hot tea. It was the Ginger Twist kind she loved and I kept here for her. She handed me a mug and I wrapped my hands around it. The warmth that radiated into my hands reminded me of riding in his Porsche with the heated seats. A sob caught in the back of my throat and I took a sip of tea to push it down. The tea had honey in it. A lot of honey. Just the way I liked it. I gave Piper a watery smile.

"He drove me nuts. From the minute I first laid eyes on him, he got under my skin. And then he kidnapped you. When he walked into the DMV that day, all I could think of was calling the cops. But I couldn't."

Piper nodded and sipped her tea.

"Instead, I vowed that I would get in his way. Stop him from doing to anyone else what he did to you." I took a breath and finally admitted the truth. "But that was just an excuse. An excuse to be near him."

"You loved him even then," Piper said and I shook my head in vehement denial.

"No. Maybe." I sighed. "I don't know."

"But the more I saw him… the more I saw. You know? There are so many layers to him… so much he hides."

"He was like a puzzle that you wanted to figure out. Pieces that you just had to align."

"Yes," I said, the butterflies in my stomach acting up again. She did get it. She knew exactly what I meant. "I could never make excuses for what he does, what he's done. I hate it, but…"

"But you don't hate him."

"No. I don't."

"Maybe he is just as much a victim in all of this as everyone else," she said quietly, shocking the crap out of me.

"How can you say that?" I asked, fortifying myself with more honey with tea.

"I don't know why Charming became an Escort, but if he was in any kind of position like Dex was, then he probably didn't have a choice. Sometimes people get caught up in things and then they don't know how to get out."

"Dex did," I said, the words falling from my lips before I could stop them.

"Yes, he did. And it cost him his life." Her eyelashes swept down, hiding her hurt. I started to apologize, but her quiet words shocked me, cutting off whatever I was about to say. "Sometimes I wish he hadn't found a way out because then he'd still be here. With me."

Her words sank into me, squeezing my heart and making it hard to breath. "Piper," I whispered.

"I know. For him to still be here would mean I would have to be dead. But sometimes I still think…" She shook her head.

What it must be costing her sitting here talking to me about this. She'd already been through so much. I let the subject drop, not wanting her to have to relive anymore. As hurt as I was by Charming, I knew that it was nothing compared to what I would be feeling if he were dead.

"Did he try to kill you?" she asked.

I laughed. "No." That probably would be easier than this. "He… he showed me the person he was beneath the charm. I thought it was the real him. And then he disappeared. It was all just to get me into bed."

She gasped. "You slept with him?!"

I looked at her. "Well, I never claimed to be a nun!"

She grinned. "Well?"

"Well, what?"

She rolled her eyes. "How was it?"

I sighed. "He totally rocked my world."

She grinned again.

"He used to be a boxer. He has these boxing gloves…" I felt heat pooling between my legs and I clamped my lips shut. Reliving sex with Charming wasn't going to make this any easier.

"You know what we need?" Piper declared.

"What?"

"Pizza. Soda. Candy. And a bunch of horror movies where the dumb virgins run up the stairs instead of out the front door. It will make us feel better about ourselves for not being that stupid and for not being virgins."

I lifted an eyebrow. "Who you getting it on with?"

"Please. It's been so long I might as well be a virgin."

I laughed. "Someday, sista, someday."

"Not anytime soon," she said, getting up and grabbing the phone, but not before I caught yet another flash of hurt in her eyes. "I'll order the pizza. Go raid the stash of candy you have hidden in your underwear drawer."

I made a sound of mock surprise. "I do not have candy in *there*." Then I went off to get it because that's exactly where I kept it.

In my room, I pushed past the lace panties knowing they were all gonna have to go in the trash. I would never be able to wear another pair of those again without thinking about the things I did with Charming while wearing a pair. I loaded up on candy and then I remembered my emergency stash. The box of truffles I kept hidden in my closet.

I dumped what I was holding on my bed and went to my closet, pulling open the door.

My eye caught something it didn't recognize.

I looked.

I looked again.

I forgot all about the truffles, stood there, and stared.

At the body hanging in my closet.

# Chapter Thirty-Seven

*"Joke - something said or done to evoke laughter or amusement,
especially an amusing story with a punch line."*

## *Charming*

He took me to his office, but he could have taken me to
the depths of hell and I wouldn't have cared. I was just glad
we left before he could take his shitty mood out on Frankie.

I didn't know what she would think when I wasn't there,
but I was hoping I could get back without being gone too
long. And then I could explain. I wasn't exactly sure how I
was going to explain the fact that I pissed off the Grim
Reaper even more than I already had by stealing some of his
favorite bodies and jamming his pet soul into a jar.

G.R. didn't waste any time but instead went behind his
desk, reaching under the chair for the secret button. I
expected the wall to open immediately and when it didn't, I
looked up.

"How do I know you just aren't playing more games?"

"You should know by now I don't play games when it
comes to a job."

He just stared at me and I realized he was trying to
decide if I was just grasping at straws, if I was trying to find
out his secrets by saying I already knew them. Because the
minute he pressed that button, I would know for sure that he
did have a secret stash of bodies and a wayward soul. He
would know that I found his weakness.

"You gonna push that button?" I said. "The wall isn't
going to open itself."

And just like that he knew. Cold seemed to seep into the
room around me, the kind of cold that stiffened your limbs,
the kind of cold that crept over bodies when they died.

He pressed the button and the section of the bookcase opened, just as silently as it had the first time. He walked past me and into the narrow hallway that led to his closet-sized safe and stopped. "Get in here," he commanded.

I walked over to the door but didn't go any farther.

He drew a key out of his pocket, unlocked the door where the bodies wouldn't be, and opened it wide.

The silence that surrounded us was so thick you couldn't even cut it with a knife. He pivoted around to stare at me, his eyes glowing an odd shade of violet. Then he turned away again, opening the second door, the door to the secret apartment.

He called out for the soul, not calling her by name, and I wondered if that was on purpose or if she just didn't have one. I stepped forward, looking toward the entrance, and I knew when he realized she was gone because a chair flew by and hit the wall, smacking whatever was there and shattering some glass.

I prepared myself for his wrath as he faced me.

"How did you manage to pull this off?" His voice was deadly calm.

"You'd be surprised what a man can pull off when he's aptly motivated."

"Where is she!" he roared. His anger was so intense that it was palpable energy that flew off him and barreled toward me.

It slammed into me, sending me backward, my feet dragging across the floor as it pulled me. It would have yanked anyone else off their feet. It would have flattened them into the wall and knocked them unconscious.

I wasn't just anyone. I had a few abilities that I could use to my advantage.

My body absorbed most of the energy he threw, using it to fuel my cells and pump me up for a fight. I might not win against G.R., but I could do some damage.

I dug my feet into the large area rug that covered most of his office, planting them solidly apart. What was left of the energy kept going, pulling at my hair and my clothes until it snapped away, crackling behind me and knocking over everything that sat on his desk.

My body was overfull with energy, so much so that my fingertips crackled with it, so I flung my hands out, sending back some of what he gave me. The energy had a red glow about it, and it moved so fast it looked like the retreating taillights of a car speeding along the highway at night.

The Reaper moved, but not fast enough. Speed was my specialty. It hit him in the shoulder, singeing a hole in his perfectly tailored shirt and knocking him to the side. He didn't fall down because he caught himself on the edge of a nearby club chair, but watching him stumble was pure pleasure.

His eyes flashed violet again, a color I never thought of as threatening until now. Thinking fast, I picked up one of the chairs that sat in front of his desk, the same chair I used for many of the lectures I was made to endure, and I threw it at him. It moved slower than the energy so he was able to dodge it, but it landed on the edge of his sleek glass coffee table, shattering the entire sheet of glass.

A few of his security guards came rushing into the room. They all had the telltale ring of their souls around them, marking them as Escorts. These must be new ones because I didn't recognize any of their faces.

"Take. Him. Down," the Reaper growled, pointing at me.

All three of them rushed me. I sucked in some of their eager energy and cracked my neck, ready to take them on.

The first one lunged and I kicked him in the thigh, crippling his leg and making him go down. I used the surprise of his fall to grab the next one closest to me, and I punched him right in the jaw, snapping the head on his shoulders. He came back for more and I instinctively dropped into a boxing position and began bouncing on my feet. The lighter I was on my feet, the harder I would punch.

The way my stance and body position changed, the Escort knew I wasn't some inexperienced kid—like him. I saw the doubt in his eyes when he lashed out and I smacked his arm away and nailed him again, right in the eye. Then I put him in a headlock and slammed his body into the other one, who was climbing up from the floor. Both of them went down in a heap.

I turned to the final Escort, the one who'd been silently watching. This one had an orange ring around him, and he decided he was going to use a weapon instead of his fists. He reached over and grabbed a letter opener off the desk, brandishing it like a knife.

I laughed.

"You know," I said as I kicked, sweeping both his legs out from under him and watching him fall hard onto his back, "most people who try to defend themselves with a weapon end up having it used against them." And with that I snatched it out of his hand and stabbed him in the upper thigh.

He howled in pain.

I swiped my arm across my forehead, breathing heavily, and looked over at G.R. "You got any more kids you want to send in here?"

His eyes narrowed. "So smug," he spat. "Do you think the way out of getting Recalled is by trashing my office and taking what's mine?"

"I think a little extra insurance never hurt anyone."

"I ought to Recall you right now," he spat.

"Go ahead. You'll never see those bodies or that pretty pink soul again." It was a direct challenge. A skittering of fear actually moved down my back. I didn't want to be Recalled. Only now it wasn't for the same reasons as when I took those bodies.

Before, I just wanted to win, to prove I was the best Escort there was. To get the best of G.R.

But now, now it was because of Frankie.

I wanted to be with her. In any way she would have me (hopefully whatever that way was included sex).

He lifted his hand and once again, my soul began to pull out of my body. "We have a deal," I reminded him. "My job isn't over. You can't Recall me unless I fail."

Like a rubber band, my soul snapped back into my body.

"I don't go back on my word."

It was something I'd counted on, something that throughout the years I knew to be true. The Grim Reaper always kept his word. He never went back on a deal. I was beginning to think he was going to prove me wrong this time, but thankfully, it appeared he wasn't.

"However, I never said I couldn't make the job impossible. I never said I couldn't make your life a living hell."

He lunged across the room and grabbed my arm, his hand wrapping around my arm.

The pain was severe, an instant searing sensation that started where he touched me and worked its way up my arm, like a spreading infection, a growing disease. My veins began to turn black and they showed through my skin, which was now completely white.

I couldn't say anything. I just stood there, caught between life and death, as the pain spread throughout my entire body. I opened my mouth, but no sound came out. The pain was so intense that it robbed me completely of sound.

And then my eyesight began to go. Dark spots started swimming in my vision until there were so many everything went completely dark and I could see nothing.

Is this what it was like to be touched by the Grim Reaper? I thought death by him was instantaneous, that it was swift and final. Where was this pain coming from? Why did it hurt so incredibly bad?

When my insides were completely obliterated, I slid to the floor, dead. Only I wasn't dead. Just the body I'd been using for the past twenty years. I was hovering above my body, staring down at what a mess it was. The pain of what happened still vibrated in my soul. It almost looked like I'd been electrocuted to death. Kind of felt that way too.

And just like that, I no longer had a body. Not one that I could actually live in.

"I hope that didn't hurt too bad," G.R. said, sounding rather thrilled with himself.

"I thought when you touched someone, they died instantly."

"Humans, yes. For them it is pain free and blissfully quick. But for Escorts, it's entirely different. My bodies are different. To truly destroy one of my creations, it's much harder."

One of his creations? Did he think he was Frankenstein? The guy collected bodies, bodies he stole from other people. He didn't create them.

"And what a waste this one was." He frowned. "It was a good one." He looked at me. "But you certainly didn't deserve it."

"That body was more mine that yours," I spat.

He looked at me and lifted an eyebrow that seemed to reach halfway up his wide forehead. "That body was never yours. It was on loan to you. I am the one who collected it. I am the one who prepared it for a soul that was not its own, and I am the one who made it possible it didn't rot like a body is supposed to. The reason that body served you so well is because I was the one who made it possible."

You know, it kind of pissed me off that he was standing there trying to take away my claim to the body I wore for twenty years.

It also occurred to me that since my body was completely unlivable, I was now in a very tough position with the Target. Basically, I was going to have to start over.

Score for the Reaper.

"Tell me, do souls need air to breathe?"

"No."

"Oh well, that's good, because I forgot to poke holes in the lid of the jar I stuffed your soul in."

"*You did what?*"

"I know," I said. "I was surprised she wasn't willing to go with me either. I mean you would think any woman would choose me over you. When she refused to come along, I had to take matters into my own hands."

"Do you think I won't find her? Find the bodies?"

"That's another thing… What was my body doing in your secret stash? You haven't been using it, have you?"

"You don't have a body. Not anymore."

"Well, if you want your thirty million dollars, you're going to have to give me one."

"I thought we already determined that I never really cared about the money." There was a gleam in his eye that I wasn't liking.

"So?"

"So, I think I have better things to do than spend my day arguing with you."

He raised his hand and pushed me backward toward the opening in the wall. I tried to steer away, to wiggle from the control he seemed to have over my soul.

He laughed—a happy and joyous sound. "Fight all you want, but I am the Grim Reaper. I own your soul. I control it."

I was pushed through the tiny hallway, past the closet where the bodies once hung, and right into the small secret apartment. He appeared in the doorway, blocking the only exit.

"Let me tell you how this is going to go," he said smoothly, happily. He actually kind of reminded me of the Grinch after the green guy stole all the gifts from the town and he was so jolly and thrilled.

"On my word, I cannot Recall you until you fail to kill the Target. So you will remain here, in this makeshift prison, without a body, without contact to the outside world. When the six-month time limit I gave you is up, I will let you out. And then I will Recall you."

"And what about the bodies I took. The soul I stuffed into a jar? Do they mean nothing to you?"

"On the contrary. But while you whittle away your last few months on Earth here, alone, no doubt replaying everything you did that brought you to this unfortunate end over and over again…"

Was it just me or was he a bit dramatic?

"I will be searching. And you should know by now, I always get what I want. So when I at long last open that door to send you off into the void for your final exile, you will not only see me, but the possessions that you dared to steal."

"I'll be looking forward to that day." I quipped.

"You joke. You're funny."

The joke was on him if he thought I was just going to sit in here and wait for my punishment.

He began to pull the door closed behind him. I rushed forward, thinking I could at least try to slip by except my soul didn't move the way I wanted it to. Instead, it moved sideways.

"Oh, and might I suggest while you are in here that you think about your weaknesses. The things you're leaving behind."

"You already played that card. You can't use my sister against me anymore."

"Actually, I can," he corrected. "However, I have discovered that your sister is not your only weakness."

Everything in me stilled.

He smiled.

"I was always partial to blondes, too."

"Don't you go near her," I growled.

"Perhaps it's time I started adding some of the female variety to my collection," he said, his voice turning thoughtful and mean.

I tried to rush him again. This time I flew backward, hitting the wall with a poof.

He laughed and shut the door.
I didn't think it was funny.

# Chapter Thirty-Eight

*"Doorbell - a bell, chime, or buzzer outside a door that is rung to announce the presence of a visitor or caller."*

## *Frankie*

What does one do when they find a body hanging in their closet? Scream? Run? Try it on?

I didn't do any of those things. Instead, I walked out of the bedroom and directly into the living room where I grabbed a Cherry Coke, popped the top, and took a huge drink. Piper watched me with an amused expression on her face.

Finally, I pulled the can away from my lips. "There's a body hanging in my closet."

Her mouth opened and closed. I walked back into my room and she followed and we both stood there just staring at it. It was on a hanger, like a dress or a nice shirt. It was a guy who had shaggy blond hair that fell well over his forehead. He was dressed in a pair khakis, a white button-down shirt, and an ass-ugly sweater vest. His chin lay against his chest and his eyes were closed. The body itself was flat and lifeless.

It didn't move.

It didn't jump out and yell, "Boo!"

It might have been less creepy if it had.

"Where did it come from?" Piper asked.

"Is there a body store in Alaska I didn't know about?" I quipped.

She took the can out of my hand and gulped a long drink. "It isn't a coincidence that your boyfriend works for the Grim Reaper and now you have a body in your closet."

"Charming isn't my boyfriend," I argued. Though she was right about one thing. This was not a coincidence. But after what happened, I couldn't exactly call him up and say, "Did you happen to leave something at my house?" Charming slept with me and then disappeared. He left me. I wasn't going to call him for help the first minute a body turned up.

"Why is it here?" Piper asked.

I shrugged. Then I leaned forward and poked it. The hanger swung back and forth on the rod. Piper smacked me in the arm. "Don't poke it!"

I couldn't stop staring at it. But not because it was morbid. Because there was something familiar about it. I'd never seen this person (or whatever you wanted to call it), but there was still something about it that felt recognizable. "He's actually not bad looking."

Piper gasped. "First you poke it and now you're hitting on it!"

"I am not hitting on it," I grumbled. "Give me my soda." I snatched the can back and drained it. "It seems to me that we should be much more traumatized about finding a body in my closet."

"Well, we already decided we needed therapy."

"What should we do with it?"

"Guess we can't call the cops."

"Not without looking like we put it there."

"You could call—"

"No." I interjected. "I am not calling him. He made his choice."

"So it's over between you two?" She seemed a little sad at the thought.

The pain that sliced through me was swift and strong. But I didn't flinch; I might as well get used to it. "Yeah, it's over."

And then the doorbell rang.

# Chapter Thirty-Nine

*"Message - a usually short communication transmitted by words, signals, or other means from one person, station, or group to another."*

## Charming

I wished the Reaper's last words didn't bother me. But they did.

I wasn't used to worrying about someone. I wasn't used to caring. But I did.

All I could think about was Frankie. What if he wasn't just making idle threats? What if he really did go after her? What if he touched her? My God, would she feel the pain that I felt when my body was killed while I was in it? Would that searing pain seize her veins and bloom outward until it stopped the beating of her heart?

The questions were relentless. The worry was indescribable. And what made it worse was that I had no body to expel the extra energy. I couldn't do pushups or punch a wall; I literally just had to hang there and do nothing but hope she was safe.

I wasn't good at doing nothing. I needed a plan, a way out of here. If I had to kill that Target without a body, then I was going to figure out a way to do it.

I hadn't lost yet. I was still in the game.

A game that now involved Frankie.

I wanted her safe more than I wanted anything, including not being Recalled. A memory flashed over me from the day Dex lost it in G.R.'s office and threw a couple well-placed punches to my face. I'd taunted him about Piper, about trying to save her, about being weak and caring about someone else over himself.

Is this how he felt that day? Desperate and willing to do anything to save the woman he loved? I couldn't understand it then, but now… now I understood all too well. I was wrong to think of him as weak because it seemed to me that putting someone else above myself was the strongest thing I could do.

Well played, Dex. Well played.

"Dude, I saw your body. Did that hurt?" said a voice from behind me.

I turned, red scattering everywhere, and faced at a cloud that looked just like me, only this one was black. "Storm! How the hell did you get in here?"

"Dude, you don't have a body. You can go right through the wall. You've seen me do it more than once. Why are you still here?"

"Are you serious?" Sure, I'd seen Storm go through walls and borrow bodies, but I thought those were abilities unique to him. It never occurred to me that I might be able to do those things too.

He snickered low and I watched as he pushed half his form through the wall and then pulled it back in.

"Why didn't I think of that?" I muttered, feeling like a complete idiot for the little bit of panic I felt when he locked me in here and threw away the key.

"Because up until now you've spent maybe an hour out of your body in your entire life," Storm suggested. "And because G.R. doesn't want you to know that stuff. He wants you to think you're stuck here."

But Storm spent most of his life as a ghost and unbeknownst to G.R., he used a lot of that time to learn to do things he wasn't supposed to be able to do.

"So I can just walk, or whatever it is souls do, right out of here?" Excited, I looked at the wall and moved toward it, thinking I would go right through like the ghosts I'd seen on TV.

I went sideways instead of forward, but I was heading toward a wall so I went with it. Only I didn't go through.

Once my form touched the wall, it puffed out like I was a chalkboard eraser being banged against the side of a building. "Uh, I'm thinking not all souls can go through walls."

"Operating as a ghost isn't as easy as I make it look," Storm replied smugly.

"What?"

"You're going to have some control issues. Operating a soul isn't like operating a body. Your body has weight. It obeys the laws of gravity. A soul doesn't."

"Shit," I muttered. Then I thought of something. "How is it you aren't completely ghost anymore, yet you're still able to get through a wall?"

"It ain't easy. Sometimes I get stuck. *That's* a real pain. Half in and half out of a wall? I wouldn't recommend it."

"Then why do you keep doing it?"

"Because it's convenient. Because if I didn't, you would still think you were trapped here. And because it's cool."

Yeah, okay. It was cool.

"C'mon, I'll show you what to do," Storm said.

"How long is that going to take?"

"Don't know. Depends on you I guess."

Judging from the way I'd been moving around so far, it wasn't going to be something I got the hang of in five minutes.

"How long have I been here?"

"Not quite a full day, but a while. I waited until G.R. left to come in."

That long? Why is it time always passed so quickly whenever you really wanted it to slow down, yet when you wanted something over and done with, it seemed to take forever?

"Do you know where Frankie is?"

"She's here, at her apartment."

"Did you see her? How did she look?"

"I didn't really notice. I was just there to, uh… make sure her and her apartment was secure."

That was kind of an odd response for someone whose life was spent observing the details about other people. But I didn't have time to ask him about his weirdness. I had enough to worry about.

"G.R. is on the hunt for the bodies. You need to move the two you hid. Put them in separate places. Make sure they're where no one would think to look," I stressed. I left the female body in L.A. and hid the soul in Scotland. I was hoping the fact they weren't here in Alaska would buy me a little bit of time to get there and move them before they realized the bodies might not be here.

"Well, let's get you out of here so I can do that."

"No. There isn't enough time," I said. "Go move the bodies first. And check on Frankie. Make sure she's safe. Tell her…" My voice trailed away. There was so much I wanted to say to her. So many things I wanted to apologize for. But those were all things I needed to tell her myself.

"What about you?" Storm asked.

"After you move the bodies and check on Frankie come back, that should buy us some time for you to show me how to get out of here." I thought about telling him to warn Frankie about the Reaper and possibly tell her to get out of town. But I didn't want to scare her. And I really didn't think her leaving town would protect her. The Reaper would find her. Besides, I was hoping G.R. would be too busy searching to bother with her. The safest place for her was with me; I would keep her safe. "I need to get out of here," I whispered to myself.

"I'll hurry," Storm promised as he moved toward a wall. I was envious at how easy he made it look. So envious that I tried to follow him, trying again to have some control. I ended up floating upward and getting stuck against the ceiling. I felt like a stupid balloon.

"Keep practicing," Storm said, watching me. "Concentrate on giving yourself the feeling of weight."

"Give Frankie a message for me," I called as he slid halfway through the wall. The words rushed out of me quickly and then he was completely gone. I didn't know if he heard what I said, but I hoped he did and I hoped she understood the message when she heard it.

*Don't give up on me yet,* I thought.

Then I started concentrating.

# Chapter Forty

*"Borrow - to adopt or use as one's own."*

## Frankie

I almost expected it to be the cops. That they somehow figured out I was harboring a body in my house and they had come to drag Piper and me off to jail.

I stood behind the door, wishing I had a peephole so I could at least prepare myself for whatever I was about to be accused of. I cast a glance at Piper who was standing behind me, a worried look on her face.

The person banged on the door again and I jumped. "I know you're in there, Frankie. Open the door!"

I frowned at the unfamiliar voice calling my name.

That settled it. The only strangers that could know my name were cops. "Go hide," I whispered to Piper.

"Yeah, 'cause that's not suspicious," she retorted.

This time when he banged on the door, he didn't stop, just kept on hammering.

I took a breath and yanked it open, trying to look surprised as to why a group of cops would be on my doorstep.

There was no group. There were no cops. Just a man, a lone man standing there with a look of impatience (and constipation?) on his face.

"Can I help you?" I asked tentatively.

"Me?" he said. "No. But I've come with a message from Charming. And to collect… what I left here."

It wasn't often someone rendered me speechless. I don't think a complete stranger ever managed it, until now. I stood there staring at him, trying to decide the best way to answer him. He let out a sigh and walked in the apartment, his gaze going directly to Piper and holding for long moments.

"Excuse me?" I managed, drawing his attention away from her.

"You might want to shut the door," he said, glancing at me.

I did and walked farther into the room, not once taking my eyes off of him. I searched my mind for any kind of recollection, some kind of memory of meeting him or seeing him somewhere.

He was tall, well over six feet. He was lanky, not at all that muscular, and was dressed in jeans and a sweatshirt. He had sneakers on his feet and sandy-colored hair. There wasn't anything remarkable about his appearance, but the words that came out of his mouth were.

"My name is Storm. I work with Charming."

"You're a Death Escort?" I asked, taking in the look of pain on his face. He didn't look like a killer. He looked like he needed to sit down.

"Sort of," he said. "Listen, do you mind if I drop the body?"

I glanced at Piper who shrugged and then I looked back at him. "Ummm, sure?"

He let out a great sigh and then dropped his head onto his chest and closed his eyes. I was about to tell him this wasn't the best time for yoga or meditation, but then something weird happened.

Black smoke started leaking from his ears. It puffed out, curling up around his head where it formed a dark cloud. Then it began curling out his nose, in great long tendrils that rose up to join the growing mass of black.

"What the hell?" I said, reaching for Piper and pulling her over toward me and the door. We weren't going to be like those idiot virgins who ran farther into their house when a killer was after them. We'd be going out the door.

The black cloud kept growing, until it pretty much surrounded the body, swirling around like smoke. And then the man dropped to the floor. He fell in a heap, landing in a tangle of limbs, right there beside my couch.

Now not only was there a body in my closet, but one in my living room, right next to a black cloud thingy.

"Let's get the hell out of here," I whispered to Piper and yanked her to the door. As my hand closed around the handle, the man/cloud thingy spoke.

"Whew, thanks. That guy did not like to share."

I glanced down at the body and then back up. "You have exactly two seconds to explain before I start screaming my head off."

"If you were gonna scream, you would already be doing it."

"You said you work with Charming?" I asked, not acknowledging he was right. "And how is it you can talk?"

"I'm a Ghost Escort. An Escort who doesn't have a body. I don't kill people. I just watch them for the Reaper. And I have no idea how my voice works. It just does."

"You watch people," I repeated.

"Yes. Not having a body and being black makes it easy to stick to the shadows and remain unseen."

"But we can see you," I pointed out.

"That's because I'm letting you."

"What about him?" I said, gesturing to the body. "Is he dead?"

"Nah, just out of it. We should probably put him outside. He's probably going to wake up soon."

"We?" I said.

"Well, I don't exactly have arms to move him."

"Right." I went over and grabbed the man by his arms and dragged his body toward the front door. Piper was there to open it and then took one of his arms and helped me pull him the rest of the way out into the hall, where we left him, and went back into my apartment and closed the door.

"You're sure he isn't dead?" I asked again, picturing one of my neighbors coming home and screaming at his body lying there.

"Positive. Borrowing doesn't kill people. It just makes them tired and disoriented."

"Borrowing?" Piper asked. It was the first time she'd spoken since he walked into my place, and although I couldn't exactly see him staring at her, I did see his cloudlike form turn toward her.

"It's something I can do," he replied. "Get in someone else's body and borrow it. I don't do it that often," he explained. "It's kind of painful depending on the size of the personality inside the body. That guy was bigger than most. Felt like I was a sardine jammed in one of those tiny cans."

Piper laughed.

I looked at her like she had ten heads. "This isn't funny," I reminded them. "Why are you here?"

"Actually, I just came to pick up something I left here," the cloud replied.

"*You're* the one who put the body in my closet?" I asked.

"You saw that, huh?"

"Well, it's kind of hard to miss,"

"You were supposed to be in Scotland."

"I wasn't about to stay there after he left me without a word," I snapped.

"Your boyfriend didn't leave you. He was taken. By the Reaper, who he has managed to piss off in every way possible."

"He is not my boyfriend," I replied automatically, but then the rest of his words caught up to me. "And isn't the fact he pissed the Reaper off old news?"

"He pissed him off some more. In new ways."

"The level of idiocy that man displays is beyond me," I muttered, thinking that the next time I saw him I was going to smack him upside the head.

But then my thoughts caused everything in me to still.

I really thought I would never see him again. I really thought it was over.

But it might not be.

Amongst the stillness, the butterflies erupted.

Maybe he really hadn't meant to leave me. I looked down at his T-shirt that I was still wearing, the T-shirt he'd put on my bed to presumably put on after he joined me in the shower. Someone who was going to leave wouldn't have bothered to do that. Would they?

"What did he do?" Piper asked, drawing me out of my thoughts.

"The Reaper had a secret stash of bodies kept under lock and key because they were important to him."

"Okay," Piper said, urging him to finish.

"Charming stole them and I helped him. I put one here. One at your house," he said, gesturing toward Piper, who made a choking sound. "And he took one out of town with him. Not sure where he left that one."

The garment bag. The one on the plane I teased him about. It hadn't been a suit at all. It had been a body.

I was so out of my league.

"You put a body at my house?" Piper said, her voice hollow.

"Yeah," he answered, sheepish. "I needed somewhere the Reaper wouldn't look."

"How do you even know where I live?" she asked.

There was a very heavy, drawn-out pause. "I knew Dex," he finally replied.

My eyes shot to Piper, whose face went white. "You knew Dex?"

"Um, yeah. I was assigned to watch him and sorta you too."

"Oh," was all she managed to say.

I gave him a dirty look for upsetting her. "The body is still where you left it." I was hoping he would take the hint and leave.

He nodded. "I'll get it out of here."

"Where are you going to take it?"

"It's needed," was all he said. Then he turned to Piper. "I'll get the one at your place when I leave here."

"I'm supposed to work later."

"You don't need to be there. I can let myself in."

"That's how he's been getting into my apartment!" I burst out. "You've been helping him!"

"I make a pretty good key," he said smugly.

Escorts were weird. They bragged about being criminals.

"I'll just get the body and get out of here." He moved off toward the hall.

"Wait, you said you had a message from Charming?" Maybe I should have acted like I didn't care, but I did.

"Oh yeah. He wanted me to tell you he was working on making room for the sun and he'd see you later."

Piper looked at me with a question in her eyes, wondering if I understood what he meant.

I smiled. I knew exactly what he meant. It meant he was coming back.

"Why couldn't he tell me that himself?" I asked.

"About that," he explained. "The Reaper took his body away. Right now he looks like me, except he's red."

Awww, he thought that would be a sufficient reply.

"That's not going to cut it. I need more info. Pronto."

Cloud guy sighed heavily, and with his sigh some of his body (or whatever) puffed out like breath on a winter's day. "G.R. took away Charming's body and locked him up at his mansion. He can't Recall him because the only way an Escort gets Recalled is if they don't finish a job. Charming still has a few months left to the job he was assigned, but the Reaper wants him gone. So he took his body and trapped him. He's going to keep him there until time runs out for the job and then he'll be able to Recall him."

Some people might say he was getting what he deserved after all these years of killing people who didn't deserve to die. But somewhere along the line, I stopped thinking about him as a killer and started thinking about him as a man, a man trapped in an impossible situation. And thinking about him being Recalled—or truly never seeing him again—made me want to go to the Reaper's house myself and start ripping stuff apart.

"But what about the bodies he took?" Piper said. "Won't that keep him from getting Recalled?"

"Yeah, but the Reaper already has guys searching. Eventually he's going to find them. That's exactly why I need to start moving everything. The more I move it, the harder it will be to find."

"What's your name, anyway?" I asked.

"Storm."

Huh. It fit him perfectly. "All right, Storm, go jump in that body and let's go."

"Oh, uh-uh. No. You are not coming with me."

"The hell I'm not."

"Do you have any idea what Charming would do to me if I let you go anywhere near the Reaper's house?"

"Do you have any idea what I will do if you don't?" I ground out.

"Sorry, but he's scarier than you are."

I crossed my arms over my chest.

He sighed. "Look, I don't have time to argue with you. Getting this body to him is already hard enough with having to worry about you two."

"Why is it so hard?" Piper asked.

"Because the body is empty. There's no one in it and because of that I'll have a black cloud around me that every Escort would see. If I get caught, they're going to know it's me before I even say a word."

"There was no cloud around you when you got here," I observed.

"That's because there was someone else in the body. Best I can figure it, their soul hides mine."

I glanced at Piper to see if she thought this conversation was as unreal as I did. She seemed to be having about the same reaction.

"Look, I gotta go. Time is of the essence. He's gonna flip when he finds out I hid his body here at your place."

"What do you mean *his* body?"

"That's Charming's original body. The one he died in. He seemed pretty shocked when he saw it."

Is that why it seemed so familiar to me? Did something inside me recognize it immediately?

I rushed toward the bedroom, wanting to look at him again. I wanted to take in every detail about that body. I stopped just shy of touching it. It was so different from the way he looked now… so unpolished, so… flawed. But yet when I looked at him, at the overly long blond hair and full lips, it seemed perfect for him. For Olly.

"Well, what are you waiting for?" I told Storm.

"Some privacy might be nice," he muttered. "Can't a guy get dressed in peace?"

Piper giggled. What was with her? Geez, he was not funny.

I was about to point out his un-funniness when there was a noise in the living room. It sounded like the front door opening and closing.

All three of us froze, listening for more sounds.

"Honey, I'm home!" called a voice I didn't know.

"Holy shit!" Storm whispered.

"Who is it?" I demanded.

"It's the Reaper."

# Chapter Forty-One

*"Balloon - a flexible bag designed to be inflated with hot air or with a gas, such as helium, that is lighter than the surrounding air, causing it to rise and float in the atmosphere."*

## *Charming*

Not having a body was weird. I couldn't really sit or stand… or do anything other than sort of hover over the floor. It was like existing but not existing. It made me think about Storm and I suddenly understood why he started trying to learn how to be more solid. I understood why he figured out how to borrow other people's bodies. Because not having a shape of your own was like being caught between life and death.

It also had a way of making a man feel very small and very out of control. And the more I concentrated, the harder it seemed to be. The second I moved or tried to go across the room, my body kind of dissipated away from itself. It didn't hurt, but it was kind of alarming to watch what was left of you drift out and away.

After a while I was so frustrated that I gave up and settled for just kind of floating there.

I thought about Frankie, about what she was doing right then. If she was angry with me or if she was hurt. I wondered if she was eating a pound of candy and cursing the day I ever walked into her life. I hoped Storm was there by now. I hoped she at least knew I didn't just abandon her.

Of its own accord, my form started drifting down, moving toward the floor. I tried not to get excited that I was going down instead of up. Figured the minute I stopped trying to do something was the minute my damn body did it.

I wished there was a clock in here. I wished I knew how long ago Storm had left. That's the other thing about not having a body. There's no internal clock to keep you posted on time.

"Hey," Storm whispered, coming right through the wall beside me.

"Did you get to the bodies before he did?"

"Yeah. I brought yours with me. It's outside in the trees that border his property. You might as well use it."

"That's one way to keep it on the move."

"Yeah. But you gotta stay out of sight, man. For many obvious reasons, including the red ring you'll be sporting.

I highly doubted I would be strolling down the street.

"Let's get the hell out of here," I said, trying to rush toward the wall. I ended up going in the opposite direction with a trail of red following behind. I made a frustrated sound. "How in the hell do you control yourself?"

"It's not that hard. You just have to concentrate."

"All I've been doing is concentrating. My freaking brain hurts." Wait. Did I even have a brain? Not having a body was so weird. I took a deep breath and tried again. I got the same results as before. A few colorful swear words slipped between my lips.

"I told you it wasn't easy," Storm said. "It's a good thing I brought the body here."

"Where was it anyway?"

"I stashed it at Frankie's."

"You stashed it at Frankie's!" I growled, mad that he would involve her more than she already was.

"You said to put it somewhere it wouldn't be found."

The guy was an idiot. When I got my body back, I was going to deck him. Maybe she hadn't seen it. I didn't notice I was drifting down to the floor.

"She's something else," Storm said, watching me. "She didn't even freak out when she found it."

*Well, shit.* "She saw it," I said, flat. Drifting even closer.

"Yeah, and I also sort of borrowed a body in front of her."

Double shit. "Where is she now?" I growled, wondering how I was ever going to make this up to her. I wondered if I could. Then I noticed I was right beside Storm.

"I'm on the ground," I said, shocked. I hadn't even been trying. I was too busy wanting to deck him in the eye.

"Yeah, apparently pissing you off about your lady is like an anchor for you."

Huh.

"You ready? We need to get your body out of the woods."

"Let's do this."

Storm moved over toward the far wall. "This wall is an exterior wall. Once you're through it, we'll be outside. You're not going to be able to blend into the shadows as good as me so once we're out there, we gotta move fast. Just stick with me. Follow me."

Yeah, moving fast was a lot better in theory. Trying to cram a body, or non-body as it was, through a wall and outside wasn't exactly easy. It took me four tries to get half my body out of the house and then another three tries to get the rest out.

By the time I made it out and across the open yard and into the trees, I was pissed off and in a very foul mood. It didn't help that I was staring down at my body—a body that was still kind of shocking to see. I wasn't sure what it was going to be like to literally be back to my old self again.

"I swear the next time you get your ghost ass in a body, I'm going to give you a black eye." I threatened Storm. Threatening him made me feel better. And it kept my anger at the surface, giving my body a little bit of weight. If I started flying up here, there would be no ceiling to catch me.

"Promises, promises," Storm taunted. "Focus on the nose or the ears," he instructed. "Aim for that and once you're in, it will be a lot easier because it'll be like going into a tunnel. There won't be anywhere for your soul to go but inside."

My feet (or what would be my feet) were already close to the ears of my body so instead of trying to bend down and go in headfirst, I kicked out my foot, aiming for the ear. As I thought, some red went out and around the head, but some of it made it inside, creating a red trail leading inside and so I kicked again, shoving even more of myself in.

Then something happened.

Something I hadn't expected.

It was almost like the inside of my body was a vacuum and I was being sucked up through the hose. "Storm," I whispered, trying not to sound as freaked as I was. "It's sucking me in."

"Well, that's a first," he said, sounding a little surprised. It didn't make me feel any better. "Just go with it. You want to get in there. This will just make it easier."

And so I went (like I had a choice). My body seemed to know exactly what to do with my soul and I began to move faster and faster. The body, which had been lying flat and lifeless on the ground, began to plump up and fill out. It became less like a piece of clothing and more like a living, breathing man.

And then the red was gone.

I was completely inside a body I thought I would never be in again.

I stood up, looking down at my arms and legs, tossing the light-colored hair out of my eyes. I wasn't really sure how I felt in that moment. I wanted to rush to a mirror, to look in and see if I recognized what I saw. I wanted to stand there in the yard and take stock of every part of me—to know if I felt any different, or if I felt the same…

"Maybe it's because it's your body," Storm was muttering to himself.

"What?"

"I was thinking that maybe the reason your soul went right in was because that was the body it actually belongs in."

We didn't have time for theories on bodies and souls.

"Let's go to Frankie's," I said, my eyes darting around to make sure none of G.R.'s staff was lurking. "We can talk there."

The silence that came from Storm was anything but silent.

"What?" I demanded.

"Well…" he began, drawing out the word. "There's something about Frankie you should know."

She didn't want to see me again. She was pissed I left her, pissed Storm stashed a body at her house, and he didn't want to tell me back there. "Just tell me."

"When I was there getting the body," he said, pausing.

"Spit it out already!" I barked.

"G.R. showed up," he rushed out.

"*What?!*" If I hadn't already been inside a body, I knew all the red that made up my soul would have scattered for miles. The thought of Frankie and G.R. in a room together made my skin crawl.

"He walked in like he owned the place."

"How did you get him out of there?"

He didn't say anything.

"Tell me you *did not* leave her there with him," I ground out.

"We didn't want him to find your body!"

Screw him not having a body. I reached out and punched the air where he floated. Then I stuck my other hand inside of him and shook it, scattering him all around.

"What the hell, man!"

"You deserve so much more than that," I spat. I didn't even wait for him to reply or come back into some kind of shape. I took off, racing along the edge of the neighbor's property, drawing in every last ounce of kinetic energy I could and using it to propel me right out of the fancy neighborhood without being seen once.

I was supposed to be lying low, to not let G.R. know I was out, that I had a body.

Screw that.
He was messing with my girl.

# Chapter Forty-Two

*"I Love Lucy - an American television sitcom starring Lucille Ball, Desi Arnaz, Vivian Vance and William Frawley. The black-and-white series originally ran from October 15, 1951 to May 6, 1957."*

## Frankie

The Grim Reaper was in my house. He just walked in like this was some episode of *I Love Lucy* and he was Ricardo telling Lucy he was home and ready for his supper.

But this wasn't a sitcom. This was real life.

And he was the ultimate life stealer.

All three of us were frozen, staring at the closed bedroom door like it was a bomb about to explode. I clutched my stomach so hard it hurt, but I was afraid if I let go I would hurl all over the floor.

"Come out, come out wherever you are," the Reaper called in a morbid singsong voice.

It was his voice that spurred me into action. "Storm, get that body and get the hell out of here. Do not let him see you."

"What about you?" he said, sounding unsure.

"I can take care of myself. Charming needs you. Use the fire escape." I pointed to the window next to the bed.

"Piper, go with him," I ordered quietly and rushed toward the door.

"You can't go out there," Piper insisted. "Come with us."

If I didn't go out there, he was going to barge in here and find all three of us sneaking out the window. He'll see Charming's body—the one that wasn't supposed to be here—and he would likely take it and do who knows what with us.

I couldn't risk them all. I couldn't risk Charming's body. I had to do this.

I mean how bad could the Grim Reaper really be?

I glanced at Piper and shook my head. Her eyes widened, but before she could yell at me and give away the fact I wasn't in here alone, I opened the door, slipped out, and closed it directly behind me.

An older-looking man who oddly looked a lot like Mr. Burns from *The Simpsons* was just coming down the hall.

I jumped, putting my hand to my chest like he startled me (okay, maybe he did even though I knew he was there. This guy was just creepy) and said, "Holy crap! Who are you? Why are you in my apartment?"

"We have a mutual acquaintance," he replied, looking me over.

"We do?"

"Yes, and I think you know exactly who I am. Why are you pretending you don't?"

I thought about my friends just on the other side of the door. "Could we go talk in the living room? The hallway is kind of close quarters."

He pursed his lips. "Okay."

I breathed a sigh of relief when he walked out into the living room. I followed, watching his every move.

"Marilyn Monroe," he said, staring at the wall of posters of my idol. "She was very full of life." He turned to look at me. "Until I killed her."

I gasped. "You didn't kill her. She died of an overdose."

"Did she?" he asked, lifting a brow.

"If you killed her, why didn't you take her body? I hear you have a little problem with hoarding." In truth, I had no idea how many bodies he did or did not have. Charming and I hadn't spent our time talking about him. Now I kind of wished I knew more. I felt very unprepared for a confrontation with him.

He laughed. A real laugh. "I don't usually collect female bodies. But I'm thinking maybe it's time for a change."

*Oh, that's great, Frankie. Inspire the body collector to start collecting women, starting with you.*

"Why are you here?" I asked, hoping to steer him away from the idea of hanging my body in his closet.

"I seemed to have misplaced something. I was wondering if you had it?"

I almost told him this wasn't the lost and found, but I bit my tongue. I didn't think he would appreciate my sarcasm. "What did you lose?"

"You don't know?"

I shook my head.

"I don't like liars."

"I'm not lying. I don't have whatever it is you're looking for."

"Then you won't mind if I take a look around."

Oh, I minded all right. "No," I burst out and his eyes narrowed. I took a breath. "I mean, now isn't really a good time."

"Really? What were you doing in your bedroom when I got here?"

I put my hands on my hips. "I don't really think that's any of your business."

He smiled, then came across the room, holding out his hands. "Step aside," he warned. "Wouldn't want me to accidentally touch you."

I jumped out of the way like he was a speeding car and I was a squirrel.

He went down the hallway and yanked open the door and went inside. "Well, what do we have here?" he said.

They didn't get out. I didn't stall him long enough. Now he was going to take Charming's body and kill us all.

I ran down the hallway, skidding to a stop just inside the doorway, ready to beg for our lives. But Storm was gone. So was Charming's body.

Piper, however, was still here. She was standing beside the bed, staring daggers at the Reaper.

"Ahhh, the one that got away," he said, looking at her. "How are you enjoying life knowing I will never be able to come for you?"

"Why are you here?" Piper asked, her voice completely calm.

He ignored her question, going over to my closet and going through all the hangers and clothes.

"Did you want to borrow an outfit?" I quipped. "I don't think I'm your size."

Piper gave me a *shut up* look.

"They aren't here," he murmured.

"What's not?" I said, still playing dumb.

"My bodies!" he yelled. Piper and I both flinched. "Where are they!"

"I don't know," I replied, backing up as he stalked toward me. "I really don't know."

"Hey! Get away from her," Piper called, moving across the room toward us.

"I wonder," the Reaper mused, "if Charming would be a little more forthcoming if I brought him your dead body."

Oh, this wasn't going well. Not at all. "I don't really think that would help."

"I think it might be worth a try." He yanked his hand out of his pocket and reached for me, all five of his fingers waving about like they were snakes trying to slither away.

I shuddered and backed up some more, coming up against the wall.

I was trapped.

He came closer, his hand just inches from my face. I squeezed my eyes closed.

"I said Leave. Her. Alone." Piper cried, her voice so close that I opened my eyes to tell her to run.

But it was too late.

Piper grabbed the Reaper by his wrist, yanking his deadly touch away from me.

"Piper, no!" I yelled, my chest seizing up so hard that I fell backward against the wall. If it hadn't been there for support, I would have crumpled to the floor. "No!" I cried again, staring at where her slender fingers wrapped around his wrist. She was dead. She was going to die. She went and wasted a perfectly good death pardon from the Grim Reaper by touching him.

I waited for her body to fall to the floor.

I waited for her to die.

Nothing happened.

I blinked, trying to clear my eyes of the tears that filled my vision, thinking I was just seeing things.

I wasn't.

She was still breathing. Moving. Living.

And her hand was still wrapped around his wrist.

She was staring down at where they touched, frozen in shock.

I looked at the Reaper, thinking maybe he knew what was happening, that he wouldn't be surprised. But he looked just as shocked as the rest of us.

"You're touching me," he said in awe.

Piper snapped back to reality and snatched her hand away. She backed up, pulling the ends of her sweater down over her hands.

"You didn't die," he said, looking at her with a creepy sort of reverence.

"Still breathing," Piper said, like she still couldn't believe it herself.

"Wait. You didn't know that was going to happen?" I burst out. "What the hell were you thinking!"

"That I didn't want you to die," she said quietly.

"You shouldn't have done that!" I rushed over to her side, grabbing her by the shoulders and shaking her. "That was officially the stupidest thing anyone has ever done."

"You're welcome?" she said, a hysterical laugh bubbling out of her throat. I pulled her against me and crushed her in a hug.

"If you had died I would have been so pissed." I pulled back and looked at the Reaper. "Why didn't she die?"

He shook his head, still staring at Piper.

"He lost his claim to me when Dex broke that stone. You heard him just now. He can never come for me."

"I guess I just thought that meant he would never kill you, not that he *couldn't*."

"I kind of thought that too," she whispered.

We both looked at the man who should have all the answers. He looked rattled. Like he couldn't even form a sentence. "I… I didn't know," he muttered to himself and I had to strain to hear.

"Are you saying you didn't know that was going to happen?" I asked.

He looked up at me. His eyes were still a little glassy and vacant. Beside me, Piper shifted and his eyes fastened on her once again.

"No."

It was a simple word, a single response. But the weight behind it was immense.

"I have to go," he said, shaking himself and walking back through the apartment and toward the front door.

We rushed after him, watching to see what he would do. On his way past the coffee table, he stopped and looked down at the vase of white carnations I put there just before I went away with Charming.

Without saying a word, he reached out and fingered the snowy petals of one of the flowers. It died instantly, turning an ugly shade of brown as the petals dried out and curled in on themselves. He looked down at his hand and then back at Piper again before walking quietly out the door.

We stood there for a long time. The only sound was the ticking of the clock on the nearby wall. Finally, I snapped out of it and rushed forward to throw the lock on the front door, turning around and collapsing against it.

Piper sat down on the couch, staring at the single dead flower in a vase full of living ones.

"I touched the Grim Reaper," she said.

"You saved my life."

"I didn't die."

I pushed away from the door and joined her on the couch. "You're badass."

She looked at me and grinned. "Yeah, I guess I am badass."

I nodded. "But never do it again."

"Definitely not. I hope I never see him again."

I hoped that, too. Still, I couldn't help but think that he was trying to kill me. The Grim Reaper wanted me dead. He wanted to use me to get to Charming. I was lucky and got a reprieve from death because my BFF seemed to be the Reaper Whisperer.

I just wondered how long my reprieve was going to last.

# Chapter Forty-Three

*"Freedom - liberty of the person from slavery, detention, or oppression."*

## Charming

I ran for about a mile after leaving G.R.'s upscale neighborhood. I knew I could keep on running to Frankie's apartment, that I would likely be able to keep pulling in energy, but it still would have taken me longer than I wanted. I wanted to be there with her now. I couldn't even call because I was afraid he might still be there and I didn't want him to even think I might have figured out I wasn't as trapped as he wanted me to think.

So I stole a car.

A plain four-door sedan that I wouldn't have normally driven to save my own life. Yet it appeared I was willing to do just about anything to save Frankie. I was just about to pull out of the back of the parking lot when Storm appeared in the backseat.

"Man, you would have lost it and I never would have gotten you out of the house if I had told you that shit before you got into your body."

"I'm still going to deck you if you ever get a body."

"Don't hate the playa. Hate the game."

I glanced in the review mirror as I drove. "Did you seriously just say that?"

"Just keepin' it real."

I focused back on driving and trying not to speed too noticeably. Now would not be a good time to get pulled over by the cops. The drive seemed to take forever and with every passing minute, I grew more worried I would be too late.

About a block from her apartment, I pulled the hotwired car over and parked it in a parking garage. I hurried to use a napkin that was in the glove compartment to wipe down all the surfaces I touched. I knew my fingerprints weren't in the criminal system, but I wasn't taking any chances. I had a feeling if I managed to get out from under the G.R., this was the body I'd be keeping.

The thought drew me up short and I stood outside the car, staring down, doing nothing but thinking.

*Get out from under the Reaper?* Where did that thought come from? The way I thought it just now seemed like it was something that had already been decided—like my head knew something it didn't inform the rest of me about.

Was it even possible?

Could I somehow manage to get completely free of him?

I didn't mean I could pull of this job, kill the Target, and use those bodies to get myself out of being Recalled. Because even if I managed to do that, G.R. would just keep assigning me impossible jobs until I failed. I would spend the rest of my existence scrambling around trying to do his bidding.

I didn't want that.

I wanted a life. A real life. One that meant I didn't have to kill anymore. One where I didn't have to switch bodies and identities, one where I was the only person in charge of what I did.

It wasn't possible. Was it?

Could I somehow trade everything I had of his for true freedom?

Frankie wouldn't have to make peace with me killing because I wouldn't have to kill. We could live without looking over our shoulders. I could love her the way she deserved to be loved.

I'd never had such thoughts before—such hope.

"Dude, how long you gonna stand next to the car you stole?"

I jerked up, reality crashing back in. My feet started moving; I jogged away from the car and toward Frankie's apartment.

"Okay, yeah," Storm called from behind. "I'll just meet you there."

I finally figured out what I wanted and I was going to get it. I just had to figure out how to get there. But before I did any of that, I had to see her. I had to make sure she was okay.

When her apartment building came into sight, I wanted to rush down the sidewalk and barge right in. But I couldn't. G.R. might be watching the building. I ducked into an empty stairwell across the street and watched for signs that someone else might be out here watching or waiting.

After a few minutes of seeing nothing suspicious, I had enough and decided to just use my speed and zip inside. Just as I was preparing to run, the door to her building opened and a man stepped out.

It was G.R.

My breath hissed out between my teeth and I ducked back into the opening when what I really wanted to do was beat his ass. But then my anger dissolved and fear spiked through me. He had been upstairs, inside that apartment with her for a long time.

What if she was hurt?

What if she was dead?

His car pulled down the road and I flew across the pavement. I don't even know if my feet touched the ground. I stopped only when I came to her door. I tried turning the handle to just barge right in, but it was locked.

I pounded on it. "Frankie!" I yelled. "Frankie, open the door."

Storm appeared behind me.

"You need to go in there, unlock the door."

The lock on the door slid free and the door swung wide.

"Frankie," I said, relief making my voice weak.

"Olly?" she said, her eyes going wide as she stared at me.

I nodded. "I know I look different, but it's me."

"You look..." Her voice trailed away as she just stood there and stared.

I wanted to snatch her up, to crush her against me, but I wasn't sure if she would want that. I finally knew exactly what I wanted, but I had no idea if she wanted the same.

"Can we come in?" Storm said.

Frankie stepped back, allowing us in and then closing the door. I stopped short seeing Piper was here. There were too many people here… too many eyes.

I turned my back on them and looked at Frankie. "I saw the Reaper leaving. Are you okay? Did he hurt you?"

"Your eyes are still green," she murmured, staring at me.

I smiled.

"He tried to kill her," Piper announced. I spun around. "What?"

"He was going to touch her. Got a couple inches from her face."

Bile rose up in my throat and my hands fisted at my sides.

"But he didn't touch me. Piper stopped him."

"How could Piper stop him?" Storm asked.

"She touched him first."

I swung my head in the direction of her words. "Come again?"

Frankie nodded. "Piper touched the Grim Reaper and she didn't die."

Everyone stared at Piper. Her cheeks turned pink. "I really need to be going. I have to work."

"You mean to tell me G.R.'s touch didn't kill you?" Storm said.

Piper nodded. "It's because he already promised not to kill me."

I wasn't sure that was entirely it, but I wasn't about to start an hour-long discussion. I wanted to be with Frankie. Alone.

Piper grabbed up her bag off the floor and went to the door where Frankie hugged her. "Thank you. Why don't you stay here tonight after work? You probably shouldn't be alone."

Instead of answering, Piper glanced at me.

I nodded. "Thank you. For saving her life."

Her cheeks bloomed pink again and she hurried out the door.

"Is she safe?" Frankie asked when Piper was gone. "I mean, obviously the Reaper can't kill her, but I mean… that's kind of rare, isn't it?"

"I've never seen this happen my entire career as an Escort," I replied.

"Won't that kind of make her… I don't know… interesting to certain people?"

I had no idea what it meant. I could barely think about it with her standing so close yet so far away.

"How about I keep an eye on her while she's at work?" Storm volunteered.

Frankie expelled a breath. "Would you?"

"Yeah." Storm looked at me. "You got my number."

I nodded.

He didn't wait for someone to open the door. He just went right through it.

And then we were finally alone.

# Chapter Forty-Four

*"Suspenders - fabric or leather straps worn over the shoulders to hold up trousers."*

## Frankie

His eyes were green.

The same exact green they were before. The same green that matched the rolling hills of Scotland.

I didn't know what it was going to be like the first time I saw him in his body, but it was better than I thought it would be. Seeing a body on a hanger was nothing compared to seeing it alive and breathing in front of me.

"Are you okay?" he asked, concern darkening the eyes I was so glad hadn't changed.

"Yeah."

My answer must not have been very convincing because in three great steps he was standing before me, gripping my shoulders and bending down so we were eye to eye. "Are you really okay? Did he hurt you?"

I shook my head. "No. I—" I lost my train of thought. "You're taller."

The corner of his mouth pulled up and he stepped away. "I'll give you one minute to get used to this new body."

"Only one?"

He grinned.

"What's with the khakis?" I laughed as my eyes perused his body.

He scowled. "I didn't dress myself today."

I watched as he glanced down at his body, like he was just seeing it for the first time, and make a face. Then he yanked the sweater vest up over his head and tossed it onto the floor.

Holy hot suspenders.

I never ever in a million years would have dreamed that I would ever think a guy in suspenders was attractive.

Apparently, Olly was attractive in anything he wore.

They were pulled taut across his wide shoulders and hugged his body all the way down the sides of his chest until they stopped at the waistband of his pants, which encircled a narrow, trim waist. I couldn't look away. I wanted to slide my hands beneath them, starting at that waist, and move up his solid chest until my hands wrapped around his neck and buried in his blond hair.

"I'll find a pair of jeans later," he muttered. I suppressed a smile.

"What about you?" I asked seriously. "Are you okay? What happened?"

He blew out a breath and sat down on the couch, leaning back against it lazily. "It's a long story."

"I've got time for you."

"Do you?"

"Yes."

"Come here."

I really had no clue how he could be so calm after everything that happened. My heart was still pounding just a little bit too fast. Of course when he looked at me like that it didn't help.

As I stood there and tried to figure him out, he crooked a finger at me and curled it toward him as if I were on a string and he could pull me closer. Maybe I was because my body obeyed the command of his finger and I found myself directly in front of him.

He moved swiftly, taking me by the waist and pulling me down onto his lap. I wrapped my legs around him, my feet sandwiched between the softness of the sofa and the solidness of his back. He rested his hands between us, his fingers playing idly with the hem of my T-shirt—*his* T-shirt.

"Whatcha got there?" he said. His voice was deep and slightly raspy. It wasn't the smooth-talking voice he used to have. Shivers raced up my back.

"You left it on my bed."

"You thought I left you."

I bit my lip, looking down at his hands. "You kind of did."

"Was it easy for you?" he asked. "Leaving my house, thinking you might not see me again?"

I glanced up. I didn't really want to answer. It felt like he was asking me to bare my soul to him—to tell him my most secret feelings. I wasn't sure I could trust him with those things.

He seemed to perceive my reluctance to reply, so he said, "Is that why you took my shirt? Because it made it a little less harder to leave?"

"I took your Ferrari, too. I left it at the airport."

He smiled. It was a crooked smile and he had a dimple in his chin. I wanted to reach out and touch it. So I did.

"I didn't like that car anyway. So pretentious." He caught the fingers that were tracing his dimple and pressed a kiss to the palm of my hand. "What if I told you it was just as hard for me to leave as it was for you?"

"I didn't say it was hard."

"You didn't have to."

I felt like an ice cube outside on a hot summer day… slowly melting…

"There's something I need to know," he said, taking a fistful of my shirt and towing me closer.

"What?" I have no idea if he even heard the word because it sounded like a sigh.

His lips didn't just touch me; they didn't just brush against mine… They captured me. I couldn't even be considered their hostage because even if he pulled back and offered freedom, I would have stayed. I would have begged for more.

He kissed me like he'd never kissed me before. Slow. Soft. Gentle. He was so utterly and agonizingly slow, tilting his head one way and then the other. The friction of his lips meeting mine again and again filled every part of me with something warm and liquid, until I was so overfull with longing I couldn't sit still.

My body started to move, a slow rocking motion in his lap, like we were lost at sea and our boat just followed the waves. Too soon, he pulled back gently, dropping a kiss to the tip of my nose before leaning his head against the back of the couch to stare at me with heavy-lidded eyes.

What did you say to someone when they kissed you so good you couldn't even remember your own name?

Nothing. You said nothing.

You sat there and prayed they would kiss you again.

The side of his mouth curved upward and a lock of blond hair fell into his eye. "That answers that."

"What?" I said, my voice sounding far away to my own ears.

"I wondered if you would still be attracted to this new body, to me."

I pushed my fingers through the hair falling over his eye, gripping it on top of his head. "There's something I need to know," I told him.

He lifted one of his blond brows and stared at me.

I reached for the buttons on his shirt and began at his throat slowly unfastening them one by one. He watched me with his arms at his sides, not trying to help me. Not trying to stop me. Just watching. I left the ends of his shirt tucked into his pants and the suspenders where they were. My hands slipped inside the opening of his shirt, pushing it open wider, and I looked down.

Washboard abs.

I ran my fingertip down the center and they contracted, the separate muscles rippling at my touch.

"Well, that answers that," I said, looking at him mischievously.

"What?"

"I like this body a lot better."

He grinned, flashing his teeth. One of them had a tiny chip in the corner. "My other body had abs too."

"True. And Charming was very hot," I said, running my palm across his stomach. "But Oliver… he's my guy."

His eyes darkened to the color of thick moss that grew under a tree. "You know I didn't leave you behind. I only went to protect you. I don't want him near you."

I didn't bother to point out that it didn't matter because the Reaper had me in his sights. I liked this conversation far too much to bring that up again. "I know that now."

"Listen to me," he said, moving quickly, speaking fiercely. He captured my head between his hands and sat up so he was staring directly into my eyes. "I'm going to get us out of this. Both of us. And when I do, you're never going to have to worry about me leaving again."

Yep. There I went. I melted completely into a puddle.

"Are you trying to charm me?" I said, though my voice was too watery to hold the sarcastic tone I meant to have.

"I don't have to charm you," he said.

"No?"

He released me and shook his head slowly. "No. Because you've already charmed me. Completely."

"Ahhh, so the charmer has finally been charmed?"

"What can I say? You look good in my shirt."

I pulled it up over my head and tossed it beside him. "What about when I'm not wearing your shirt?"

His hands were on my chest instantly, cupping it and massaging. It didn't take him long to see the closure was in the front, and with a single movement of his hand, it burst open, spilling out everything I had for his waiting eyes to see.

"I've never wanted anyone the way I want you," he confided. I made a sound in the back of my throat and moved a little closer, inviting his touch.

But he didn't touch me.

"Tell me, Frankie," he demanded.

"Tell you what?"

"Tell me you're mine. Tell me you didn't bring my heart back from the dead only to make it die all over again."

And there it was. My choice. But I'd already made it. I made it a long time ago. It just wasn't until today that I admitted it to myself.

I pushed the hair in his eyes up and away from his face. I wanted him to see me clearly. I wanted him to know without a doubt he was who I chose.

"I'm yours," I whispered.

I didn't know what it said about me that I could love someone like him. That I could love a killer. The worst parts of him were really bad. But looking at him now, vulnerability shining from the depths of his eyes and the feeling of him beneath me, I knew—*I knew* without a doubt—that even his darkest parts could never compare to his best ones.

His kiss started on my lips but didn't stay there very long. His mouth slid down my neck and across my collarbone where he nipped along the line of it, making me laugh. Finally, I got to do what I'd been imagining since he took off that ugly sweater. I slid both my hands beneath the suspenders, running my hands along the thick muscles in his chest, and then gently pushed them over his shoulders, sliding them all the way down his arms.

His hands caught mine when they drifted over his, but I shook my head and pulled the hem of his button-down out of his pants. It joined the sweater on the floor.

This body was bigger than the one I knew before. This one had a few scars here and there marring its perfection. But to me it was those imperfections that made him perfect.

I traced along the outline of a circular-shaped scar on his chest. "What happened here?"

"I got it in the ring."

I leaned down and kissed it and ran my tongue over its surface. He groaned and kissed me again. This time it was more demanding and not so slow. His arousal pressed between my legs, making me impatient, turning me into some sex-starved harlot, and I began to make small noises in the back of my throat.

His long fingers found the button of my jeans, releasing it, and then delved down into my waistband, cupping my butt. He tore his mouth from mine. "Your pants are in my way."

I rocked against him one last time, smiling at his intake of breath, and then climbed off his lap. Before I could do anything, he swiped the jeans and my panties down my legs. The cool air brushed against my skin and I shivered slightly as I stood there completely bare before him. It was a good kind of shiver.

His green eyes heated as they took in my every curve and then his khakis were flying over the back of the couch, disappearing from sight. I thought he would pull me beneath him right there on the couch, but he didn't. He settled back against the cushions just as he had been before and pulled me back into his lap.

His arousal jutted up between us, his hard length practically begging for my attention, and I was only too happy to oblige. His skin was smooth as satin and I wrapped my hand around him and slid upward, watching his eyes lose all focus. This was something I could definitely get used to—being in the driver's seat, being the one in control. Olly was such a strong and willful man; he always seemed to be in control, to know exactly what he was doing. But right now, as I stroked him, he was completely under my spell.

Letting go, I rocked forward, bringing our bare chests together, skin touching skin, and teased his arousal with mine. He groaned when my slick warmth slid against him.

His hands splayed around my rib cage, lifting me so I was poised just above him, but I didn't slide down. I didn't connect our bodies just yet. Instead, I let the tip of him flirt with my opening as his mouth drew in one of my rock-hard nipples and rolled it around on his tongue. My head fell back at the sheer bliss—the sheer anticipation of being with him—and I moaned.

Never in a million years did I ever think anyone would ever make me feel like this.

When he released my nipple and placed a kiss between my breasts, I looked at him. I watched him as I slowly lowered myself onto him.

His fingers dug into my ribs to the point of almost being painful, but it was the kind of pain I would ask for again and again because there was nothing as sweet as welcoming him inside me.

When I was completely surrounding him, I began to move. At first my movements were slow, but they began to take on a more feverish insistence, and I moved faster and faster, searching for that release just out of reach.

I must have made a sound because he caught my face and looked into my eyes. "What's the matter, love?"

"Can't get close enough," I whispered as I moved.

In one fell swoop he wrapped his arms around me and moved, spinning so I was lying on the couch and he was over me. He did it so fluidly that our bodies never lost contact.

The weight of him pressed me farther into the couch and I wrapped my legs around his waist to pull him even closer. He was in me. Around me. Over me. He was the only thing I could see. He was the only thing I could feel.

It was exactly what I wanted.

He pulled himself out but just as quickly pushed back in, repeating the motion over and over again until the only word I could murmur was his name.

When I thought I couldn't possibly take anymore and I was surely going to die with need, he pressed his forehead against mine and whispered, "I want you to come with me," and pushed in deep. So blissfully deep that a tidal wave of pure ecstasy rolled over me. It was so strong my entire body surrendered, going limp and boneless against the couch.

Olly collapsed against me, his chest slick with sweat, as he sucked in lungfuls of air. We didn't say anything for a long time… The chemistry swirling between us said more than any words ever could. When he finally shifted, removing some of his weight from me, I grabbed on to him, trying to keep him close.

"I'm not going anywhere," he murmured as he fitted himself between the couch and me, coercing my body to spoon against his, and he wrapped his arm around my waist, securing me firmly beside him.

I turned my head so I was looking up at him. "Olly?"

He made a sound in the back of his throat.

"Everything's going to be okay, isn't it?" Even the passion swirling inside me, the feeling of being safely in his arms, couldn't keep away all the fear. If anything, those things made the fear worse because I knew how much I had to lose.

I couldn't lose this. I couldn't lose him.

But we were up against death and the odds were stacked against us.

He brushed the hair away from my face, his touch so tender that my heart ached anew. "Everything's going to be fine. I'm not going to let anything take this away from us."

I nodded, snuggling in even closer. Part of me felt better because I knew he meant what he said. But the other part of me…

The other part of me whispered that Death didn't care.

# Chapter Forty-Five

*"Tears - a drop of the clear salty liquid that is secreted by the lachrymal gland of the eye to lubricate the surface between the eyeball and eyelid and to wash away irritants."*

## Charming

She was asleep when I slid out from beneath her and went into the bathroom. I flicked on the light and smiled down at the sink. There were bottles of product and hairbrushes scattered everywhere. She was an utter disaster. Clothes all over the floor in her room, her closet looked like it exploded, and her bathroom was clearly no better.

I loved it.

I hoped she never changed.

I looked in the mirror, the first time I actually looked at myself since taking back my body. Frankie never changed, but I sure as hell did.

It was startling to look in the mirror and see someone you didn't expect to see. Kind of like being out in public and seeing a person you hadn't seen in a long time. At first glance you don't recognize them so you do a double take. The second time you look it clicks, and you realize you know who it is.

I knew this face. I knew this body. I was familiar with it. There was a scar on my knee from when I fell off my bike when I was five. I got the blond hair from my grandfather who worked in a factory all his life and brought me a lollipop every time he visited. This was the body I grew up in. I had history here.

And now I had a future here too.

Two arms appeared from behind, wrapping themselves around my waist and hugging tight. Frankie pressed her cheek against my back and let out a small sigh of contentment. "I forgot to mention how much I like that tattoo."

I turned so I could stare at the black scroll design that stretched across the side of my shoulder. I got it when I turned eighteen.

"I forgot to mention that I like when you don't wear clothes."

Her laugh was throaty. "Oh, I think that came up."

"Want it to come up again?"

"I think you better tell me what's going on first."

Reality had a way of getting in the way. "You have any coffee?"

I watched her put on my shirt—and nothing else—and go out to the kitchen to make coffee.

I looked down at the khakis and boxer briefs on the floor. I hated those pants. So I threw on the boxers and went to the living room.

"Do you always hang out in your underwear?" Frankie asked as she was cracking eggs into a large bowl. Coffee was already starting to brew.

"When my only clothes are dorky? Yes."

She snickered. "I like those suspenders."

I poured some coffee and sat down at the round table in the small kitchen. "Better than my jeans?"

"I haven't seen this new body in a pair of jeans."

I raised an eyebrow over the rim of the mug and looked at her. "Are you saying this body won't look good in a pair of jeans?"

She smiled slyly. "That remains to be determined."

I grunted and drank more coffee. She was going to eat those words later.

"So… how bad is it, Olly?" she asked after a few moments of silence.

"Not so bad."

She gave me a withering look and I shrugged. "He locked me in a room and told me he would let me out the day the time limit on the job runs out. Then he was going to Recall me."

"How long do you think until he realizes you're gone?"

"Hopefully a couple months."

"So what? You're just going to lurk around Alaska and hope he doesn't see you?"

"That and kill the Target."

Her shoulders sagged as she scrambled the eggs over the stove. "You really have to kill her, don't you?"

"If I want a shot at getting out, yes."

"Getting out?" She glanced at me. "Like *out* out?

"Yes."

She abandoned the spatula to the pan and turned around to look at me. "You're going to quit being an Escort?"

The look on her face made my insides go hot. "I'm going to try. Don't get your hopes up. No one's ever walked away from the Grim Reaper before."

She squealed and threw herself into my lap and rained kisses over my face. "I can't believe you're going to give it all up."

I caught her chin in my hand. "What I'm walking away from is nothing compared to what I'm walking toward."

"I love you."

My heart skipped a beat. Then it skipped some more.

"Say it again."

"I love you, Oliver."

If I hadn't been sure about walking away before, I was now.

"I love you, too."

Her eyes rounded like she was shocked and then she jumped off my lap. "My eggs!" she cried and ran over to take the pan off the stove.

"That's what you say to a guy who hasn't told anyone he loves them in over ninety years? You worry about your eggs?"

She laughed and launched herself at me again. "Well, it's a good thing you told me before I demonstrated my cooking skills."

I kissed her nose. "I hear you make some good cupcakes."

"You don't eat sugar."

"Hmmmm. I don't need sugar. I have you."

"Olly?" she said. Her smile faded away and she looked at me seriously.

"What?"

"Are you sure? Like, sure about this? You're going to give up a life of living forever, money, and power."

"I have enough money to last us both our entire lives and then some. I don't need power. And living without you isn't living at all."

Her eyes softened. "Well, when you put it that way."

"I need to know what the Reaper said when he came here."

The softness left her eyes, replaced by wariness.

"It's okay. I'm going to keep you safe." I assured her. Even if that was the only thing I did.

"He was looking for the bodies. And a soul?"

I nodded. "I took a soul he had hidden away too."

"I told him I didn't know where they were." She bit her lip and looked at me. "Then he said he was going to start adding women to his collection and he tried to touch me."

My arms encircled her waist and I pulled her tighter against me. The pain of being touched by him still lingered in my memory, and while he said it wasn't like that for a person who wasn't an Escort, I didn't tend to believe everything he said. If he touched her, if he even so much as thought about killing her again, I was going to find a way to make his life a living hell.

"But Piper grabbed him." Her eyes filled with unexpected tears. I wasn't prepared for tears. "I thought she was going to die."

I pressed her head against my shoulder and brushed my lips over the top of her head. "It's okay. Piper's fine." Which truthfully shocked the shit out of me. She had to be the first person *ever* that didn't keel over from coming into contact with G.R.

"She's the only family I have." She glanced up. "Well, I guess I have you now too."

Warmth spread throughout my chest. "Yeah. Yeah, you have me now too."

"My parents live on the other side of the state. We don't talk. I wasn't the kind of daughter they wanted and they weren't happy when I refused to change. Piper doesn't have any family either. It's just us."

"Shhh," I told her, wanting the tears to stop. I could feel them falling onto my chest and sliding down my skin.

"You should have seen the Reaper's face, Olly. He was shocked. Just as shocked as we were. I don't think something like that ever happened to him before." She sniffled. "He looked at Piper… like she was some kind of miracle."

A shiver ran up her spine and she shook in my lap. I stroked her hair and made her a promise. "I won't let anything happen to Piper, either."

She nodded against me, the words actually seeming to make her feel better. It amazed me how just months ago I was completely alone and now here I was vowing to take care of these women. It didn't work out so well the first time I tried to take responsibility for two women. My sister paid the ultimate price. And the guilt from that would haunt me for the rest of my life. I wasn't going to make those mistakes again. This time was going to be different. This time we were all going to walk away with our lives.

Frankie's tears turned to hiccups as I held her, rubbing her back while all the coffee went cold before we could drink it.

And as she quieted, I began to plan.

# Chapter Forty-Six

*"Money - assets and property considered in terms of monetary value; wealth."*

## *Frankie*

Just as suspected, I got fired from my job. I called in to tell them I was better and coming back and the witch cackled and told me not to bother.

I couldn't really say I was disappointed. In fact, I kind of felt relieved. Okay, not kind of. Totally. I was surprised by how much relief I actually felt. I used to joke that place was sucking away my soul, but now that I didn't have to go back, I realized it hadn't really been a joke.

Lost in thought, I wandered over to the window, looking down to the street. Olly's Porsche was still sitting at the curb where he left it before we went to Los Angeles. He wasn't going to be able to drive it around for a while; the expensive car wasn't exactly made for blending in, and since he was supposed to be locked up in a room without a body, taking it for a spin wasn't on the to-do list.

He came out of the bedroom, dressed in the khakis, white button-down, and suspenders. I noticed he styled his hair so it wasn't in his eyes anymore and resembled the way he wore it in his other body, though it was longer now.

"I need to go get some clothes and my laptop. You're coming with me. I'm not leaving you here alone in case G.R. comes back."

I nodded. "We can take my Jeep." I went to grab my coat and noticed I was still holding the phone, so I sat it on the coffee table next to the vase of flowers. My eye caught the single brown one, and I was reminded all over again of Piper's brush with death.

"I didn't hear the phone ring," Olly said.

"It didn't. I called work. I got fired."

"Saves you from having to quit," he said, not in the least sorry.

"I guess so," I said, rather non-committal. Yes, I was glad I didn't have to go back there, but on the other hand, I kind of felt like my life was unraveling at the seams. Not too long ago I had a steady job, a normal routine, a best friend I told everything to, and a weekly habit of going to the donut shop. Now, I had no job, my routine was non-existent, I was dating a Death Escort, and the Grim Reaper wanted to kill me. Not to mention my best friend almost gave up her life for me after I all but ignored her for weeks.

Oh, and the donut shop was probably wondering if I fell off the face of the earth.

"You know you don't have to worry about money anymore, right?" he said, catching my hand and towing me against him.

"I know," I said. "But I can't just let you support me."

"Why not?" He frowned.

"Because it's not your job."

"Yes, it is."

"No. Your job is to love me. And to put up with me. Not to be my sugar daddy."

He chuckled. "Putting up with you *is* a challenge sometimes."

I scowled.

"But loving you… that's a lot easier than I ever thought possible."

"I'm so irresistible."

"How about you don't worry about money until all this is over and we can finally move on. Then if it will make you feel better, you can find a job."

"Sounds good to me." I moved to the door. "On the way back from your place, can we swing by the diner and get Piper? I don't want her to be at her apartment alone tonight."

"Yeah," he replied, but he seemed distracted, still standing in the center of the room, making no attempt to leave.

"Olly?"

He glanced up swiftly.

"What were you thinking?"

"Nothing. Let's go."

He ushered me out and we went down to the street where the Jeep was parked. I walked out alone and got in, reaching over to unlock the passenger door and then starting up the vehicle and putting on my seatbelt. A few moments later, Olly climbed in, ducking a little lower in his seat.

I didn't waste time and pulled away from the curb. The entire way Olly kept a lookout for following cars and gave me directions for a route that took us half across town. Then we doubled back before finally turning into his neighborhood.

"Shit," he swore when I pulled up on the darkened end of his street.

"What?" My eyes immediately went outside onto the street, thinking the Reaper had somehow found us.

"I don't have my keys. They're still in Scotland."

"Oh, that's okay." I fished around in my bag and pulled out a credit card. "I'll let us in."

His teeth flashed in the dark and I took that as a "You're brilliant, Frankie" and climbed out of the Jeep. I took great pride in letting us into the house while he stood by and looked pretty.

But once we stepped inside, much of my amusement and lightheartedness evaporated. He didn't want to turn on any lights because he didn't want anyone to know we were there. So we stood there in the dark (which, frankly, was creepy) while he listened or felt or whatever he did for signs that anyone was in the house, waiting for us.

"All clear," he said, moving into the kitchen a few moments later.

"Where are you going? Aren't your clothes upstairs?"

I heard the opening and closing of a drawer.

"Olly, now is not the time for a snack break."

He appeared beside me soundlessly, causing a strangled sound to erupt from the back of my throat. "Seriously!" I demanded as he ushered me up the steps toward what I assumed was his bedroom. The whole way up he kept one hand on my lower back and the other straight down against his side.

When we made it to the top of the stairs, he went first, rounding the corner and disappearing into the first room on the left. A light came on, sending light out into the hallway and making it much easier to see.

"I thought you said no lights?" I stepped into the doorway of the lit room. It was a bathroom. A very nice, upgraded bathroom with granite countertops and tile floors.

"There are no windows in this room. It will give us a little light to get my stuff from the bedroom." He turned around. And that's when I noticed it.

He was carrying a gun.

I felt my eyes round as I stared at the lethal weapon clutched in his hand. "What's that for?"

"Protection."

"Do you really think we need it?"

"I think I would rather have it than not."

"Get your stuff so we can go."

I followed him into his bedroom where he moved quickly, packing a black duffle bag with stuff while I sat on his giant king-sized bed. From what I could see, the room was really nice. But all my attention on the room was lost when he started taking off his clothes.

"I hope I never see another pair of khakis again," he muttered, throwing them on the floor. Everything else soon joined the pants.

"I agree they look better on the floor."

He spun in my direction and prowled to the end of the bed. He grabbed my ankle and slowly towed me down the bed until he was standing between my legs. "If we weren't in a hurry…" he said, letting the words dangle suggestively. My skin heated from just the hint of seduction in his voice.

I extended my fingers so I could trail them down his torso, but he pulled back, saying, "Oh no you don't. One touch from you is all it would take."

He pulled on a pair of jeans and with his back to me, reached for a dark-colored long-sleeved shirt. Even in the dim lighting, I knew even in this body he could totally rock a pair of jeans.

After he was fully dressed and his bag was zipped, I assumed he was ready to go so I hopped off the bed and moved toward the door.

"Frankie, I want to give you something."

"What?"

He tucked the gun in the waistband of his jeans, slung the bag over his shoulder, and came forward with something clutched in his hand. "Here," he said, holding it out.

It was a credit card. "I already have one of those," I said, patting my pocket.

"It's an ATM card to one of my accounts. I want you to hold on to it in case you need it."

"Why would I need to hold on to it? Why can't—" The answer slapped me hard and I flinched. "You don't think you're going to make it out."

He stared at me without blinking for a long time. It's like he was weighing his words, not sure of what he should and should not say. Finally, he spoke.

"Take it, Frankie," he said, thrusting the card at me. "I just want to know you're going to be taken care of." I opened my mouth to argue with him, but he held up his hand and continued on. "I know you don't want my money, but I want you to have it. If something happens and I get Recalled, you go to the nearest ATM and pull out everything you can. The pin is nineteen twenty-two. Then you transfer the rest into another bank account in your name."

I took the card and slid it into my pocket. "Tell me you're going to make it out."

"I'm going to make it out."

"Well, don't say it if you don't mean it!" I snapped. Oh God, my eyes were filling with tears. I hardly ever cried and now here I was trying for number two today. I couldn't help it. The idea of never seeing him again… it was incredibly overwhelming. It was the kind of hurt that had the power to crush everything inside me. There wasn't enough money in the world that would ever take away the kind of pain I would feel if he somehow got Recalled.

He rolled his eyes and grabbed my chin. "Listen to me. Even before I fell in love with you, I was determined to not let G.R. get the best of me. But now I have you. I have even more reason to fight. I'm not going anywhere, Frankie. Just take the damn money. You can give it back when this is over."

I sniffled.

He yanked me against him. His shirt was really soft and I snuggled against it. "And stop crying, would you? I really don't like it."

A laugh broke through my tears, but it sounded kind of like a sob. His arms around me tightened. I took a deep breath and straightened. I didn't like crying either. "C'mon, it's probably about time to pick up Piper."

He took my hand and pulled me behind him down the hallway, reaching into the bathroom to shut off the light.

"So what's the plan anyway?"

He glanced over his shoulder at me. "Kill the Target and trade the soul and the bodies for my freedom."

"And you think the Reaper will go for it?"

"I'm not going to give him a choice."

We were halfway down the stairs when Olly stopped moving and in one quick move pulled the gun out and used his arm to usher me behind his body. I was afraid to talk, to ask him what he thought was going on; because it was clear he thought we were no longer alone.

My body went on high alert, listening for every little sound that could mean something. I watched the bottom of the stairs like a cat about to pounce on my dinner, but I still didn't seem to hear what he did.

After several very tense moments, his shoulders seemed to relax and he started moving again down the stairs, keeping the gun at his side.

We made it all the way downstairs and into the yard.

The Grim Reaper seemed to appear out of nowhere. I couldn't understand how one minute we were walking along with nothing in our path and then there he was, standing in front of us with electric-blue energy crackling from his fingertips.

Olly's muscles bunched beneath his clothes and he turned, shoving the gun at me. "Safety is off. If he takes one step toward you, shoot his ass and don't stop."

"You cannot kill Death," the Reaper intoned. I don't know if it was because I was scared or because it was dark out, but his voice was much more ominous and frightening than it had been at my apartment.

"No. But she sure as hell would slow you down." Olly pinned me with a stare. "Shoot and then run."

"What about you?" I whispered, clutching the gun.

"Don't you worry about him," the Reaper called. "He knows when Death has someone in its sights, it always gets what it wants."

Without warning or any kind of pause, he threw out his arms and tossed some of that electric-blue energy at us. Olly didn't seem surprised. He didn't duck. He didn't run. He planted himself directly in front of me and he *absorbed* most of what came our way.

"Go to the Jeep," Olly said. Then he threw out his hands, tossing back more of the same energy.

Did he think I could just leave him there?

"Go!" he yelled when I just stood there debating.

Apparently he did.

"I won't leave you here!" I argued.

The Reaper laughed and raised his hand, pulling like he
was holding an invisible rope. A red cloud appeared around
Charming, half in, half out of his body.

"Come along, Charming," G.R. called. "You're supposed
to be locked up tight until the clock runs out!"

I watched as Olly seemed to stumble forward like his
body was following his soul. I reached out and grabbed his
hand, holding on like I could keep him right there with me.

The Reaper laughed again and pulled harder. Olly's hand
ripped from mine and he fell forward onto his knees. Red
was a giant cloud around him, growing bigger every second,
and the more red I saw, the more limp his body became.

I wanted to scream. To scream and never stop. I'd never
seen such a thing before. *Is this what everyone looked like inside?
Could the Reaper just rip out my soul right here and now?*

I didn't scream.

Instead, I raised the gun, pointing it at the Reaper.

I didn't hesitate.

I pulled the trigger.

The bullet slammed into his shoulder, knocking him
backward, but not hard enough to knock him off his feet.
The shock was enough to get him to stop doing whatever he
was doing to Olly, and his soul snapped back into his body,
the red disappearing from sight.

He scrambled to his feet, pushing me backward, toward
the side of the house. "Get the hell out of here, Frankie. Go,
now!"

Over his shoulder I saw the Reaper recover. I saw him
look up at us and smile. He released more of that energy
from his fingers and sent it spiraling right at Olly.

"Look out!" I yelled.

But it was too late. Just as Olly turned, the energy hit him
directly in the chest. He flew backward, hit the ground, and
slid into a large shrub that lined the property. I rushed over
and fell to my knees beside him. Blue energy glowed around
him before fading away into the darkness.

"Olly," I worried, leaning over his body so I could see his face.

"Find Storm." He said the words so low I barely heard them, and then he leapt up so fast that I fell backward from surprise. The Reaper had been closing in, taking advantage of my preoccupation over Olly. When our eyes connected he smiled. He was going to kill me.

I lifted the gun once more.

But I never got the chance to shoot it.

Olly was there, throwing himself between us and plowing into the Reaper like a bulldozer. I screamed, watching the man I love come into contact with the man whose touch kills.

Olly made a sound of pain and he shoved the Reaper away, but then he jumped back and stayed steady on his feet. "I'll go with you now if you leave her be," he said, out of breath.

"No!" I protested, panic taking hold.

"How about I kill her now and take you after?"

"If you kill her, I'll make sure those bodies are burned and that soul is dropped to the bottom of one of the many oceans on this planet."

The Reaper's eyes flashed violet. His eyes flicked to mine and then back to Olly. Then he waved his arm and a doorway appeared out of nowhere. "Come along, Charming. It seems locking you up in the *body you stole* will make it more convenient to keep you contained."

Olly walked toward the door; he didn't look back. Just as I was about to rush forward, to do something, anything that would keep him here with me, he turned, looking at me over his shoulder. He shook his head slightly. "Remember what I said."

He stepped into the makeshift doorway and it closed instantly. I was left standing there all alone with trembling hands.

I didn't completely understand what happened in
Scotland, how Olly had disappeared without a trace so easily.
I understood now.

The only difference was this time I understood what was
happening. This time I wasn't going to go home and cry. Olly
left because it was the only way he knew how to make me
one hundred percent safe. He became an Escort because it
was the only way he knew how to keep his mother and his
sister safe. Olly had been fighting for a long time… fighting
for his family, then for his job, and now for me.

Who had ever fought for Olly?

No one.

Until now.

# Chapter Forty-Seven

*"Making plans - stupid." *Definition provided by Charming.*

## *Charming*

Making plans was stupid. That's why I was the kind of guy who liked to wing it. I liked to make decisions based on the here and now and not before things happen. Because things always change and a man needs to be flexible.

I should have spent less time making plans and more time thinking things through. Like going back to my house. I shouldn't have gone there, but really, what were my other options? My wallet and all my credit cards and keys were in Scotland. I needed access to money and I really needed to get out of those hideous khaki pants.

So now in an attempt to keep G.R. away from Frankie *again,* I was back here in his office *again.* "I see you got the place put back together from my last visit."

"Don't even think about making a mess," he said. "You're just passing through on your way back into confinement."

"As much as I'd love to stay and be locked up by you, I think I'll pass." I walked toward the door. I wasn't staying here. I came to buy Frankie some time to get away. That was accomplished and now I was leaving.

If he wanted to try and stop me he could. I was up for a fight.

"I was there the night you died." His voice was calm, almost conversational.

Something in my stomach hardened, but I kept walking, knowing he was just playing games. "I think that's obvious." I wouldn't be in this fun position now if he hadn't been there.

"I was in the crowd, watching the fight. My money was on you."

My steps faltered. Those words… *My money's on you.* I knew those words. Someone said them to me right before… right before I died.

"It was you," I murmured, pushing through the ninety years of memories to bring back the night I spent a lot of time trying to forget. "There was a man. He came up to the ring, helped me with my water." He had dark hair and a wide forehead. *"It was you."*

"Ahh, you do remember," G.R. said. "I knew you would make a good Escort. I could see it in your face. Your determination. Your stubbornness. Your unwillingness to back down from someone who desperately wanted to hold on to his title."

"I should have won that fight."

"Yes. You should have."

I glanced up swiftly. Had he somehow interfered with the fight? Had he somehow made me lose?

"That was your downfall, you know. You underestimated your opponent. You let your human side get in the way. You didn't expect someone to cheat—someone to kill for what they wanted."

He was right. That was my downfall. I hadn't been expecting a dirty fight. My entire life I'd been honest; I'd worked hard. I thought that was the way to get the things I wanted. The respect and recognition I deserved.

But there were people out there who didn't care about hard work or integrity. There were people out there who wanted to take the shortcut to success and their shortcut involved knocking down the people in their way.

"Your loss was my gain that night," G.R. said. "I knew you would become my greatest Escort. I was right. All you needed was a little push."

"A little push?"

He smiled slyly. "All I had to do was get rid of the humanity that seemed to hold you back."

Dread began to build within in me. My humanity? After I died, the only humanity I had was…

My sister.

"You son of a…" My words trailed away as the knowledge of just how bad he played me was born. "You killed her. You killed my sister."

"I thought maybe as time went on, your preoccupation with her would diminish, but then you killed that boy. You broke my rules and you killed someone who wasn't a Target."

"You knew?"

"I know everything. I knew the minute you killed him. But I wasn't ready to Recall you. I knew your potential, but in order for it to be realized, she had to go."

Fury burned through me. It swept over my entire body like a forest fire in a bone-dry mountain of trees. He killed my sister. He robbed her of her life. He robbed my mother of her daughter. If I hadn't hated him before, I hated him now.

"It worked," he taunted. "As soon as she was gone, you became the perfect killer. So quick and precise. You never strayed from a job and the charm you exuded was the perfect bait for just about any Target."

I thought she killed herself. I thought what I had done made her end her life. All these years I carried around guilt that some days threatened to crush me when all along I hadn't killed her at all. It was him.

My sister lost her life so he could create the perfect Escort.

I flew across the room, leaping over his desk and grabbing the chair he sat in like it was his throne. Moving fast, I grabbed the chair and hurled it, sending him and the black leather monster spiraling against the wall of closets behind him.

The chair crashed to the floor, half pinning him to the ground, and one of the closet doors sprang open, revealing the row of neat bodies.

G.R. tossed the chair away and stood, swiping at a rivulet of blood that trailed from the corner of his lip, and faced me.

I sent a swirling ball of white-hot energy at his chest, making him leap to the side out of its path. The energy hit the bodies, blowing them off the racks and scattering them on the floor. I went over and snatched one up, snarling at the ugly-ass khakis and threw it at him. "Better pick a new body now because when I'm done with the one you're wearing, it won't be worth salvaging."

He caught the body and lowered it to the ground like it was delicate and then turned his eyes to the other bodies that lay around my feet.

He barreled toward me, and I knew he was going to try and touch me. From the last time, I understood just a simple touch from him wouldn't kill me like a regular human, but any longer contact would completely kill the body I was in. This was my body and I wasn't about to lose it.

I rushed around the end of the desk and lifted, using it as a shield against him. All the contents that sat on top slid down and rushed across the floor, making the Reaper dodge the falling office supplies.

I shoved the table away, pushing it toward him, and it teetered on its one side before falling over, crashing toward him. He narrowly missed being crushed, and the desk landed on the floor with a hard smack.

His office door flew open and several of the Escorts rushed in, looking at G.R., the mess, and then settling on me.

I smirked and looked at G.R. "You didn't fire them after the ass kicking I served them last time?" I shook my head. "Your business is going to hell."

His response was to shoot more of that electric-blue energy that crackled from his fingertips. This time it connected.

I flew backward, hitting the sofa in the center of the room and knocking it over. I landed behind it on the floor and lay there stunned for a few minutes.

One of the Escorts (the blue one) hauled me up and drew back his fist to punch me, but I kicked him, sending him sprawling into the one behind him.

All three of them went down like dominoes. It's like they were the three stooges of death.

I faced the Reaper once more, my brain rapidly running through ideas of how I could cause him extreme pain.

But my thoughts were stalled when I heard the telltale cocking of guns behind me.

I looked over my shoulder to see the three stooges hadn't come alone this time. They'd brought some friends. Friends that were much more lethal than they were. And right now all three of their friends were pointed at my head.

Well, damn.

My options just got a lot more limited. I could (and would) fight back, but the odds were at least one of them would get off a good shot. If this body died, the chances of getting G.R. to give me another one were slim to none. Not to mention not having a body made moving around a real pain in the ass. I didn't have time to get shot.

G.R. smiled like he knew he won and made his way through the mess to dig out his chair and press the button underneath of it. The secret wall slid open, revealing the doors inside.

"Your new home awaits," he said, gesturing toward the room.

I wasn't going back in there. I glanced at the closets, at the closed doors lining the small hideaway. *Keep him talking,* the voice in my head told me.

"Why did you keep my body? My sister's body?" As I talked, I moved slightly toward the wall, pretending I was going to do what he wanted. All three guns followed my movements.

"After she was gone, I decided to put her body away for safe keeping, your body too. In case I ever needed something to control you. In case that humanity reared its ugly head again. I never thought it would end like this, Charming. But you're becoming a liability. And that is why I must Recall you."

His words angered me all over again. He had taken so much away from me, so much more than I ever realized. He's the reason I was who I became, and now he wanted to punish me for being too good at exactly who he wanted me to be.

"You're not Recalling me because I'm a liability." I snarled. "You're trying to get rid of me because you're scared. You created me a little too perfectly and now that I've decided I won't be your puppet anymore, you know you won't be able to control me. That was your mistake. You gave me too much power."

I saw the truth in his eyes. The acknowledgement of my words. I was right. He was scared of me. I wasn't being punished because I overlooked what Dex had done. That was just an excuse. If it hadn't been that, he would have found something else. I was being punished because he saw me as a threat.

I took my opportunity and grabbed the closest gun that was pointed at me. I ripped it out of the Escort's hand, snapping his wrist in the process. He howled in pain but didn't go down like I thought he would. Instead, he plowed into me low, catching me around the legs and sending me forward to fall over his back. I fired the gun, but the shot went wild, the bullet burying into the wall.

"Get him!" G.R. demanded.

I fell onto my stomach and rolled, trying to bring up the gun from beneath me to fire again. But before I could get a shot off, one of the Escorts was there, using the butt of his gun and slamming it into my temple. I collapsed back onto the floor.

Everything went black.

# Chapter Forty-Eight

*"Sinister - suggesting or threatening evil."*

## Frankie

The diner was closing just as I pulled up to the curb. I rushed inside, ignoring the dirty look of the waitress who thought I was there to order, and hurried over to the counter where Piper was standing, refilling a napkin dispenser.

"Hey," she said, looking up, her eyes traveling behind me. I knew she was looking for Olly.

"Is Storm here?" I said, lowering my voice so our conversation would remain private.

"I'm not sure. He said he would be around. Whatever that means."

I glanced outside toward the sidewalk. "Meet me outside when you're done here. Hurry."

"What's wrong, Frankie?"

"I'll explain later," I said, halfway out the door.

The sidewalk outside was vacant, the hour late enough that most people were already home for the day. I looked around, trying to see Storm and then giving up with an irritated groan when I realized there were just too many dark places here from him to hide.

"Storm!" I whisper-yelled.

A few seconds ticked by and I opened my mouth to yell louder this time when I heard him up ahead. "Here."

I moved up the sidewalk, looking for the source of his voice, and when I passed by a darkened eave for a shop, he said, "I'm here."

"Get in the car!" I whisper-yelled again. I went around to my side and climbed in, leaving my door open so he would be able to get inside.

A few minutes later, black fog filled up the back seat.

"That is seriously sinister," I said, looking in the rearview mirror.

"You're dating an Escort," he pointed out dryly. "I would say that's worse."

It was the first time I didn't bother to correct someone when they said I was dating Olly. I wasn't really sure if that was our official title, but since we both confessed to love and I was ready to do anything to get him back, I figured dating wasn't too far of a stretch.

Piper climbed into the passenger seat, her eyes going to the black cloud in the back and then doing a double take on the gun I clutched in my lap.

"Where is Charming and why do you have a gun?"

"He's with the Reaper. I'm going to get him out," I said, pulling away from the curb.

"You're going the wrong way," Storm pointed out.

"No, I'm not. I'm taking Piper home."

"What!" she exclaimed. "No, you are not."

I gave her a look. "Yes, I am. You're my best friend. I don't want you to get hurt."

She snorted. "I'm the only person in this car who is safe from the Reaper."

We all sat there silently, realizing she was right.

"That's exactly why you should go home," I pointed out, using her reasoning against her. "You've already suffered enough at the hands of the Reaper."

"I agree," Storm said.

"You don't get a vote," she snapped over her shoulder.

I grinned. "Tell him!"

"You don't get a vote, either."

The grin I was sporting vanished. "Excuse me?"

"This is my decision. I'm not going to go sit at home while you rush off to do God knows what without me."

"She's just going to sit in the car," Storm put in from behind.

"Be quiet!" we said at the same time.

She looked at me and I sighed. "Fine." I didn't have any right to make her stay home. No one could keep me from being involved if this was about Piper.

The tires screeched as I did a U-turn in the center of the road.

"Tell me where to go," I told Storm.

"Oh, am I allowed to talk now?" he quipped.

"You may give directions," Piper told him, glancing over her shoulder.

"Women," he muttered.

"Tell us what happened," Piper said when we were headed in the right direction.

As I drove, I explained what happened at Olly's house. The whole time I had to keep reminding myself not to speed, that a speeding ticket would only make things worse. When I was done explaining, I thought for sure they would tell me I was crazy, that we couldn't just go to the Reaper's house and expect to get him out.

But they didn't bother to tell me it was a stupid idea or that Olly wouldn't want me to go there. Maybe they saw the determination in my face. Maybe they knew it would be a waste of breath. I didn't really care what they were thinking because it didn't matter.

"We're here," Storm said quietly.

My attention went beyond my thoughts to the homes of the upper class. Every home here had lush, sprawling lawns, winding driveways, and homes that belonged on the cover of magazines. So this was where Death lived.

It didn't seem fair he got to live here and I had to stand behind the counter at the DMV every day for little more than minimum wage. Well, technically I didn't do that anymore.

"Slow down and then stop here at the curb," Storm instructed and I did as he asked, stopping the Jeep between houses, hoping no one would notice there was a car that looked like it didn't quite belong.

"G.R.'s house is that one," he said, pointing at the one just ahead. It was just as nice as the others with its stone façade and big windows. "I'll see what I can find out. I'll be right back."

"I'm coming with you," I said, shocked he thought I was going to sit in the car.

"Are you kidding me?" he said. "The whole idea is to not draw attention. You're like a freaking red flag waving in the wind."

"Excuse me?" I said. "Was that some kind of fat joke?"

He let out a frustrated sigh. "What is it with women? Always thinking men are insulting you…"

I glared at him.

"*No*, I was not calling you fat," he explained. "I was saying that you aren't exactly unnoticeable. You've got a happening body, bright blond hair, and you have a problem keeping your mouth closed."

I'm pretty sure that last part was an insult. I let it go because he complimented my body.

"Look, just sit in the car. Arguing with you is wasting time."

"Fine." I sniffed.

I unzipped the window and he didn't waste any time disappearing into the night. I let out a nervous sigh. Waiting around sucked.

I lasted for about five minutes.

Then I popped open the door and jumped out.

"Frankie, what are you doing?" Piper whispered.

"If he thinks I'm sitting in this car, he's nuts."

"What are you going to do?"

"I don't know yet," I said. "Wait here."

I got no more than four steps down the street when she appeared at my side and we both made our way to the house silently.

"What the hell are you two doing?" Storm demanded from a dark area at the edge of the Reaper's yard.

Both of us let out a little squeal. "Seriously! That was mean!" I pressed a hand to my chest to hopefully keep it from beating right out.

"You deserve it. I told you to stay in the car."

"You took too long!"

"I was gone five minutes."

Felt like a lifetime to me.

"What did you find out?" Piper asked, grabbing my hand and pulling me closer to wherever Storm was.

"Charming's here. Getting him out isn't an option this time." His voice sounded a little funny.

"Why not!" I demanded.

"Well, because he's still in his body. He won't be going through walls anytime soon."

"So let's create a distraction. He'll know it's us and he can escape." It was a perfectly reasonable plan.

"Uh, that's not going to work."

"Why not?" I demanded again.

"Because he's unconscious."

If that wasn't a bucket of ice-cold water right in my face. I sucked in a breath. "What happened to him?"

"I don't know. He doesn't look bad, just unconscious."

If he was unconscious, then it was bad. A person didn't just pass out for no good reason. My worry over him increased tenfold. I really thought we would be able to find a way to get him out of there. Now I was starting to worry it wasn't going to happen at all. Olly would sit there for months, only to be Recalled. The ATM card he gave me felt like a twenty-pound weight in my pocket. Had he known this was going to happen all along? Had his confidence been just so I wouldn't worry?

"No." I said, "This isn't how this is going to go."

"Let's just go back to your place and we can come up with some sort of plan," Storm said reasonably.

I was done with being reasonable.

I marched ahead, stepping onto the Reaper's property and toward the front door.

"Frankie!" Piper called, running after me. "What are you doing?"

A man came around the side of the house and stopped short, seeing us approach. "This is private property," he said.

"I know exactly whose property it is," I spat. "Now step aside."

"I'm afraid I can't let you go any farther."

I snorted and walked around him. "Fine, then. Come along."

He raced after us as I walked up to the front door and banged on the solid wood with my fist. He probably had a doorbell, but I felt like hitting something.

The door swung open a few seconds later. "Oh, well, isn't this a surprise?" The Reaper smiled. "I'm afraid your boyfriend can't come to the door. He's indisposed."

Piper stepped up behind me and all his attention zeroed in on her. Again, that weird look of reverence overcame his features and it made me wrinkle my nose in disgust.

"She's only here because of me," I said, trying to take the attention away from her.

He blinked, his stare coming back to me, only for it to wander right back to Piper.

I slapped my hand against the partially open door. "Hey!" I snapped.

Irritation crossed over his features until I spoke. Once the words had left my mouth, I had his complete and utter attention.

"I came to make a deal."

"You came to make a deal with me?" he said, interest clouding his eyes.

I nodded.

"Come in." He held open the door as Piper and I went inside, both of us sticking very close together.

In his office, he sat in a massive black chair behind a desk that was completely bare, and my eye caught a few shards of broken glass lying on the rug beneath it. It made me wonder what happened and if it had anything to do with Olly.

The Reaper steepled his fingers beneath his chin and pinned me with a cold stare. "What's the deal?"

I swallowed, not really believing what I was about to do. Yet I'd seen too much to simply ignore or deny anything that had happened recently. I could no longer just tell myself there was a way out of this that didn't require anyone to die. In the world of the Reaper, death was king. Death was the be all and end all of everything.

If there was one thing I learned through all of this, it was that death wasn't fair. No one wanted to die. No one wanted to simply cease to exist.

Yet there wasn't a choice.

At least not for me.

"If I kill the Target for Charming, will you consider the job complete?"

Beside me, Piper gasped. "Frankie! Do you know what you're saying? You want to kill someone?"

No, I didn't. Killing Rosalyn was the very last thing I wanted to do. But it was her or Olly. I suppose it was selfish to choose Olly because I wasn't just doing it for him. I was doing it for me too because I couldn't fathom living in a world that he wasn't in.

"You—a human—want to take on the duties of a Death Escort?" the Reaper asked.

"Not all the duties. One kill. One Target. I kill her for you, and you agree to let Charming go."

He sighed. "I really did want to Recall him. However, this is just too fun to pass up."

So he was going to accept. And I was going to agree to murder.

"But first, let's see what Charming has to say about this."

"No!" I said, not wanting him involved. I already knew what he would say to this. But it was too late. He wasn't going to stop me.

"Send him in!" the Reaper yelled and the door opened and Olly was thrust into the room. He stumbled a bit, like he was out of it, but when he saw me his eyes widened and cleared. He had a gash on his temple, one that was red and swollen.

"Frankie?" He looked at the Reaper. "I told you to stay away from her!"

"Apparently you forgot to tell her the same. She came to me."

He looked at me like I was insane and rushed across the room to grab me by the shoulders and give me a hard shake. "What the hell were you thinking?"

"I was thinking it was about time someone fought for *you*."

Something behind his eyes shifted. His hard grasp on my arms gentled. "Frankie—"

The Reaper interrupted whatever he was going to say.

"Your lady here has offered me a deal."

Olly's eyes widened and he shook his head. "No."

"She has agreed to kill your Target in exchange for me not Recalling you."

*"No."*

"I was just as shocked as you." The Reaper went on. He was totally enjoying torturing Olly. "But it made me realize perhaps I was being too harsh. You are, after all, the best Escort I have. I thought maybe you were losing your touch. But this is the first time you've ever charmed anyone into killing for you."

"She's not killing anyone!" Olly ground out. He grabbed me again. "You are not doing this."

"Ah, but she's already agreed."

I looked at Olly and nodded. Anguish filled his eyes. "You can't do this. I won't let you."

"You don't have a choice."

"Just Recall me!" he burst out, turning toward the Reaper, stepping up in front of me. "Recall me right now."

"No!" I cried, pulling Olly back.

"As tempting as that offer is, I'm going to have to pass. It's clear the best way to punish you for everything you've done is by letting her sacrifice herself for you."

His shoulders slumped. That single gesture did more to me than any denial he could have made with his lips.

"Frankie," he whispered, hoarse.

"So, then. We have a deal?" The Reaper looked at me with glee in his eyes. "You will kill the Target and I will agree to let Charming live."

Olly looked at me, a plea in his eyes. I looked away. "Yes."

And so it was done.

I just hoped Olly could forgive me for what I was doing.

I also hoped I would be able to forgive myself.

# Chapter Forty-Nine

*"Hotwire - to start the engine (an automobile, for example) without a key by short-circuiting the ignition system."*

## Charming

*She made a deal with the Grim Reaper.* After everything I'd done to keep her away from this, to keep her safe.

She freaking comes here *to his house* and makes a deal.

Was it really too much to ask for a guy to be allowed to protect the woman he loves without her going and ruining it all?

When I got out of here, I was going to kill her. G.R. would be the least of her worries.

And I was getting out of here.

All I needed was for the opportunity to present itself.

It took forever. I waited hours, keyed up and pacing the room. The longer I waited the more afraid I became that I was going to be too late to stop her. If she killed someone for me, I would never forgive myself.

I knew what it was like to carry around guilt like that. I carried it around longer than Frankie had been alive. All these years… all these years I thought my sister killed herself because of me. Because I killed the man she loved. But she didn't kill herself.

She was murdered, by my boss, in an attempt to control me. And then he stuffed her body in a secret closet in case he ever needed to control me again.

The worst part was it worked. He managed to turn me into a cold-hearted killing machine. Whatever he saw in me when I was in that ring, he'd been right because with a little manipulation, I turned into exactly what he wanted.

I was done being manipulated and controlled by him. I wasn't a puppet whose strings could be pulled for a desired effect. My sister was gone… and while I realized I wasn't directly responsible for her death, I was still involved. If I hadn't taken the job as an Escort, the Reaper never would have killed her. There was nothing I could do for my sister now, but Frankie was here. I could actually save her. History didn't have to repeat itself.

I heard footsteps drawing closer so I put my back up against the wall, the same wall with the door.

Seconds later the door cracked open.

Someone swore. "He's not in here."

"What! How the hell did he get out this time? Let me see." The door swung all the way open and one of the newer Escorts stepped inside.

I rushed him from behind, taking him by surprise and putting him into a headlock and ramming him straight into the wall. He fell out of my grip, unconscious.

"That's for earlier," I spat, reaching up to finger the knot where they hit me with the gun and then turned to leave.

Stooge #2 was waiting. I used all the anger and frustration built up inside me to power out a burst of pure energy, which struck the man and sent him back out into the hallway, slamming him into the wall.

I made it through the house in seconds and out into the driveway. I planned on running, but as I passed by his BMW Roadster, I changed my mind. Using the heel of my foot, I kicked out the driver-side window and let myself in.

Hotwiring it didn't take me very long. Ninety years of practice made a guy pretty good at getting a car to go when you wanted it to.

G.R. rushed out into the driveway as I sped away. In his car. Before I pulled out onto the street, I stuck my hand out the window and gave him the finger.

# Chapter Fifty

*"Gun - a weapon consisting of a metal tube from which a projectile is fired at high velocity into a relatively flat trajectory."*

## *Frankie*

I called Rosalyn to see if she was back in town, remembering that Olly told me she had to go away on business. She was just arriving back—her trip being cut short by a few cancelled meetings. I told myself her cancellation was good luck for me. Then I told myself it was wrong to have good luck when you were trying to murder someone.

I lied and told her Charming was still out of town and that he felt guilty about leaving her to do all the work and he asked me to step in and help plan the fundraiser. We agreed to meet at her house tomorrow for lunch where we could tackle what remained on her to-do list.

I was basically a basket full of nerves.

The moment I left the Reaper's house, the reality of what I agreed to do sank in.

How was I going to do this? How was I going to look someone I considered a friend in the eye and then rob them of their future? The weight of it was crippling. How did Olly live with this weight? How did he live knowing he took countless lives?

He turned it off.

He turned off his emotions—his humanity. That's how he survived all these years. His cold exterior when we first met made so much more sense now.

"What the hell happened in there?" Storm said as we drove toward my apartment.

I didn't answer. All I could do was stare out the windshield, like I was on autopilot and going through the motions of driving the car.

I heard Piper explaining. I heard him exclaiming about how messed up it was. But I tuned them out. I didn't need to hear how messed up it was. I already knew.

It's true I had a choice here.

I could have walked away. I could have let Olly figure this out himself.

But he wouldn't have walked away from me.

I knew what I was doing was wrong. But I was going to do it anyway.

I didn't know what time it was when we walked into my apartment. It was very late and all I wanted to do was go to sleep.

But I couldn't. I lay there and stared at the ceiling, contemplating things I never contemplated before. Like how to execute a murder.

I thought about all the movies I watched where there was a killer on the loose. I thought about all the crime shows on TV I never watched because it was too gruesome to bear. I was no shrinking violet, but there were some things not even the strongest of people should have to endure.

I heard Storm and Piper whispering out in the living room, but I didn't bother to join their conversation. Piper had been relentless in trying to make me see I couldn't do this.

I asked her what she would have done if it were Dex.

She didn't say anything else after that.

It didn't matter anyway. I made a deal. I made a deal with the Grim Reaper. There was no going back. If I didn't do this, Olly would get Recalled and I would get killed. Yet I couldn't bring myself to feel like a victim because the only real victim here was Rosalyn.

After a while I fell asleep, but it was fitful and I woke feeling more tired than when I lay down.

Piper and Storm were already in the kitchen when I surfaced for some coffee. Piper stared at me as I poured a mug full of the stuff, black, and took a big gulp.

I pinned her with a stare over the rim of the mug. "I haven't changed my mind."

She nodded.

We didn't talk after that. I basically stared at the clock and counted the minutes until finally dragging myself off to shower and get dressed.

When it was time to go, I stared down at the gun that Charming had given me. If he had known what I would end up doing with it, he never would have given it to me. But it was the only way I knew to do this. It would be quick and hopefully relatively painless. I didn't think I had it in me to do it any other way.

I picked up the gun and shoved it into my bag.

Piper was standing beside the couch when I went to the door. She couldn't come with me. I had to do this alone.

And then I left. I didn't look back.

# Chapter Fifty-One

*"Deal - to do business; trade."*

## *Charming*

*Please don't let me be too late.*

It was the mantra that repeated over and over again in my head the entire way to Frankie's apartment. I knew I didn't have long, that G.R. would be coming for me yet again, but it didn't matter. I wasn't going back into confinement.

Confinement was stupid.

Besides, I tried it twice, all in the name of keeping Frankie out of this mess, and that worked about as well as using leaves for toilet paper.

There was no way in hell I was going to let her kill someone for me. That kind of thing would ruin her life. The guilt would swallow her whole until she was just a mere shell of herself.

I illegally parked the stolen Roadster and ran as fast as I could up to her apartment and flung open the unlocked door. It hit the wall with a bang.

Piper jumped off the couch and Storm shot across the room to put himself in front of her. "Charming! How did you get out?"

"Where's Frankie?" I demanded.

"She left," Piper replied.

"The Target is here?" I'd been hoping she was still out of town.

"She got back last night. Frankie's going over to her house now."

"How long ago did she leave?"

"There's still time," Storm said.

Relief made my limbs weak. "Good, let's go."

The entire drive over, Storm argued with Piper about why she should have stayed behind. It annoyed the hell out of me. "Would you two shut up?!" I demanded, pulling up as close to her gated property as I could.

I was nervous because it took so long to get here. I prayed Frankie was having an attack of the nerves and wasn't able to do what she came here for.

"It doesn't matter if she came or not. We're here and I'm sure as hell not driving her home."

The pair fell silent.

"Piper, sit in the car," I ordered. "Storm, you're coming with me."

Once we were out of earshot from Piper, I said, "This probably isn't going to end well for me. Will you watch out for Frankie?"

"Yeah, I'll watch out for her."

"Thank you."

He hesitated like he wanted to say more, but there was no time. I had to get inside. Her property was gated, but otherwise, it didn't have any extra security other than a regular alarm system (this is why learning background information about a Target is crucial. It's a real timesaver later). So once we got past the gate, it wasn't any trouble to make it up to the house. I knew the security system was likely off because it was afternoon, so I didn't hesitate to walk up to the front door and try to open it.

It opened.

I ran into the house, yelling Frankie's name, praying all over again that I wasn't too late to stop her from making the biggest mistake of her life.

"Olly?" she called, coming around the corner and stopping in the wide archway that led into the large kitchen.

"Please tell me you didn't…" I rushed forward.

Her face went pale and the bottom fell out of my stomach. No. Please. No.

Rosalyn walked around the corner behind Frankie. "Who's this?"

All the air whooshed out of my lungs and I felt myself smiling. I grabbed Frankie and pulled her against me, crushing her into a hard hug. "Thank God I made it in time."

"How are you here?" she asked me, her voice muffled against my chest.

"It doesn't matter. We need to leave."

"What's going on?" Rosalyn asked. "Frankie, is everything okay?"

I released Frankie so we could make up some lame excuse and get the hell out of there, when a black cloud rose up behind Rosalyn. It looked like one of those heavy rain clouds that blow over entire towns quickly and unexpectedly just before dumping a ton of hard rain over everything.

He acted fast, holding out what I assumed was both his arms, and then placed his hands over both her ears. His soul worked fast, funneling itself inside the Target, slipping into her head in seconds before she even knew what was happening.

She lifted a hand to her head to wipe her brow like she had a headache, and when she looked up, Storm had taken over.

"I figured it would be easier this way," Storm said, his voice now the voice of the Target. "Plus, now you won't have to hear her ask a bunch of questions."

"Thanks, man."

Then I swiftly snapped her neck.

She fell to the floor instantly. Dead.

Yes, it was that quick. I wasn't about to draw it out and make things harder than they already were.

And this was hard.

This wasn't something anyone wanted. Least of all me. I was weary of killing. Weary of death.

"Oh," Frankie gasped. "Is she…?"

I stepped aside so she could look down at the body. So she could fully understand what she was getting into when she said she wanted a life with me.

No, I didn't want her to change her mind, but I didn't want her to one day look in the mirror and wonder who the hell she had become. I understood that feeling well.

"She's dead," I said, flat. "Give me your cell phone."

She pulled it out of her pocket and handed it to me. I dialed G.R. and handed the phone back. "Tell him it's done and then hang up."

He answered a few seconds later.

Frankie did as I told her and then stared down at the body. So did I, but not because of the incredible guilt I felt (though, I admit I did feel guilt), but because I was wondering where Storm was. Why was he still in that body?

I didn't try to comfort her because there was no comfort in this and coming from the man who just murdered someone without blinking, the comfort probably wouldn't be that good anyway.

The Reaper appeared like he always did and Frankie looked at me swiftly, fear in her face.

"He already knows I'm out. I'm not leaving you alone with him."

"Well done!" G.R. said, looking at Frankie. I hoped she realized she was going to be taking the credit for this. She was the one that had the deal to fulfill.

"Don't congratulate me on her death like it's some sort of sport. You make me sick," Frankie said.

It appeared that whatever kind of shock she was in from all of this was now gone.

"I like you," the Reaper said, smiling. "Such spunk. You would make a wonderful Escort."

I stiffened and stepped a little closer to her.

"Tell me, though…" he began. "I'm surprised you were able to snap her neck like that. Is it something you've done before?"

"No," Frankie replied.

His eyes speared me. "You, on the other hand, know how to snap a neck quite well."

"Can't take the credit for this kill," I said, shrugging.

"We had a deal," Frankie reminded him.

"Did you think I was stupid!?" he spat. "Charming is the one who made the kill, not you! We had a deal. A deal that you would finish the job in exchange for his freedom! The deal has been broken!"

"No, it was me!" she exclaimed, rushing forward, but I yanked her back, angling myself in front of her.

I could have told her to run, but really, what good would it have done? You can't outrun Death.

"You can't protect her, Charming. Not anymore."

He started coming closer, wiggling his fingers in anticipation for his touch. I began to build up energy in the palm of my hand, knowing it would only slow him down but wanting to do everything I possibly could to help her.

Just then Storm began to rise up out of the Target. He was making a weird sound like he was struggling to get out. All three of us turned to look at the black smoke that trailed out the Target's ears and nose as he groaned as if he were in pain.

The mist seemed to surround the body, filling up the space around her, until he came together, creating more of a shape.

"Damn. I didn't know being in a body when it died was going to be like that," he said. Then he realized the Reaper was standing there watching him. "Uhhhh…"

"How did you get in that body?" the Reaper hissed.

"It's something I know how to do."

"You mean to tell me that one of my Ghost Escorts knows how to take over a body and use it as their own?" He seemed more intrigued than angry.

This could be good… I nudged Frankie toward the exit.

"Yeah, but sometimes it hurts."

"But you can do it. And what about the soul already in the body?"

"It's still in there. I just take over."

"What else have you been doing without me realizing?" he said shrewdly.

"I was just bored. I was gonna tell you," Storm said. I could hear the nerves in his voice.

"Of course you were," he replied. "What else can you do?"

"Well… I've sorta been becoming more solid."

"But you can still get into another person's body?"

What was his obsession with getting into another person's body?

And then I knew.

The soul in a jar. She said she needed a body.

"That soul, the one I took? She said she needed a body, that she couldn't get into any of the ones you tried."

"That's none of your business," he snapped.

"No. But it seems to me that Storm might be able to teach her how to borrow a body. You know, one that isn't empty. Maybe that's the kind of body she needs."

I saw it in his face, the intrigue, the desire. And here was where his weakness lay.

"The Target is dead," I told him. "That's what you wanted. Does it really matter who killed her?"

G.R. looked at me.

"Let me out. Completely out, free of being an Escort and free of being Recalled. I'll give you back the soul I took." I looked up at Storm.

"And I'll teach her how to borrow a body," he added.

It was then that Piper rushed into the house, calling out for Frankie. She dashed around the corner and stopped, staring at us all standing there over a dead body. "You were gone a long time. I was worried."

"I'm fine," Frankie told her. "Go back out to the car."

"Wait," the reaper called, stopping her.

He was looking at Piper like she was some sort of miracle or something, like he was enthralled with her.

"I'll agree to this. If she lets me touch her again."

"No!" Frankie shouted immediately. "Kill us all now because that isn't going to happen."

The Reaper shrugged. "Fine." He stepped toward Frankie.

"Wait!" Piper cried, rushing over. "If I let you touch me, you won't kill them? Any of them?"

He stared at her, taking in all of her face, scrutinizing every detail about her as if he were committing it to memory. "I will not kill or Recall any of them."

He lifted his fingers, looking at her again.

"Piper, no," Frankie insisted.

"He's already touched me once, Frankie."

"But what if it was just a fluke?"

Piper bit her lip. "Guess we'll find out."

The Reaper chuckled eagerly. "Can I touch you now?"

"Wait," I said and he looked at me, annoyed. "I want your word that Frankie and I will be completely free of you."

"You have my word," he said, looking back at Piper.

"She can't do this," Frankie argued. "I won't let her."

Piper looked at me. "Hold her." I wrapped my arms around Frankie, locking them into place, and she struggled against me, begging Piper not to do this and telling me she would never forgive me if I let her best friend die.

It was a risk I was willing to take. This was it. We were down to no other options. If this didn't work, we would all be dead in minutes.

"Do it," Piper said, looking directly at the Grim Reaper.

While Frankie continued to struggle, G.R. reached out tentatively, extending his hand like he was touching something so delicate it might shatter with the merest hint of a touch. He drew closer and Frankie began to cry.

Piper just stood there, stock still, waiting, and then the tips of his fingers brushed her cheek.

She blinked.

She drew in a deep breath and smiled, looking over at Frankie, who practically collapsed in my arms.

"It's been so long," he murmured, becoming braver and cupping the side of her face with his palm.

Piper stiffened at his caress and lifted her foot like she wanted to step away, but she didn't. She glanced at me instead.

"You got what you wanted," I told him.

It's like he didn't even hear me speak at all. He was so entranced by her that it was like he saw nothing else. He began stroking the side of her cheek like she was a treasure he had searched out for hundreds of years. "You're soft. And warm. I forgot how warm live skin could be."

Okay, he was just being creepy now.

"We had a deal." I reminded him, my voice hard.

He drew away from her slowly, like he didn't want to let go. Maybe he didn't. I would think that never being able to touch anyone ever would make a man feel a certain hunger—the kind of hunger that never really went away. It was the kind of hunger that not even Death would be able to get away from.

When he stepped away, Piper let out a huge sigh of relief and stepped back.

The Reaper looked at me. "Charming, I release you from the employ of myself, the Grim Reaper. From here on out, you will no longer possess immortality. You will no longer have the abilities that were bestowed upon you during your work. You will live and die like any other human who walks this earth. You have my word that I will not come for you or the girl."

I was free.

Free from death. Free to live. Free to love.

It was something I never once thought was even possible and now it was mine.

Frankie wrapped her arms around me and squeezed. Her laughter made me smile and then my smile turned into a laugh.

*I am free.*

"Now I want what's mine," G.R. said, cutting into my happiness.

I nodded. "We can go right now." I pulled away from Frankie. "Go wait in the car. I'll be there as soon as I can."

She bit her lip and glanced over at the Reaper. I couldn't really blame her.

"I do not go back on my word," G.R. said. Then he looked at Piper. "Perhaps we will meet again."

That got Frankie moving. She grabbed Piper's hand and towed her toward the door. G.R. watched Piper until she was out of sight. Once they were gone, he turned abruptly, pinning Storm with a hard stare. "You've been very busy."

Storm didn't say anything, but his cloudlike body shifted.

"You're going to make it up to me."

"Yes, I'll show your soul how to borrow a body."

G.R. smiled and gazed back to the door Piper and Frankie just went through. "Yes, how to borrow indeed."

I glanced at Storm. It was one of the times I really wished he had a face so I could read his expression. Because what G.R. said just now… it sounded kind of ominous.

Before anyone could ask him what he meant, he was ushering us off through his insta-doors so we could give him back what we stole. It didn't take long and once he had gotten exactly that, he sent us back to the Target's house where he said we were responsible for the body. Apparently he wasn't interested in keeping it or eating it (I certainly didn't ask him about that).

He didn't even say good-bye to me.

I didn't care.

When his doorway closed for the final time, all I felt was relief. I was never going to have to kill again. And maybe, somehow, with the life I had left, I could try to make up for some of the lives I had taken.

But first I had a body to dispose of.

"What the hell are we gonna do with her?" Storm complained. "Why does she have to be the senator's daughter?"

"It doesn't really matter who she was," I said. "Because even if she had been a nobody, someone would have loved her and that someone's entire world would be over."

"If I had a face, I would be crying right now," Storm said.

I laughed. "Smartass."

He made a heavy groaning sound and I rolled my eyes.

"What I said wasn't that bad," I replied.

"That was *not* me."

Someone groaned again. I looked down at the Target. It was her.

"Dude, I thought she was dead," Storm said.

"She was. Wasn't she?"

"I-I don't know. When you snapped her neck, everything went black. It was like I was unconscious. The next thing I remembered was trying to get out. I was so disoriented though, it was hard."

She moaned again. This time her head moved back and forth.

"Can someone survive getting their neck snapped?" Storm asked.

"No." But she wasn't dead. Clearly.

"Maybe you didn't do it right?"

She groaned again; this time her hands moved.

"Is it possible that somehow having your soul inside her protected her from dying?" It was a crazy thought. Wasn't it?

"I don't know. I've never been in someone's body when they died before."

"Olly?" Frankie whispered, stepping in from the other room. I jumped a little, surprised at her appearance. Then I realized she hadn't just appeared; she walked into the room like any normal human would do. Except this time I couldn't hear or feel her coming.

I was completely human now.

I smiled.

"Is she *alive?*" Frankie said, completely ignoring the fact that I was having a moment. It was likely the first of many private moments I would be having due to my newfound freedom.

"I think so," I answered.

She gave a great shout of joy and pulled out her phone. "I'm going to call for help."

"What will G.R. say if he hears about this?" Storm worried. Frankie lowered her phone and frowned.

"It doesn't matter. He's already made the deal. He can't go back now."

Frankie grinned.

"You guys get out of here. I'll wait and tell the ambulance I found her like this when I showed up for lunch."

"I don't want to leave you here alone."

She caught my hand and smiled. "I'll be fine. See you at home."

Home.

I liked the sound of that.

# Chapter Fifty-Two

*"Marilyn Monroe - (June 1, 1926 - August 5, 1962) was an
American actress, singer, and model."*

## *Frankie*
*3 days later...*

We had one perfect day. One perfect day of freedom and happiness.

Then I started worrying.

When I woke up and reached for him, he wasn't there. I sat up, pushing the hair out of my eyes, and called out his name. I thought he was in the kitchen, making coffee, or would come bounding in from the bathroom.

He didn't.

I wandered through the apartment, noting he wasn't there.

The familiar ache from the day in Scotland tried to make an appearance. I shut it down. I wasn't going to go there. I knew he wouldn't leave me. Not after everything. Not even the parts of him that made up Charming could ever make him leave.

Still, something was off.

He was gone already today and yesterday... yesterday he'd been gone most of the day as well. When he returned home (looking mighty lickable in those jeans he wore so well), he acted like everything was fine. He grabbed me up and kissed me senseless, almost making me forget to ask where he'd been.

But I didn't forget.

I asked.

He was shady.

And now he was gone again.

I really thought the honeymoon period of my happily ever after would last a little longer.

I decided to give him hell when he got home. But in order to properly give a man hell, a lady had to make sure she looked hot. Hot as in *you better watch it because if you don't treat me right someone else will* kind of hot. My heart would never belong to another man, not even if Olly never came back today, but he didn't need to know all my secrets.

I rushed into the bathroom and took a hot shower. I shaved, I exfoliated, and I did things to my body a man would never even dream of doing to his. Then I lotioned and potioned and styled until I stepped out of the bathroom in a way that if I walked down the street, every man would turn his head. Some would probably even follow.

And then I waited.

I heard the key in the door not too much later, and I smiled, sitting sideways in the armchair with my legs flung over the side and an open magazine in front of my face.

When he walked in, I flipped down one corner and looked at him. "Oh, hey," I said casually.

He raised an eyebrow at me. "That's quite the dress."

"This old thing?" I scoffed and stood, tossing the magazine onto the coffee table. I gestured toward the red body-hugging dress I wore. "I found it in the back of my closet."

"I'm surprised *you* found your way out of your closet."

I narrowed my eyes.

"I'm guessing all this is because I'm in trouble," he said, waving his finger at me.

*Damn.* "All what?"

He smirked. "Before you give me a lecture—I *hate* lectures, by the way—why don't you open your present?"

"Present?" I perked up. Oh, he was good. He got me a present before he got in trouble.

He handed me a white envelope. "What's this?" I stared down at it.

"The million dollars I owe you."

I rolled my eyes. "Olly, that was a joke. I hated that job anyway, which you well knew."

He rolled his eyes. "Just open it."

I ripped open the seal and slid out a stack of papers. I read the first document, looked up, and reread it again. I couldn't believe what I was seeing. My eyes had to be playing tricks on me. "Are you— Is this for real?"

He grinned. "Yep. You now are the new owner of the Iced Princess."

"Holy pink cupcakes!" I exclaimed and threw myself into his arms. I couldn't believe he bought my favorite place ever. My job was now literally playing with sugar all day long. "Is this why you've been acting all shady the past couple days?" I said, bouncing around in his arms. I was just too excited to stand still.

"I was not acting shady. I was acting secretive."

I pulled back. "But my cupcakes aren't as good as the ones at the Iced Princess."

He kissed my cheek. "Yours are better."

I squealed and hugged him again. "I love you."

"I know."

He pulled me back. "Now about that lecture…"

"What lecture?" I batted my eyes.

He scowled. "You thought I was already changing my mind, didn't you?"

"No. I know you want to be here with me, but I thought maybe you were having second thoughts… maybe a couple regrets. Losing all your abilities and your immortality can be a lot on a guy."

"A friend once told me something I didn't really understand until I met you. *We should all start to live before we get too old. Fear is stupid. So are regrets.*"

"Marilyn Monroe said that."

He smiled. "She was right. You don't have to worry about me having second thoughts. I'm not going backward. I'm only going forward. With you."

I kissed him.

But then I pulled back once more. "You know you really need to tell me what happened with Marilyn Monroe. I want the truth."

"I can't tell you all my secrets at once," he said slyly.

"Well, then it's a good thing we have an entire lifetime. I have a feeling you're going to keep me very well entertained."

This time he kissed me.

# *Epilogue*

*"Icing - a sweet glaze made of sugar, butter, water, and egg whites or milk, often flavored and cooked and used to cover or decorate baked goods, such as cakes or cookies."*

## *Olly*

The pink cup slid across the counter toward me and I gave it a dubious stare.

"What's the matter, Olly?" Frankie taunted from the other side. "Is pink not your color?"

I grinned. "You tell me," I said and picked it up and took a drink. "Does it match my eyes," I asked, batting them.

"I knew you were gay," she muttered.

"That's not what you said last night." I wagged my eyebrows at her and a feeling of smugness came over me when her cheeks turned pink.

"Olly, I'm at work," she hissed.

"Just like last night," I drawled, pointedly looking behind the counter toward the floor where all the naughty events took place after closing.

"That's the last time I let you sample my new icing recipe." She sniffed, her cheeks still pink.

"Give me a cupcake, woman."

She gave me a surprised look. "*You* want a cupcake. Something filled with sugar?"

"Someone once told me food should be enjoyed."

She reached in to pull out the Iced Princess's signature cupcake. "Oh no you don't," I said. "I want one of your creations."

Her hand moved past the signature one and grabbed up a pink cupcake piled high with white frosting and sprinkles that looked like pearls. Frankie called it "The Marilyn." She handed it over on a very pink plate and shooed me away from the counter. "You're holding up my line."

I took the very girly cupcake, the pink plate, and the pink cup and went to sit at the empty pink table near the back. If a guy wasn't careful, he might find himself turning into a pansy in this place.

One bite of the cupcake and I forgot about all the pink. My God, she was good at baking. And she was right; food was a lot better when you actually enjoyed it.

I could get used to this living thing.

The chair across the table pulled out and Piper dropped herself into it. We regarded each other for long, silent moments. She was the first one to break the silence. "You bought this place for her," she said. "She looks really happy. Happier than I've ever seen her."

I glanced over at Frankie. She was putting several cupcakes into a large pink box and she was laughing. "About what I did to you…" I said, not really knowing what to say. Apologizing seemed stupid, especially when I wasn't really sorry. I'd been doing what I had to do. I knew I had to say something, though, because this was Frankie's best friend, her family, and Frankie was, well… my life.

Piper held up her hand. "That's not what I want to talk about. That's in the past."

"Then what?" I asked, setting the cupcake down and giving her my full attention.

She took a deep breath. "Give me your hand."

"My—" I stopped because I knew exactly what she wanted to do. There was only one reason she would want to touch me.

She wanted to see what my future entailed. She wanted to be guaranteed that I wasn't going to do something awful to Frankie.

I actually wanted to know too.

Slowly, I stretched my hand across the table. She looked at it for long moments, no doubt deciding if this was really what she wanted. We both knew whatever she saw might not be good.

I heard something clatter to the floor and we both looked. Frankie was staring at us with a pale face and round eyes.

I was about to pull away, to change my mind, when her hand covered mine.

Maybe I would get lucky and she wouldn't have a vision. Maybe nothing would happen.

I knew from the look on her face the instant a vision overwhelmed her.

Her hand covered mine for several minutes and then she pulled away, her eyes coming back into focus and looking at me.

I couldn't read her. Her face was closed off, tight. I knew it was bad.

I swallowed. "How bad is it?" Maybe there was a way to somehow change whatever she saw.

Her face softened and a small smile played on her lips. "Well, that depends. How do you feel about kids?"

*Kids?*

I stared at her dumbly. Was she saying Frankie and I were going to have kids?

She nodded. "With green eyes just like his daddy."

A boy. I was going to have a son.

A huge grin broke over my face. It hurt my cheeks because I was positive I had never smiled so big in my entire life. After everything—after the fighting, the killing, the heartache—I was finally going to get a chance to live.

And damn, living was so much better than death.

# The End

# Acknowledgements

I would like to acknowledge you—why? Because you are taking the time to read these acknowledgements. I have been hearing through the grapevine that many readers do not read the acknowledgements of a book. I admit that I didn't always read them either… until I started writing. It seems to me that the best way to get even a glimpse into an author's world is just by reading the acknowledgements in the back of their book.

You're probably thinking, "Uhhh, I *already* know the author. I just spent, like, a bunch of hours reading the stuff they wrote." (C'mon, you know you say "like" too). But here's the thing… a book (well, at least my books) aren't really me. Yes, you get a glimpse into my head, but what I'm writing isn't me; it's my characters. It's the people in my head who talk to me constantly. I'm totally going to make you roll your eyes with this next confession: sometimes I feel like one of those mediums that see dead people.

Yup, go ahead. Get it out. Roll your eyes real good.

Okay, now I will explain. You know how sometimes you see the interviews with the mediums who are with a family and the spirit of a lost loved one is there and telling the medium what to say? Well, that's how I feel. Except my characters aren't spirits (well, most of them, lol) trying to talk to loved ones. They're people with a story to tell. In many ways, I feel like the medium for them to tell their story through. A lot of times, I have no idea what's going to happen in one of my books. I sit and I stress about it. I worry I won't be able to fill a page let alone an entire novel with a story. I surf Facebook, Pinterest (I swear I have, like, every recipe known to man saved on there and no time to cook them), and well, do just about everything other thing than start writing. But then I do. And the answers come… because the characters know them, because it's their story to tell.

While some details in my novels might reflect on me (for example, I used to drive a red Jeep Wrangler like Frankie), these stories are not *me*. I just listened well enough to the people in my head while they were talking. Does that mean I'm bipolar? Whacko? In need of therapy? Likely.

Anyway, the point I'm trying to make here is that by reading this part of my novels, you get a chance to hear something from me and not my characters. So it means a lot when you take the extra couple minutes to actually see what I want to tell you. Oh, and I promise to never just make a list of people I would like to thank (though, I will be thanking people) like some of those incredibly bad speeches you see on TV from some celebrities at award shows who get up there to accept their award and pull out a notecard. *facepalm*

I know some of you read this part… like Mommom, Aurora Bray, who actually reads all my books and acknowledgements. I know because in the acknowledgements of *Recalled* I begged someone to find me that Ginger Twist tea that fell off the face of the earth. Well, my mommom, fabulous lady that she is, called Lipton. Turns out I was, like, the only person who liked that tea and so they quit making it. (Note: I have no idea if anyone else liked that tea). So, thank you, Mommom, for reading my entire books, for calling Lipton, and oh yeah, for being my grandmother. And a really great one at that.

I would also like to acknowledge my new personal assistant, Katy Austin. Without her this book might never have been done. Trying to keep up with everything social media, messages, marketing, etc. leaves very little time to actually write. Katy stepped in with her super powers and organization and started handling a lot of that for me so I could write. Oh, and thanks for putting up with me and my messages too. Hopefully you aren't considering running away screaming yet.

My editor, my book doctor, Cassie McCown, you rocked it out. Thanks for making my books a lot better than they would be otherwise. Congratulations on starting up

Gathering Leaves Editing. I just know you are going to be booking up like crazy. Save me a spot on your calendar.

And just as in every acknowledgement I have written so far, I must mention Regina Wamba of Mae I Design. I mean, seriously. Did you see the cover of this book? You know you licked it. It's okay because I licked it too (more than once). Thank you, Regina, for always designing book covers that make me have butterflies in my stomach. You truly are an artist.

To my third child, Cocoa. Thank you for always lying beside me during the many, many hours I spent finishing this book. Cocoa is definitely the best dog I have ever had. And, of course, to my two human children—thanks for the suggestion that Charming fight the "demons" in this book by making those incredible abs he has dance so the demon just passes out.

To Shawn, my husband, thanks for putting up the pool in the backyard. It makes a great babysitter. And always thanks for sitting up until midnight some nights while I went on and on about the plot.

Also, I need to acknowledge thefreedictionary.com where I got all the definitions for the chapter headings (except for the one provided by Charming, lol). If any definitions are inaccurate, it was through my error and not theirs.

Finally, thanks to all the fans. The bloggers, the Facebook peeps, all the sharing and enthusiasm you give me and all my books keeps me going. You deserve a donut. Or two.

Cambria Hebert is the author of the young adult paranormal *Heven and Hell* series and the new adult *Death Escorts* series. Watch for her upcoming new adult series, the *Take it Off* series, debuting in late summer 2013. She loves a caramel latte, hates math and is afraid of chickens (yes, chickens). She went to college for a bachelor's degree, couldn't pick a major, and ended up with a degree in cosmetology. So rest assured her characters will always have good hair. She currently lives in North Carolina with her husband and children (both human and furry) where she is plotting her next book. You can find out more about Cambria and her work by visiting: http://www.cambriahebert.com

"Like" her on Facebook:
https://www.facebook.com/pages/Cambria-Hebert/128278117253138
Follow her on Twitter: https://twitter.com/cambriahebert
Pinterest: https://pinterest.com/cambriahebert/pins/
GoodReads:
http://www.goodreads.com/author/show/5298677.Cambria_Heb
ert

Turn the page for an exclusive
look at Cambria Hebert's first
new adult contemporary novel
TORCH
part of the brand new
*Take It Off* series!

# TORCH

By Cambria Hebert

# 1

The pungent smell of gasoline stung my nostrils and my head snapped back in repulsion. I opened my eyes and lifted my hands to place them over my mouth and nose to hopefully barricade some of the overwhelming scent.

Except my hands didn't obey.

I tried again.

Panic ripped through my middle when I realized my arms weren't going to obey any kind of command because they were secured behind me.

What the hell?

I looked down over my shoulder, trying to see the thick ropes binding my wrists. The lighting in here was dim.

Wait. Where was I?

My heart started to pound, my breathing coming in shallow, short spurts as I squinted through tearing eyes at the familiar shapes around me. A little bit of calmness washed over me when I realized I was in my home. Home was a place I always felt safe.

But I wasn't safe. Not right now.

I sat in the center of my living room, tied to my dining room chair. I was supposed to be in bed sleeping. The boxers and T-shirt I wore said so.

I started to struggle, to strain against the binds that held me. I didn't know what was going on, but I knew enough to realize whatever was happening was not good.

Movement caught my attention and I went still, my eyes darting toward where someone stood.

"Hello?" I said. "Please help me!"

It was so dark I couldn't make out who it was. They seemed to loom in the distance, standing just inside the entryway, nothing but a dark shadow.

My eyes blinked rapidly, trying to clear the tears flowing down my cheeks. The gasoline smell was so intense. It was like I was sitting in a puddle of the stuff.

"Help me!" I screamed again, wondering why the hell the person just stood there instead of coming to my aid.

The scrape of a match echoed through the darkness, and the catch of a small flame drew my eye. It started out small, reminding me of the fireflies I used to chase when I was a child. But then it grew in intensity, the flame burning brighter, becoming bolder, and it burned down the stick of the match.

The dark shadow held out the matchstick, away from their body, suspending it over the ground for several long seconds.

And then they dropped it.

It fell to the floor like it weighed a thousand pounds and left a small glowing trail in its wake. I watched the flame as it hit the floor, thinking it would fizzle out and the room would be returned to complete blackness.

But the flame didn't fizzle out.

It ignited.

With a great whoosh, fire burst upward, everything around that little match roaring to life with angry orange flames. I screamed. I didn't bother asking for help again because it was clear whoever was in this house wasn't here to help me.

They were here to kill me.

To prove my realization, the dark figure calmly retreated out the front door. The flames on the floor grew rapidly, spreading like a contagious disease up the walls and completely swallowing the front door. The small side table by the door, which I'd lovingly scraped and painted, caught like it was the driest piece of wood in the center of a forest fire.

Smoke began to fill the rooms, curling closer, making me recoil. How long until the flames came for me?

I began to scream, to call for help, praying one of my neighbors would hear and come to my rescue. Except I knew no one was going to rush into this house to save me. They would all stand out on the lawn at the edge of the street and murmur and point. They would click their tongues and shake their heads, mesmerized by the way the fire claimed my home. And my life.

I wasn't going to die like this.

I twisted my arms, straining against the corded rope, feeling it cut into my skin, but I kept at it, just needing an inch to slip free.

I tried to stand, to run into the back of the house. If I couldn't get loose from the chair, I would just take it with me. But my ankles were crossed and tied together.

I called for help again, but the sound was lost in the roaring of the flames. I never realized how loud a fire truly was. I never realized how rapidly it could spread. It was no longer dark in here, the flames lighting up my home like the fourth of July, casting an orange glow over everything. The entire front entryway and stairwell were now engulfed. I could see everything was doused in gasoline; the putrid liquid created a thick trail around the room. Whoever had been here completely drenched this house with the flammable liquid and then set me in the center of it.

I managed to make it to my feet, hunched over with the chair strapped around me. It was difficult to stand with my ankles crossed. But I had to try. I had to get out of here. I took one hobbled step when a cough racked my lungs. I choked and hacked, my lungs searching for clean air to breathe but only filling with more and more pollution.

I made it one step before I fell over, my shoulder taking the brunt of my fall, the chair thumping against the thickness of the carpet. I lay there and coughed, squinting through my moist and blurry vision, staring at the flames… the flames that seemed to stalk me.

They traveled closer, following the path of the gas, snaking through the living room, filling it up and rushing around me until I was completely circled with fire. The heat, God, the heat was so intense that sweat slicked my skin, and it made it that much harder to breathe.

It was the kind of heat that smacked into you, that made you dizzy and completely erased all thought from your brain.

I was going to die.

Even if I were able to make it to my feet, I wouldn't be able to make it through the circle of fire that consumed everything around me.

I pressed my cheek against the carpet, not reveling in its softness, not thinking about the comfort it usually afforded my bare feet. Another round of coughing racked my body. My lungs hurt. God, they hurt so bad. It was like a giant vise squeezed inside my chest, squeezed until all I could think about was oxygen and how much I needed it.

My chin tipped back as I writhed on the floor, making one last attempt at freedom before the flames claimed me completely. I heard the sharp crackling of wood, the banging of something collapsing under the destruction, and I blinked.

*This is it.*

*The last moments of my life.*

*I'm going to die alone.*

I started to hallucinate, the lack of oxygen playing tricks on my fading mind, as a large figure stepped through the flames. Literally walked right through them. He held up his arms, shielding his face and head as he barreled through looking like some hero from an action movie.

My eyes slid closed as my skin began to hurt, like I sat outside in the sun for hours without the protection of sunscreen.

I heard a muffled shout and tried to open my eyes, but they were too heavy. Besides, I preferred the darkness anyway. I didn't want to watch as my body was burned to death by fire.

Pain screamed through me and the feeling of the carpet against my cheek disappeared. My first thought was to struggle, but my body couldn't obey my mind. I felt movement, I felt the solidness of someone's chest, and I could have sworn I heard the sound of a man's voice.

"*Hang on,*" he said.

The shattering of glass and the splintering of wood didn't wake me from the fog that settled over my brain. The scream of pain at my back, the extreme burning and melting that made a cry rip from my throat still wasn't enough to get my eyes to open.

And then I could hear the piercing wail of sirens, the faraway shouts of men, and the muffled yell of one who was much closer.

I really thought heaven would be more peaceful.

And then I was sailing through the air, the solid wall of whatever held me ripped away. I plunged downward, and with a great slap, I hit water, the icy cold droplets a major shock to my overheated system.

My eyes sprang wide; water invaded them as I tried to make sense of what was happening. I thought I was burning. But now I was… drowning.

The water was dark and it pulled me lower and lower into its depths. I looked up. The surface rippled and glowed orange. I almost died up there. But I would die down here now.

I wanted to swim. My arms, they hurt so badly, but they wanted to push upwards, to help me break the surface toward the oxygen my body so desperately needed.

But I was still tied to a chair.

The chair hit the ground—a solid, cold surface—as my hair floated out around me and bubbles discharged from my nose and mouth.

It wasn't hot here.

It wasn't loud, but eerily quiet.

It was a different kind of death, but death all the same.

The ripples in the water grew and the chair began to rock. I heard the plunge of something else coming into the water and I looked up. Through the strands of my wayward hair, I saw him again. My hero. His powerful arms pushed through the water in three great stokes. He reached out and grabbed me beneath the shoulder, towing me upward toward the orange surface.

When my head cleared the water, my lungs automatically sucked in blissful air. It hurt so bad, but it was the kind of pain I had to endure. Another cough racked my body, and as I wheezed, the man towing me and my chair through the water said, "Keep breathing. Just keep breathing."

And then I was being lifted from the water, the chair placed on the cement as I coughed and wheezed and greedily sucked in air.

"Ma'am," someone was saying. "Ma'am, can you hear me? Are you all right?"

I looked up, blinking the water out of my eyes, but my vision was still blurry. I tried to speak, but all I could manage was another cough.

The ropes around my wrists were tugged, and I cried out. The pain was so intense that I thought I would pass out right there.

"Stay with me," a calm voice said from behind. It was the same voice that instructed me to keep breathing.

When my arms were free, I sagged forward. The pain splintering through me was too much to bear. And then there were hands at my ankles; I heard the knife against the rope. When I was completely untied, my body fell forward, sliding off the chair and toward the ground.

But he was there.

I slid right into his arms, my body completely boneless.

A low curse slipped from his lips as he yelled for a medic. Yeah, a medic. That seemed like a good idea. I hurt. I hurt all over.

I cried out when he shifted me in his arms, bringing me closer to his chest. I pressed my face against him. He was wet, but his clothes were scratchy against my cheek. I tried to look at him; I opened my eyes and tilted back my head. I caught a flash of dark hair and light eyes, but then my vision faded out, pain took over, and I passed out.

# Ready for more blazing action and romance? Purchase TORCH August 2013!

## *ALSO CHECK OUT THESE EXTRAORDINARY AUTHORS & BOOKS:*

Alivia Anders ~ Illumine
Cambria Hebert ~ Recalled
Angela Orlowski Peart ~ Forged by Greed
Julia Crane ~ Freak of Nature
J.A. Huss ~ Tragic
Cameo Renae ~ Hidden Wings
A.J. Bennett ~ Now or Never
Tabatha Vargo ~ Playing Patience
Tiffany King ~ Meant to Be
Beth Balmanno ~ Set in Stone
Lizzy Ford ~ Zoey Rogue
Ella James ~ Selling Scarlett
Tara West ~ Visions of the Witch
Heidi McLaughlin ~ Forever Your Girl
Melissa Andrea ~ The Edge of Darkness
Komal Kant ~ Falling for Hadie
Melissa Pearl ~ Golden Blood
Alexia Purdy ~ Breathe Me
L.P. Dover ~ Love's Second Chance
Sarah M. Ross ~ Inhale, Exhale
Brina Courtney ~ Reveal
Amber Garza ~ Falling to Pieces
Anna Cruise ~ Maverick